SONG

OF THE

HUNTRESS

Praise for

Lucy Holland and
SISTERSONG

"A captivating spell of myth and magic. Holland's lyrical prose and powerful storytelling will lure you into an eerie, intriguing world in which enemies lurk unseen, the threat of betrayal hangs heavy, and sisterly loyalties are tested to their limit."
—Jennifer Saint, author of *Ariadne*

"*Sistersong* truly reads like a ballad—beautiful and mournful, a melody that sticks in your head. An absolutely stunning book."
—Hannah Whitten, author of *For the Wolf*

"From its opening pages, *Sistersong* transports you to a time period often overlooked and spins a tale of family, loyalty, and triumph. I was utterly captivated from the beginning to the tragic, bittersweet end."
—Genevieve Gornichec, author of *The Witch's Heart*

"*Sistersong* is a fresh and gripping retelling of an ancient tale. Set in a realistic, gritty world, the nuanced, compelling characters are the heart of this story about family, love, loyalty, and identity. I loved it."   —John Gwynne, author of *The Shadow of the Gods*

"An enthralling fantasy....Fans of reimagined folklore and mythology like Christina Henry's *Horseman* and Genevieve Gornichec's *The Witch's Heart* will be enchanted."   —*Booklist*

"Holland delivers an enchanting queer retelling of the English murder ballad 'The Twa Sisters.'... [Her] fast-paced plot and fresh, inventive take on a little-known classic make for a stirring experience. Fans of folkloric fantasy will be spellbound."

—*Publishers Weekly*

By Lucy Holland

Sistersong
Song of the Huntress

SONG

OF THE

HUNTRESS

LUCY HOLLAND

REDHOOK

Redhook Books/Orbit
Hachette Book Group
1290 Avenue of the Americas
New York, NY 10104
hachettebookgroup.com

First Edition: March 2024
Simultaneously published in Great Britain by Tor, an imprint of Pan Macmillan

Redhook is an imprint of Orbit, a division of Hachette Book Group.
The Redhook name and logo are registered trademarks of Hachette Book Group, Inc.

The publisher is not responsible for websites (or their content)
that are not owned by the publisher.

The Hachette Speakers Bureau provides a wide range of authors for speaking events. To find out more, go to hachettespeakersbureau.com or email HachetteSpeakers@hbgusa.com.

Redhook books may be purchased in bulk for business, educational, or promotional use. For information, please contact your local bookseller or the Hachette Book Group Special Markets Department at special.markets@hbgusa.com.

Library of Congress Control Number: 2023949620

ISBNs: 9780316321655 (trade paperback), 9780316321860 (ebook)

Printed in the United States of America

CW

1 3 5 7 9 10 8 6 4 2

*For my mother, Deirdre, and in memory of
my grandmother, Iris: women who chose to fight*

Twrch Trwyth will not be hunted until you get Gwyn son of
Nudd, in whom God put the fury of the demons of Annwfn, lest
the world be destroyed. He cannot be spared from that.

"Culhwch and Olwen," *The Red Book of Hergest*

She knew what made the horses kneel.
Here was the heart of all wild things.

Alan Garner, *The Moon of Gomrath*

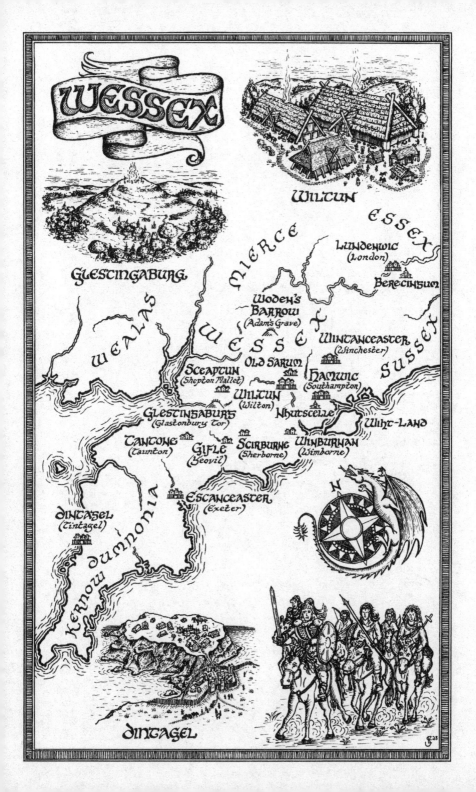

WESSEX

WILTUN

GLESTINGABURG

MIERCE

ESSEX

LUNDENWIC
(London)

BERECINGUM

WODEN'S
BARROW
(Adam's Grave)

WEALAS

WESSEX

SUSSEX

WINTANCEASTER
(Winchester)

SCEAPTUN
(Shepton Mallet)

OLD SARUM

HAMWIC
(Southampton)

WILTUN
(Wilton)

GLESTINGABURG
(Glastonbury Tor)

NHUTSCELLE

WIHT-LAND

TANTONE
(Taunton)

GIFLE
(Yeovil)

SCIRBURNE
(Sherborne)

WINBURNAN
(Wimborne)

ESCANCEASTER
(Exeter)

N

DINTAGEL
(Tintagel)

KERNOW

DUMNONIA

DINTAGEL

bISTORICAL NOTE

This book is foremost a fantasy. While I have chosen to explore the early medieval period, I have always been more interested in the way history intersects with myth than with rendering a detailed portrayal of an era. Saying this, I have striven to recreate early eighth-century Britain with some accuracy; any errors are likely due to the sparse detail available, and to the inevitable nature of storytelling. I have been liberal with the birth and death dates of historical personages, as well as the posited dates of certain events. Other events, I have entirely invented.

Ine and Æthelburg, whom you will meet in these pages, might have been what we would call a power couple today. According to the Anglo-Saxon Chronicle, Ine was King of Wessex for thirty-seven years, an immensely long reign in this period, and Æthelburg bore the title of queen before its use was discontinued amongst Wessex royalty. Even Ealhswith, wife of Ælfred the Great, was not granted it. Æthelburg is also popularly held to be one of the few female Anglo-Saxon warriors. The Anglo-Saxon Chronicle intriguingly records her leading an army to destroy her husband's fortress at Taunton, while William of Malmesbury, writing in the Norman period, was quite taken with her character. Ine himself is famous for creating one of the earliest Anglo-Saxon law codes, part of which Ælfred appended to his own laws—thus ensuring its survival. Ine's law code points to the evolving nature of kingship, with a new emphasis on upholding justice, maintaining social order and legislating for a population that included native Britons as well as his own Saxon subjects.

While Britons lived in Saxon Wessex during this period, relations were still poor between the two peoples. The Old English word for the natives was "Wealas"—the root of Wales. It carried a derogatory connotation and was used to distinguish all natives from the Saxons, not just those in the Cymric kingdoms. The Dumnonii were a native British tribe that had controlled the West Country for hundreds of years, but West Saxon incursions were pushing them ever further into Devon and Cornwall. Geraint of the Dumnonii, who was killed in battle around 710 AD, is considered by some historians to be the last ruler of a consolidated Dumnonia.

Despite this ongoing struggle, the Saxons were still given to warring amongst themselves, and a king's authority could be challenged by any ætheling: a prince or noble with sufficient credentials for kingship. A royal court, therefore—with its shifting tides of power and influence—had the potential to become as perilous as a battlefield. It is against this turbulent historical backdrop that I have set my story.

History offers a wonderful canvas for writers, especially when primary sources are contradictory and relatively scarce. This has allowed me the space to interpret situations in creative ways, with an eye to including identities and themes chronically underpursued in historical narratives. Similarly, the elements of Welsh myth I have incorporated only hint at the extraordinary depth of Celtic folklore. I hope readers will be inspired to explore it further.

PERSONS OF THE STORY

THE ROYAL HOUSE OF WESSEX

Ine—King of the West Saxons
Æthelburg—wife of Ine, Queen of the West Saxons
Ingild—younger brother of Ine, ætheling of Wessex
Cuthburh—sister of Ine, wife of Aldfrith of Northumbria, now
   a nun
Cwenburh—sister of Ine, also a nun
Cenred—father of Ine, Ingild, Cuthburh and Cwenburh
Frigyth—wife of Ingild, *deceased*
Eoppa—son of Ingild and Frigyth

PEOPLE OF WESSEX

Hædde—bishop of Wintanceaster
Earconwald—bishop of Lundenwic
Nothhelm—King of the South Saxons
Thryth—wife of Nothhelm
Gweir—a warrior gesith
Leofric—a warrior gesith
Edred—a warrior gesith, sworn to Ingild
Sælin—wife of Edred
Winfrid of Crediantun—a Christian priest

Godric of Wintanceaster—an ealdorman
Osberht—an ealdorman
Beorhtric of Hamwic—an ealdorman
Gefmund—gerefa of Gifle
Merewyn—daughter of Gefmund
Eadgifu—a lady of the court
Sinnoch—master of the king's stables
Deorstan—chief stablehand
Eanswith and Alis—maids to Æthelburg

DUMNONIA, KINGDOM OF THE BRITONS

Geraint—King of the Dumnonii
Cadwy—son of Geraint, prince of Kernow
Goeuin—sister of Geraint
Dinavus—steward of Dintagel
Ulch—Lord of Carnbree
Beruin—a local lord
Cigfa—a witch
Emrys—a wandering storyteller
Eiddon—a warrior
Celemon—a warrior
Brys—a warrior

THE WILD HUNT

Herla—leader of the Wild Hunt, formerly an Eceni warchief
    sworn to Boudica
Corraidhín—a hunter, Herla's second-in-command
Senua—a hunter, sister of Gelgéis
Gelgéis—a hunter, sister of Senua
Orlaith—a hunter
Nynniaw—a hunter
Ráeth—a hunter, *deceased*

ANNWN, THE OTHERWORLD

Gwyn ap Nudd—King of Annwn
Olwen—daughter of Ysbaddaden, chief of Giants
Culhwch
Rhiannon
Pwyll
Pryderi
Bwlch, Cyfwlch and Syfwlch
Cædwalla—former king of Wessex, *deceased*
Centwine—former king of Wessex, *deceased*
Ceawlin—former king of Wessex, *deceased*

A NOTE ON PRONUNCIATION

The ash character Æ/æ used in Old English is pronounced like the **a** in "cat."

The Welsh names Gwyn ap Nudd and Annwn appear so frequently throughout the book that I wanted to provide a phonetic pronunciation for those unfamiliar with the Welsh alphabet. While it is difficult to create one that is both easily understood and incorporates the whole sound, an approximation would be "Gwin app Neethe" (to rhyme with seethe) and "Ah-noon."

SONG

OF THE

HUNTRESS

PROLOGUE: THE WILD HUNT

I should never have sought him, he of the silver eyes. When I followed stories into the wilderness to find him, and he turned a face towards me, it was ancient and sad. When I asked his name and he denied it, the face he wore was wild; a stag stirred to madness by the harvest moon. When, finally, I told him what I wanted, he laughed and his face changed again. A low anxious hum rose between us, as if wasps nested in his heart. I remember stepping back. But I did not step far enough.

My queen's name once sang in the throats of our people. It rang above the thunder of chariot wheels, and the horses that drew them into the maelstrom of battle. We washed the Romans' blood from our skin together, Boudica and I, just as we lay cradled in the same dark, imagining a world without fighting, tithes and overlords. A world without Rome.

My own story should have ended like hers, in the dance of spear and shield. I should have lived and died simply like the warrior I was. But I had heard the stories. Druids warned of hollow places, where worlds touched and dreams became flesh. They spoke of a guardian—someone with the power to challenge Rome. Boudica's bravery could not defeat an empire.

The day I met him, the King of Annwn had eyes like cold stars. He was both huge and humble: a giant one moment, a man the next. I found myself on my knees, his hand atop my hair. "So," he said in the voice of the wind that scoured high crags. "You wish for the power to drive Rome from these shores."

I forced aside fear. "The druids call you guardian—of land, life and law. Will you help our people?"

"I have heard your plea, Herla." He raised me up. "All that remains is the price."

I felt myself stiffen. "Price?"

"It is customary to bring an offering to the Folk of Annwn." His lips parted; a gleam of teeth. "What have you brought me, Herla?"

"I have brought nothing." Who was I to know of offerings and etiquette? Such things were the province of priests.

"Not true." He extended a hand towards me. "You have brought yourself." When I did not speak, he continued, "Come to my feast. Come to the merry halls of Caer Sidi. Give me but three days and I will give you three gifts."

Unable to help myself, I asked, "What gifts?"

He smiled. "Power your enemy cannot withstand."

Ah, how those words pulled. And yet—"Boudica marches on Londinium in three days. I must be at her side."

"You will be." His hand turned gracefully so that it hovered, palm up, before me. "You will be there with the boons of my people."

Power your enemy cannot withstand.

I called the best of my warband, nineteen women in all. Among them Corraidhín of the swift spear; passionate Ráeth; sisters Senua and Gelgéis; and sweet-voiced Orlaith, whose sorrowsongs were as haunting as her battle cries. I kissed Boudica, swore I would meet her on the grassy plain before the Roman capital. In three days, I whispered, the war would be won.

I looked back only once. The Queen of the Eceni met my eyes, her tawny hair snapping like a pennant and a promise of blood. It always tangled hopelessly around her face whenever we lay together. My fingers had combed those fiery strands more times than I could count.

I never saw her again.

The Otherworld king met us at the foot of a great cliff, and my heart shuddered to hear how the stone cracked and groaned open at his touch. Darkness leaked into the world. We flinched, but the king's smile was light. "Fear is for the weak, Herla, do you not agree?"

A flowery shore waited to greet us, deep beneath the earth. "The steeds of Llŷr," the king said of the horses that fled across that meadow sea. A golden road lapped at my feet and, like every mortal who had strayed into the Otherworld, the desire to tread it gilded my bones. I ached to go where it led, but I remembered Boudica. When the king whistled, twenty horses broke from their herd-kin. "They will carry you swift and sure," he told me, "if you will accept them?"

Like a fool, I nodded, and found a shining bridle in my hands. "Beautiful." When I ran my fingers across its glossy flank, the horse's white coat deepened to dark. I watched that silken hue flow over the rest and paid it no mind; how glorious we would look, riding down the Romans, crushing them beneath hoof and blade.

The following day—although it was difficult to tell beneath the misty, cavernous skies of Annwn—the king threw a feast. Mead flowed from the doors of Caer Sidi. The Folk of that dread castle, touched neither by age nor by infirmity, welcomed us, flattered and plied us with the finest foods. Pellucid honey, apples and blackberries, tiny cakes, and cheeses white as winter. Songs were sung in that place, jests made. And if our hosts' laughter had an edge, we did not hear it. *I* did not hear it.

At the end of the second day, I remembered the vow I had sworn to Boudica. My heart pounded at how nearly I had forgotten her. The more I thought on it, the stronger it grew, and no amount of fairy wine could numb the sense of urgency that beat like a war drum within me.

"My second gift to you." The king snapped his fingers and my mind filled instead with the sight of the sword that lay across his palms, mist-pale. "Will you accept it?"

Like a fool, I took the sword. It was the most beautiful thing I had seen, more beautiful than the wilderness of my queen's hair.

But in my hands it had a hilt of shadow and a blade darker than the space between stars. As I lifted, swung it, I could have sworn it cut the world itself. "Great Culhwch's axe can draw blood from the wind," the chief of Annwn said, and his voice held a strange joy, "but this is sharper."

As the third day ended in frolic and feast, I found myself pacing before the doors of Caer Sidi, the glorious sword sheathed at my side. "I am grateful for your gifts, lord, but they are useless without an enemy against which to wield them. Is it not time to return?"

He tutted, as if at a restive child. "Will you not accept my third and final gift?"

I had become complacent then, and greedy for more. "What is it?"

"Mount."

Like a fool, I mounted. Soon we would be at Londinium. Soon I would win Boudica victory and the Eceni freedom.

"Here." The king passed me a small hound and I frowned as it draped itself before my saddle. It was all white save for two unsettling blood-red ears. "One of the Cŵn Annwn, hounds of the Otherworld. He is Dormach, my favourite." His voice, usually so smooth, was harsh with regret. "Do not alight in the mortal realm until the hound leaps down."

"Why?"

"You desired the third gift. Remember—" his eyes glinted—"stay in the saddle until the dog leaps down." And without another word, the chief of Annwn lifted his hand and sent us from his kingdom.

I knew we were returned—the wind had all the boisterous imperfection of the real world and I bared my teeth at it. "We make for Londinium. For victory." When my warband hollered, their voices had an odd resonance, as of horns blowing across a distant plain.

Llŷr's steeds ate up the leagues, but the land looked different. Unfamiliar. Stones were missing from the great road that led to Londinium, and weeds straggled up between the cracks. My unease grew. A ragged group were building a wall with the stones of the road and I reined in. "You are fortunate we go to break Rome's power in these lands, for they would not be pleased to find you dismantling their work."

"Your speech is odd," one of the men replied, face paling as his eyes swept over us. "And the Romans are gone—or nearly. They will not care what we do."

"Gone?" My heart stuttered. "Boudica has won?" *Without me?*

He chuckled. "Boudica is three hundred years dead. If she lived at all. There are some as believe her a story."

"*Lies,*" Ráeth cried, and before I could stop her, she leaped from the saddle. The instant her foot touched earth, her body crumbled, collapsing into dust.

I screamed. The labourers fled.

One day, my heart told me, *one hundred years*. The others screamed too. We threw back our heads, shrieked our grief at the sky, but what emerged were howls; a predator's cry. Dormach turned to look up at me, his muzzle a hideous grin, and in his eye, I saw the wasp-hearted King of the Otherworld for who he really was. I read his name there: Gwyn ap Nudd, the ancient shepherd of souls.

From that day forth, we rode, for the bloodhound showed no sign of leaping down. Every month, when the moon grew old, Gwyn's blade woke us from our damned slumber beneath the tor to slay any who crossed our path. It was indeed sharper than the axe that drew blood from the wind: it sheared soul from flesh. Those souls rode with me, a host of spirits whose bitter lamentations withered my heart. I had no need to dismount to become dust. I forgot the Eceni. I forgot Boudica. Even mortal language was lost.

The Britons called us the Wild Hunt and learned to dread the ageing crescent of the moon. The Saxons that came in Rome's wake threatened their children with tales of our savagery. To the priests of Rome's god who stayed to finish the conquest the empire had abandoned, we were the Devil's kin. And Gwyn ap Nudd? He never once showed himself. So it went through three more centuries, and the only thing that stirred the dust of my heart was the bloodlust that drove me to hunt.

Until the night I met *her*. Until the night the hound of Annwn leaped down.

1

ÆTHELBURG

Tantone, Somersæte
Kingdom of Wessex

"Burn it," she says.

Faces turn to her in the waning light. "*Burn it?*" Leofric repeats. "But Tantone is a strategically important piece in your husband's—"

"You want Ealdbert to control it, or worse, the Wealas?" Æthel casts a dark glance at the fortification beyond the wall. Unornamented and squat, with greening planks of stout wood, it would still go up—with a bit of effort on their part. "Let us burn him out."

Leofric shakes his head. It's a shade greyer every time Æthel sees him, and more than likely, she is the cause. "I want Ealdbert dead as much as you, but firing Tantone is a step too far."

"We did not bring a force to garrison it," Æthel argues, starting to pace. "Do you think the king will be pleased to hear we left it behind for the taking?"

"My queen, Ine king himself ordered Tantone built. At least send word to him before making an impulsive decision."

Æthel comes to a sudden stop. "Ine king is my husband, and he trusts me," she says coldly, stamping on the flicker of doubt her own words sow. "He will support my *impulsive* decision."

"I agree," comes a new voice.

Edred is dressed a little too well for battle; a golden brooch pins his cloak to his shoulder, and his tunic is linen fine enough to wear at court. "The Wealas still roam these lands," he adds with a vague gesture westwards, and Leofric frowns. "You know the natives—always searching for ways to undermine Saxon rule. Unless the king posts men here, Tantone is better off ruined."

Æthel seizes the chance to say, "And he informed me of no such plan to do so."

"Maybe true, my lady, but equally he gave no instruction to destroy it." Anger mottles Leofric's cheeks. "I must insist—"

"Insist, Leofric?" Edred raises an eyebrow. "To the Queen of Wessex?"

Æthel straightens her mail shirt while the man splutters, although she would rather not win this battle by rank. *It's a sensible decision. Any good commander would make it.* Edred's agreement is a surprise, however. He is her husband's brother's man and not one she knows well. Æthel regards him through narrowed eyes. Perhaps he seeks to win a favour from the king and hopes for her support. Whatever the reason, she'll make use of it.

"All I meant," Leofric says through gritted teeth, "is that—"

"The queen has decided. Your protests now are improper, if not downright defiant."

Æthel presses her lips together before a smile can ruin her poise, but she has probably made an enemy this day. *Well, it can't be helped.* "Burn it," she orders her men.

After a moment, Leofric nods infinitesimally, and that small motion kills any humour Æthel had in her. How dare he give his permission—and the men look to him for it? It gnaws at her heart: the knowledge that Ine's gesiths think nothing of her prowess in the field. No matter how many successful campaigns she fights, how swift her thinking or strong her arm, to them she is still only a woman. "Burn it all." Her tone is harsh and Leofric walks away. Ostensibly to supervise, but his displeasure is a chill that even the rising conflagration cannot banish.

When the buildings beyond the palisade are fully ablaze, she picks up her spear, unshoulders her shield and ensures her sword and seax are loose in their sheaths. "To me." A yell from the assembled men, and Æthel bares her teeth as she leads them up and over the earthen ramp, covered by arrow fire. Her blood thrills. Wild-eyed men are tumbling from the fortress as the flames spread, and she cuts them down, her anger at Leofric turning her blows savage. It is only after a dozen have fallen that she remembers they ought to take prisoners. And where is Ealdbert, the traitor she came here to fight?

They have brought a hellish dusk. The night is orange, the air choking and thick as old stew. A man—*boy*, she amends on seeing his thistledown beard—lunges at her out of the stables, carrying with him the frightened squeals of horses. She parries the blow, but the boy's eyes lock with hers beneath her helm and widen.

"The queen," he shouts, "it's the queen!" In moments, another five of Ealdbert's men surround her. *Shit.*

"Lady Æthelburg," the eldest says with a mocking bow. "How considerate of you to provide my lord with such a fine ransom. How much will your husband pay to have you back unharmed?"

Æthel flinches at the thought of Ine's face if she were to arrive trussed like game at the gates of Wiltun. She can picture his pained look perfectly. *He* would not blame her—he never did, even if he should—but the men of the Witan are a different story. Ine would be forced to make her excuses. Æthel's fist clenches on the hilt of her sword. "I doubt he'd pay a silver penning," she tells her assailants, already hearing the apologetic speech he would give the Witan. "I am far more trouble than I am worth."

The man chuckles: her only warning before she is forced to parry a backhanded blow meant to knock her unconscious. The others are grinning too—at least for the first minute. One by one, their smiles fade as each attack fails to land. Æthel can feel her face set in a frozen grimace. Batting aside the sword of the man who mocked her, she sees an opening and takes it, thrusting her spear into his ribs. His leather slows the strike, but does not stop the spearhead sinking deep.

"*Bitch*," the boy snarls as his companion staggers. Æthel tries to pull her spear free but it's stuck fast. She draws her sword just in time to block the boy's rage-fuelled swing.

A second man lunges for her. She catches the blow on her

shield and spins to deflect a third that slices into her arm. *Damned if I'll let them take me.* Yelling wordlessly, Æthel launches a flurry of blows hard and fast enough to send the boy to his knees—if it wasn't for the fact she is facing four other men too. All of whom are starting to wonder whether she needs to be taken alive. Dodging a blow aimed unambiguously at her kidneys, she thinks, *How dare they?* Fighting for her life against the Wealas—Britons—is a given, and against the men of Mierce and the east to be expected. But these are her own people, Wessex born. How dare they raise arms against her?

The roof of the stables is afire now; Æthel can see her men hustling the valuable horses out of danger. Most of Ealdbert's small force seems to be fleeing into the night, but where is *he*? A horrible thought hits her, along with another glancing blow. Was he ever even here? He had fled west; she'd spent a month driving him from place to place until she had cornered him here at Tantone. At least, she had thought him cornered.

Her sword is knocked aside. Throat sore from gasping smoke, Æthel watches it thump to earth cracked by summer sun and pulls the shorter seax from its sheath. Another man goes down with the weapon planted in his neck, and she snatches his sword as he falls. It is a poor substitute for her own pattern-welded blade, but they are forcing her onto lower ground where she cannot reach it. She coughs; the smoke is thickening, making her eyes stream. Æthel drags an arm angrily across them.

Blinking, she thinks she sees Edred's face, but grey rolls across and a streak of silver swings at her in the dark. Everything slows. Æthel watches the blade part the smoke and knows she cannot raise her shield in time to block it. *How ridiculous*, a stray thought says. How incredible.

The iron stops an inch from her flesh. Still braced for the blow, Æthel blinks again, but the sight before her becomes no clearer. The boy warrior's mouth is open, his eyes bulging. With the sureness of a woman born to the battlefield, she knows that he is dead.

Screams pierce the dark. Not the cries of the wounded, or the desperate fury of those fighting for their lives, but lost bitter wails.

Æthel shudders. The next instant, sheer instinct throws her flat just as a blade scythes the spot where she was standing. Her helm slips; she pulls it off before it can blind her, to see riders among them like ragged ghosts, steering their mounts through the spear-din. Men are falling beneath sword and hoof; the slaughterhouse stench of spilled guts is thick in her nose. Æthel frowns, trying to gauge numbers, but the chaos is absolute. That is, except for one still point. She raises herself, sticky with mud and blood, and looks.

Like the eye of a storm, unreally calm, a woman looks back. Mounted atop a horse larger than any Æthel has seen, armoured in leather and fur, one of her gauntleted hands is curled around a blade as dark, surely, as the roots of the world. Many small braids tumble out beneath a horned helm pushed back from her face.

Something inside Æthel stutters, stops…and the figure is gone, become the chaos. She licks dry lips, tastes blood. Perhaps she has taken a blow to the head. "Leofric!" she yells, staggering to her feet. She does not expect a response, but the gesith answers from somewhere east of her and Æthel follows his voice to the edge of the earthen ramp that guards the fortress. "What's happening?"

He is grim-faced. "That traitorous bastard must have had horsemen. They swept through and cut down two dozen of us before we even knew they were here."

She curses. "If they're Ealdbert's, where are they now?"

Leofric shakes his head and Æthel wonders whether he saw what she did: that person—wild and beautiful and dangerous beyond all measure. She grimaces. A trick of the smoke and the pain of her wounds. More likely the riders belong to Ealdbert and she is a royal fool for failing to find them before the attack.

"You're bleeding," the gesith says, and she is surprised to hear a note of concern in his voice. Probably concern for his own hide—it will not look good if she dies on his watch.

Æthel shrugs. "It's nothing." And it mostly is, but the wound on her arm will need stitching up. "What of Ealdbert himself?"

"No sign."

Although Leofric's tone remains neutral, condemnation is writ large in his lowered brows. Tantone, he thinks, has burned for nothing. Men have died for nothing. Æthel looks away. "It's one less place for him to hide." Their losses are heavier than she had planned for. "Did we take any prisoners?"

"Two."

Edred emerges out of the night, wiping his sword—the only dirty part of him—on his cloak, and Æthel recalls her brief conviction of seeing him among the men who cornered her. "Where have you been?"

"Ensuring we have these to question." He gestures over his shoulder. His men are dragging a pair of smoke-stained prisoners, their wrists bound.

"Soften them up." Æthel makes sure they can hear. "I will question them later. If they do not talk, kill them. I won't feed traitors."

Leofric nods approvingly and Edred bows. "Your will, my queen." The men are led off, staring wide-eyed at the fortress that sheltered them. Clearly it had never occurred to Ealdbert that she would choose to burn the place. Æthel adds the absent ætheling to the list of men who have underestimated her…or think her merely unhinged. It is a long list.

Tantone is a beacon in the night. Those riders…She cannot convince herself they were Ealdbert's. *Else they'd have stayed to rout us.* But if the fire had alerted them, it would alert others. Æthel turns her head west. "Gather the dead and bury them quickly. Geraint may have eyes in the area."

"The King of Dumnonia is not brave enough to face us," Leofric says. But he too turns to look westwards, where the land rises and falls in the first of the valleys that give the people of Dumnonia their name. Night blankets those forbidding dales; Æthel shivers at the thought of them. She was raised in open country, on a plain disturbed only by the ancient tombs of people gone before. Gentle, grassy mounds—unlike the tangled hills that hide the Britons. Space for a horse to run without pause while she clung to the reins and the wind and the sound of sun drying the grasses.

She used to plait them while she waited for her horse to catch his breath. *Keep your hands busy,* her mother had said, *and they won't suspect your mind is at work too.*

Æthel smiles at the memory; the sad smile that comes with knowing her mother cannot give her more advice. "I could do with it," she murmurs under her breath and goes to oversee the collection of the dead. Despite her attempt to banish them, a pair of eyes burning brighter than the fire goes with her.

"Holy God, Edred. I said *soften* them, not beat them to within an inch of their lives." Æthel crouches in front of one of the rebels. In the dawn light, his cheek is split and blood crusts his swollen mouth. "They do need to be able to speak."

"Crazy she-wolf," the man slurs.

Before Edred can raise a hand to strike him, Æthel catches it. "Peace. I don't care what he calls me."

"By insulting you, he insults the king," Leofric remarks, and she keeps her expression blank with an effort. She would bet that *crazy she-wolf* is exactly what he thinks of her after tonight.

Æthel forces down exhaustion, leans forward and grabs the rebel's chin. If he wanted a she-wolf, he could have one. "Where is Ealdbert?"

His lip curls. "If the king seeks him, why didn't he come himself?"

"We are not talking about the king. Where is Ealdbert?"

"Gone." He spits. Æthel ducks aside and it lands on Leofric's shoe. The gesith makes a sound of disgust. "Ine won't find him."

"Few places would extend him welcome." She flicks her eyes at Leofric. "Sussex?"

"Nothhelm would not dare. After the beating Cædwalla meted out, the realm's sworn to your husband now."

"You don't know where he is, do you?" she says to the rebel. "Might as well admit it and save me the trouble of torture."

The man glues his lips together, but she knows she is right. Both are likely no more than ceorls pressed into the ætheling's service with promises of wealth. She tips her head on one side, considering what to do. Ine would probably exile them…and they'd swiftly join up with Ealdbert again. The hard decisions always fall to her. "Kill them," she says and forces herself to watch while it is done.

The events of last night are blurring in the late-summer dawn. Searing heat, metal on metal, the scream of tired muscles—all seem a fancy. Except *her*. Æthel could not forget those eyes if she tried. They are there even now when she shuts her own, along with a face haunted by pride and grief. She shakes herself. Foolishness.

"The riders," she begins and stops. A blackbird pipes gaily; the breeze is gentle. From where they are camped, Tantone is a slur on the green, its watchtower a smoking ruin. But something is moving. Æthel squints at a ripple in the grass, and her blood chills. "Leofric!"

"What is it?"

Æthel nods at the frisks of distant movement. "Look."

Leofric follows her gaze, raising a hand against the glowing sky. "Deer, surely."

"No," Æthel says. "Wealas."

"What?" Edred joins them. "Dumnonii—here?"

"I *knew* Geraint would investigate. He'd be on us already if we hadn't moved our camp."

"I cannot see any men."

"And you won't until it's too late." Æthel wheels round to bark out orders. "Move! Strike camp. Be quick about it." No man looks to Leofric this time. They can hear the alarm in her voice.

"Why not face them?" Edred catches her injured arm and Æthel winces. "If Geraint is foolish enough to bring the fight to us—"

"Foolish?" She almost laughs. "Our forces spent the night fighting, burying bodies, and then marching out here to put some distance between us and Tantone. They are in no shape to take up the sword again so soon. Geraint is not foolish. It's the perfect opportunity."

"What do you mean we won't see him until it is too late?" Leofric asks slowly.

Æthel hesitates. Plenty among the court do not believe what she has witnessed with her own eyes. And the bishops come down hard on such talk. "Geraint employs... unusual methods," she says meaningfully, and prays he takes the hint. "You know the Wealas and their superstitions."

"Superstitions can't make up for strength of arms," Edred says.

Æthel grinds her teeth, determined not to spell it out. Her credibility has taken enough of a knock. "Look at the men," she says in a low hard voice. "They have been up all night while Geraint's forces are fresh. Only a fool would stay and face him."

"What forces? Some scouts, perhaps, but nothing more."

I have seen them appear as from air, she tells him silently. As if Geraint and his men could blend seamlessly into the world around them. No battlefield prowess can explain that. And if those flashes of movement are anything to go by, he—or whatever power he prays to—is doing the same now. The Dumnonii will be on them while they stand here and argue.

"Enough." She lowers her voice, so only Edred and Leofric can hear. "You know I value your opinions in the field." Æthel draws a breath. "But, as you pointed out last night, Edred, I am queen. If I say to retreat, you will retreat, and I am not beholden to state my reasons."

They glower. She has had this conversation more than once, and every time she wonders whether *this* will be it—the time they openly defy her. She wonders what she would say, how she would react. They are important men, trusted in court, and have proven themselves good counsel. It would cost Ine to exile them, but he would do it if she asked. He has never denied her anything. Except *that*. And as the years pass, she—not he—bears the consequences of his decision. In her darker moments, Æthel wonders whether it is guilt that urges him to support her, to defend her, rather than belief in her ability.

Between blinks, the blood drains from Edred's face. There they are: lining the brow of a hill. She does a clumsy count—at least five score warriors—and shock courses through her, leaving no room for the pleasure of vindication. Only an overwhelming force would have the confidence to declare themselves so openly.

"We'll pull back to Gifle," Leofric says tightly into the silence. "Once we have walls around us, we dispatch scouts to keep an eye on Geraint."

"And send a message to the king," Æthel adds, eyeing the Wealas—more and more appearing by the second. "I have never seen the Dumnonii show themselves or their forces so blatantly."

Leofric grunts agreement and Æthel mounts her horse, her thoughts in turmoil. First Ealdbert, then the nameless riders, and now Geraint. Foreboding cramps her chest like a winter ague. As she turns her horse south-east, she imagines she can feel Geraint's eyes across the intervening distance, the mass of Dumnonia brooding at his back. *What does he want?* And more to the point, why did he show himself? His decision to drop his disguise, to threaten them openly: bluster or something else?

Æthel bites her lip. After years of uneasy truce, it's as if the King of Dumnonia wants war.

2

ĐERLA

They sleep beneath the tor...until the moon is old and it is time to ride. Then Gelgéis raises a horn to her lips and Orlaith raises her song and they pour forth, their horses darker than the night. Herla needs no horn; her cry is a wild thing, and deadly. Life shudders when she throws back her head. The scurrying beasts of the grass burrow into it, and the owl on the wing veers sharply. Smaller shapes fall from the sky.

The shy deer are stirred to frenzy. Herla's head is as proud as theirs: the horns of her helm upswept, one broken, its bone tokens a rattle. Beneath it, her hair is a mane of dark braids, her smile animal. The bloodlust is upon her, and she welcomes it.

Her hunters tumble after in a rough cavalcade. At the forefront are Nynniaw and Corraidhín, spears bundled behind their saddles. Then come Orlaith, Senua and Gelgéis. Others fall in behind. Their faces are cold as the ice that splits trees in winter.

Raising her eyes moon-ward, Herla catches a scent on the wind. *We ride.* Her order is not words, but impulse. The Hunt-tongue is simple. *We ride.* Draped in front of her saddle, the bloodhound adds his own curdling howl to their chorus. Herla's shadow shrouds them and withers the late-summer leaves. If any person were to step outside, they might hear it: the echo of Gwyn's laughter in Herla's.

Mortal distance is nothing to the horses of Annwn; she closes quickly on her quarry. The fools have even lit a fire to announce themselves. Fire on the night of the old moon. Either they court death, or no one remembers the stories.

Or—she soon discovers—they are enmeshed in battle. Herla watches the tide of it, the ebb and flow of slaughter, and it tugs at something in her, buried deep. *Smoke, stench, banners.* The black sword hungers to join the fray and she lets it, swinging it in bloody arcs as she thunders among them. It takes the combatants some moments to realize she is there, for the screams to begin as her hunters cut a brutal path. The sword of Annwn shears through armour and flesh alike—all the frail tethers that bind souls to bodies—and Herla laughs, as the bright threads break before her.

Blood on her lips, she seizes a young man. *Son of the dust. Will you ride with me?*

"I don't want to die," is all he says, over and over until his soul is swallowed in the host. Her hunters toss down a score of warriors and the black sword sings. More this night to ride with her, hunt with her, sleep with her under the tor until the moon is old again.

A mailed figure catches Herla's eye. The earth beneath the warrior is scuffed; she can see weariness in the set of their shoulders, in the way their weapon hangs low. Wheeling her horse, she charges, swings—and the warrior throws themselves flat, leaving Herla's blade to cut air. Momentarily stunned, she watches as they rip off their helm with one bloodied hand and eyes like chips of blue ice meet hers. Short fair hair dampened with sweat. A woman, fierce-faced in the lurid night.

That gaze pierces Herla like the Otherworld blade. Her bloodlust falters, her head abruptly tumbling with colour. *Smoke curls sweetly; a rabbit spitted over a cookfire; a tawny-haired woman leaning back on her hands. Faint lines crease the corners of her eyes.*

The dog howls, and night returns. There is pain in her chest, and a terrible weight on her spirit: the souls of the reaped ready to crush her. With a gasp, Herla tears her gaze away, urges her horse into a gallop. It is only when she is running that she realizes she is running; from what is unclear. Obediently, her hunters follow. Although Gwyn's hound thrashes, howling his rage, the hill and its flames, and the woman with ice-sharp eyes, are left behind.

The night is young, but she rides for the tor, spurred on by something nameless. Is this fear? Herla's skin prickles with a feeling she is sure she knows, but cannot recall. Her memories are darkness, riding, killing, and dreamless sleep to ride again. And yet it lingers—the brief vision of the fire with its rabbit, watched over by a tawny-haired woman.

"Lord," Corraidhín calls, and her voice cuts through Herla's wild musing. How long has it been since she heard it? Like her, the Hunt speak horn. Their words are the flexing of horse muscle, the beating of shield and spear. That is language enough. Herla ignores the word, that slip of the old tongue. Still pursued by the thing unknown, still plagued by souls whose true weight she has not felt until this moment, she makes the only choice left to her: enchanted slumber in the deep halls of Glestingaburg.

Oblivion.

For the first time, Herla dreams.

She climbs steps she has climbed before, dread kerbs of stone that end at a door many enter and few leave. She is walking, each footfall remarkable because it is her own. Her hand, as she pushes on the wood, is unfamiliar. Skin browned from the marsh sun, knuckles rough. That hand, she knows suddenly, has braided leather, scrubbed pots with sand, cut kindling and laid fires. She cannot stop staring at it, wondering what else these strange fingers have touched. Cloth worn thin from river stones. Wool. The skin left on warmed milk. Softer things. Hair tawny as an owl's wing.

She drops it with a hiss, as if the wood of the door has turned to forge-fire iron. Those new words are massing in her mind. Scrub. Sand. River. Milk. Tawny. No, not new. Old words she has forgotten how to say. She wants to hold them close. She is frightened of holding them close.

Caer Sidi swallows her footsteps. The Folk of Annwn are busy inside it—wasps in the nest of their chief's heart. She sees him before she is seen. He is moving from group to group with determined, agitated strides. He looks up and shock rules him for so brief an instant she is sure she imagined it. Then his face relaxes into a smile. The same smile that bought and shredded her trust.

"Lord Herla." Gwyn ap Nudd gathers a retinue around him. "I am surprised to see you. How are you enjoying my gifts?"

She opens her mouth. Her words are a howl, and the Folk laugh.

"Ah, yes." The King of Annwn shakes his dark head. "As you have discovered, the art of conversation is no longer required from you. A relief, is it not?"

Herla's eyes burn.

"Do not look at me like that." With a nod to the sword sheathed at her side, "I gave you what you asked for, after all. Power your enemies could not withstand."

She keeps her lips shut, keeps the savage language locked away, but in her dust-dead heart are the ashes of Rome. Slain by time. Along with her people and everything she loved.

Love? It is something from the old language, a word the Hunt-tongue cannot shape. Like fear, Herla thinks she felt it once, but it is far from her grasp.

"Please do not bear me too much ill will." Gwyn ap Nudd comes closer and Herla fights the urge to retreat. "You are the unknowing architect of my deliverance. Of all this." He spreads his arms at the pavilions beyond the castle's doors, proud with pennants: a black hare; two golden rings linked with a chain; a wing on a bloody field. More banners hang above her, emblazoned with the famous cauldron of Annwn, the one that can heal death.

"I am grateful," Gwyn whispers.

There is no remorse in him. No acknowledgement of his crime. She had not thought it a crime until now—the Hunt is everything. But here in the halls of the fortress that changed her, Herla is closer to herself than she has been in centuries. Other memories pile up behind her eyes; she has only to let them in.

And then Gwyn waves a hand. "You have trespassed long enough, Herla. Take my blade and return to your rest."

Annwn unravels around her. She cannot refuse the order, but something has shifted. Scales tipped ever so slightly in her direction, away from the King of the Otherworld. Perhaps he feels that shift; her last sight of his face shows it frowning.

Herla wakes in darkness.

She has never dreamed before and she has never woken before. Her waking is the Hunt and when she does not hunt, she sleeps. So it has always been.

She cannot move. Her arms and legs are bound to her side like a sacrifice laid in the mud. Neither can she turn her head, but she senses them there, her hunters, bound and slumbering as she is supposed to be. Their horses sleep beside them. They lie as if in death, as if waiting for the world to catch fire at the end of days.

She makes a sound. It takes her a moment to realize it is a word, a real word, like the ones she spoke before. "No," she says to the suffocating dark. *Free me, or let me sleep.* She strains, but it is like straining against fate. Invisible strings she has never wanted to believe in.

Weight on her chest is her only answer. Hot breath, claws. The dog has come to sit there and he is no longer small. She can feel how massive are his paws, how wide his muzzle. The Cŵn Annwn's true form. Has he leaped down? *I should not be awake to ask the question,* Herla reminds herself. Three hundred years have passed the same way: waking, riding, sleeping. If breaking the curse were as easy as this, she would have thrown off the yoke long ago.

Sleep does not come. What comes instead is tawny hair. Tawny hair and green eyes, which change, slowly, to icy blue. A smudged face in the night, battle-weary. Not a face Herla knows, but she recognizes the spirit behind it. So familiar. So like another's. She strains after a name, finds none. Only that lingering foxfire colour and a scent of cedarwood.

3

INE

Wiltun, Wiltunscir
Kingdom of Wessex

"Your own *wife*," Ingild says, slamming down the missive that brought the news. "That woman will be the ruin of this realm."

With a surge of anger—anger he rarely feels—Ine rounds on his brother. "Lower your voice. As you point out, Æthelburg is my wife."

"Even you must admit she has gone too far this time," Ingild says in the same forceful tones. They are in the Witan chamber at the back of Wiltun's great hall and only a partition separates them from the bustling space beyond, always full of servants tending the firepit, providing food for the men coming and going. Far too many ears to hear Ingild slander the queen. "*You* built that fortress at Tantone," his brother continues. "Our enemies will not see us as strong or united if your wife—"

"Prevented Ealdbert from gaining a foothold."

"Ealdbert wasn't even there."

"But he is of noble blood." Ine struggles to lower his own voice, taking two deep breaths. "Remember that an ætheling with a fortress is no small threat."

"Especially in a kingdom without an heir," Ingild retorts and Ine looks away, profoundly glad that Æthelburg cannot hear. His chest aches with her absence. There are more and more of them lately, as if she is finding reasons not to be at home. With him.

His brother comes around the table to grip his arm with

sudden solicitousness. Ine tells himself not to believe it; Ingild has blown hot and cold since they were children. "You must understand, Ine. Women are not built for war."

"Please tell her that to her face. I want to be there when she hits you."

Ingild ignores him, darting a glance at the door instead. The others are expected any minute. "Put her aside. Take another wife. One who'll give you an heir before the kingdom tears itself apart."

"You've never liked her," Ine says flatly, pulling his arm free. He remembers how much relish Ingild took in comparing Æthel to his own bride. And Frigyth was a good person, kind and honest, until the fever took her and their second, unborn, child. Ingild has never been quite the same since.

"It's not that I dislike her, it's…well, we *are* talking about the woman who set a pig loose in your bedchamber."

"That was a long time ago," Ine says with a wince, because the mess really had been awful. "And she was just proving a point."

"Proving a point? Ine, listen to yourself. She's a madwoman."

"Apologies, lord." The door bangs open, revealing Nothhelm of Sussex, followed by Gweir, Ine's most trusted gesith. Bishop Hædde comes next with ealdormen Godric and Osberht. And then his father, Cenred, seeming no more lucid than usual. Ingild's expression darkens on seeing him.

"You called for us?" Nothhelm prompts, a flush in his cheeks. He has been drinking, despite the hour.

"Indeed. It concerns Geraint of Dumnonia." Ingild opens his mouth, no doubt to mention Tantone, so Ine snaps, "Æthelburg is pinned down at Gifle with Leofric and Edred."

"Pinned down?" Gweir asks sharply.

"By a host of Britons larger than we've seen in a decade."

"Has Geraint stopped them from leaving?"

Ine slowly shakes his head. "The missive said only that he has hawk eyes on the settlement. But since they have not returned, I assume so. What could he possibly intend?" The question is directed at Gweir. Bastard son of a Briton, Leofric fondly likes to call him, but the gesith does have an insight that the rest of them lack.

The table holds a map, secured at each corner by weights carved in the shapes of beasts: dog, horse, bull and a wyvern like the one that rides the Wessex banner, proud head caught on the cusp of striking. Gweir leans over it, his finger tracing the river: an old meandering border between Wessex and Dumnonia.

"The destruction of Tantone may have given them heart," Ingild says before Gweir can speak, and in his sinking heart Ine knows the news is spreading beyond this room even now. "Geraint could use the opportunity to take back lands west of the Parrett."

"He has not ventured so far east in years." Gweir looks at Ine. "I do not believe the loss of Tantone can account for it." There is a question in there, of course, but Ine pretends not to hear it.

Nothhelm squints at the map. "It *may* have given Geraint new heart. But I agree it seems out of character. Unless he plans to drive us from Escanceaster?"

"I've been too focused on the trade at Hamwic," Ine mutters, nodding at the inked settlement on their southern coast. "The Britons may think we don't have the resources to fortify Escanceaster."

"If so, they should be disabused of the idea."

A predictable Ingild response, but the others agree with him; there are nods all round. And it is true—a determined Geraint could easily retake Escanceaster. But Ine cannot swallow his distaste at the thought of fighting the Britons, and he suspects Ingild knows it. That's what his brother really meant when he claimed Æthelburg would be the ruin of the realm. Easier to blame a woman, rather than a king. Fresh anger burns in his throat. Or perhaps it is simply disgust at himself for letting Æthel take the brunt of his brother's scorn.

Distracted, he turns to his father. "What do you counsel?"

Cenred smiles benignly, and that mild expression turns Ine cold. He has heard the whispers; once so incisive, his father's mind is fading. Ine keenly misses the days they spent together on the law code, here in Wiltun. Days filled with ink and parchment, rather than mud and fighting. Æthelburg had spent those same days far away from talk of hides and fyrds and wergelds. She'd been hunting down exiles heading unerringly for the East Saxon court, despite Sigeheard's promise not to shelter them. *What would I do without her?*

Ingild's snort intrudes on the memory. "Why do you ask *him*? Father is no more use than a babe-in-arms."

Ine almost expects Cenred to cuff his son for his rudeness, but the old man has not heard. He wanders over to one of the unlit braziers that warm the room in winter, and pokes it absently.

"If Geraint wants a fight, why not give it to him?" Ingild leans on the map. "You've ignored him long enough."

A sick feeling growing in his gut, Ine studies the faces of his advisers. "You agree?"

"Geraint's certainly made it impossible for you to ignore him any longer." Nothhelm is Ine's kinsman and King of the South Saxons, whom Cædwalla beat into submission some years ago. He shakes his head at the thought. Loyalty is better won with gifts of power.

"If he threatens your wife, he knows you will come yourself," Gweir argues. "It could be bait designed to coax you into the open."

"Oh, it is certainly bait." Ingild stabs his belt knife into the parchment heart of Dumnonia. "But we'll take advantage of it."

As the blade quivers to a stop, Ine turns reluctantly to Hædde, already knowing what the bishop will say. "Would such a campaign find favour with the Church?"

"The Britons are still in need of guidance," Hædde says crisply. His small dark eyes flit across the map. "Removing a heathen king from power would certainly aid the Christian cause."

"I don't want Geraint killed." Over Ingild's splutters, Ine adds, "Dumnonia is a huge territory and needs a capable ealdorman to govern it. I cannot be everywhere."

"Geraint an *ealdorman*?" Ingild is almost choking. "Have you lost your mind?"

"You believe he'd rather die than answer to me?"

"I don't care what *he'd* rather do." Colour has risen in Ingild's cheeks; he is almost as flushed as Nothhelm. "I care that you would be leaving a man certain to rebel the moment your back was turned. You are all but sanctioning a revolt."

"Ingild ætheling is right," Osberht says amidst other sober nods. He and Godric are eyeing Ine as if he has indeed lost his mind. "Victory in Dumnonia hinges on removing Geraint from power."

Ine lets his gaze fall on the table, imagining the pages of the law code spread there. He had done what he could for the Britons in Wessex. But for those in Dumnonia—"Killing their king will antagonize them needlessly. And there is a precedent, remember." He directs his words at Hædde. "Rome might have let Dumnonia govern itself, but technically it was still part of a conquered nation. What I am proposing is really no different."

"Rome was far away, lord. Whereas Dumnonia is on your doorstep. They speak a different language, practise a different religion. If you want them to integrate, they must change." He nods at Ingild's dagger still buried in the map. "And I do not think they will, at least while Geraint is alive. He is a powerful figurehead."

"Ine king." After the raised voices of Ingild and Osberht, Gweir's hushed tone is strangely ominous. "I advise caution fighting him on his own land. There are forces in Dumnonia that have kept Wessex at bay since the days of Constantine. Or you would long ago have taken it." Ine frowns to himself. Gweir's use of *you* is an unusual slip for him.

Bishop Hædde presses his lips together so hard that they whiten. Godric studies the wall, and even Ingild seems at a loss for words. It is not the first time Ine has heard of such a thing—Æthelburg has reported similar. Stories of mists rising on dry days, men vanishing in woodland no larger than a hide. But whatever the truth of such claims…"My mind is made up," he says. Being king must count for something sometimes. "I do not want Geraint harmed unless there is no other option." Ine takes a deep breath. "Call the gesiths together, Nothhelm. We march for Gifle."

He can see protest in the glances they exchange as they leave. Like a child following his elders, Cenred drifts out after them.

Ingild is the last to go and his stiffened back plainly says, *You are a fool.* Ine raises a hand to his forehead. The skin there feels rubbed raw.

Leaning over the map, examining his realm's fragile boundaries, the hairs on his neck suddenly lift as one. Ine whips round, but the room is empty. Beyond the door the sounds of the hall continue unabated; the low mutter of gossip, the scrape of benches. And yet the sense of being watched is so acute that he seizes a light, splashing radiance across the wall where shadows cluster thickest. An old shield hangs there. Once wielded by the warmonger, Cædwalla, its nicks and dents are battle scars, testament to blood spilled. Ine brushes a finger across it—before snatching his hand away with a gasp.

The shield is *cold.* Wood hanging in a summer-heated room should not feel like ice. Heart thumping, he raises a finger, hovers it above the painted middle. That prickle of watching eyes sharpens.

When he touches it again, the shield is just wood, rough and cool beneath his fingertip.

Ine shakes his head. It must be weariness, concern over Æthel, worry over Geraint. *Have you lost your mind?* Ingild's voice asks again, and Ine turns his back on the shield, wishing abruptly for the noise of the hall.

That night, the court is a frenzy of talk. Ine sits brooding in his chair on the platform set along one wall. On either side of him, the benches that can easily seat two hundred are only half-full. It will take a few days to gather the fyrds, to call men in from across the shire. Dumnonia is on everyone's lips. And so, as he feared, are whispers that Æthelburg not only burned their stronghold at Tantone, but managed to provoke a horde of Wealas, from which she must now be rescued. For the umpteenth time that day, Ine rubs his forehead. Although they are careful not to criticize her in his hearing, he can guess what words are exchanged under breaths. While he has pretended not to notice the ill feeling rising against his wife, it has grown like a weed unchecked, until it is large enough to strangle. A weed it was *his* responsibility to uproot. If only Æthel were here more often—

There is a hollow inside him. Ine grabs his goblet to fill it and wine slops over the rim. Servants have vanished his untouched meat, but they have kept the beaten metal full. He doesn't know how much he's drunk; the idea of carrying on into insensibility is overly appealing. Maybe he will sleep with his head pillowed on his arms and wake to a bleary dawn like the regular sots of his court.

"Are you well, lord?"

Ine sighs. "Too full of thoughts."

"Your wife is the most capable woman I know," Gweir says, leaning in to lay a hand on his arm. "Do not be concerned for her."

"I'm not." *Please don't do anything foolish, Æthel. At least wait for me.* Catching the gesith's sympathetic grimace, he pulls himself together. "Gweir, what did you mean when you spoke of Constantine and forces in Dumnonia?"

Gweir stiffens. Ine follows his gaze to see Hædde sitting with Earconwald—the bishop is newly arrived from Lundenwic. The men have their heads together and glare in tandem at a particularly raucous peal of laughter from further along the table. "Speak freely," Ine says, interest stirred by Gweir's obvious unease. "They can't possibly hear."

"My king." The gesith's shoulders are still hunched, as if expecting an attack. "It is not a subject that the Church looks favourably upon."

"I am not the Church."

Doubt is clear in the curve of Gweir's brow. *No wonder*, Ine thinks, *with all the charters I've issued.* Gold, land, protection. The Christian cause wants for nothing in Wessex. "You know it has more to do with politics," he admits in a low voice. Not an admission he would make to just anyone.

Finally, Gweir nods. "I have heard that there is a...spirit in the land." The gesith's voice is a murmur, and Ine strains to hear him over the banging of cups, the roar of the fire as another log is heaved onto it. "It's tied to the blood of Dumnonia, the royal line

specifically, although some Dumnonii have use of lesser powers."
He is speaking quickly, as if frightened he will otherwise lose his
nerve. Or perhaps it is the sight of the bishops in close conference,
their chains of office burnished by firelight. "Geraint can use this
to help his people, or hinder his enemies."

Ine steeples his fingers, resting his chin upon them to think.
"Are you saying he can call upon the land to fight for him? Ask the
fog to mask his movements, the rain to wash away the tracks of
his men so that they pass unnoticed? Trees to uproot themselves
and confuse an opponent?"

Gweir does not reply. When the silence starts to stretch, Ine
sits back. The gesith has an odd expression, enigmatic enough
that it proves impossible to read. "Gweir?"

"Sorry." He shakes his head. "You have quite the imagination,
lord. Yes, I suppose Geraint could do all those things."

"Pagan heresies, of course," Ine says, taking a larger gulp of
wine than is good for him, and Gweir swiftly agrees. Flicking
what he hopes is a surreptitious glance down the table, he wonders what Hædde and Earconwald think of such stories, whether
they view his reluctance to kill Geraint as heretical. The Church
might not be powerful enough to remove a king, but they could
certainly back one of his rivals.

Shouts interrupt his musing. Men are slapping an indistinct
figure on the back, urging them on in drunken tones. Now that
night has fallen, the only light comes from the fire, torches and
the stone cressets burning at intervals along the walls.

"Tell of the Spear-Danes from across the sea!"

"No, the battle at Finnsburuh."

They want a story, Ine realizes. His eyes are stinging from the
smoke, or sleeplessness, or simply too much wine. Hands help
the scop onto the table, where they rise slowly to their feet. Ine
frowns. Beyond their creased brown skin and greying hair, he
cannot tell whether they are male or female. "I have not seen that
person beneath this roof before," he murmurs to Gweir.

"Storytellers travel widely," the gesith says with a shrug.

It is remarkable—watching men sit up like eager apprentices.

A scop is a scop first and foremost, no matter their gender, age, or their place of birth. No other person is granted that same kind of acceptance... not even a king. Ine smiles to himself, recalling what Gweir said about his imagination. *Perhaps I ought to take up storytelling instead.*

"Honestly, poet," Nothhelm calls out, "whatever tale you choose will suit us. We've all had too much to drink to remember it come morning." Shouts and more thumping of cups make a truth of his words.

"Then perhaps I will tell of the forty tasks set by a giant for his daughter's hand in marriage." The scop's voice is a melody of ages, resonant and rich. Silence falls. "It begins with a hill and an order to plough it and sow wheat enough for a giant's table." Their eyes are impossibly blue in the gloom. "It ends with a sword and sleepless nights. But nothing challenged the young hero more than the seeking of Gwyn ap Nudd, Lord of the Hunt."

Where another scop's story would be scattered with the hoots of their listeners, the hush tonight is religious. Ine tears his gaze away to Hædde and Earconwald. The bishops sit as still as the warriors and nobles, but there is a bitter curl to Hædde's lip as he stares at the scop, and his brow is dark. As well it might be, at pagan tales.

"Now they must have Gwyn, for the great boar, Twrch Trwyth, cannot be hunted without him." The scop is warming to their story. "Trwyth is no common boar, you see, but a prince who carries a comb between his ears. No other comb can tame the giant's tangled hair without breaking in pieces. It is a treasure like the cauldron of Annwn, or Garanhir's basket, which can feed a hundred men on a single man's share."

Ine rubs his eyes, blinks them furiously, but the sight before him does not change. The shadow of a boar looms over the scop's shoulder, its eyes a violent shade. Between its ears lies the horn comb, its prongs chased with silver. If he is seeing things, he has certainly had too much to drink.

"Or the pots coveted by the warlord, Gorr," the scop continues—and the boar fades. "They will keep their contents warm until the last days." Ine is breathing relief when a new vision shimmers into being: stoppered earthenware jugs sitting amidst the debris of the table. Though men's elbows touch the jugs, no one spares them a glance.

"Or Teirtu's harp, which needs no harper to pluck it."

In place of the jugs stands a harp as high as the storyteller's thigh. Its graceful neck is stretched like a dancer's, and its strings glow with their own light. Ine swallows hard. He knows he has gone pale, is thankful that his face is mostly hidden. Not one person blinks at the harp as it fades.

"Marvels all." The scop spreads their arms and Ine tenses. "But we are concerned with Gwyn. His skill is needed to hunt the boar. His skill, his horse and red-eared hound." Palms turning up, they meet the eyes that meet theirs. "But how is our hero to get him? Before this land ever felt the step of man, higher powers summoned Gwyn to Woden's Barrow, and there he was charged with a solemn duty."

The fire, chuckling a moment ago, sinks. Torches burn lower in their brackets and the shadows become cavernous. "His feet are meant for the field." Now the old scop's voice is a bared inch of blade. "Where black wings mock the slain. He alive—they in death, their souls a-wander." Ine cannot look away as a figure appears framed in the doorway, sword in hand. Antlers crown his head like the gods of their heathen past. "It is his task to take those souls up, though where he takes them—" the scop shrugs—"I cannot say." That bladed voice drops to a whisper. "Perhaps to Annwn, to Caer Sidi or Caer Wydyr, from where so few return."

It covers the doors and the carved wooden pillars on either side. It spreads all the way to the ceiling, swallows the beams, the weapons mounted on the walls: a glittering citadel, gold-fair, not unlike the images of Heaven Ine has seen scribes sketch in their margins. Illuminated like manuscripts, the towers are of glass and whitest stone. The doors—three times the height and width of his own—are thrown wide and stairs lead up to them. A thin rivulet of blood is creeping over that dread stone. Ine watches it wend its way towards him like a worm lifting its blind head to the sun.

He pushes his chair back. Men flinch at the noise, turning to look. Heart racing, Ine rises—half staggers—to his feet. The scop is staring at him now too, proud and unblinking, as if they are equals. He does not care, has a desperate urge to flee the bloody stairs and the boar's shadow and the horned man with his red-eared hound. It is the drink, Ine tells himself, making him see things, making him sick to his empty stomach. He ought to know better.

He laughs weakly, waves a hand, says something like *please continue*. Then the King of Wessex flees his own hall, guards throwing open the doors before him into a summer night that is blessedly empty of visions. The scop's eyes follow him. They burn like a spear thrust between his shoulder blades.

4

ÆThELBURG

Gifle, Somersæte
Kingdom of Wessex

Gifle is a small community with walls that do not deserve the name, but it is easier to defend than open country. Part of the dirt streets are laid out faintly in the Roman style, a remnant of days long past, and the folk here are Æthel's own people with a scattering of Wealas. No one looks happy about a bunch of warriors descending on them, and they are even less happy when they catch sight of Geraint's threatening ring. The Dumnonii patrol the low hills, showing their strength but keeping their distance. Æthel hates it. She paces up and down the gerefa's shabby hall, cursing.

Over the past sennights, they have tried to break for the old Roman road several times, but Geraint has men enough to guarantee a wholesale slaughter and does not pursue them as long as they retreat to Gifle. He has them penned like livestock. Æthel grinds her teeth. She knows what Geraint wants—the king. And if this goes on any longer, he will get him. Along with half the men of Wiltunscir.

"To hell with it," she growls, sweeping up her sword. "Bring my horse," she snaps at a young woman who gazes back, her mouth a little round "o." Æthel supposes she has not seen a female in battledress. After a stunned moment, she hurries off.

"My queen." Nostrils flared, Æthel turns to find the gerefa, Gefmund, whose roof currently shelters her. He is a large man with the build of a warrior gone to seed, the creases worn deep in his face. "You have news from the king?"

"No. I am going to speak with Geraint myself."

She might as well have said she planned to run naked through the streets screaming pagan curses—his face pales and she is halfway to the door before he finds a response. "Stop. Æthelburg queen, you can't."

"Can't?" she says, halting with her hand on the latch.

"*Shouldn't*," Gefmund amends, closing the distance. Æthel flashes an icy look and he backs off a pace. "It is too dangerous."

"If Geraint intended to kill us, he'd have done so. He wants my husband."

"A plan to lure the king here?" He scratches at the sagging skin beneath his beard. "For what purpose—other than harm?"

"If I die, Ine will not stay to hear his words. Which is why I will be safe." *If I died, he would be free of me.* Æthel catches her breath at the horror of her own thought; a thought nurtured by the doubt that has grown quietly over the last few years. *He could marry again.* She feels sick. Is this what their marriage has come to? With her wondering exactly how much her husband cares if she dies?

"You will be safe from *what*?"

Although they are the last people she wants to see, the arrival of Leofric with Edred on his heels is a merciful distraction. Anger is easier to embrace. Gathering up the emotions churning inside her, Æthel turns a hostile eye on them. Have they been conferring without her? She starts to pull open the door. "I am going to ask Geraint what he wants."

"Unwise." Leofric shuts it with a bang. "My queen, Geraint knows your value. If you are captured—"

"I won't be captured." With sheer brute strength, she wrenches the door open and Leofric stumbles. After the dimness of the hall, the sunlight stabs her eyes, only making Æthel angrier. "I am not some sheltered flower. I can look after myself."

"Edred, you must agree that Lady Æthelburg is taking an unnecessary risk."

"If she wishes to speak with Geraint, we cannot prevent her," Edred says—and it is the second time since leaving Wiltun that he has surprised her. Æthel frowns, not liking it. "I think the effort pointless, however."

"Pointless or not, I will know what he intends." Fed up with men and opinions she did not ask for, she swings a cloak around her shoulders and marches across the yard to her horse, which the young woman already has saddled and waiting. "What's your name?" She had been about to add *girl*, but in daylight, the woman looks to have seen at least five and twenty winters.

"Merewyn, lady queen. My father is gerefa here."

Æthel swears. "I am sorry. I treated you like a servant."

"I *am* a servant," she says with equanimity, "to Wessex and to you," which only makes Æthel feel worse.

It seems crass, but she nevertheless presses a coin into the woman's palm. "For your speed. It is appreciated."

Merewyn smiles. She has lovely eyes, clear as lakewater.

"Wait!" Leofric is calling for his own horse, snapping out orders for men to join him. Æthel ought to do as he says, but a reckless-ness is in her, fuelled by impatience and anger, and that awful doubt bubbling away beneath the surface of her thoughts. She swings swiftly into the saddle.

When she reaches the gates, however, they are open. The air is full of shouting and horn blasts—Æthel shivers at the memory of the horns she heard the night Tantone burned, now near a month gone—and she stands up in the stirrups to see better. A long dark column marches towards Gifle, golden wyvern rippling above it. There are a dozen horsemen at its head.

She stares at them, knowing she ought to feel relieved. What she feels instead is…conflicted. Like a child who has climbed a tall tree, lacking both the courage and ability to return to the ground. Now others are come to fetch her down.

"Ah," Edred remarks from behind her. "That was a fast march. The king values you highly."

Æthel says nothing. She has not seen him for two months. Instead of waiting to greet the party, she returns to the gerefa's courtyard, stables her horse and sets to polishing the nicks out of her blade. The sharp, rhythmic motions are soothing. Seated on an upturned barrel, she lets her thoughts wander until a hustle of voices intrudes.

Half a dozen people make for Gefmund's hall. The gerefa himself is among them, alongside a bunch of gesiths, Nothhelm of Sussex and—Æthel blinks—the king's brother, Ingild. All of them are talking at once, their words washing over the one silent person in their midst.

He looks tired, is her first thought. Æthel crushes it. For some reason, holding onto her anger seems very important. She clutches it before her like a shield, as she rises to her feet. When Ine glances round and sees her, his face brightens, and she has to clutch it even closer. The sun picks out the golden flecks in his eyes.

"Oh, Æthelburg," Ingild says lazily, following his brother's gaze. "How good to see you well." He nods at her arm with its puckered scar. "Ealdbert's men put up a fight, then."

Ine comes over immediately. "Æthel. You're hurt?"

"It's all but healed," she says, backing away from his worried hand. Some of the light leaves his face; she tells herself she does not care.

"Still as charming as ever," Ingild remarks. Ine gives him a hard glance and Æthel thinks, not for the first time, *How can brothers be so different?* Not just in looks, but in character too.

Ine is dark where Ingild is fair. He is slender for a man, and lacking Ingild's temper; Æthel recalls her father grumbling that her husband-to-be seemed more scholar than king. Of course, he had never protested the match, not when it would make his daughter Queen of Wessex. Neither had Æthel. She and Ine had met a few times as children, and she remembered a boy with serious eyes. Awkward, shy almost, but when he spoke, people listened. She feels a pang at the memory, and yearning for those that came after it. Happier times, when they were younger, keen to know each other, full of plans for Wessex and its people—

An unexpectedly cold wind scatters the thoughts like leaves, and Æthel is left staring at Ingild with his sneer and his quirked brow: an expression he reserves just for her. They lock horns every time they meet. She is the opposite of everything he expects to find in a woman.

Ine offers his arm and, since it would cause comment if she were to refuse it, she lets him walk her into the hall like the graceful lady she and Ingild both know she is not.

The moment they are inside, Gefmund all but hurls himself before her husband. "Ine king, it is an honour to have you beneath my roof."

"Thank you for your hospitality towards my wife and gesiths," Ine says and stops, gaze twitching to one side. Æthel does not miss the eyebrows raised between Ingild and Nothhelm. What has happened since she left Wiltun? "You will be compensated," Ine says, almost an afterthought. In the dim hall, he looks unwell.

"Generous, my king. Please sit. We lead modest lives here, but I will send for food and drink."

The hall is less than half the size of those at Wiltun and Wintanceaster and consists of just a single floor with sleeping quarters at the back. There are no windows save for the holes at either end of the roof to let out smoke, and the paint on the wooden walls needs refreshing. The firepit burns lowly, requiring a dozen torches to light the room. They add their own smoke to the pall that hangs in the air and makes Æthel cough.

The table shows signs of being hastily swept free of crumbs, but a few mead spills remain, fanning white against the wood. They sit: she and Ine, Ingild, Nothhelm and the gesiths. Gefmund deposits himself on the end of a bench. No one talks as servants lay out fresh-baked bread, beef, stewed apples and a cheese so large it could serve in a shield wall. Despite her unease that *something* is going on, Æthel's stomach growls. She has been too angry to eat today. As soon as the jugs of ale are down, she reaches for bread, dips it in the apples and stuffs it in her mouth while pouring with her free hand. Gefmund is watching her with a crinkle of distaste between his brows. She pointedly tears off another hunk of bread and chews it, staring at him all the while. He looks away.

For a few minutes, no one speaks, as they help themselves to the food. Æthel watches Ine wrestle with the cheese and swallows a bubble of mirth alongside her bread. "The message we received was somewhat lacking in detail," Ingild says, and the bubble pops. They all know who sent the message. Ingild might as well come out and call her useless to her face. Æthel hacks off a piece of meat with unnecessary force.

"We knew nothing of Geraint's motives," Leofric admits with a glance at her. "We still don't. Only that there are over five hundred men out there in the hills and they do not want us to leave."

"But there have been no losses?" Ine asks, yielding in his battle with the cheese. As he settles for beef instead, Æthel tuts. Seizing the meat knife, she stabs the cheese, cuts downward and then, with a flourish, offers him the chunk she's skewered. "Thank you, Æthel," he says mildly, adding it to his trencher.

With a wince at the mangled cheese, Leofric shakes his head. "Incredibly, none. We lost more at Tantone fighting against Ealdbert. Or his men at least."

"You forget," Æthel snaps, "that we cannot be sure the riders who slew our men were Ealdbert's."

Ine pauses with the cheese halfway to his mouth. "Riders?"

"They vanished as they came," she says, seeing between each blink the woman on the horse. *Wild braids woven with feather, bead and bone. The sword in her hand like a remnant of the darkness before the world was made.* "Swiftly. From nowhere."

"What do you mean, Lady Æthelburg?" Edred is frowning.

She stares at him, then at Leofric. "You saw them, Leofric."

The gesith scratches his cheek. "With the greatest respect, Æthelburg, your description is a little…fanciful. While I admit their behaviour was odd, there is no cause to paint them as anything other than warriors on horseback."

"Leofric is right," Edred says and grimaces sympathetically. "It is easy for the mind to play tricks in the midst of battle, all that fire and smoke—"

"Do not patronize me. I have been fighting battles since before you earned your first sword." It seems Edred's unexpected support of her is at an end. Æthel cannot say she is surprised. She glares at Leofric instead. "You admit their behaviour was odd. If they were truly Ealdbert's men, they'd have stayed to rout us."

"You do not call Tantone a rout?" the gesith asks, in a quiet, but carrying voice.

They are all looking at her. Æthel's heart pounds sickly. The food, welcome a moment ago, sits like lumps of flour in her mouth. She takes a swig of ale, swallows hard, can feel her husband's eyes searing as all suns. Determined not to look at him, she sits back. "I find I am no longer hungry. I will visit the scouts. Geraint will not have failed to notice your army."

"Æthelburg…" Ine says, but she swings a leg over the bench and is gone in a few quick strides.

Outside, she leans against the wall and lets the breeze cool her flushed face. She could believe bad of Edred—he *is* slippery—but what game is Leofric playing? The two of them painting her as hysterical, fanciful…

With a growl, Æthel pushes off the wall and makes her way to the main gates. Folk glance up from their work as she passes, clad in tunic and trousers, weapon belt slung about her waist like a man. Not all their gazes feel friendly. She suspects she offends a lot of people just by being herself.

Are the gesiths right? Were the riders no more than traitorous men? *Perhaps I really did inhale too much smoke and dreamed her.*

Thunk.

An arrow shivers in the post beside her head. With a cry, Æthel throws herself down, but no others come. Slowly, she looks up and back. There is a message wrapped around the shaft.

The gates are a swirling mass of men. A couple rush to help, but she waves them off. *This is what you get for daydreaming.* Æthel yanks the arrow out of the gatepost, then, raising her hand against the sky, squints at the distant archer shouldering his bow. "Stand down," she calls to men in the act of strapping on weapons. "It is only a message."

"What does it say?" one asks.

She glances at the note and curses. "If you can read it, feel free to tell me." Folding her fingers over the incomprehensible words, she marches back to the hall. It is galling to return so soon, but there is no help for it. Æthel throws open the doors, letting sunlight pour inside. "From the Dumnonii," she says, thrusting the note at Ine. Her husband speaks three languages, so she assumes he can read it.

"How?"

"An arrow shot a little too close to my head," she admits.

Instead of reading the thing, Ine's eyes crinkle in concern. "You're not hurt?"

"For God's sake, I'm fine. What does it say?"

Faced with her glower, he looks down. "Geraint wants a meeting. Out in the open, under a flag of truce." He passes the note to Gweir. "Do I have that right?"

The gesith runs his eyes over it. "Yes, Ine king. At midday."

"What's the hour?"

"...Almost midday."

Ine shoves the bench back and the others are forced to their feet too. "What are you doing?" Ingild demands, an ugly mottling in his cheeks. "He whistles and we come—like obedient dogs?"

"Ingild." Ine runs a hand through his hair, mussing it, and Æthel feels a sudden urge to smooth the dark curls at his neck. She stubbornly tramples on it. "Geraint has done me the courtesy of *not* attacking an inferior force that included my wife."

She knows he means numbers, but cannot help wincing at how the gesiths will interpret the word. *You're so good with languages, couldn't you have spoken more carefully?*

"But that does not place you at his beck and call. Who does he think he is?"

"A king," Ine says drily.

"Ingild ætheling is right." Nothhelm comes around the table. "It will make us look weak—before Geraint and our own men."

For a moment, Æthel swears her husband's eyes flick past them to something in the corner of the hall. She follows his gaze, but sees only furs stacked haphazardly, and a sad ball of yarn fallen from a weaver's basket. Ine's shoulders slump. "Then what do you advise I do? Ignore him?"

"For now," Nothhelm says. "If he takes offence and chooses to fight—" his eyes glint—"well, he won't find us so easy to intimidate."

"I was not intimidated, Nothhelm." Æthel rounds on him. "I simply did not have enough men to force an exit without taking heavy losses."

"I wasn't aware that bothered you," Ingild says and the temperature in the hall drops considerably. While Æthel wouldn't mind punching him, the swirling mass of guilt in her chest dampens the urge. No matter that her men were slain by riders she is almost certain weren't Ealdbert's. Dead is dead.

The creases around Ine's mouth tell Æthel he's not happy, but he makes no further argument. That irks her too. *You are king,* she thinks at him. *It's your decision.* But since the law code, he puts too much value on the advice of others. *All of whom have their own plans.* Æthel knows it is just as dangerous to turn your back on your allies as on your enemies. At least enemies can be trusted to do the obvious.

Midday comes and goes. The afternoon dies in a blaze of glory. Although watchers line the palisades of Gifle, no more message-bearing arrows find their mark. What might Geraint be thinking? Their refusal to meet him is part of a power game Æthel has no taste for. The stakes are always ordinary lives.

She returns to Gefmund's quarters, only to find Ine already there, white-knuckled hands clenched on the back of a chair. Partitioned off from the main hall, the room is softened by baskets of embers, and furs that have seen better days. He is muttering under his breath. "You know what they say of folk who talk to themselves."

Ine starts. "That they hate company?"

"Quite." Æthel leaves it a moment too long before asking, "Does that include mine?"

"Of course not. Why would you say that?"

She unbuckles her sword belt, tosses it on a nearby table. "You would not be in this mess if it wasn't for me. I chased Ealdbert out here, allowed Geraint the opportunity to corner me, to lure you—"

"No." He rubs his forehead, a recent habit that has been growing worse. "This confrontation is long overdue."

"But you would prefer to have it on your own terms. Instead we're dancing to Geraint's tune."

Ine is silent. In the brazier, wood cracks and settles.

"The others think I am a danger," Æthel says. She tells herself she does not care, but her voice is like a river flint, hard and cold. "They would prefer I remain at court with the other women and leave *men's business* to men." She draws a breath. "What tales have they told?"

Ine hesitates. She braces herself for the worst before he says, "Ingild did bring up the pig."

"Oh." Despite everything, a weak chuckle fills her throat. "I'd forgotten the pig."

"How could you forget something like that? The mess was so bad I considered retiring to a monastery."

"It was absurd to sulk over that cloak," she retorts. "A person shouldn't place so much value on possessions."

Ine looks aggrieved. "It was part of the wergeld Cent paid for Mul."

"Which should have been fully in *gold*." She nods at the cloak he is wearing. "That one is much more sensible."

"Yes, well. I couldn't risk any more pigs."

This time she laughs aloud, real laughter like she used to, and her heart aches at the sound. Her hands want to do foolish things like pat his cheek, or tug a lock of his hair until he winces. Æthel keeps them stiffly folded across her chest. He will not touch her, after all, so why should she touch him? Her laughter fades.

Ine must sense her change of mood because he comes a few steps closer, frowning. "Æthel. What's the matter?"

"You know what's the matter," she says—and is aghast at herself. It is not the time for this conversation. Not here, not when the morning will likely bring battle. "You know why they judge me, why they are so hostile." *No, no, no.* But the words spool out of her like thread too long unspun. "You have no heir. And they blame me."

Ine stops, only a step away.

"You know it is not fair," she whispers. "I have borne the fault for years when I could have told them."

"Æthel—"

"I need to *know*." The word is ragged. In one swift movement, she seizes his hands, presses them against her body. "Am I so abhorrent to you? Can you not think of me without disgust? Or is there someone else? Another woman?"

Ine pulls his hands away as if she is scalding water. Æthel's tears harden in her throat and suddenly she does not want to see his face. She turns, snatching her sword belt back off the table.

"Æthel, it's not, *I'm* not…"

She lets him stutter into silence—always his refuge—before taking a slow, steadying breath. The tears have become needles piercing the corners of her eyes. "You have made your feelings clear, husband. I only wish *I* did not have to pay for them."

Without giving him a chance to say anything more, she blazes into the hall, her face a patchwork of hot and cold. Æthel knows it will raise questions. She is tired of questions. She pulls up her hood as she strides past the curious eyes of Nothhelm and Gweir. Someone calls her name, but she keeps walking.

Out under the night sky, she dashes one of the needle-tears from her cheek, trying to dispel the memory of Ine ripping his hands away from her. It is answer enough. Why then hasn't he put her aside? He could do it—no one would protest, not even her own family. To them, she has failed in her duty, after all.

They do not know that her husband refuses to lie with her. They cannot imagine such a thing—unless of course Ine was the most devout of Christians. Far easier to think Æthel herself unable or unwilling to conceive. She is too stubborn, they say. Too warlike and wild. Too much like a man to become a mother. But the realm needs an heir. Surely Ine can swallow his indifference for the few minutes it would take?

A thieving wind grasps at her cloak and Æthel clutches it tighter. Rounding the side of the hall, she sinks down, elbows on her knees. *Do I want a child?* She does not know. In her younger days, it rarely crossed her mind. But the whispers in court are louder now. People no longer lower their voices when she passes by. She is *supposed* to hear. She is supposed to reflect on her failure.

She wants to scream. She wants the wind, that winter harbinger, to carry her away from the sick knot of longing in her chest. Most of all she wishes she could hate her husband. That would make it bearable. Instead, she rests her head against the wood, still warm from the day, and thinks of the nameless riders. And of the woman who led them, astride her horse like a queen of chaos.

5

INE

Gifle, Somersæte
Kingdom of Wessex

Ine stares at nothing. Æthel's voice has joined the others crowding his brain.

I have borne the fault for years.

Can you not think of me without disgust?

He hates himself for being unable to speak. He hates himself for letting Æthel believe he despises her. How is that better than the truth? Is the truth so terrible that he'd rather she shoulder the court's contempt when it should rightly be his? Is he so frightened of what they would say? Ine looks at his hand; his fingertips are trembling, and he can almost hear them: the whispers spilling over into open ridicule when they discovered how much he dreaded the idea of intimacy.

Is there someone else? Æthel demands in his head and he shakes it. "I have never loved anyone but you." Useless to speak the words—she cannot hear him. Even if she could, she would not believe him. They were intimate so rarely and when they were...

Unwillingly, Ine finds himself thinking of the last time he gave in to her, when Æthel had roused him under her insistent hands. He remembers her quick, urgent breaths as she pulled at their clothes. How she placed his hands on her waist as she moved, her own on his shoulders, rocking herself to a climax astride him. The sounds she made: a hushed cry and a moan, as she rested her hot cheek against his neck. His own release left him curiously empty.

Discomfited even. As Æthel slept, contented, he lay beside her thinking that surely, this was not how it was supposed to be. The way other men spoke of lovemaking was foreign to him, a language he did not understand. Thinking of it sparked no heat in his belly, or stirring between his legs. What in God's name was wrong with him? Because it must be him. It must.

The memory leaves behind an echo of that despair. Of the dread he felt whenever his wife wanted to lie with him, and the shame of making excuses, sick at heart. Always excuses, never the truth. Because he has no name for this truth. As the years passed, and they both grew older, even guilt at Æthel's disappointment lost the power to make him give in. Or perhaps she simply stopped trying. And now here they are. At a point utterly beyond the reach of words. Ine squeezes his eyes shut, wishing he could find them. To explain, even to himself, what he feels. And what he does not feel.

Hours crawl by and Æthelburg does not return. He tries to sleep. The pallet is a cheap one, stuffed with straw and hidden beneath rough goatskin blankets. The only source of light is the embers glowing warmly in their basket. The storyteller's eyes find him in the darkness, blue and burning. That night remains hazy, but they and their tale are quite clear. The tale…

Ine turns over, punches the pallet into better shape. Possibly he sleeps. Gwyn walks towards him, blade trailing through bloody dirt. The hound at his side is a nightmare, white save for the splash of crimson across its blunt head. Laughing, each of Gwyn's steps covers a vast distance until he comes beneath the lintel of the very hall in which Ine rests. Past the long table, the alcoves piled with firewood, foot kicking at the yarn unrolling in his wake. Towards the back where only a curtain separates them.

A shadow in the room. Ine sits up so fast, it spins. He snatches his seax from the belt he shed before sleep. "Stay back."

"Peace," a deep voice says in the Britons' tongue. "I did not come to harm you."

His mind is still muddled with Gwyn. Ine scrambles to his feet and the figure backs off, folding a pair of powerful arms. They are inked with marks favoured by the natives: intricate spirals, dots and lines drawn to some significant but unidentifiable design. He follows them up to muscled shoulders, a reddish beard and a pair of eyes like the bark of a young hazel. Disbelief ties his tongue until he manages to say, "Geraint."

"Ine," the King of Dumnonia acknowledges.

"You—" he switches languages—"how did you enter here?" There are no sounds from the hall beyond, no cries of alarm, just the sleepy silence of a building at rest. Ine forces down the dream of Gwyn.

"I can avoid being seen if I wish," Geraint says, "just as none will hear our words. Though it is a strain, here in the borderlands." Ine does not miss the accusation in his voice. "King Constantine's power stretched far beyond this settlement into territory we have not held since he walked the forests and valleys, and called the slumbering gods out of the land."

Constantine again. The Britons speak his name with a somewhat wearing reverence. "He was just a man," Ine says. He lowers his blade but keeps his hand curled tight about the hilt.

"He was more than a man, Saxon," Geraint rumbles. "Unlike your Christian god, he is with us still."

"I assume you did not come to debate religion. My gesiths are nearby."

Geraint indulges his glower for another second before he nods. "You did not answer my message."

Remembering Ingild's indignation, Ine pushes down his first response. "I don't appreciate being commanded, especially by someone who threatened my wife and caused me to take men from fields that need harvesting."

"I did her no harm." Geraint seems abruptly uneasy at Æthelburg's absence, as if he fears she lies in ambush. Knowing Æthel, it isn't an absurd idea. "In fact, it is better this way, that we talk alone."

He speaks the Kernow dialect, a swift-flowing river that must part around occasional stones. It makes Ine think of the secret glades that priests condemn, of the brooding valleys carved, as if by giants, into the land. *Tangled hair, the comb between a great boar's ears. Fields of wheat like golden sail-roads—*

"I need safe passage across your land," Geraint says, pulling him back to the present. "For me and at least two score men."

Ine blinks. "Two score?"

"Safer to bring more," the Briton says grimly. "But that number must serve. At least until I discover the truth."

"What truth?"

Geraint's smile is mirthless. "Not something that would concern a Christian." The blue of his markings is the same shade as the old storyteller's eyes.

"It concerns *me*, however," Ine says while another part of him marvels at the sheer improbability of this meeting, that neither of them holds a weapon to the other's throat. Ingild would froth at the mouth if he knew. "You will bring no force into Wessex without telling me why. And where."

They glower at each other. Ine reaches a silent count of five before Geraint says, "Ynys Witrin. You call it Glestingaburg."

"The abbey?"

"It is not the abbey I want, but the isle." Geraint's lip curls. "You hold land you know so little about." Outside, the wind is picking up. A draught stirs the trailing threads of the tapestry on the wall, commands the torch to dance in its iron bracket. "The isle of Ynys Witrin is a hill. A tor. The highest point on the plain."

Ine nods. "I know it. Berwald, the abbot, wishes to build a chapel there."

Geraint snorts at that. "It is funny how Christians condemn us as heathens and yet claim so many of our sites and practices for themselves. The tor is far older than your god and saviour. It towered before the surrounding lands rose from the water. Ancient peoples sang the first songs there, spoke to their dead...honoured the ones who went beyond."

Ine feels the words as a breath on the back of his neck and only just stops himself from whipping round. Since that day with the shield, the sense of being watched has grown. "Went beyond?"

"To the Otherworld." The Briton lowers his voice, as one wary of eavesdroppers. "To Annwn."

Perhaps to Annwn, from where so few return. The scop's voice is in his head again. Ine shakes it, but cannot dislodge the image of Gwyn, the reaper, walking the crow-black fields.

"You have heard the name before." Geraint is eyeing him speculatively. "You surprise me, Saxon. It is not something your priests would entertain."

Ine remembers the chilly expressions of Hædde and Earconwald as the scop's tale unfolded. He licks dry lips. "Annwn is just a story. I heard it told in Wiltun a few weeks ago."

Geraint raises a shaggy brow and says in a tone that could either be amused or contemptuous, "Do your people not prefer stories of bloody battle and monster slaying, or feuding families murdering each other during feasts?"

"Yes," Ine admits, thinking of the calls for the usual tales. "But stories cross boundaries that we may not. Countries, religions... time. I bar none from my hall, and welcome those that tell them."

"A shame we must be rivals," the Briton says after a long moment. "I believe you have more in common with my people than you think."

Unsure how to answer that, Ine folds his arms, trying not to feel so intimidated by Geraint's bulk. "You haven't answered my question. What do you hope to do at the tor?"

"I cannot say."

"Not good enough."

Geraint draws himself up. It is not unimpressive—he is taller than Ine by a head at least. "Allowing me to reach the tor is in your interest as well as mine. This is beyond rivalry, beyond *us*. It is part of my responsibility to the land and its people." There is a strange light in his eyes. "You would not understand."

If Ine were anyone else—Ingild, Nothhelm, Leofric—he would have called for his guards long ago. Or flown at Geraint with blade bared. *I'd probably be dead if I had.* Unlike Æthelburg, his skills do not lie on the battlefield. And he cannot forget Gweir's warning. After all, Geraint had reached this room without anyone raising the alarm. Ine studies him, noticing how lightly he is armed. Impossible, surely, for an ordinary person…

"If I were to grant your request, what of tomorrow?" he asks. "We outnumber you and my gesiths are spoiling for a fight. Better to retreat—"

"There is no time." That light in Geraint's eyes blazes. "I must reach Ynys Witrin before Lughnasadh."

Lammas, the harvest festival. "That is barely two sennights away."

"Thus the need for *haste*."

Ine's back is still nettled with the sense of a gaze. He glances over his shoulder, but there is nothing to see save for shadows piled up in one rough corner. *Where are you, Æthel?* Her absence is starting to worry him.

"I count Bishop Hædde amongst my advisers," he says slowly, dragging his thoughts back to the matter at hand. "If he discovers I have allowed you to further a heathen cause…" He shakes his head. "I cannot afford to cause a rift with the Church."

"It is to further *peace*." Geraint has held himself still so far, unthreatening, but now he clenches a fist. "It concerns the safety of *both* our peoples."

Ine stiffens. It is not anger he sees in the clench of Geraint's fist, but fear. "What do you mean?"

"I cannot say more until I know more. Besides, there is not time enough to explain it to a man who believes our ways are pagan superstition."

Ine has an urge to ask about this *connection* Geraint shares with the land, but better to keep his moves hidden. Instead, he finds himself unexpectedly thinking of Æthel's words during the meal. Of the riders only she claimed to see. He did not ask her what she meant.

A creak and rush as the main door opens, letting a sliver of windy night inside. Both of them turn their heads, on edge. God knows how it would look if they were discovered like this. "All right," Ine murmurs. "I give you my word that you will not be harmed in my land. But if I find you anywhere other than Glestingaburg…"

"You will not."

"And you cannot travel as yourself. Wealas pilgrims I can permit, but not the King of Dumnonia."

Geraint's expression darkens. "I know a little of your language, Saxon. I will not be called a foreigner in my own country. And you ask much—that I should come to Witrin disguised as one of those craven suppliants."

"And yet, those are my terms," Ine says sharply. "Perform your heathen rites and then leave my kingdom."

They return to glowering at each other until Geraint sighs. After all, how many others would allow him to speak, let alone preserve his life? He must realize it. Ine is far from certain that he has made the right decision, however. On every level it sounds like madness, save for the foolish hope of a king who believes peace gained by the sword is no peace at all. Perhaps this could be a beginning.

"Agreed." Geraint holds out a hand and they grip each other's wrists for a few astonishing moments. Surely none before them have met like this, struck clandestine deals at midnight, hidden from advisers and peoples alike. And although Ine remains decidedly uneasy, something in him trusts Geraint, or at least trusts the fear he can sense in the other man. Whatever drives him to this truce, it is indeed larger than their rivalry.

"Should I be worried?" The thought prompts him to ask: "About this…whatever this is."

"Worried over *heathen rites*, Saxon?" Geraint is still gripping his wrist, staring at him with a hard hazel gaze. "You have my thanks." He lets go. "You have been more…gracious than my lords expected, so I will give you a warning." His gaze flashes upwards. "Keep your men within these walls. Tonight the moon is old."

Perhaps Ine imagines it. Weariness, the strain of their fast march…there are half a dozen reasons why his senses might deceive him. But in the lee of Geraint's words is a feeling. A change in the air. As on the day when a chill wind cuts through the heat, revealing the worm in summer's heart, slowly eating the season away. That is what he feels now. The certainty of winter.

Geraint leaves as he came—invisibly. After a harried moment raking the room, Ine sinks back to the goatskins, elbows on his knees, and releases a breath. The Briton's words have left him with the sense of something slipping out of his control. *Keep your men within these walls.* The words of a pagan, Ine reminds himself. The Dumnonii are given to fancy. And yet it was not so very long ago that his own people followed ways the Church now calls heathen. Not all his predecessors were Christian. Cædwalla for instance—

Pale flits on the edge of sight. Ine looks, but there's nothing. Just like earlier when he entered the hall. Something in the corner of his eye. *Maybe I'm losing my mind like Father.* The thought brings a lump to his throat and he wishes Æthel would return. Well, no point wishing. She probably expects him to find her. Of course. Cursing himself, he rises to his feet.

Ine manages three steps—before agony rips through him.

He is on his knees, the floorboards rough beneath his palms. And then all he sees are trees. Branches wind around his limbs; he bucks, twisting viciously to break free. He gasps for breath, but instead of air, chill earth pours into him, filling him with root and loam until his bones must surely break, flesh giving way before the power of it.

Laughter in his ear. Words like the howl of wind and water. He blinks—and he is on a hill: the giant in the story. Its thighs are other hills, its groin the slopes of a valley. An abdomen rises to rolling moorland, and the giant's barrel-chest is thick with trees, the same trees that hold him. Beyond lies a face in repose. A mouth with creased corners; this giant laughed once. Now its shuttered lids are cruel, and hidden eyes rove. They know him. He is seen.

Is this death?

He screams as two forces pull him apart, like horses racing in opposite directions. The floorboards are back and leaves are pushing up between his fingers. He cannot tell what is real any more except that, somewhere, another battle is being fought. Ine can feel the surging of men and metal, screams and battle-sweat. He tries to stand, but his legs are too heavy, his arms like mist and rainwater. *What is happening to me?* As if they walk upon his own skin, he can sense men flooding out of the settlement. *No.* He must stop them. Geraint said the moon was old.

Geraint. He has a sudden knowledge of the man nearby. Without choosing to, Ine reaches out and Geraint reaches back to him, and he knows at once that the Briton is dying. He can sense breath fading, blood seeping into the ground. Geraint clings to him and he to Geraint because there is nothing else for him to hold but the giant—and he is terrified of that huge life.

Impossible, Geraint's ebbing presence says. *Who* are *you?* They are his last words. Ine feels him slip away into the soil where root and stone enfold him like a mother. Inside Ine, the pain soars and flings him into the roaring dark.

6

ꝹERLA

Sweet Mother, the dark. Time should mean nothing to one who has weathered centuries, but Herla has spent much of them asleep. During the long month without it, she has come to realize that sleep was perhaps the only thing holding madness at bay.

Bound in the belly of the tor, with the dog's breath hot on her face, Herla has lain unmoving as the moon died, rose and grew old again. Without sleep to save her, she clung to the ancient patterns and practised the sounds that she once used to form words. As the moon aged, she held that learning close, unwilling to fall back into the savage shapes of the Hunt.

But now Herla can feel it growing: an iron tang in her mouth, a widening of her nostrils. The bloodlust stirs the roots of her hair, fills her limbs with a storm, until the binding suddenly loosens and the full weight of the curse falls upon her.

Herla screams. It wakes the others, their horses snorting. It is not the scream of the Hunt. It is the sound a woman makes when she fights, a desperate struggle against impulses seeking to smother her. Gwyn's impulses. The black sword twitches in her hand; she closes her fist around it, pictures throwing it from her. Her arm trembles. The sword does not move.

"Lord," Corraidhín says. She is frowning as she comes before Herla, aware of her struggle. And Herla realizes that they are tied to *her*, just as she is tied to him. As long as she resists, so too can they. She struggles harder.

"Corraidhín," she says. And then all their names—"Gelgéis, Orlaith, Senua, Nynniaw—" as if they are a chant to ward off evil. If she can say their names, the bloodlust cannot have her. It cannot have *them*. They followed her to Annwn. They followed her and she doomed them.

Gwyn's hound is growling now, muscled body ready to spring, as if he yearns to tear out her throat. Herla grits her teeth, steels her heart. She will make the curse work hard to take her back. Red mists the corners of her vision and her blood thrills at the promise of the Hunt.

Mounted, she bursts from the tor and her hunters follow, filling the night with their horns. Herla's own voice is ragged-edged: a fading part of her knows she fought a battle and lost. Out in the darkness, she turns her horse south. More mortals risking the old moon. Inside her, a hundred thousand souls shriek their want. *Join us and live forever.*

Torches burn on the walls of a settlement. There is a great multitude of life here and more in the hills around. Herla smiles, raising the sword. Her hunters let out a chorus of cries.

Then, without warning, *something* seizes her horse's legs. Her mount struggles, shrieking his rage. Other shrieks tell Herla the rest are gripped too. The earth has sprouted silver vines which tangle about the horses like twisting snakes. Furious, Herla looks across the darkened ground to where a man stands, inked arms outthrust before him. Silver pools at his feet; the vines are feeding on it, drawing the strength they need to hold her.

The black sword swings, a vine snaps and the man staggers. A moment later, two more burst from the earth and Herla cuts again, wildly with teeth bared. But the more she kills, the more spring up, tangling, snarling, and her mind sharpens beneath the assault, the bloodlust wavering. This is not the power of Annwn. *Who is he?*

"Fools," she hears the man shout in the Saxon tongue as warriors surround him, blades pointed at his heart. "You fools. Flee—I . . . I cannot hold her."

Herla turns her head at a rumble and roar to see another host spilling down from the hills. Their bare arms are inked like the silver man's and they carry short spears. "Father!" A boy sprints at their head. Only leather protects his chest. "Run! They are our enemies. They are not worth it."

"Get back, Cadwy."

The bloodlust coursing in her veins weakens further. *This power can fight Gwyn's,* Herla thinks, just as another figure rises up behind the silver-footed man and plunges a knife between his shoulder blades.

The boy, Cadwy, screams rage. He and his men hurl themselves forward—straight onto enemy blades swung with cold and savage precision. More screams split the night: the agonized cries of the dying.

Fury will only carry you so far, but it is far enough.

The thought feels old, dredged up from somewhere muddy and full of remnants. An image comes with it: tawny hair, bright eyes, arms inked with patterns not so very different from the silver man's. A Briton, Herla realizes, as he sinks to his knees. The blade in his back shudders with every gasped breath, and the vines holding her start to wither. Unbidden, a whimper fills her throat. Gwyn's dark geas is tightening in their place; red floods the corners of her eyes.

"Why?" Her keen ears pick out the word. The Briton coughs blood onto the earth, silver ebbing beneath his fingers. "You doom yourself, Saxon."

"I think not," the one behind him says. His fair hair shines in the torchlit night. "Go to your grave, *wealh*, knowing Ingild of Wessex sent you there."

The man chokes. "How did you—" The rest of the words are lost in a howl as the silver pool boils around him. He turns his eyes to the boy still fighting fiercely to reach his side and there is stark horror in them. "Run, Cadwy. Go!" But the boy will not run; Herla has seen that look on a thousand faces before. It only ever ends one way.

The vines holding her are all but gone, and the black sword

yearns for the souls it can sense. She will ride amongst them, and the song she and the sword will sing burns in her mind. There is no melody more perfect than the Hunt. Her teeth bare themselves.

"*No!*" a part of her shrieks—the part that fought and lost—and it is louder than the thud of metal meeting painted shield. For a few stunned moments, everything stops. Or nearly everything. The boy seizes his chance. Dodging beneath his opponent's swing, he throws himself at his father, one dirty hand gripping his shoulder.

"Father. Father." The other hand goes to the earth, fingers cup-curled as if he can catch the silver before it drains away. All he comes up with is mud. "Father, please." He shakes him. "I do not understand."

The elder Briton's gaze moves from his son to the settlement. "Impossible," Herla hears him breathe. "Who *are* you?" Then he looks at the fair-haired man and begins bizarrely to laugh. The Saxon's brows draw together. He wrenches his blade free and blood sprays. The scent gets into Herla's nose, and her horse snorts, and the hound bays, where it lies draped across her saddle. She can taste the iron on her tongue.

Still laughing, the Briton slumps. He turns his face to the sky where the first drops of rain fall into his open, staring eyes.

The curse rears up, sending her hunters straight at the battling men. Most turn too late to deflect the spears that come for them. Corraidhín pierces a man through the heart and, with an effort-less tug, rips the spear free to stab another. They cut down Briton and Saxon alike. Herla feels each death—*revels* in each death—and reaches out to gather their souls, as she has done for seasons beyond counting.

"*Father!*" The word is a grief-stricken scream. Weaponless, uncaring of the dead and dying, careless even of the Hunt, it seems, the boy bows his head over the body. The fair-haired Saxon lifts his blade and lets it fall, contemptuously.

Another catches it. The scrape and clang of metal. Herla's blade stops too, at the sight of the one who stands over the weeping boy, eyes flashing. *Her.* The woman who faced her at the last moon, bloodied and defiant. The one who dodged her blow.

"Æthelburg," the man grates out. "What are you doing?"

"I should ask you the same, Ingild," she snarls. "Ine told you to preserve Geraint's life."

It is all Herla hears before the world around her flares gold. For one mad moment, she thinks the sun has risen—the sun she has not seen since the day she left Annwn. But this gold races over the ground like a greedy tide reclaiming the beach. The Britons' faces are slack with wonder. The Saxons eye it fearfully, flinching when the earth beneath them glows. As it nears, the black sword wheels Herla around and she gasps. The curse fears this power.

Her hunters are driving men into the hills, but they come at her cry. The golden wave is almost upon her, and Herla uses the bloodlust's own rage to throw back her head and pull her horse around to face it. If this is her death, *finally,* she will not flinch and she will not flee.

The mysterious power passes under her horse, and a song, different from that of the Hunt, soars in her mind. A clamour of images. *She is running muddy-footed across fenland, deftly leaping from tuft to tussock. Ahead of her, laughter, a streak of reddish hair. The wind is wet with the lush green of the marsh. Home. Alarmed wings lift around her; feathers drift down. Ahead, smoke curls up, still distant. They will be waiting for her. They will be waiting for them both.*

The soft thump of paws hitting earth is deafening. When Gwyn's hound leaps, Herla feels it in her bones. Her soul aches, scarred from the chains that have bound it. On some blazing instinct, she hurls herself after the dog—into oblivion.

Except it is not. She is lying on earth—*earth*—and she is laughing. Laughter that would chill a mortal heart. It is sharp enough to cut, to shear through all the stories they have told of her. All the years that have imprisoned her. Is this madness? She clutches herself, as she laughs, face to the earth Gwyn had said would unmake her. Some patches are dry after the summer. Dusty. She laughs harder. Not *her* dust. Just honest sun-baked dirt.

Even the word *summer* is wondrous. She has not measured the centuries in seasons, but in the pounding of hooves and the wild blowing of horns…and in the swing of the shadow-hilted blade. Now, laughter withering, Herla presses both palms to the earth, as if she can sink right through it to the time she left. Earth remembers. Somewhere in this land are the impressions of their bones: her battle sisters, blood brothers, her mother and father— she cannot now recall their names. But one name comes back to her. *Boudica.* Bright-haired Boudica, who she loved, who she would have followed to the last.

Who she abandoned. Who died alone without her.

A cry escapes, a red cry of rage, a black cry of grief. Centuries have passed in a savage flood, leaving nothing behind but the riding, the reaping. Now the weight of it comes down on her: what he did, what he took—

A hand touches her shoulder. "Herla," Corraidhín whispers.

They cluster round her, bewitched by the earth that would, moments before, have turned them to dust. "What now?" Orlaith is murmuring. "What now?"

There is wet on her cheeks and Herla lifts a shaking hand. Then it comes back to her: the battle. Britons, Saxons, the golden light. The woman. She looks around, but the gold is gone. Not far away, Gwyn's bloodhound stands with legs locked and trembling, growling deep in his throat. He did not leap willingly, then.

Unmarked, the black sword lies beside her. She can still feel its leashed hunger, the chains that bind her to it. Does this mean the curse is *not* broken, after all? She curls flinching fingers around the hilt, but it is quiescent in her hand. Herla turns her eyes to the battlefield, dark with the dead and dying. She stares at the fair-haired Saxon. His face is very pale, arrogance ripped away to expose uncertainty. Only one pair of eyes looks back at her without terror, ice-blue.

Æthelburg. Herla cannot stop staring. Her heart beats strong in her chest; a feeling like the bloodlust, but sweeter, lighter. Without thinking, she takes a step forward.

The Saxon throws out an arm. "Æthelburg. We must go, get back behind the walls."

"Why?" the woman asks, watching Herla as if mesmerized. Herla takes another step.

"Save your questions. Bring the boy, if you must."

"I will not go with you," the boy spits. "You killed my father. I would die here, rather."

"I would rather you did too." The man raises his voice. "Back to the walls!"

Finally, Æthelburg looks away. She binds the boy's hands with her belt, and—when he struggles—hisses something in his ear that even Herla's preternatural hearing cannot distinguish.

About half the Britons remain. The boy's father—*their leader*, she assumes—is hurriedly dragged away. Saxon warriors each hold one of his legs, letting his head and torso scrape across the earth. When the boy sees, he screams curses at them in his own language and twists in Æthelburg's grip. Herla starts forward, towards the chaos of limbs and downed weapons, but the horizon stops her. A line of light, brighter every second. *Dawn.* Real, this time.

She does not know why her blood chills at the sight. After centuries of darkness, she fears the sun. She fears its fire. Finding herself back on her horse, she turns west, away from the home of the morning. Having followed her so long, her hunters follow her again, and they race the rising, leagues crossed in mere strides.

She stops amidst the wilderness of the Dart lands, dismounting in a thicket whose branches hide the sky and its terrible light. Herla flinches as her foot touches earth again, but the ground has lost its power to unmake. The hound has run alongside them. Now it comes beneath the trees, a demon with ears dipped in blood and tail held rigid. A crow caws from some near and hidden place.

"Why does it not return?" a voice asks: Corraidhín. The words are halting. She too has not used human speech in centuries. "It belongs to *him*."

"He belongs to me," Herla hears herself say, though she does not care at all for the creature that gaoled her. "Remember he is Dormach, Gwyn ap Nudd's favourite." The hound pricks up his awful ears at the name. "As well you should," she says, and laughs coldly. "You must do as *I* say now."

She is aware of Corraidhín's glance. Of all their glances. Perhaps she truly is mad, but Herla does not feel so. Inside her is a maelstrom; a confusion of feelings she does not yet have names for. Except anger. She gathers it close. Anger and something else...a face in the darkness, an ember glowing amongst the ashes. Blue eyes.

Beyond the trees, the light grows stronger and she can only look at it through a prison of her fingers. "Are we free?" Orlaith asks in a small voice. She is the youngest of them, fifteen when she followed Herla to Annwn...and ancient now by mortal standards.

Free. Herla smiles bitterly. "We may walk instead of ride, wake instead of sleep, but can you not feel it?" She extends a wrist and, after a moment, smoky links become visible, wrapping her arm. "Our chains have loosened, not broken. We are still cursed."

"What does it mean then?"

That light. First silver then gold, but the same power, Herla thinks. Strong enough to weaken Gwyn's curse, to force the loyal hound from his oath. "A shame the man who wielded the magic that aided us is dead," she remarks.

"What of the boy?" Corraidhín turns her head eastwards. The sun will be rising on a grim scene this morning. That is something Herla remembers: the eager hop of the crows, the stench, a prickling awareness of larger scavengers watching from concealment. "We could seek him out."

None of them have moved from the place they dismounted. They all stand unnaturally still. *We will have to learn how to walk again*, Herla realizes, half-disgusted at the thought. How to converse, how to pass as human. She forces herself to move, taking careful, hushed steps to the trunk of a tree. Laying both palms against it, she can feel the warp of the bark; she presses hard so an impression comes away—of the glorious, imperfect world that birthed her. Because she did not spend a mere three days in

Annwn, or even three centuries. Her fingers crook into claws. She is still its creature. She has never truly left it.

The others are watching her, waiting on her. *Friends* is the word she once used for them. Not hunters. *Battle sisters.* In the hollow of her chest, that barely burning ember flares. They *do* have an enemy still. Not the empire, but the one who promised them the power to fight it. The one who deceived them: Gwyn ap Nudd, King of Annwn. Herla bares her teeth at the thought and pushes away from the tree.

"We may still be cursed," she says, meeting every eye, "but we are not without purpose." She recalls her dream: pavilions and pennants, the bustle of the fairy Folk spilling down the steps of Caer Sidi. Bright spears in racks. Air humming not with songs, but with serious-throated talk. She has seen many a war camp in her time. Her sisters look on, silent. "I dreamed of Annwn," Herla tells them, "and its green slopes were planted with banners, and the people who walked there walked like warriors. Gwyn is setting something in motion. I would know what it is." She clenches a fist over the bark shape on her palm. "And I would stop it."

"Then we must learn." One of Senua's hands still fretfully clasps the bridle of her horse. "About the power that aided us. About the one who wielded it."

"We must go amongst people," Gelgéis says on the heels of her sister. There is blood beneath her nails. "Without them suspecting."

Stocky Corraidhín nods, disturbing her auburn braids bound with bead and feather. Their colour reminds Herla too painfully of another's. "We must have somewhere to plan. Somewhere to gather our strength."

"Then let us return to Glestingaburg," Herla says. "Although it remains closed to us, the tor is a gate to the Otherworld. We will guard it, make it our home." In a softer voice, "Rather than our prison."

Her words are a pebble tossed into still water. She watches the ripples spread in widening circles until the whole wood seems to undulate. More than purpose, they have a *choice*. For the first time in centuries, Herla's dust-dead heart puts forth a flame.

7

ÆTHELBURG

Gifle, Somersæte
Kingdom of Wessex

She finds him sprawled in a pile of leaves.

Æthel cries out, falling to her knees beside him. "Ine." Her voice is very small. He can't be—*he can't be*. She lifts a trembling hand to his lips, slightly parted...and feels warmth. *Oh, God.* Her heart is hammering, the breath burns in her throat. What would she have done if—she can hardly bear to think it—she had found him lifeless? In her head, repeating awfully, are the last words she spoke to him: cold and angry. Stricken with hurt, she meant them at the time. Æthel swallows hard. She still means them. But at the sight of Ine crumpled on the floor, she has no room for anger. Only terror at the thought of losing him. Only relief that she has not done so.

Gweir must have heard her cry: he is beside her in moments. His eyes travel over the king and his strange bed. Æthel cannot read his face. It is hard and gentle, deeply odd. But no odder than the scene before her. Broken twigs are stuck between the floorboards, as if some force has pushed them up from below.

Shakily, Æthel sits back on her heels. *Alive* is not *awake.* "Gweir, what's wrong with him? Who did this?" She plucks at one of the twigs and pulls it right out of the floor, trailing a long root.

Shouting from the hall behind them. Gweir's hand comes down hard on her shoulder. "Clean this up," he says in a hushed voice. "Quickly, Æthel."

She frowns; he has never addressed her so informally. "Why?"

"Just make sure no one sees."

Her brow is still furrowed as she dumps the leaves on a blanket, the twigs and unsettling roots. "Burn it later," Gweir says. He has eyes on the curtain, braced against anyone wishing to enter. The ruckus in the hall is growing.

"Please check on the boy. Geraint's son. I don't want Ingild making an example of him."

When Gweir raises an eyebrow, Æthel adds in a low voice, "Ine will be furious. The least we can do is ensure the boy survives. For now."

He nods before his gaze moves to her husband. "Do you need help lifting him onto the bed?"

"He probably weighs less than I do."

Gweir pauses with a hand on the curtain. "If anyone asks, the king took a sleeping draught. Nothing out of the ordinary."

"He *has* been taking them," Æthel says, gesturing at the cloth pouches she had spotted earlier amongst his things. "I intended to ask him about them. Do you know why? It isn't like him."

Gweir hesitates and she is sure he *does* know something, but ugly voices reach them, mingled with the higher tones of a boy. Whatever he says—he speaks the Wealas tongue—Gweir's face tightens and Ine stirs in his sleep. The gesith leaves without another word.

Æthel slides shaking hands under her husband's shoulders and heaves him onto the bed, which is low, thank God. Despite what she said to Gweir, he is not light. Or perhaps she is simply exhausted. Her head is a mess: that argument with Ine; Ingild's night-time ambush; Geraint's death; the woman on horseback—the same whose eyes have haunted her this past month. And now this.

She shoves the leafy bundle under the bed and then sinks onto its end, chin in hand. The woman, the riders. Æthel is quite sure no one who saw them could claim they were ordinary. All *women*—she feels a thrill at the thought—but who were they? Geraint had considered them dangerous, that much was certain.

As for the power he summoned against them...Æthel bites her lip. The only person who could tell her more is Geraint's son. How likely is he to talk after the way Ingild slew his father? Attacks from behind are a coward's way to kill.

Ine's hands have curled into claws on the blanket. Æthel thinks about taking one. Instead she leans down; he is muttering in a slurred tongue, words she cannot distinguish. Perhaps whatever power Geraint called up is responsible for this unnatural slumber. For the leaves. Although why it would target Ine, presumably safe in the settlement, she cannot guess.

Her heart is slowing, the shock growing less with every breath he takes. Still, the taste of terror lingers. What would her life be like without him? Æthel realizes she has never considered the question, has actively shied away from it. She has built herself around being queen and all the duties that go with that role. Without Ine...Too old to be married again, she would be relegated to the back of a court that despises her. Ingild, unrestrained, would make her life a living hell. The thought is so awful, she shudders and squeezes Ine's hand. Their problems abruptly seem small. *You will not like what awaits you,* she tells him silently, *but please wake soon. For me.*

The hall is a strange place: jubilance at Geraint's death punctuated by grim faces, Nothhelm's and Leofric's chief amongst them. It seems only Edred and his men knew that Ingild planned something. The other two missed the engagement entirely. Æthel would have as well, were it not for the argument with Ine that had driven her from the hall. While others slept, she had discovered the gates open. After that, it was a mad dash to the scene of battle.

Nothhelm and Leofric are biting their tongues; they must have questions. Æthel has questions of her own. What was Geraint doing so close to Gifle last night, outside the protection of his camp? And how did Ingild know he would be there?

"My brother took a sleeping draught?"

"Yes, Ingild ætheling," Gweir says as the two men stride into the hall. The doors are open and weak sunlight falls across the floor.

The rain that began in the night has subsided, leaving behind the wet green scent Æthel loves. She takes a breath of it, and imagines it chases away her weariness. "It was perhaps a stronger dose than he required. He does not stir."

"But he is well?" Ingild asks sharply.

"Quite well." Æthel does not care that her tone is grating. "When he wakes, he will no doubt be keen to hear your reasons for disobeying him."

Ingild smiles, a small and infuriating curl of the lips. "Are you saying Geraint's death does not benefit us?"

"No, but—"

"Well then. My brother has some strange ideas." His eyes sweep over her. "He will make a show of being angry to save his pride—I would do the same—and then he'll accept that Geraint's death was necessary."

Nothhelm drops onto the bench at the long table, bangs it for food. "If I recall, Ine king said he didn't want Geraint killed unless there was no other option." He raises a brow at the rest of them. "*Was* there no other option? We forwent the meeting he offered."

Ingild's look is unfriendly; he does not move to sit. "I saw an opportunity and I exploited it. Geraint is the source of his own demise."

"What was he doing outside his camp?" Æthel seizes the chance to ask. "It seems reckless in the extreme." When Ingild does not answer, she adds, "Perhaps his son knows. Is he...secure, Gweir?" They both understand that what she really means is *safe*.

"He is, Lady Æthelburg," the gesith says neutrally. "I've men watching him."

"See he is fed."

To her satisfaction, a vein twitches in Ingild's temple. "Send word to me when my brother wakes," he snaps before turning on his heel and leaving before she can question him further. How collected and confident he is now, but Æthel remembers his expression when *she* stood and looked at him across the battlefield.

She sits beside Nothhelm, Leofric opposite, while Gefmund

sends for trenchers of mutton. The other warrior gesiths join them, jostling for jugs of weak ale and splashing them into each other's cups. Talk, however, is quiet; they lost friends last night. It has not escaped her that Ingild took only those men loyal to him, who would not question. There are whispers too of what they witnessed: the strange powers summoned by the Dumnonian king. She had been close enough to hear Geraint when he yelled at the men to get away. *Was he protecting them? Protecting Saxons?* The question brings her right back to the woman on the horse.

Æthel's heart gives an urgent kick. *I must speak to the boy.*

"Give him time," Gweir says and she realizes she has spoken aloud. "He is a storm of rage and grief."

"Can't blame him," she mutters. "Seeing his father slain so dishonourably."

Nothhelm and the gesiths exchange looks. Ingild is ætheling; even if they agree with her, they would not choose to utter it aloud.

"The act may have been necessary," Leofric concedes after a long pause. He wipes the ale-froth from his beard. "Geraint was a dangerous man."

"You have spoken with the men then?" Æthel leans forward. "Did they tell you of the riders they saw? The riders that Geraint summoned his power against?"

"They say only that Geraint used some sort of witchcraft."

"Do not play ignorant," Æthel snaps, swallowing too large a chunk of meat in her anger. "They were the same riders that attacked us at Tantone." She coughs. "Once Geraint was dead, they set about killing our men and his alike."

The silence around their end of the table is thick enough to sink teeth into. "As I have already told you," Leofric says delicately, "we were attacked by Ealdbert's men at Tantone."

The mutton is turning sour on her tongue. "Then ask those who fought last night what they saw." She pauses. "Ask Ingild."

"I am sure Ingild ætheling will give us a full explanation as soon as your husband recovers," Nothhelm says to smooth the moment over. Æthel will not be smoothed. She sits and seethes.

There are people here holding back things she wants to know. Ingild, Gweir, Geraint's son. *I will have those things from them.*

But when she goes to visit their prisoner, locked in a storehouse, she hears ragged sobbing, and hesitates outside. Peering through a crack reveals a hunched form. The boy sits on sacks, although Gweir has left a blanket for him, she is pleased to see. His hair is cut long, the colour of mead, and his face is hidden in his knees. Each sob racks his narrow shoulders and brings a lump to Æthel's throat. Behind her eyes is a memory of a fair-haired girl, no more than twenty, clutching at the limp hands folded across her mother's chest. A hot swell in her eyes, Æthel backs away, leaving the boy to his grief. What is he? Fifteen? She does not know if Geraint's son has a mother. But he is too young to have lost a father. Especially at the hands of someone as craven as Ingild.

She takes a moment to gather herself. Then, pausing to look back at the storehouse, Æthel bows her head. "I am sorry, boy."

The sun is setting by the time Ine finally wakes up. Æthel had gone to check on him, found him still asleep, and had just lifted the curtain to leave when he suddenly called her name. She looks back to see his eyes darting wildly, as if he is still in the grip of a night-terror.

The worn furs on the bed are rucked, pushed every which way. Æthel lays her hand on Ine's forehead, but it's cool. No fever. Without warning, he seizes it, clasps her fingers like a fraying rope. "What's wrong?"

"I..." His eyes cease their darting. "He's gone then?"

"Who's gone?"

"Geraint."

A shiver, cold as meltwater, runs down Æthel's back. "How could you possibly know Geraint is dead?"

"Dead?" He drops her hand—she feels a sink of disappointment—and sits up. "What do you mean?"

"You just said you knew he was gone."

"I thought it was a..." Ine coughs. "Is that ale? I'm so thirsty."

Æthel pours a cup for him and watches as he downs it in one. Some of the mist clears from his eyes. "Why say Geraint is gone?" she asks, taking it back, although a prickling suspicion has joined the shiver on her skin.

"Gone from here." He turns his palms up as he says it, as if they hold secrets now vanished.

"Ine." Her tone is dangerous. "Geraint was *here*? In this room?"

Faint colour creeps across his face. "Yes."

Before she realizes it, Æthel has sprung to her feet. "How did he get in? How *could* you have been so foolish?"

He flinches, but the gaze he turns back to her is steady. "I fully believe Geraint intended no harm. He wanted to talk."

"Sometimes I do not think I know you at all." She is angry with herself, but it is easier to direct it at him. Geraint should not have come within a hide of this hall. Æthel stops her pacing as it falls into place: *this* was why the King of Dumnonia was outside his camp. This was why Ingild had the chance to corner him. And yet it still does not explain how Ingild *knew*.

"Æthel." Ine swings his legs off the bed and winces. "What has happened? Why was I asleep?"

"I hoped you could tell me." She remembers the roots beneath him like bony reaching fingers—he has not mentioned them— and that makes her remember the terror. The panic which coursed in her blood when she thought he was dead. Æthel fights the shadow of it down. "What did Geraint say?"

"That...doesn't matter now." Ine closes his eyes briefly. "How did he die?"

"Ingild," she says, and watches his hands clench on the blanket. "Geraint was distracted. Your brother took the chance to stick a sword in his back."

"Holy God." That colour in Ine's cheeks has entirely fled. "But Ingild's no warrior. What distraction could possibly have given him the opportunity to kill a man like Geraint?"

"The boy could answer you. We captured Geraint's son." Æthel smiles thinly. "Ingild wanted to kill him too, but I thought he'd caused chaos enough for one night."

Ine is blinking—trying to take it all in, she thinks. "One night? What hour is it?"

"It's æfen again. You slept all day. Which reminds me." She picks up one of the cloth pouches stuffed with God knows what. "If you must take sleeping draughts, at least have them mixed by some-one with proper leechcraft." She wrinkles her nose at the smell. "You will make yourself ill."

Ine shakes his head. "I didn't drink one. I think I was dreaming."

"Well, the others are waiting on you. No one has yet managed to extract an answer from Ingild." Æthel admits, however, that Ine looks in no shape to hold a meeting. His forehead is furrowed as if it pains him and she is sure he's lying about the draught. "I don't need to tell them you're awake," she says quietly.

"No, I have been absent too long. Æthel." He rises unsteadily to his feet. "I would be grateful if you kept Geraint's being here to yourself. The others will not understand."

"Only if you tell me what he said."

He hesitates. "Afterwards."

Æthel holds his arm to keep him upright. It is not a good idea for Ingild and the others to see him like this, but Ine can be stub-born when he chooses. He pushes the hanging aside and immediately squints against the brightness of the hall.

"Brother." Ingild rushes over. He tries to take the king's arm from Æthel, but Ine does not relinquish it. "You are pale," Ingild says instead, trotting beside him. "Perhaps a night's rest—"

"I have rested enough." The sharpness of his tone cuts through both clatter and chatter. The men look round.

"Lord." Nothhelm and the warrior gesiths rise from table and wait for Ine to be seated before settling back themselves. "It is a relief to see you awake."

"I am sure," Ine says darkly. He is still squinting in the glare, as if the torches are little suns. "It seems you have been busy in my absence."

Edred, four places along, has the grace to drop his gaze. Ingild, however, sits himself on Ine's right and starts heaping food onto a trencher for him, apparently uncaring of the king's glower. "Yes. We have won a great victory."

"A victory, you call it." Ine ignores the meat, the roasted vegetables and bread set before him, though they steam invitingly. He should eat something, Æthel thinks, before he faints dead away. She cannot be the only one who's noticed. Indeed, Gweir is staring at Ine with the same contradictory face he wore when they first found him. "I told you I wanted Geraint alive."

"That was never a realistic option," Ingild says breezily. "The Britons won't fall into line if they have their king to lead them." He pokes a piece of meat towards Ine as if he is a reluctant child. "Eat something."

Ingild had spoken earlier of an opportunity exploited. Had he somehow anticipated Geraint's visit? Æthel chews her lip, uneasy at the thought. Besides, what was so important that Geraint risked walking right into the heart of his enemy's stronghold?

"Whether it was realistic or not, I gave you an order." Still, Ine does not touch his food. "Do you forget who is king?"

"Don't be like that, brother. I have always had the kingdom's best interests at heart."

Æthel feels herself frowning at the lightness of his tone. Even Nothhelm is eyeing Ingild apprehensively, as if expecting a fist-fight to break out. Ine takes a deep breath. "Tell me what happened." His hands are hidden in his lap, but Æthel can see the knuckles are white.

As Ingild begins to speak, she stares hard at him, eager to hear what he might say of the riders. But to hear him tell it, their men were slain by Britons furious at Geraint's death. Fortunately, losses were minimal, while the fields beyond Gifle were left dark with Wealas dead. Æthel meets Ingild's eyes. He knows she saw the riders, and that Geraint used some mysterious power to hold them at bay. When, however, his words dry up without a mention of them, she slams a fist on the table. Knives jump.

"Ingild neglects to tell you that Geraint was fighting the riders I saw at Tantone. The ones Leofric claims were Ealdbert's." The gesith bites an awkward lip, and Æthel's next words are a hiss.

"He's wrong. These riders were all women. Led by a woman. I think they are something very dangerous. And not...ordinary."

By forcing her to tell it, Ingild has made her out to be confused at best, unhinged at worst. "I know how it sounds," she says, striving to put a lid on her anger. "But I saw what I saw. Geraint was holding them back. The killing began after he died."

"Did you see these riders, Ingild?" Ine asks.

"Perhaps some of the Britons were on horseback," the ætheling says with a shrug, and Æthel almost chokes. "Once daylight comes again, we can check the ground for hoofprints."

She stabs her knife into the table, scarring the wood. "They were there. Ask the boy. Geraint's son will tell you."

"Geraint's son should have died with him," Ingild retorts, losing his nonchalance. "Your intervention has complicated matters. As usual."

The statement falls into a silence only Gweir is kind enough to break. "I do not think Lady Æthelburg was wrong to spare the boy. She knew Geraint's death would displease the king."

"Quite," Ine bites off the word. "Thank you, Æthel, for stepping in when you did. Perhaps I can salvage something from this mess."

"I do not understand, brother." Ingild has given up on persuading Ine to eat. Now he leans back on the bench, his brow furrowed. "What mess? We have turned a difficult situation to our advantage."

"That's right. You do not understand. I have never wanted to beat the Britons into submission. Many of them live in Wessex already, contributing to our wealth. They are *subjects*." That flush is back, rising in Ine's cheeks, and his eyes are overbright. "Yes, they must earn their rights—I accept that much. But I would rather have them as allies, not enemies."

Nothhelm exchanges a glance with the warrior gesiths, and Æthel's stomach clenches. *You are good, I give you that,* she thinks at Ingild, who is smirking. She is not the only one manipulated into saying things that might later be regretted.

Perhaps Ine realizes it, for he lifts a hand to his head. "I find I may need to rest, after all. I am still a little muddled from…the draught."

"It is only natural," Ingild says, all solicitousness again. He helps Ine to his feet. "Tomorrow, events will be clearer."

The other men return to their meat and drink. Æthel picks up Ine's untouched plate and leaves them discussing next steps: what settlements might easily be taken, where the Wealas could make a stand, what advantage, if any, could Geraint's son bring.

"That was foolish of me, wasn't it?" Ine says as soon as she ducks into the room at the back of the hall. "I shouldn't have let him goad me. It is too delicate a subject for a mead hall, for heads that are still fixated on battle." When Æthel silently hands him the food, he sighs and sits down. "Thank you. As soon as I left, I regretted not eating it." He looks up at her. "What am I going to do about Ingild?"

"He's *your* brother." But she agrees it is a valid question. "You can't let him get away with undermining your every decision."

"I know." Ine chews the meat slowly. "Easier said than done, though. He has his supporters, and this will only increase his popularity."

"Supporters?" The word is sharp. "I do not like the sound of that."

Ine waves her concern away. "I only meant he has men who listen to him."

"That's not better, Ine."

He sighs again. "No."

"Eat your supper."

"Now you sound like him," he grumbles, but spoons up some of the roasted vegetables.

"You promised to tell me what Geraint said," she prompts in a low voice, sitting beside him on the bed. "Why he thought it so vital to sneak in here."

"Only if you promise to tell me more of these riders," he returns and, after a long moment, Æthel nods. But she cannot find the words. Behind her eyes, the tall woman hacks at the power trying to bind her, screams at the sky; a scream of storm, dark earth, of blood and tears. Æthel can still hear it echoing somewhere deep inside her.

Despite claiming he did not drink a herbal draught, Ine's eyes slide closed while the trencher is still in his lap. She catches it before it falls, and, oddly relieved, pulls a fur over her husband.

The memory of the scream drives Æthel back to the storehouse where the boy is locked. There are guards posted outside; they look at her strangely when she asks them to stand down. But they obey and, taking a torch, Æthel slips inside.

He is lying curled, his hands bound. Gweir's blanket has been kicked aside. By the light of her torch, she sees his eyes are open. "Good æfen," she says, sticking the torch in a bracket by the door.

He cranes his neck, spits, and Æthel calmly wipes it from her cheek. He is probably expecting death. "Can you understand me?"

"Why do you care?" His voice rasps, perhaps from grief, perhaps because the cracked shell of his boyhood still half-shelters him.

Æthel raises a brow. "You speak Englisc. What's your name?"

When he presses his lips together, she sighs and perches on a barrel. "I am not here to kill you."

"Why not?" he snarls, rocking himself into a seated position. "You killed my father."

"No." Æthel leans forward in her anger—not at him, but at the memory of Ingild's cowardly attack. "I would not have dishonoured the man. King Geraint deserved a better end than the one he got."

"That should make me feel better?"

"Not really," she says honestly. "But it is the truth."

Almost a minute passes before he speaks again. "You stopped them from killing me."

"My husband did not desire Geraint's death. I assumed that extended to you."

The boy narrows bloodshot eyes. "Your husband?"

"I am Æthelburg of Wessex. As I am sure you know." In a softer tone, she adds, "Will you not tell me your name, Geraint's son?"

He considers a moment, and then his chin comes up proudly.

"Cadwy ap Geraint." The syllables of his father's name are choked. "Of Dumnonia."

Neither of them speaks while footfalls and voices pass outside. When all is quiet again, Æthel says, "You have no reason to believe him, but Ine is sorry for Geraint's death. It was not what he intended when he came here."

"You are right," he retorts, "I do not believe him. I hear your men. They are *happy*."

"Can you blame them?" Æthel says without thinking. "They have been taught to see you as enemies." *Christ, I sound like Ine.*

As expected, Cadwy's expression hardens, but the sort of hard that might shatter at a word. "Go away."

"I wanted to talk to you—"

"*Go away.*"

"—about the woman Geraint fought last night."

The same order on his lips, he freezes. His eyes are a glitter in the dim, his cheeks blotched with his earlier crying.

"Who is she?" Æthel whispers, knowing it is too late to hide the depth of her interest. She sounds urgent and he hears it.

Cadwy scoffs coldly. "She is something you ought to fear." There is bitterness in every line of his body when he adds, "You did not deserve Father's protection."

"So he *was* protecting us." She had guessed it, but to hear Cadwy confirm the fact only hammers home the injustice of Geraint's death. If he had rejoined his people instead of calling on his power to defend his enemies, perhaps Ingild would not have had the chance to kill him. Æthel shakes her head. "Why did he do it?" she asks softly. "Why did he risk his life for us?"

"He was a good man." Tears are threaded through Cadwy's voice. He pulls his legs in closer. "And because in the face of Herla and the Wild Hunt, we are all the same: human."

Æthel goes very still. *Herla.* The name suits her. It has her darkness in it, and savagery. It has her grief. She tucks it away like a keepsake. Then she frowns. "Aren't the Wild Hunt a story?"

"A story?" Cadwy's gaze burns. "Then what was my father fighting last night? The moon was old."

She is striving to remember it, something she heard only in passing, as a child. Their kitchen maid had been a slave, taken young, who Æthel's father had given her mother as part of her morning gift. Even after she'd had her freedom, she stayed on in their household. Æthel remembers her hands best of all: big and scarred from the oven. Her hands and her tales. All sorts of stories, some Saxon, some Wealas, some from Íraland, across the narrow sea. Æthel screws up her face. "But in the story, the leader of the Wild Hunt is a man. An ancient king."

Cadwy's look is hostile as his eyes travel over her trousers and tunic, and her belt with its twin scabbards. "Perhaps no one believes a woman capable of such things."

His words hit true as an arrow to the heart; Æthel sucks in a breath. She has spent most of her adult life being underestimated, scorned, doubted. She licks suddenly dry lips. "If Herla is real, who is she?"

Cadwy gives a humourless laugh. "No one has ever lived long enough to ask, Saxon. Why don't you try it when she rides again at the old moon? As long as you do not mind it being the last question you ever ask." He pauses. "Now leave me alone. I'm tired of speaking your ugly tongue."

Æthel regards him a moment more before hopping off the barrel. From the bag at her waist, she takes bread and a chunk of cheese, silently laying them on the blanket Gweir left behind. Cadwy turns his face away, staring hard at the dark. "Thank you," she murmurs. "I will not let Ingild harm you." But even as she says it, Æthel is far from sure she can keep that promise.

The boy knows it too. When he speaks, the words are half-sob. "I hope every last one of you rots in your Hell."

8

ꝟERLꝒ

Glestingaburg, Somersæte
Kingdom of Wessex

Herla is learning to walk again.

She is like a child, frightened at turns, triumphant at others. Just the act of stepping forward is a challenge; she has lived with the threat of the earth for so long. In the beginning, before the bloodlust stole such thoughts, she had considered unmaking herself, as Ráeth had unwittingly done. But she was too proud for the act, and too frightened. Her soul, she feared, would find no rest after death. The thought of it roaming the grim halls of Caer Sidi, or bound like the Cŵn Annwn to Gwyn's side, paralysed her.

"There is no door."

Herla breathes out, savouring the sound of Corraidhín's voice. The other woman is staring at the tor, and a heavy dusk shrouds them all.

"It looks an ordinary hill," Senua says, raising a hand to her head. "But my mind is fogged. I cannot recall entering or leaving."

"It is the way of the curse." Herla remembers how she battled it yestereve, struggling to escape the red mist that stripped her of will. "There *is* a door."

No sooner has she spoken than it appears: a yawn on the green. Worn pillars flank it, sunk in the skin of the hill. Their carvings are long faded, but Herla recognizes the topmost tower of Caer Sidi, with its cauldron-emblazoned flag. A stone wind wrinkles it. The longer she stares, the more it appears to move. Uneasy, she looks away.

"How did you do that?" Corraidhín murmurs.

Herla eyes the threshold apprehensively. "I did nothing. It was always there."

"What if we sleep again?" Orlaith this time. "I do not want to sleep again."

"We will not sleep," Herla says, although she is far from sure. "If the curse tries to make us, I will fight it." *Fighting or fearing. Is that all you are capable of now?*

Thrusting the voice down, her every sense alert, she pushes inside, but no unnatural slumber awaits them. And no battle either. She feels the urge to laugh and laughs. After a surprised instant, so do the rest of them. Herla listens to their voices, doomed long ago to rise in wails and horns, rise instead with mirth, and something small shifts inside her. It is a something that wants to gather them up, her battle sisters, wants to touch lips to each of their foreheads. But her limbs are clenched, as if they do not bend in so gentle a way.

"May the Mother hold our fallen sister close," Corraidhín whispers, and yes, none of them had spoken rites for Ráeth. Her dust had blown away in the wake of their first ride. Herla murmurs her name, and the others echo it. Then they lift their heads.

The place of their slumber was no doubt built with the blood and bone of Annwn. The smell is the same as in Herla's dream, as in her distant memory: a heady scent of flowers and saltwater, of things indefinably *other*. The hill has been hollowed, its floor and curved walls made of the same sparkling earth, the refuse of stars.

There is space enough for them all: the earth still holds the impressions of their bodies and the bodies of their mounts, laid out like the dead in three neat rows. "How we must have looked," Herla says, "to any who found their way here."

"As if we were sleeping heroes." Gelgéis drifts to the spot where she had lain and, after an instant's hesitation, scuffs the dirt over it. They watch her skin boot kicking and smoothing until her earth-shape is gone.

"Good," Herla says. "Flatten it over. It will make a fine Saxon mead hall." She laughs again, this time with an edge to it, and leads the way deeper into the hill.

Instead of erasing her own shape, Corraidhín drifts towards the back of the long chamber. There is dread in her voice when she calls Herla's name. She nods at a blank rock face: the twin of the gateway that took them to Annwn. Herla recoils. She can still hear the grind and boom as it sealed behind them. The hairs are standing up on her arms. "It is a passage," Corraidhín says. "A way."

"Yes." Herla presses her palm against the rock. How might one open a door to the Otherworld? She closes her eyes. Searching in the darkness behind them, all she finds is a chasm, and in it are the souls of the damned. She catches her breath as they reach for her, and backs away, thrusting them down.

"There is something else," Corraidhín says. "Look."

Herla crouches, studying the faint outline on the earth: a footprint. The sort of print a fairy might leave on stepping from one world to another. She has no better name for them: the lords and ladies, the heroes and hosts of Annwn. Some were human once, like her. Others are of Gwyn's ilk: old or older than the world.

"One of them has passed through," she says to Corraidhín, rising to her feet again. "Maybe at Beltane." A spoke on the wheel of the year. "It is easier to open the gates during the old festivals." She lifts her face, sniffs. No wonder the Otherworld scent is so strong. There is a trail.

"You believe whoever it was came through on *his* orders?"

"Who else's?" Unconsciously, Herla's hand strays to the black sword at her hip. "He has always had an unnatural interest in humans."

We are alike, you and I.

She drops her hand, turns angrily, putting the door at her back. "Guard it. It may open at Lughnasadh."

"Wait." Corraidhín's mouth creases. "I remember that tone. You are leaving?"

"To follow the trail." She is the Hunt. No quarry can escape her, not even one of the Folk.

Warmth on her arm. Herla's skin twitches and she slowly looks down to find Corraidhín's hand curled there. "Let me come with you," the other woman says.

They have been together so long, the nineteen of them. The Hunt has always had Herla to lead it. In the six centuries that have passed since the day they left for Annwn, not once has she parted from her battle sisters. "There is no need. It will be fine, Corra." The name slips out of a hidden pocket, as if from a garment she had forgotten she owns.

Corraidhín's green eyes grow huge. She opens her mouth.

"At least one of them is here in this world," Herla says, forestalling her, reclaiming her arm. For some reason, the touch makes her uncomfortable. It is too like the gentle urge of earlier, something that will shrivel in the violence that burns beneath her flesh. "Together we are conspicuous. I would rather the chief of Annwn remain ignorant of us a while longer."

"But if you are seen…" Corraidhín's gesture takes in Herla's armour, the horned helm tucked under her arm. "You will stand out."

It is a good point. When Herla turns her attention inwards, the image of the fair-haired warrior rises in her mind. She had not meant to think of Æthelburg, but she is quite clear, everything from her blue glare to her mail shirt, to the sword sheathed at her waist.

Corraidhín sucks in a breath. "How did you do that?"

Herla examines her new tunic, cut long in the Saxon style. Her arms are covered by light linen. Gwyn's sword is an ordinary blade in an ordinary scabbard, and a belt pouch hangs beside it. Reflected in Corraidhín's eyes is the image of the warrior herself. The sight sparks a new emotion, a curling nausea Herla recalls from the time before. Or rather, like language, it is an old emotion long forgotten. She has no right to wear this woman's face.

She changes it back to her own—or something similar to her own—and her friend raises an eyebrow. "I do not think most women wear men's clothing. Certainly not this metal armour." Corraidhín is right. Somewhat regretfully, Herla makes the shirt a dress, the tunic an overdress, and her boots into shoes that tie at the ankle.

Orlaith joins them—and gasps. "Your face, Herla." She waves vaguely. "I can tell it is you, but you look…less clear somehow."

Herla shrugs. She is unsure how much power came with the sword, whether this ability to alter appearance is even Gwyn's at all. Annwn is a land soaked in magic. None who venture there return unchanged. All she did was *will*. A shame the same method cannot be used to break the curse.

"It is a good disguise," Corraidhín says, "but why not go invisibly?"

Trying to dispel the lingering effects of the feeling that had seized her so suddenly, Herla folds her arms. "And how will I talk to folk if they cannot see me?"

"Talk to folk," Orlaith repeats, as if it is bizarre in the extreme. She has slain those same people in Herla's wake—they all have.

Herla pushes the thought away. The only thing that matters is finding Gwyn's spy. Her blood heats. And when she does… "Watch the gate while I am gone."

"How long will you be gone?"

"As long as it takes to follow the trail to its end."

They gather to bid her farewell. Their fierce ageless faces would terrify any human who happened upon them, but Herla feels a wrench when she turns her back. It is unutterably strange to mount her horse without them, to lift her own face to the stars, silent-throated. She is a lone hunter this night. No horns will sound in her wake, or wail before her on the wind. At her side, the black sword hangs quiet.

Nostrils flared to pick up the overripe scent of the Otherworld, Herla urges her horse into the dark. It leads her east, deeper into Saxon lands. Thick woodland presents no barrier. Neither do rivers—whether they flow swift, or wide and slow. Without the bloodlust dyeing her world red, Herla can see all the night-shades that were hidden from her before: blues and browns and wells of green. The creatures that usually flee her creep back to watch her pass.

After a while, she realizes she is not alone. "I wondered where you had gone," she growls at the huge dog running beside her. "You will ruin my disguise. Stay away from me."

Dormach gives her a baleful glare, stretches his neck out and disappears into the night. Herla watches uneasily. Does this mean he obeys her orders? Or is only appearing to obey them? She rides on.

The scent of Annwn is growing stronger, but so too is the light in the sky. Herla reins in on a low hill and forces herself to watch the blue blossom into pink and orange until the sun crests the horizon.

She hisses as it stabs her eyes, so long in darkness, and raises a hand to shield them. *I will not run. I will stay and watch.* Soon her cheeks are wet and her teeth gritted, but the pain is worth the price as the late-summer land blazes gold. It is harvesttime. Figures labour in distant fields for the crop that will see them through winter. The sight stirs memories in Herla. She had helped bring in the harvest once. Almost, *almost*, she can recall the weight of the bushels, the rough stems scratching her arms. Wheat dust turned the air hazy. People laughed and toasted their labour come evening, and groaned at knowing another strenuous day waited on the morrow. The Roman governor of course took much of their yield. She had stood with the others and watched their work loaded onto carts and borne away to feed the citizens of Camulodunum or Londinium, to be divided amongst men who had her people's blood on their hands. That was the day her heart first hummed with hate.

Rage will overwhelm her if she lets it. Savage and unthinking, no wonder it was the first emotion that returned to her. She cannot let it. She has a quarry to chase. Herla retreats to the leafy shade of an oak to study the landscape. In the distance is the henge, its stones arranged as if by giants. Much nearer, to the south, smoke stains the sky. A large settlement, walled and ringed by farmsteads, sitting at the confluence of two rivers. An impressive hall rises above the other buildings. When the sun strikes its golden roof, Herla catches her breath. It could be the abode of gods. Surely it is a house of kings.

She sniffs. The Otherworld trail cuts straight to the settlement. Interesting. She can sense Gwyn's hand in this. And yet it has been so long since she found herself among people, since she saw them as something other than prey. Herla narrows her eyes. Well, they are still prey—to whatever spy the King of Annwn has sent. While he is ignorant of her freedom, she will make use of it. She glamours her horse as an old nag, grimacing at the skirts she must hike up to ride. How anyone moves about in them is beyond her.

On the packed dirt of the road, Herla tries to settle into her disguise. She does not know how to be a labourer, farmer or trader. She is warrior, bondswoman, hunter. She is used to giving orders. Fortunately most people are dressed as she is. It is easy to spot the richer travellers; the couple conversing ahead of her wear cloaks pinned with silver. "The king *is* heading back to Wiltun?" the man asks the young woman riding beside him. "I do not want to have come all this way for nothing."

"That's what I heard this morgen." The woman loosens her cloak in the growing heat. "Fought against the Britons at Gifle. It's rumoured their king is slain and his son taken prisoner. I forget his name."

"Geraint of Dumnonia," the man supplies. His tone is thoughtful. "They are strange folk, most are still heathen. If you ask me, Wessex's laws give them too much freedom. Some even own land here."

While the woman purses her lips in seeming disapproval, Herla's mind races back to the night the dog leaped down. Geraint of Dumnonia—could he be the same man who called up power to hold her? His son might know more of the magic that weakened Gwyn's curse. *If* his captors have kept him alive.

As expected, the trail leads right through the gates. Herla dismounts, her hand tight on her horse's bridle. She will have to be careful: if she can sense the Otherworld trespasser, they may well be able to sense her too. Secrecy depends on how convincing she can make her disguise. She swallows a grim new uncertainty. The Hunt had left no room for uncertainty.

"What is your business in Wiltun?"

The guards are stopping random travellers; she is pleased to see the rich couple questioned, for wealth had always oiled Rome's way. When her turn comes, she is waved through unmolested. It is a novel experience: being thought unthreatening. But her flush of victory fades once she is inside the settlement. The trail leads in different directions, tangles in the marketplace. Whoever it is has gone *everywhere*. She curses. Scent alone will not help her now.

There are more people here than she has ever seen in one place save the battlefield. Sparks fly from open-fronted smithies; farriers fit horseshoes; red-cheeked women stir dyeing vats and children run through it all, presumably on errands, though it looks much like a game to Herla. It is almost overwhelming—the noise, the voices, the press of lives against her own. For one red instant, she wants to lash out in animal rage, to shed bright blood, to strip flesh from soul. In its guise as a knife, Gwyn's sword is heavy on her hip. Herla grits her teeth and masters the urge. *I am more than this.*

She turns that rage against the quarry she is failing to find. She extends each of her honed senses; nostrils flared, ears pricked, eyes narrowed...and the scent strengthens imperceptibly. Baring her teeth in triumph, Herla heads uphill towards the great hall. Its doorway is expertly carved with stags and hounds, leaping fish, cattle and wind-rustled wheat. She stops. In the curve of the stag's proud neck are the hills that hide the groves of the druids. In the fish's scales, the foaming shore. The wheat bends like the people before war, but it does not break. They do not break.

We do not break.

She is in the village, drawing a whetstone across the edge of a spearhead. Cross-legged on the rushes, sweet cedar in her nose. Nearby sits a tawny-haired woman. Boudica's whetstone has paused in its work, and her gaze is distant. She is thinking of Prasutagus again. Warm light spills into the hut; their knees are touching.

Shouts shatter the memory. Herla tears her eyes from the

carvings. More shouts come, and an animal screech. Curious, she leads her horse to a stable to find people clustered around a stallion, trying to calm him. Boys cling to ropes tied to his bridle, but they are being flung around like chaff on the wind. The animal looks crazed, eyes wide and rolling with fright. Herla stiffens. The scent of the Otherworld is very strong.

"It's no good." A man dodges the thrashing hooves. "Find the stablemaster. Though even he will be hard-pressed to manage him." Hands up, he eases back from the horse, while a woman, mud thick on skirt and shoe, races in the direction Herla came from. The woman who is left, almost as muddy as the first, makes soothing noises at the stallion, but something extraordinary has spooked him. And not only him; Herla can hear frenzied kicking coming from the stalls, as other horses pick up on his fear.

"How long have they been like this?" the woman asks, nervously eyeing the hooves.

"All was calm earlier. Must've caught the smell of something, I suppose. But only a wolf could spook them so."

A wolf or something worse, Herla thinks. She leaves her horse standing placid in the shadows and steps out, flinching as the sun strikes her eyes. It takes the shocked shouts of the stableboys before the man and woman notice her. By then, Herla is level with them and walking unconcernedly towards the kicking horse.

"Lady—no!"

She ignores the warning, dodges a hoof, and lays a hand on the sweating horse's chest. He quietens at once. The man's voice dies mid-shout, becoming a strangled gasp as the stallion kneels before Herla. Satisfied, she pats him before heading inside the stable, dark after the bright sun. She merely looks at the other horses and they still. The smell is even stronger here. A hand catches Herla's sleeve, and she only just stops herself from lashing out.

"Mistress." Beyond the man, the stallion stands on trembling legs. Perhaps she is not much better than her quarry—they both smell strange. "That was dangerous," he says, shaking her sleeve. Herla looks at him, the same look she gave the horses, and he lets go. "You could have been killed."

The missing woman arrives out of breath, accompanied by a man in a tunic with sleeves rolled up. The stablemaster, Herla assumes. A few scars crisscross his arms and he is exceptionally lean, as tall as she. He stares at her with eyes the same green as his tunic. On reflection, it might not have been a good idea to draw attention to herself. *I should have waited until they were gone.*

"Never seen the like," the man blurts as soon as the stablemaster reaches them. "He was ready to draw blood, but she calms him with a touch. And the rest too."

"I find that hard to believe. Who are you?"

It is a shock to be spoken to in such a way. Herla reminds herself she did not dress as a woman of status. "My name is—" she grasps for something appropriate—"Ælfrún."

The man frowns. She braces for suspicion before he says, "You speak with an Anglian accent," and she swallows against a sudden tightening in her throat. It seems something of her homeland still travels with her. "Do you hail from there?"

"Yes." Herla hopes she has not unwittingly named herself an enemy.

The stablemaster grunts. "What has brought you to Wessex? Where is your husband?"

About to say she does not have one and has never wanted one, Herla stops herself. "Dead." Her voice sounds flat even to her. This is harder than expected. "Killed when our homestead was burned by men jealous of his talent." Perhaps he will take her impassivity for pain. She presses her lips together.

The man grunts again. "I've heard the like of that. But you're good with horses, Deorstan says."

"It really was incredible, Sinnoch. Just a touch. She's fearless."

Deorstan's words are backed by the enthusiastic nods of the stablehands. Watching them, Sinnoch pushes his tongue into his cheek. His is not a Saxon name, Herla notes. "So you come here seeking what—work? A new start?"

"Work is good," Herla says, seizing on the chance to explore. Perhaps she might question the others.

"You should take her on," her unexpected ally, Deorstan, says.

"This isn't the first time the horses spooked. They were restless yestereve too." Herla looks at him sharply. "A gift like hers could save lives. I only just escaped injury today."

The stablemaster narrows his eyes, as if he does not quite believe her story. "A trial period then. I cannot pay much."

"I will take what you give me."

"The king's horses are the best in Wessex and require the best care." Sinnoch's voice softens a little as he speaks of the animals. "Grooming twice daily, before and after exercise in the fields outside the walls. Clean and ordered stalls. Deorstan will show you around." He turns on his heel.

"Don't mind him," Deorstan says as soon as Sinnoch is out of earshot. "He is a surly one and his tongue can be rough, but I've never seen a finer stablemaster."

"He has a Briton's name."

For the first time, Deorstan's expression cools. "He is a good man. Served Wessex loyally for years."

Somehow, she has offended him. "I meant no disrespect," Herla says, thinking of her earlier flippancy over talking to folk. She is already weary of talk.

The art of conversation is no longer required from you.

She cannot swallow a growl at the memory of Gwyn's words, and Deorstan takes a step back. That will not do. "You said the animals were uneasy before?" Herla prompts, hoping to distract him. But the anger remains inside her. Anger and…a stone sinking in the pit of her stomach. A creeping heat at her neck. After a moment, she remembers the word for it: shame. She is weary of talk because it requires nuance, tact, *thought*, and she has lived too long as a beast, on the merciless edge of instinct. The garments of her disguise feel flimsy, as if they will fall to pieces by simply rubbing against her flesh.

Herla is a wolf in a sheepskin.

"Yes," Deorstan says, regaining some of his wind. "Been a few times in fact. But today was bad. You probably saved me a cracked skull, Ælfrún."

She pushes past the unwelcome feeling in her belly. "Has anyone new visited the stables?"

"Folk come and go all the time." He chews his lip a moment. "But no one stands out. Let me show you where everything is."

After saying she would work, Herla must work, tossing out soiled hay, raking over fresh, and while she stays with them, the horses are quiet. She attacks her tasks with a violence that causes Deorstan to raise his brows. But a part of Herla is determined to prove she can wield a shovel as skilfully as a sword. She can soil her hands with dirt as well as blood. *You waste time,* the hunter in her snarls, and she snarls right back before remembering the humiliation she felt at Gwyn's callous words. After that, she shovels more sedately, and hears Deorstan let out a long-held breath.

When the others retire, Herla takes up watch in the hayloft. She feels no need to sleep, which is just as well—her Otherworld quarry could appear at any moment. But the night passes with only the shuffling of the animals to disturb the quiet. Undeterred, she spends a second day with the horses, another vigilant night, and then a third and fourth. On the morning of the fifth, she is shaken from her listless watch by a horn.

She sits up, arrow-straight. For one wild moment, she thought it the Hunt, her sword sisters grown weary of waiting. But this horn has a honeyed tone. It does not take long for the news to reach the stables: the king's party has returned. And if the king's party has returned, so has *she.*

Without thinking twice, Herla joins the excited flow of people keen to break up the morning routine. Whispers bob around her. *Was the battle one for the stories? Were men lost? Did the Wealas summon their heathen gods to aid them?* She does not care about any of that. Only one face is in her mind. Only one need.

She finds a spot just off the road that winds up towards the mead hall, and stiffens when she recognizes the fair-haired man, supercilious in the sunshine. She remembers his hand holding a bloodied knife. He rides at the fore of the group, chin raised like the king he must be. Other men come in his wake, one slumping in his saddle as if wounded.

Herla's eyes rake them, searching. She is dimly aware of her heart in her throat.

Æthelburg has stopped to talk to one of the watching women, and so lags behind the rest. In the summer heat, her browned arms are bare to the shoulder, and dusty from travel. Her lips curl at something the woman says. Then her gaze strays to the group of men almost hidden by a bend in the road. "Of course, lady queen." The commoner bows and, with a brief word of parting, Æthelburg heels her horse after them.

Herla watches the dust settle. "Æthelburg." She likes the shape of it in her mouth. But a queen... the thought of Æthelburg married to the fair-haired man is unexpectedly unpleasant.

About to follow, Herla stops. *What is this?* she asks her thumping heart. She is here for one purpose: Gwyn's spy. As soon as she finds them and shakes the truth out of them, she will no longer need to run around with mortals. Still she stands there, staring, long after the people return to their tasks and the streets teem again with the bustle of morning.

9

INE

Wiltun, Wiltunscir
Kingdom of Wessex

Nobody suspects. Ine does not know how long he can keep it up. In the beginning, he seized upon the sleeping draught: an ideal excuse for appearing vacant, or retiring early. But as the golden-tipped roof of Wiltun catches fire in the distance, he accepts it is time to drop the act of being poisoned. Which means he must pull himself together.

Æthelburg isn't entirely fooled. She has always been able to read him. Gweir too, he fears, sees more than the others. They are the only people who know of Geraint's visit. Although Ine had found a quiet moment to take both aside, none of them can make sense of the Briton's words. At least puzzling out their meaning has distracted him from what must be the onset of madness.

I thought I would have more time. He should not be surprised; it is taking his father, after all. Riding near the head of the column, Æthel at his side, Ine still has the sense of being watched.

"What *is* the matter?" Æthel is staring at the back of his blood-less hands clenched on the reins. "Aren't you relieved to be home?"

Relieved? His own unstable mind travels with him; it does not care if he is among enemy or friend. He forces something out. "I suppose so."

"Fine," she snaps, "don't talk to me."

Ine studies her stiff posture as she canters off. She is always moving away from him; he is always looking at her back. Where would he even begin? His inability to trust her with the truth about himself is bleeding over into an inability to trust her with anything at all. His heart is like a lump of charred wood in his chest. *You are always so angry,* he thinks. *You never used to be so angry.*

Just the thought of explaining what he saw the night Geraint died makes his mouth dry. Ine has tried hard to dismiss it as delirium. What else could it have been? The giant's shuttered eyes stare out at him from his memory, and he shivers, pushing away the thought of his body bound by root, dissolving in soil.

What would Æthel say if he told her he was losing his mind?

"Ine king, are you well?"

"Quite well." It is his turn to snap, but he regrets it when he meets Gweir's concerned eyes. He must keep the gesith close; the man knows too much. "I was wondering what to do with Cadwy." It isn't wholly a lie. Geraint's son is yet another itch in the anthill of his mind. Encouraged by Ingild, there are loud calls for his execution. Others, like Nothhelm, think the boy a potential bargaining piece. Æthel seems unusually protective and insists on taking his meals to him. *He* is not the only one behaving oddly.

"The boy must live," Gweir says, and Ine nods. Since he cannot keep his promise to Geraint, the least he can do is protect his son. "Nothhelm is right. He is a bargaining piece. But he could be more than that." The gesith lowers his voice. "Cadwy must know Geraint came to see you. His father paid for that decision with his life."

"Glestingaburg." An abbey Ine was happy to fund. The tor Geraint called an isle could be seen a league away, rising to an unlikely height from fields that still flooded when the rains were heavy. But to hear Geraint speak of it . . . "He called it Ynys Witrin. He talked of the Otherworld."

Although Ine readies a dismissive laugh, Gweir nods. "Yes. The tor is a place sacred to the old ways and those who follow them."

"But the Otherworld is giants and boar princes and—well, you heard the story." Another night he does not care to recall.

"There is always some truth in stories," Gweir says soberly.

Ine does not know what to make of that. "Do you think Cadwy would be more forthcoming with you?"

"I will try, lord, but I doubt he sees me in a kinder light. Perhaps he even believes me worse for choosing to serve you, my mother's kin, rather than return to my father's."

"Why do you?" Ine asks after a moment.

Gweir looks at him with eyes that remind Ine quite suddenly of the scop, who stood on his table and filled his hall with visions. "I—"

A horn blares, drowning whatever Gweir intended to say. The guards on the gates have spotted their mounted party and set about clearing the road of travellers so that they may ride through unimpeded. There are not as many as usual; most folk are busy in the fields, working to bring in the crop.

When Ine next raises his eyes to the settlement, everything has changed.

In place of the high hall is a grove of trees, the bent-backed children of giants. The wind carries singing, and a veil of twilight dims the sun. A green path fringed with stones unfolds before him, each scored with a pattern he almost recognizes. The song from the grove and the twisted trees are part of it. His heart kicks, and sweat chills his skin. Ine tears his eyes away with a gasp.

"My king?"

The sun beats down, the morning is bright. In the distance, the roof of his home glows like a dragon's hoard. Ine blinks. No grove, no mossy path. Only the wide dirt road splintering into the smaller streets of Wiltun. His gasp has attracted attention. Folk pause in their work and guards in their duties, to stare at him. Gweir is frowning.

Ine forces a smile, though his belly roils and he thinks he might be sick. It is too hot. Scared to blink lest the grove return, he has no energy to conjure up an excuse, so he urges his horse faster, deeper into the settlement, leaving the gazes behind. *I have to be more careful. Can't let it show.*

After a few moments, Gweir catches up with him. "What did

you tell them?" Ine asks in a quiet voice, eyes still fixed on the hall in case it changes again.

"You do not need to explain yourself to common folk."

"The king serves the people, not the other way around. I do not want them to think I am losing my mind."

The vision has unsettled him, caused him to speak too candidly. But Gweir only says, "You are not losing your mind."

"How do you know? I might be. Everyone has seen how my father is."

"Lord Cenred's illness is a result of the head injury he was dealt many years ago, I am certain of it." Gweir is being considerate. Ine hopes to God he won't mention the incident to the others. He could order his silence, of course, but that would only look suspicious.

The ride up to the hall takes forever. All he wants is to step beneath its cool shade, to seek silence and solitude, but the moment the guards throw open the doors, a man walks towards him, and every single hair on Ine's body tries to rip itself free. The figure is dressed for battle in mail and leather. His beard is close-cropped, his nose like the beak of an eagle, hooked and prominent. A veritable arsenal swings from his belt. His shoulders bear a cloak, madder-red, and his black eyes are fixed on Ine, as he strides unhesitatingly towards him.

The man's name is Cædwalla. And he is fifteen years dead.

Before Ine can do anything other than gape, his predecessor walks right through him. It is worse than winter. It is the grave-cold that came from the shield a few weeks ago. The cold is oily, leaves him feeling soiled. He spins around, but the dead king is gone. Only Gweir stands there, one eyebrow raised.

Fighting down panic, Ine nods jerkily at him, but his steps are uneven as he moves deeper into the hall, flinching at shadows. To conjure up Cædwalla so...his illness is worse than he thought. *What is happening to me?* Did Geraint do something to him before he died? Brought down some malediction upon his head? But he had asked for Ine's help.

"My king." It is Bishop Hædde—the last person he wants to see.

Ine clasps his shaking hands behind his back. "Word has reached me of your victory." His smile bares a brown tooth. "May I offer congratulations."

"Thank…" the word rasps and he has to cough his voice free. "Thank you, bishop. But I fear Geraint's death will not benefit us in the way you anticipate. I would rather have him alive."

"The Britons will be in despair and disarray, lord. I do not share your belief that this will damage your campaign in the west."

"I know you don't," Ine mutters under his breath. "Feel free to join me in council after we have eaten and rested from the road somewhat. There is a matter to discuss." The sooner he secures Cadwy's life, the better. Ingild has gone behind his back once already, and Ine wants the boy alive. *Only he knows why Geraint asked to take two score warriors to a quiet hill in the middle of farmlands.*

Instead of finding silence and solitude, Ine spends a restless hour pacing the Witan chamber, glancing at the shield and nibbling the bilberries a servant brings. Finally, others join him: Ingild, Edred and Nothhelm; Gweir and Leofric; both bishops; ealdormen Godric and Osberht, and lastly Cenred with Æthelburg. His father seems unsteady today—she is guiding him by the elbow. The sight of them together chases away a little of the horror the vision of Cædwalla left in its wake.

"Good to have everyone here," he begins, as they find places on the benches that fill the space.

"Are you well, Ine king?" Hædde asks. "Your brother says you were indisposed at Gifle."

What else has Ingild rushed to tell the bishop? Ine summons as calm a face as he can and says, "Quite well, Hædde. The matter I wished to raise is divisive. Which is why it needs addressing now. It concerns Cadwy, son of Geraint, whom we have brought to Wiltun."

Hædde sucks in a breath and Earconwald's eyes widen. Both look primed to jump in, so Ine rushes on. "I want no harm done him. He should be treated as a royal prisoner with what rights that status grants him."

Ingild snorts. "Your wife should have let me kill him alongside his father. It was foolhardy to bring him here, where he could serve as a rallying point for rebellion."

There are nods. Ine grips the carved wooden arm of his chair. "Have the Wealas—" that word no longer sounds right—"the Britons in Wessex shown any sign of rebellion?"

"Not yet," Edred says, "but they have never had a royal son of Dumnonia amongst them. To inspire them."

Æthelburg folds her arms. "If you think rebellion likely, Ingild has already fanned its flames by stabbing Geraint in the back."

"But why *was* Geraint outside his camp that night?" Ingild retorts. His pale eyes are narrow. "Do you know, brother?"

What perceived wrong has he done Ingild to warrant this behaviour? "I know nothing more than you," Ine says. "As you are so keen to tell everyone, I was *indisposed*."

Ingild sits back. Is that disappointment Ine can sense? He shakes his head. "Besides, *you* have not provided a suitable explanation for your own presence outside the walls."

"Because it is the fact of least importance," Ingild says coldly. "With the arrival of our army, we outnumbered the Britons who—until then—possessed the numerical advantage. I anticipated a surprise assault and I was right. Although I admit catching Geraint alone was unexpected."

Ine recalls the invisible way Geraint moved and bites his tongue before it demands to hear how exactly Ingild had cornered the Briton. Carelessness on Geraint's part? He had mentioned the strain of using his power. Ine knows far too little about it, and the only person who could tell him more—

"Cadwy may prove an asset. As I said at our last meeting—" his voice hardens—"I prefer to keep our options open."

"Alive and secure will take resources," Nothhelm comments. "He will attempt escape at the slightest opportunity."

"No different to holding prisoner a member of the Miercean or Centish nobility." There is an edge to Leofric's voice that has been there since he missed the confrontation at Gifle. If Ingild is seeking support for his ideas amongst the gesiths, his rash action may have cost him Leofric.

"I acknowledge that there are valid arguments for and against." Bishop Earconwald is a quiet man, not so outspoken as Hædde, but Ine is warier of him because of it. "However, the risks of keeping the boy alive outweigh, in my opinion, the benefits—which are still only potential."

Æthelburg meets his gaze. Ine is quite sure she wants Cadwy alive, and will fight to keep him so. She is just as angry at Ingild as he is. At least he can count on her support in a vote.

Ingild rises to his feet. "Striking a blow against the royal line has weakened Dumnonia—and Cadwy's death will weaken it further." He slaps a fist into the palm of his other hand, meets every pair of eyes except Ine's. "This readies the way for an invasion, which will make Dumnonia a permanent part of Wessex at last." A pause as he turns. "Is that not what you want, brother?"

Ine cannot deny it. But Geraint's visit has only strengthened his conviction that violence is not the way to win this struggle. Geraint was a proud man, a difficult man certainly, and yet Ine respected the Briton's integrity, his commitment to his people. *A good king.* And Ingild slaughtered him in the dark, from behind, as a brigand does his marks.

"We will put it to the vote," he says.

When the little wooden counters sit on the table, he and Æthelburg, Gweir, Leofric and Nothhelm are on one side. Ingild, Edred, Osberht, Godric and the bishops are on the other. Six to five. Ine's heart sinks. Wild plans flood his mind—how Cadwy might be spirited away, where he might go, how he could make it look like an escape, whether Ingild would suspect—before another counter clinks gently down.

Cenred's hand is shaking, but his eyes are clear when they meet Ine's. Hope blooms in his chest. "Father?"

"My vote is with the king," Cenred says before his mouth begins to shape stranger silent words and the lucidity fades from his gaze.

Ingild slams a hand down; the pieces jump and scatter. "It doesn't count. When are madmen allowed a vote at this table?"

"Father is of the royal line of Wessex," Ine says coldly. "As long as he lives, he is entitled to a place in the Witan."

Ingild grinds his teeth. He knows as well as Ine that an equal vote means the choice lies with the king. The room fills with the sound of his disgust as he throws open the door and strides out, cloak billowing behind him. Ine lets go a breath. If Ingild harmed Cadwy now, it would be tantamount to treason. This should buy the boy better protection. "Thank you, Father," he says, but Cenred's back is turned and he is humming under his breath. The other men exchange glances.

"I will see to the boy's lodging." Before she goes, Æthelburg gives him a small, satisfied nod. Not a smile, but it helps soften the burned lump of Ine's heart. Sinking back in his chair, he rubs his forehead. *That was too close.* What would he have done without Cenred's deciding vote? His own laws forbid him from going expressly against the wishes of the Witan. As the others drift out too, Ine moves to his father's side and realizes that he is staring at the shield in its quiet place on the wall.

With daylight slanting in through the high window, only half the room's torches are lit. Ine's skin prickles. Elation dying, he turns slowly. All but invisible in a gloom-draped corner, the spectre of Cædwalla watches from the darkness.

10

ÆTHELBURG

Wiltun, Wiltunscir
Kingdom of Wessex

A woman is shaking out her clothes. Æthel freezes in the doorway of her bedchamber. "Who are *you*?"

The stranger's head snaps round, before easing into subservience. "Here to serve," she mutters.

"I have a girl," Æthel informs her, "with whom I am quite happy. I do not need another."

"Æthelburg queen!" Feet thump the boards behind her and Eanswith arrives in a chaos of flapping skirts. "Sorry, lady, I meant to tell you. This is Alis. While you were gone, Father sent word to say Mother's not well after the birth and that I must go tend her. Sure it'll be only a while."

"And Alis is…?"

"The daughter of my second cousin. You won't notice the difference." Eanswith locks her fingers, eyes earnest. "She works hard."

Alis is staring at her feet. "Look up, girl," Æthel says. "I don't like servility. You are your own person."

"I said she was fierce," Eanswith hisses and the girl's lips twitch in a weak smile. "But Lady Æthelburg is kind really and won't ask much."

"Shouldn't you be going, then?" It comes out harsher than she intended. Eanswith is more friend than maid, and has always been good at drawing her out of herself. Æthel will miss her chatter at sunrise. When the younger woman's face dims, she relents and adds, "Give my sincerest wishes to your mother for a swift recovery."

Eanswith beams. "Thank you, lady. That'll mean much to her."

When she has gone, Æthel strips off her armour. "Take this to be oiled," she says to the new girl, and watches to make sure she can carry it all. "I will bathe in the river."

Clothed only in sweat-stained linen and belt—call her over-cautious, but she makes a habit of always having her knife—Æthel takes the door at the rear of the hall and follows a winding path to the stream that loops the foot of the hill. The sunlight is fading warmly into dusk. She draws a breath of it, tasting the harvest dust on her tongue. Birds flutter up at her passing. Æthel watches their small dark bodies against the sky and wishes for wings herself. *Where would I go?* She should be happy here. Nearly the highest position in the realm, servants to oil her armour, scurry at her word. Gold enough to buy gems and jewellery, if she cared for such things. Food enough to fill her belly. Safety enough—

Yes, she should be happy. That she is not content only makes her selfish. She strips off her clothes and wades into the stream. Despite the temperate water, hers is a brisk bath. Ine could spend all day here, until his skin shrivelled like a dried plum. Æthel enjoys teasing him about it. Enjoyed. They used to come together, arm-in-arm. They used to talk. Now...Something is wrong. How can she help him if he refuses to share it?

Why should you help him at all, the voice that tormented her in Gifle whispers, *when he does not help you?*

Beneath the water her belly is flat, hard as river rock. How much louder will the whispers become before she must cover her ears in the din? The thought is a ball of outrage, but hidden inside is something Æthel does not want to face. It is dark and clinging like shame and it turns the cool water cold. Gooseflesh pimples her skin. Growling as she hoists herself up—because weeping is out of the question—she has a sudden, overwhelming sense of being watched.

Naked, dripping, she reaches for her knife, but there is nothing against which to wield it. The birdsong is becoming sleepy, the light on the water has sunk to the silty bottom, and a star shines high above. Æthel shrugs back into her clothes, keeping half an eye on the trees. That hidden gaze follows until the bustle and swell of the hall rise to reclaim her.

Ine is surrounded by his usual thicket of nobles. Although he told her and Gweir about Geraint, he has not mentioned the roots. Maybe he doesn't remember, or maybe Æthel is simply failing to scale the wall building between them. As for Geraint's request to take warriors to Glestingaburg…She grimaces. Only one person could explain that and he is their prisoner.

Ingild is notably absent. Still licking his wounds then. Æthel visits the table only briefly to heap a plate with seasoned meat before going to lean against a painted dragon to eat it. She is in no mood to share the benches with men who will only condescend to her. Leaning her head back, she stares at the other creatures climbing the walls, claws reaching for the rafters. Gold leaf glows copper in the firelight.

"…could have been killed," a voice says and Æthel pricks up her ears. "Did you see it?"

"I missed Deorstan's rescue," a man replies drily: the stable-master, Sinnoch. "But I saw her calm the rest of the horses with little but a look."

"Such a gift is rare these days. Why, even *you*…" The man breaks off at Sinnoch's scowl. "I mean to say, there was a time when you could find a horsemaster in every family. Now it's once in a generation, if that."

Æthel drifts over. "There is a horsemaster in Wiltun? A woman?"

The men startle, dropping hasty bows. "Yes, Æthelburg queen," Sinnoch's companion says, a portly man whose tarnished cloak pin suggests a low-status noble. Æthel reaches for his name and comes up empty. She has not spent time enough in court to memorize the name of every hanger-on. "Saved Deorstan a battering a week or so past."

"She is still here?"

"The woman claimed to be seeking work." Sinnoch's tone says

he does not believe it. *Interesting.* "Seemed churlish to refuse her. And the horses are calmer since she came."

"They weren't before?" Æthel asks with a frown.

"They have been unsettled of late, though I can find no reason for it."

Another oddity to add to an increasing list of oddities. "From where does this horsemaster hail?"

"Sounds Anglian." She can tell Sinnoch finds the topic prickly, and swallows a smile. It would rankle—being outshone by a stranger and a woman at that. *Maybe I will pay the stables a visit.* She nods at the men, who are already turning towards the old scop tuning his lyre.

It is a warm night with little wind. Lammas Eve. The church folk will be preparing their rituals, the millers and bakers working the first of the crop into bread. The hunters will no doubt bring down an enormous boar for roasting, and there will be music and dancing and all the usual things she used to enjoy. Æthel hugs herself, but the cold is inside her. It was different when she was younger. Now, long past her thirtieth winter, the court seems a perilous place, full of barbed smiles and words spoken behind hands. How can she enjoy the festivals as she once did, knowing that so many of those words are about her?

The stables are close, just a handful of breaths from the court-yard into which the road empties. A few torches are lit, but no one seems to be there. Shrugging, she takes a slow walk past the stalls, footfalls muffled by fresh straw. The animals poke their heads out to see if she has brought food. Æthel shows them her empty palms and, snorting reproof, they retreat. The place smells musky, com-forting. She has always felt untouchable in the saddle, whereas in court…

The thought trails off as she catches sight of an unfamiliar horse at the end of the row. It is a wan beast, nearing the end of its span. Its dappled coat is well groomed but dull, and it seems underfed. When it turns its eye on her, however, Æthel freezes. She stares at the horse and the horse stares back, and into her head comes a vision: a waving expanse like an ocean of flowers. Dizzy, she stumbles—

—and arms close around her. Æthel gasps. Her instinct is to fight, but the arms are not locked; they are keeping her from falling. She hears breath catch. The grip on her tightens and, for an imagined instant, a handful of dark braids falls over her shoulder. The scent in her nose is like a night wind after rain.

She blinks, and it is gone, fleeting as the flower vision. No arms around her; nothing on her shoulder; the musk of horse and straw mingling in her nose.

"Have a care," a voice says.

Æthel turns. A woman is standing in the middle of the empty space. Brown hair braided down her back, her homespun overdress has a deep pocket at the front, and a knife hangs from her belt. Ordinary, but Æthel's heart is racing. The woman steps into the pooled light of a torch, and the eyes Æthel thought were dark have a streak of the green wild in them. "Sorry," she hears herself say and then feels ridiculous. These are *her* stables. It is the way the woman holds herself, queenlier than Æthel has ever felt. Her mouth is dry. "Are you the one they call horsemaster?"

Expression touches the woman's face: a slightly rueful smile. "Is that what they say? I have a way with horses, but I am no master."

Æthel does not believe her; the rustling in the stalls has entirely subsided. No animal moves.

"You are Æthelburg." It is not a question. Her gaze is very direct, and her tone entirely devoid of deference.

Æthel raises an eyebrow. "And you are?"

The woman pauses, as if she has to think about it. "Ælfrún."

Perhaps it is her real name, perhaps it isn't. She would not be the first woman to hide beneath a new one. "The stablemaster says you hail from Anglia." Æthel can hear it herself now, in the way Ælfrún draws out her words. "What brings you south?"

"It is no longer my home." In a softer tone, "But I would like to see it again. Before the end."

Æthel laughs. "You speak as one about to go into battle."

"I...apologize."

"No need," she says with a smile of her own now. "I rarely have a chance to speak with women outside of court. Especially about matters that aren't whose niece will wed whose nephew, whose wife has borne yet another daughter and so on. He may not show it, but our stablemaster is impressed by your skill. If you agree, I would like to make your post official."

Ælfrún bows her head and still manages to drain deference out of the gesture. "That is gracious. Should I not present myself to the king?"

"I will introduce you tomorrow." When silence falls between them, Æthel searches for something else to say. "Sinnoch mentioned the horses being disturbed?"

The woman comes closer, and Æthel feels her approach as an odd shivering on her skin. It is hard to tell how old Ælfrún is. Her face is unlined but cannot be called *young*. Her air, too, does not belong to a person of scanty winters. "I saw the effects, but cannot discern the reason," she says, eyes raking the corners of the stable. "It was as if they caught the scent of a wolf pack."

"That's impossible."

"Has anyone entered the settlement recently?"

"Plenty, especially while the king holds court here." Æthel frowns. "You believe this disturbance is linked to a person?"

"Some things resemble people, but are not. While they can fool humans, animals are another matter."

"Some *things*?" She rubs her arms. "What things?"

"Things that do not belong here," Ælfrún says darkly. Unlike Æthel, every inch of her is still. Nothing about her hints at a jest, and Æthel remembers that night: the elf-faced women on their tall horses, weapons singing. *Herla,* she thinks.

The woman twitches, clasps her hands, and warmth floods back into the moment. "I did not mean to unsettle you...my lady."

"I am not unsettled." Despite the words, Æthel cannot help checking the corners of the stable too—for what, she does not know. Outside, an owl calls, startling her. She is a mess of nerves. The sense of being watched at the river, those wild visions..."I am simply tired from the journey." *How like a wilting noble I sound.* "We can speak again tomorrow after I introduce you to the king."

"I believe I saw him earlier," Ælfrún says in a stranger tone. "A proud, fair-haired man?"

Æthel almost chokes. "You saw Ingild. And *arrogant* would be a better word." She fights down a shudder at the idea of being married to him. "My husband is his older brother, Ine."

The woman gives a soft acknowledgement. Æthel has to walk by her to reach the door and, with every step, Ælfrún seems to grow, until Æthel feels she is passing beneath the shadow of the great colossus Ine once described to her. She is considered a tall woman, but Ælfrún is taller still. How has she not noticed? Then she is out under the stars and that sense of unearthly height drops away. Æthel blinks, drags a hand across her stinging eyes. She really must be tired.

Ine is not in their bedchamber when she retires for the night, and he is not there when she wakes at dawn, but the warm shape of him lingers. Æthel runs her hand over the empty space. It is cooling, already forgetting there was another beside her.

Her belly is a band of pain. The reason becomes obvious as soon as she rises: her blood has come early. Calling for Eanswith to bring hot water, Æthel strips off the stained undergarments and rubs her back. The last time it was this bad, the herbalist gave her some leaves to chew. Not that she wants their bitterness coating her tongue before breakfast.

Just as she's wondering why the girl is taking so long, an unfamiliar face peers around the door and Æthel remembers that Eanswith is gone. "Oh—" she grasps after a name—"Alis, I had forgotten. Did you lose your way?"

The girl shakes her head. She will have to work hard with this one, Æthel thinks, hoping Eanswith's mother recovers quickly. *I really am a spoiled noble at heart.* When Alis's eyes slide to her undergarments, Æthel steps in front of them. "If you could lay out clothes for me?"

Once she nods, Æthel lifts the bucket of steaming water and

steps behind her wooden screen to wash. She can hear Alis moving about the room, still in that uncomfortably silent way. Then the soft *snick* of the latch. Drying herself, Æthel hisses at another cramp. Perhaps she will have some of those leaves after all.

Instead of tunic and trousers, an embroidered dress awaits her. "Lammas." She mutters it like a curse. Feeling mournful, Æthel dons a linen underdress before pulling the folds of woad-weld green over her head. The trim is the same madder as Ingild's fancy cloak, with gold thread outlining each diamond in the weave. No sensible garb for feast days. Today she must be a queen. Æthel opens the jewellery box, a beautiful ivory thing, but dusty, and takes out a necklace: a double-tiered string of glass beads. Garnet brooches to secure her dress at each shoulder, two rings, and tiny fish-shaped earrings, the least she can get away with.

It is only when she glances around for her belt that she realizes her undergarments are gone. Æthel stares at the patch of floor where she left them and hugs herself. *Alis has merely taken them to be laundered.* But how many will see them and know from whom Alis has come? She cannot even admonish her without drawing attention.

Every month, Æthel takes care to hide evidence of her childlessness; the fires lit against her in court do not need more fuel. Out on campaign, in the field of battle, she can bury the subject and her feelings with it. But it is always waiting for her when she returns, disinterred by the whispers and frowns of the nobles. Her jaw is clenched tight and her eyes prickle, shockingly, with tears. Ine professes to care for her, but he cannot care much if he is happy to leave her defenceless. It is like this whenever she returns home, whenever they are together, and Æthel has no sword in her hand to distract her. Here, she is forced to ask why her husband refuses to take responsibility. Here, she is forced to ask herself again whether she wants a child beyond her duty to bear an heir. This morning, with her belly cramping viciously, Æthel cannot tell how much of her desire to fulfil expectations is hers...and how much is the court's.

She swallows her tears. The jewellery hangs heavy upon her, sings a gilded song when she moves. She should not have to tolerate gossip. Her word is Ine's. She is *queen*.

It is time Æthel reminded them all.

11

ḢERLA

She is supposed to present herself in the hall. An audience with the king. Herla takes a circuitous route, drifting half-curious through the streets. The day dawned excited. People are laughing, the daily work being done with happier hands. And the waft of baking bread permeates all. It is a smell Herla remembers from the long ago. Her own hands might once have kneaded dough like this woman, skirt feathered with flour. Her teeth might have crunched their way through the hot hard crust. As if thinking has power to make it real, the woman glances out with a "Happy Hlafmas!" Breaking the bread, she tosses a piece to Herla.

Watching the steam twist up into the morning, it occurs to her that she has not eaten in centuries. She does not have to eat. Can she even enjoy it? Perhaps mortal fare will taste like ashes now that she has sampled fairy food. Gwyn's feast was the last time anything solid passed her lips.

Herla goes a little way before biting into the bread. Salt. Yeast. The warm mustiness of wheat. She swallows, presses a hand against her mouth. She can feel the morsel inside her like an anchor, like a burning coal, like a—the sensation fades and she wants to laugh. Rocked by a scrap of bread. *What a stranger to life I have become.*

Off-balance, she almost fails to notice the change. Stepping through the doors of the great hall, it hits her: the scent of the

Otherworld. Herla sucks in a breath, half expecting to be greeted by the cruel smiles of Caer Sidi, but all she sees is men drinking, throwing dice, polishing swords and stories. Nobles cluster in gossiping groups; women sit in a circle, weaving. The walls are painted, and the posts that support a second floor, half the length of the first, sport beasts and figures carved skilfully into the wood. All is as it should be...except for the overripe scent of something that does not belong. Herla's nostrils flare. She puts a hand on her sword.

"I'm afraid there's no one here to fight."

Æthelburg wears a dress of green linen. Recalling herself, Herla releases the disguised blade, finding her eyes drawn to the queen's neck, adorned with beads. "More's the pity," Æthelburg adds in an undertone. Her hands bear a warrior's calluses and, unlike the other noble women, her skin is browned from the sun. Herla knows just how brown because she watched her yestereve, while she bathed in the river. Her pulse races at the memory; she had struggled to hang back. And later in the stables, trembling at the feel of the queen in her arms, she almost lost her grip on the glamour. Something like the hunter's rage, but softer, hotter, burned in her veins.

Who is to stop her taking what she wants? Is she not Lord of the Hunt?

"Good morgen, lady," Herla murmurs. Æthelburg's lips are parted, and there is a rising flush in her cheeks, as if she has heard Herla's every thought. With a nod, she turns swiftly, and leads the way deeper into the hall.

The queen is not the only one in finery. There is a lot of gold on display and dyed cloth spun fine to serve in summer. Two seats are raised higher than the benches, and in one sits the weary man Herla saw yesterday. At first glance, he is the least kingly of the lords, with rings on their arms and oiled beards. But when he looks up and his eyes meet Herla's, she finds herself pausing. They are dark, flecked with the same gold as his jewellery. Unlike many others, he is clean-shaven. And there is something...familiar about him that she cannot place.

"Ine," Æthelburg says, her voice cutting through the male banter. "This is Ælfrún horsemaster."

When Herla bows, there are whispers. Æthelburg's lips twitch. But if she did something wrong, the king does not remark on it. Instead he steps down from his chair. "You are welcome here, horsemaster. They tell me you hail from Anglia?"

"Yes." She is still trying to trace the familiarity. "I left my home."

"Well, you are welcome to remain in Wessex if the stablemaster is pleased with your work." His strange eyes flicker to the woman standing beside her. "You have certainly impressed my wife."

The colour deepens in Æthelburg's cheeks. She shakes her head, as if to be rid of it, and says, "Will you join us for the Lammas feast, horsemaster?"

About to decline, Herla hesitates. If it means she can spend more time in this hall, where the Otherworld scent is strongest...She nods.

Æthelburg seems pleased before deflating a little. "I suppose there are rituals to observe first."

"Indeed," comes a voice: a greying man in the vestments of a priest. Hanging from his neck is an elaborate cross set with gemstones; it sways with every step. "My lords, will you follow me to church?"

The Saxon king looks as if he'd rather go into battle. Before Herla can slip away, Æthelburg catches her sleeve. "Accompany me."

She would prefer to explore while the hall is emptied, but someone of Ælfrún's status cannot refuse. And perhaps there is another reason why she lets herself be swept along, as if she really is a woman far from home, overawed by the splendour of a royal court. Overawed by the queen's hand on her arm. It is not difficult to pretend; she knows little of this era's people. A hunter does not seek to understand the hunted.

The souls in her own soul stir at the thought. If Herla concentrates, she can distinguish individual voices among the throng. That is something new. Uneasy at their growing weight, she shoves them down and asks Æthelburg, "What is this ritual you spoke of?"

"Oh, Lammas," the queen says dismissively. "We bring bread to church, the bishop blesses it, and then a piece is buried in each corner of the grain barn to protect the harvest."

"You do not sound as if you approve."

Unlike the other women who move sedately down the wide steps outside, Æthelburg picks up her skirt so as not to break stride. "I find it pointless. If God wants to burn the barn, or send a plague of pests to spoil the grain, He will. A bit of bread is hardly going to deter Him."

Herla chuckles, and almost stops in her tracks. Her laughter is not the glee of the victorious hunter, or the hollow humour of the vengeful. In the wake of it, even the weight of the souls seems lessened. She raises a hand to her mouth, unsettled.

"Is that yours?" Æthelburg asks, and the feeling blazes into anger as a small sleek shape trots up to them: Dormach in his guise as a bloodhound. *I told you to stay away,* Herla thinks at Gwyn's dog. Her hand has moved once more to her weapon; her fingers hovering over the hilt. But Dormach is a creature of the Otherworld— can he even be slain? And slain without Gwyn knowing it?

"Ælfrún?"

"He follows me," Herla says, glaring at the hound, "so I suppose he is mine."

"A hunting dog," the other woman remarks.

Herla looks at her sidelong. How much does the queen recall of the night the bloodhound leaped? Their eyes had locked. She is certain something passed between them. Unless that is her own desire speaking. What might Æthelburg think, if Herla let her disguise fall away?

Perhaps she does not like the answer to that question, for she turns her attention to the streets, ignoring, for now, the blood-hound shadowing them. People hover in doorways to wave at the king's party. Children hang on the frames. Herla watches them watching Æthelburg; the queen seems a divisive figure. Younger folk tend to smile at her, which Æthelburg returns. Older women regard her narrowly, tongues stuck between their teeth, as if to catch words they may regret.

Colours thrown across the road announce the church before they reach it. "Stained glass." Æthelburg nods at the windows when she notices Herla staring. "It is a new technique. Very pretty, very expensive."

"You are a Christian then?"

"Who isn't?" Æthelburg says quietly, flicking the small silver cross she wears. The king has one too. "Particularly with Hædde breathing down their necks."

Herla lowers her voice to match. "But your husband is king."

"Even kings must bow before God." There is a hint of suspicion in the slant of Æthelburg's brow. "I am certain Ealdwulf of East Anglia feels the same."

Her disguise will not stand up to any serious challenge. Herla has a strong urge to throw it off, impatient with niceties and idle talk. She is impatient too with ease and the hot listless sun drenching the streets. If she could run, if she could *ride*…But that is exactly what Gwyn would expect of her, and she snarls silently. She will not flee like an animal too savage to live amongst its own kind.

Æthelburg sighs when they come beneath the cool stone of the church. Her brow is sheened and she pulls at her dress, exposing collarbones Herla cannot help but stare at. Before she knows it, the sight has awakened more of those memories determined to spill into her thoughts.

She tries to push them out, but in the mesmeric cadence of the priest's Latin, she can hear soldiers and merchants, scribes and scholars. Their voices reach her from a distant place, across centuries of ground. It is the language of their freedom-takers, of the masters that flogged Boudica, stole her inheritance and raped her daughters. Herla's fists curl. She sees it again. Her hand had trembled as she staunched the blood from the whip marks. Boudica had uttered not a word. Her eyes were ablaze, but something deep in them had died and stayed dead, as she slew Roman men, and women with babes in their arms.

I sowed the seeds of my fate. The Latin is endless in her ears.

When I made Boudica's rage my own. When I too took my blade to children's throats.

She does not realize she is trembling until she feels a light touch on her arm. The queen does not speak, but her eyes ask, *Are you well?*

It is a relief when the ritual ends at the grain store: a stone building already filled with the reaper's harvest and miller's labour. The king takes the northern and western corners; Æthelburg takes the southern and eastern. Afterwards, she goes to wipe her hands on her dress, but snatches them away with a curse at the last moment. She has barely looked at her husband once. Even Herla feels the tension between them and cannot help wondering at it.

"I hope you will tell me more about yourself," Æthelburg says as they walk ahead of the king and his guards. "During the feast."

"There is little enough to tell."

"Then make up a story." Æthelburg tips her face to the sky. "You will have time during all the eating and dancing and general mead-drinking."

The queen's hair falls away from her neck, revealing a soft expanse Herla imagines grazing with her teeth. "Do you not like festival days?"

Her voice sounds strained, even to her, but Æthelburg only shrugs. "I find them tedious, to be honest." All around are the sounds of people eschewing work. Children run through the streets, bright scraps of cloth in their hands. "See?" The queen nods at them. "They tie those on the old oak by the well. Each one is a wish." She laughs, and it is a husky, lovely sound. "I used to play too."

"What did you wish for?" Herla asks before she can stop herself.

"Oh, the usual. A good marriage. A kind husband." Æthelburg stretches her green-clad arms before her, as if trying to prevent the memory escaping. "One year, I wished that Leofe would kiss me—she had such soft lips." She drops her arms quite suddenly, staring straight ahead. "God knows why I said that."

Herla's breath has caught in her throat. "How did you know her lips were soft?"

When the other woman turns, her own lips are curved, and there is a hint of a furrow on her brow. "I got *that* wish the following year," she says a little wickedly, "when we were fourteen." Before Herla can ask about her other wishes—the ones concerning her marriage and husband—Æthelburg adds, "Would you like to ride?"

The queen means it as a pastime, a pleasure. The word is so weighted with the Hunt that it has *become* it. But then Herla remembers how she rode here with the night in her ears and the wind in her face. What would it be like to ride that way with Æthelburg at her side? "Yes." The word escapes with such keen-edged desire that she belatedly adds, "My lady, do you not have responsibilities?"

"It seems you only call me *my lady* when you remember to." Æthelburg's smile is crooked. "So you might as well use my name. And no." When her eyes go to the grand hall, her smile fades. "I doubt I will be missed. Wait for me while I change my clothes. You can show me your horse-skill and I can show you the trails I rode with my mother."

Herla watches her vanish into the hall. A strange comment for a queen to make—someone who should stand at the centre of court. She follows Æthelburg over the threshold and is struck anew by the Otherworld scent. The thought of Gwyn's people anywhere near Æthelburg raises her hackles. Deep in her chest, the flame flutters. The intoxication of a hard-beating heart—where has it come from so suddenly, so unexpectedly? Herla thinks back to the night she saw the queen, stained with blood and battle. The past had yawned inside her and *something* had risen up out of it, long forgotten. Her blow had missed. Æthelburg is the first mortal she has failed to kill. The first to break the pattern of the curse. What does it mean?

Shouting reaches her from outside, and she turns in time to see a man slipping off a horse on the verge of collapse, its flanks heaving. Already a group surround him, lifting him up when his legs fail. "I must see the king," he is babbling. A dark gash mars his temple.

"What goes here?" Æthelburg is dressed as Herla saw her before—in tunic and trousers. She sweeps down the steps, her eyes moving at once to the blood on the man's face. "Who is he, Leofric?"

"Ceolmund," the man gasps, hanging onto the one supporting him. "From Scirburne. I work the gerefa's land there. I've ridden all night—" his expression abruptly crumples—"we were attacked."

"Attacked?" Æthelburg asks sharply. Something has come alive in her. "By who?"

"I...don't know." But the man's eyes slide sideways as he says it. "They went for the Wealas. As if they could tell them at a glance. And when my son, when Pæga—" the name is a sob—"tried to stop them, they slew him too. He bled out in my arms."

"What about the rest of the people?" comes a voice and Herla turns to see the king, two more men at his shoulder.

Ceolmund bows. "The killers left after that, lord. It was dark. Many fled. I rode to bring the news before the trail went cold." He bares teeth. "So that someone will pay for the blood spilled."

"You said it was Wealas blood," one of the men with the king remarks. Gold at his ears and on his hands. "Must the court really be disturbed on Lammas Day for something so trivial?"

The king's eyes flash. "Murder is never *trivial*, Edred. These people are under my protection. Our laws enshrine it."

Edred lets his lip curl as soon as Ine turns back to the messenger, and Herla is sure she is not the only one who notices. "Why the Britons? Were any of our people harmed?"

"I cannot be sure, lord. But they did not spare my son."

"It is little consolation, I know, but I will pay his wergeld myself, in thanks for bringing the news so swiftly."

"I will leave at once for Scirburne," Æthelburg says. "Verify his story. If there is a trail that points to those responsible, I will find it."

The king's face falls. His hand twitches, as if he wants to reach out to her. "You have only just returned to Wiltun, Æthelburg. Let another go."

"I will not trust it to another. This attack occurred in the heart of our territory, long considered secure. The duty is mine."

Ine briefly closes his eyes. His expression, however, is schooled in a way that seems long practised. "I thought you might stay a while with me. But if it is your wish…" He turns to the man beside him. "Go with her, Gweir."

"My king—"

"No arguments." His tone softens. "I will do without you for a few days."

The messenger is shaking his head. "They came and went like shadows. I fear they have not left many clues behind."

Æthelburg stills. "What do you mean?"

"I…nothing." Ceolmund raises shaking fingers to his temple. "I hit my head. I cannot trust my memory."

The queen leans in. "Answer me truthfully. Was it *women* you saw?"

Edred tuts under his breath. Leofric looks away as if embarrassed. After a few moments, Herla realizes: Æthelburg thinks *she* is responsible for this attack? The idea is not at all improbable, save that she has never chosen her victims. Gwyn's sword seeks souls; it does not matter to whom they belonged in life.

"No," the man answers, unaware of the tension crackling around him. He sags in Leofric's arms. "It sounds foolish. The Wealas say there were several, but I only saw the one. A man. He wore gold on his brow. Like a crown."

His words leave everyone nonplussed. Herla, though, whose lynx eyes miss little, notices Ine flinch ever so slightly. The king's cheeks are pallid when he swallows and reaches for his wife. "Æthel. Please take care."

They clasp forearms like kinsmen. Fleetingly, the ice in Æthelburg's eyes thaws before she turns away. "Bring my horse, Ælfrún," she says, "and then the day is yours."

Herla nods obediently, but she already knows she is going with her.

12

ÆTHELBURG

Scirburne, Dornsæte
Kingdom of Wessex

They are a party of fifteen by the time they reach the settlement.
It is small, but growing; squat houses creeping up around the new
abbey like mushrooms. The building is unfinished. Masons ought
to be here, making the most of the fine weather. In place of hammers and chisels is the cawing of watchful crows. Æthel cannot
help but see them as an omen. A lingering pall hangs over the
place; she has an inexplicable sense of past violence done here.

A child's shout brings people stumbling from their homes, terrified eyes raking Æthel's group. She dismounts at once, holding
up her hands. Her signet ring—the only jewellery she regularly
wears—glints gold in the sunshine. And because there is but a
single woman who wears both armour and the king's heraldry,
they recognize her. Relieved shouts travel back through the
people, until a man pushes his way to the front.

"Æthelburg queen." He is better dressed than the ceorls he over-
sees, but the clothes are rumpled, as if he has slept in them. "I am
Eadgar, gerefa of Scirburne. Is the king with you?"

"Of course not." It is more caustic than she intended. "My husband has many other duties. We have only just returned from
Gifle."

"Forgive me," he says, wringing his hands, "we are all nervous.
Please, my lady." He leads them over to the largest building.

Gweir instructs his men to comb the area before following

Æthel inside. The day is hot, and it is no cooler under the stout wooden roof of the hall—hardly large enough to be called a hall. Sweat beads on Æthel's brow and she accepts a cup of ale gratefully. "Tell me what happened."

"You will not believe me," Eadgar says flatly.

"Your man, Ceolmund, mentioned a crowned figure."

He flinches. "Yes. He was their leader."

"How many of them?"

"I only saw the leader. But the Wealas amongst us were screaming that there were others. It was unerring—as if they knew where each of them lived." He swallows. "We buried them already. Too hot to leave out bodies."

"Did any escape?"

"Some."

Æthel turns to Gweir, who has gone very still. "See if the survivors know more." When he nods, she rises with him, suddenly desiring to stand beneath the sun. "Did these intruders leave any marks behind? Any clues as to who they were?"

"Came and went without a word spoken, or cry uttered." Eadgar accompanies her outside. "Ceolmund's son tried to fight them, but he was slain like the Wealas. With a single stroke to the heart."

"An execution," Æthel murmurs. Arms folded across her chest, she stares at the village, at the houses and unfinished abbey; an improbable battlefield. Not a battlefield at all. These—she does not yet have a name for them—*killers* came here for a single purpose. "Show me where you buried the dead."

Eadgar leads her to the graveyard, which is split in two: the larger, sunnier side for Saxon dead, and the smaller for Wealas. Divided in death, as well as in life. Although it comes as no surprise, the sight strikes her a blow. *Even as corpses, we are not equal.* Ten fresh mounds cluster together. Whatever she expected to find, it is not the woman kneeling beside one of them. "*Ælfrún?*"

The horsemaster rises slowly to her feet. "Æthelburg."

She imbues the name with such intensity that Æthel almost steps back. It is because of the force emanating from the other woman, as if her skin cannot contain all that she is. Æthel shakes her head, pulls herself together. "What in God's name are you doing here?"

Perhaps Ælfrún senses her unease. She smiles and says, "I was intrigued by the man's story. I knew you would not permit me to travel with you, so I came alone."

"How did you arrive before me?"

"I rode through the night."

Disconcerted, Æthel finds herself looking up to hold Ælfrún's gaze; she keeps forgetting how tall she is. The woman is dressed as before, in a skirt wholly unsuitable for horseback. But then, she is a horsemaster. She could probably ride in a silk gown. "Did it not occur to you it might be dangerous?"

Ælfrún tips her head on one side, regarding Æthel as she might a curiosity. "Are you...concerned for me?" The idea seems to perplex her.

"Well, how do I know if you can take care of yourself?" Aware of the gerefa hovering nearby, she feels oddly flustered. "What did you think you could achieve here?"

The horsemaster wipes her hands on her skirt. They are mud-stained, Æthel notes with renewed unease, the fingers strong. What was Ælfrún doing beside the grave? "I thought that I could help you as thanks for the help you have given me."

"A simple *thank you* would have been sufficient," Æthel mutters, but buried in her disquiet is a gleam of secret pleasure. No other woman of her acquaintance would have followed her here. Away from the shelter of court, her only companions are men. She looks at Ælfrún anew, seeing belatedly the muscles in her upper arms, her supple, straight back. She stands like a warrior, Æthel realizes. The dress cannot disguise it. All at once she remembers the stable and the arms that caught her, that momentary tightening, and feels a low warmth in her cheeks.

"You know this woman, my lady?" Eadgar asks, clearly confused.

"She is my horsemaster." Æthel turns before the gerefa can frame any more questions. "Perhaps Gweir is waiting to report. Come, Ælfrún."

"My lady," she murmurs, and a strange sort of shiver cascades through Æthel, something she has not felt in a long time. It is there too in Ælfrún's gaze, whenever it meets hers. That intensity. She is almost frightened of it.

"Can we speak alone?" Gweir says at once on seeing her. He has just stepped out of a house roofed with thatch in sore need of repair. The woman at the threshold meets Æthel's eyes; under the red marks of her grief is condemnation. Gweir blinks when he spots Ælfrún and raises a brow, but Æthel gestures for him to continue. "They blame it on Geraint's death," he says quietly. "Especially as the attack came only hours after word reached them."

She frowns at the now-closed door of the house. "What has Geraint to do with it?"

"The Dumnonian birthright," Gweir says. "You know it has power. You witnessed it the night he died."

Æthel is aware of Ælfrún listening closely. "And?"

"They believe they have lost its protection."

"Protection from what?"

"Whatever hunted them." Gweir hesitates. "Nothing alive, they say."

Once, perhaps, she might have laughed, called the Wealas superstitious pagans. But the story of Herla is in her mind... and she has been laughed at herself. So Æthel stands wondering at the words while a cloud swallows the sun. "Do you think Scirburne is likely to suffer another attack?"

"No."

She waits for more, but Gweir does not elaborate. She had thought Ine had sent the gesith with her because he could speak the Wealas tongue. Now Æthel is not so sure. He knows something about Geraint and the power the Dumnonian king used to fight Herla. Maybe he is simply unwilling to speak before Ælfrún. "We will discuss this later," she decides. "If you think the settlement safe, I'll respect your judgement."

"My lord." Although his accent has the lilt of a Briton, the man approaching them is in Saxon dress like the rest of the folk in Scirburne, and he speaks Englisc. "May I make a request?"

Gweir bows his head. "If she will allow it, you may make it of the queen."

The man's eyes widen. "I have family north in Sceaptun, lady queen. Please, they are in danger."

"That is significantly out of our way." Ine should hear of this. He claimed to believe her about the riders. Where others will laugh, Æthel is sure he will listen. She feels a flicker of bitterness. He will listen to *this*, at least. "What makes you think they're in danger?" she asks the villager.

He licks lips cracked from long days spent under sun and sky, ill at ease, and then says something unintelligible. Gweir hisses and Ælfrún lets out a breath; clearly Æthel is the only one who does not understand. "You speak the Britons' language?" she demands of Ælfrún. Gweir too, is staring at the horsemaster, suspicion pinching his face.

Ælfrún shrugs, as if unaware or uncaring of it. "My mother taught me. She was a Briton."

Æthel quashes a torrent of other questions. They would have to come later. "Gweir, what did he say?"

A breeze stirs the gesith's coppery hair, which brushes his shoulders. She can see the tension in them. "His family carries the old blood."

Old blood. "Do you mean the Dumnonian birthright?"

The Briton's mouth is like the round rim of a mead jar; even the merest mention of paganism attracts strict penalties from the Church. To hear her speak the words aloud—"You may talk without fear of punishment," Æthel assures him.

"Not the birthright, the heritage, and just traces of it," he whispers after a long moment, returning to Englisc. "Only the king can commune with the land. My sister and her husband do small things, like make a spark for kindling, or ease a child to sleep. My mother too."

"Communing with the land," Æthel says slowly. "Is that what Geraint did? The silver light I saw?"

The Briton's nod is bleak, and she cannot blame him for his censure. Her own brother-in-law is responsible for Geraint's death, after all. "So whoever killed the Britons in this village did so because they bore traces of the old blood."

"It does not live in me. That, surely, is why I stand here today."

Æthel can sense the shape of *something* beneath the inky water that is everything she does not know. Geraint had intended to take men to Glestingaburg, but she has not had time to tease the truth from Cadwy. *Ingild,* she curses silently, *if only you hadn't been so rash.* "This news should reach Wiltun without delay." She grips Gweir's forearm. "You know as much as I. We will split up. I will go onto Sceaptun to see if I can learn more."

Gweir is shaking his head before she finishes speaking. "I promised Ine king I would protect you."

"Have I ever needed it?" she says with some acid, letting go of him. "If anyone needs protecting, it's my husband." She lowers her voice, so the Briton cannot hear. "I have not forgotten what we saw in Gifle." Æthel knows it is in his mind too: the memory of Ine half-strangled in roots. Gweir's brow is deeply furrowed—that of a man torn. But it is the only argument she has. "There are Britons in Wiltun too," she reminds him and he deflates. "They may be in danger."

"I will go with her."

"You." Gweir turns a hard face to Ælfrún. "You are a stranger. How can I trust you to protect yourself, let alone the queen? Lady Æthelburg, you must take my men."

"I will take half," she says and holds up a hand to forestall his protest. "And I am sure Ælfrún can look after herself, or she would not have ridden here so boldly." Her tone is sharp. Ælfrún *will* give up her secrets, or Æthel will see her banished. Despite the fact they could be friends, despite how she feels…drawn to the other woman. Æthel swiftly buries that last thought.

"Thank you, my lady," the villager says, reminding her of his presence. "I swear I will repay this kindness."

Æthel nods at him, satisfied that he at least does not doubt her ability. The gerefa is happy to resupply them for their impromptu journey north, though Ælfrún in her skirts confounds him. She could almost pass as a maid were it not for the overproud tilt of her chin. The longer Æthel spends with her, the more convinced she becomes that the horsemaster is a noble in exile. Nothing about her hints at the rude birth she claims except her clothes— and clothes can be changed.

"I won't tell you to be careful," Gweir says as Æthel mounts her horse. Ælfrún is riding the haggard beast she saw in the stable, which must be sturdier than it looks. "But if a fraction of what these people say is true…"

"I am not defenceless." Even as she says it, Æthel wonders at the truth of it. She is used to fighting rebels, or Wealas—ordinary men. Whatever happened here is anything but. The thought prompts her to look at Ælfrún, only to find the woman already studying her. Æthel shivers again and heels her horse. They will head for the settlement the Romans called Lindinis and then pick up their long straight road to Sceaptun. And perhaps along the way she will root out the real reason Ælfrún came to Wessex.

13

INE

Wiltun, Wiltunscir
Kingdom of Wessex

When new wheat grows from the buried bread, they call it a miracle.

Ine stands and looks at it, stony-faced. It is only a handful of days after Lammas. "Why just two corners?" Nothhelm asks, humour thick in his voice. He flicks a head of wheat, which comes up to his waist. "Is God only half-pleased with us?"

"Do not blaspheme, Nothhelm king," Hædde says wearily, "especially in the presence of His work."

Ine can feel the bishop's eyes upon him, can hear his carefully controlled doubt. Ironically, holy men seem to be the most suspicious of anything miracle-shaped. Hædde does not believe this a divine act. But anything *not* divine is deemed its opposite: heathen, the old ways...magic. He swallows. "I did feel His presence in the barn that day."

"The realm is blessed," Hædde says, folding his hands piously and doing a good impression of sincere. "The wheat should be made into bread for communion."

"Arrange it, please," Ine says to the servant who brought news of the "miracle." His palms are sweating and he turns away.

"A quiet word, my lord, if you will."

Ine freezes. *You are king,* he reminds himself. *You've every right to refuse him.* "In the Witan chamber then," he mutters, although it is the last place he wants to go. His mind is least stable there—he has seen the spectre of Cædwalla more than once. Climbing the steps to the hall, he drags a hand across his face. *I am running out of time.*

"My king," Hædde begins when they are alone.

Ine finds himself checking the corners of the room, but none hoard any unusual shadows. He releases a breath. "What do you want to say to me, bishop?"

Hædde comes closer. "I did not wish to air my concerns publicly, to cause alarm. But the wheat is not God's work."

"What makes you so certain? Hlafmas is His festival."

"It is also Lughnasadh," the bishop says, and Ine blinks at hearing the pagan word from his lips. "We have followers of the old ways in Wiltun."

Ine lowers himself into his chair, as if the news has shaken him. "You think they are responsible for the barn?"

"I have little doubt. Our Lord is of course capable of miracles, but this is not one of them." His brows draw together. "The heathen ways have ever been adept at mimicking the true faith."

"You speak gravely, Hædde. Making some wheat sprout hardly seems a threat."

"Not yet, my lord, but it has betrayed their presence. I've no doubt we will see further heresy." When Ine says nothing, he adds, "Do you recall the scop who performed for us?"

Ine can feel the blood receding from his cheeks, impossible for Hædde to miss. "I remember." Both bishops witnessed him running from the hall that night.

"I believe I can trace the rot to that person. The story...that is a dangerous tale. Very few know of it."

Ine eyes him narrowly. "And you do?"

"It is my business to know," Hædde barks before realizing he has raised his voice. More softly he says, "It is my duty to ward against it and others of its kind. You understand duty, Ine king."

Yes, he understands duty. He understands he is expected to follow up on Geraint's death, to march into Dumnonia and take what he wants. He understands he is expected to give the realm an heir, to preserve the vaunted bloodline that stretches all the way back to Cynric. Duty makes slaves of them all. "What do you propose?" he asks in a voice that sounds sepulchral even to him.

"I will speak with Earconwald before he returns to Lundenwic. We will increase attendance at church and reconsecrate certain areas of the settlement. And I will have people watch for the scop. There may be others."

"Good," Ine says, rising, hoping his agreement will end the conversation.

"Oh, my lord."

About to cross back into the hall, Ine halts. "Yes?"

"If you witness anything suspicious, you will be sure to tell me." Hædde's eyes glint. "The earlier we catch this plague, the better our chances of stopping it spreading."

On another day, Ine might have smiled at such dramatic language, but he cannot summon more than a stiff nod.

Geraint has done something to him. Ine is increasingly sure of it. He sits in the king's chair and hears petition after petition, but his mind wanders far from the petty concerns of ceorl and ealdorman alike. He is thinking of the night Geraint died, remembering the agony and the domed chest of the giant. So like the scop's tale. And the voices of Æthelburg and Gweir. They had spoken while he lay in his shallow, confused sleep, though he cannot recall their words. Both have behaved strangely since.

"...Something must be done, lord."

The silence into which he is supposed to speak is loud enough to wrench him from the morass of his thoughts. Ine stares at the gangling man before him, stretched thin like a weed in shade. "I have heard enough for today."

Just as protests start to spill from the man's mouth, a voice says, "Allow me to take over, brother."

Ingild hovers at the arm of his chair. They have not spoken since the vote on Cadwy, but that is not unusual. Ingild has always been the same: furiously sulking for a day or two before turning up as if nothing has happened. Ine studies him. His brother's face is earnest and, truth be told, he really would rather avoid spending the next two hours in the sweltering mead hall listening to men rant over cattle. But he has not forgotten Ingild's behaviour at Gifle. "There is no need—"

"Lord, forgive me." Gweir marches into the hall. "I have news from Scirburne that cannot wait."

The gesith is alone. Ine looks over his shoulder, a spark that had leaped at the sight of Gweir fading. "Where is Æthelburg?"

"May I speak with you?"

Ingild raises an eyebrow at him and Ine has no choice but to nod shortly and watch his brother take the seat that should be Æthel's. "Not in here," he says to Gweir, determined to shun the Witan chamber. "It is far too warm. We will go to the river." He waves away the guards that start to follow and they sink back on their benches, unabashedly relieved.

Amidst calls for cold ale, Ine leads Gweir from the hall, taking the verdant path to the river. It chuckles today, carefree in a way he envies. Leaves float by, borne on the bubbling current, and for a few brief moments, Ine wishes he were one of them. If he closes his eyes, he can see where the river has flowed, the valleys that harbour it, the trees that weep over it, the stone that is its bed, wearing out a course on its way to the sea. If a person could become one with the water, where would they go? Upriver to the caverns that birthed them. Downriver to the languid lowlands, the pastures and hamlets, where they might be drawn into buckets and given back to the earth...

He is on his knees; the water is seducing him out of his skin, but its kiss is cold, and someone has his arm, pulling him away. "Be careful, lord," a voice says.

Gweir. He must have fallen. How clumsy to slip on sun-baked riverbank. The illness, not content with stealing his mind, wants his body too. "Thank you," Ine murmurs, grasping after the reason he came here. "Yes. You have news. Where is my wife?"

"Sceaptun," the gesith says. "Trying to unravel this mystery."

He keeps his back firmly to the river while Gweir fills him in. The news is as bizarre as the wheat—and more shocking. "No one knows from where these killers came?"

"The gerefa's account tallies with that of the surviving Britons. From nowhere, it seems." Gweir pauses. "Have you spoken with Geraint's son?"

Ine briefly closes his eyes. "In all honesty, Gweir, a part of me is ashamed to face him."

"He should know what you have done for him—securing his life in the Witan."

"Scanty remuneration for the death of his father."

"Which wasn't your doing." The gesith's sigh is heavy. "War is a bloody business, lord, and resentment runs deep. You have a chance to stem it."

The river leaps coolly over its stones. A breeze steals between the leaves. "That hut he's in must be sweltering," Ine murmurs. "Perhaps he might find relief here beside the water."

Wordless, Gweir nods and turns to leave. While he waits, Ine stares at the sun slanting through branches, listens to the birds hopping between them. But not too closely; he is convinced he can hear tiny claws on the bark, the swivel of a yellow eye. He shakes himself, half-hoping Cadwy will not come, but that is a cowardly hope unworthy of him. He owes Geraint's son an explanation.

Tramping on the earthen path. Gweir is accompanied by two guards, Cadwy walking between them. When he sees Ine, his face goes from blank to boiling in a matter of moments. "You did not say *he* would be here."

One of his guards makes to cuff him, but Ine barks, "Stop," and he checks the blow. "Leave us."

They exchange glances. "Is that wise, lord?"

"Gweir is here and he is only a boy."

Cadwy narrows his eyes in the murderous way of all young people when they are referred to as children. He rips his arm from the grip of the guards as soon as they step back. "What do you want?"

"I thought you might like some fresh air," Ine says, addressing him in his own language. "It is over-warm today. I am sorry we have not spoken sooner."

The boy's eyes widen. "Your Kernish is good. For a Saxon thug. You expect me to believe you give a shit about me?"

Ine ignores his language. "If I did not," he says evenly, "you would already be dead."

Cadwy stares at him, a shimmer in his eyes, and Ine immediately regrets the callous words. *He is a child who has lost everything,* he reminds himself. "Are you being treated fairly? If you can read, I'll have books brought—"

"Of course I can read. You think us savages?"

Ine winces. This is going about as well as he imagined.

"Cadwy," Gweir says, clearly feeling the need to intervene. "The very first thing the king did upon arriving home was to ensure your safety."

"I never sought your father's death." Ine touches his heart where remorse and anger mingle. How is he able to punish Ingild for a deed everyone sees as heroic? "Truly, Cadwy, I am sorry for it."

The boy blinks, a furious motion Ine suspects hides tears. Geraint's son has only a hint of his look. His hair is fairer, his eyes grey where Geraint's were the peeling bark of a hazel. "Your wife already apologized for you, Saxon. But an apology will not bring my father back."

"I know. If there is a way to make amends…"

"You can set me free," Cadwy snarls. "You say you regret it, but if that is true, you would let me return to my people. You…" he chokes. "You would give me my father's body so that I may see the rites spoken."

The guilt in Ine's throat has the iron tang of blood. Geraint's body was burned on the road. Sparing him the indignity of being dismembered was the only thing he could do for the man. Gweir is right. War is a bloody business. "I am sorry, Cadwy. More than I can say. I did all I could for your father. I have done all I can for you. I know that it is not enough."

The boy's lips are white. "If you won't free me, return me to my prison."

"There is something I must discuss with you. Britons are being killed in Wessex."

Cadwy lifts his gaze from the riverbank, eyes blazing. "I knew your kindness was pretend. Your people have killed mine for generations. Why torture me with it?"

"No." Ine takes a step towards him, and Cadwy steps back, hands rising protectively. "This is not Saxons killing Britons. I wouldn't allow that."

"I went to a village where every Briton who bore a trace of the old blood was killed," Gweir says soberly. "With a single strike to the heart."

Cadwy's demeanour changes completely, shock softening the stiff lines of anger in his face. "You *must* release me. If it is happening here, it will be even worse at home. I am Heir. I have to protect my people."

Ine's heart jumps. "*What* is happening here too?"

"The death of the old blood. My father..." His face crumples.

"Your father wanted to go to Glestingaburg," Ine finishes for him, "where he thought he could find answers." *It concerns the safety of both our peoples.* "Why there?"

Cadwy is silent, his gaze weighing Ine. Perhaps the scales balance because finally he says, "When the killings began, he thought *you* were responsible. But then our people started dying in settlements well beyond the border, deep in Kernow. And only those with the blood, who could work the small magics."

"Herla sleeps beneath Glestingaburg," Gweir says, and Ine looks at him sharply. "Is this her doing?"

Cadwy shakes his head. "The Wild Hunt only rides when the moon is old."

"The Wild Hunt?" Surely not Æthelburg's riders? "I thought they were a story told to frighten children."

"Not everything is a children's story, Saxon," Cadwy says caustically. "Your men owe my father their lives."

Ine rubs his forehead. If only Ingild had not gone behind his back, he might have answers for all these questions. "Who is Herla?"

"You could ask your wife," the boy says in the same cutting tone. "She seemed *very* interested in the leader of the Wild Hunt."

"Æthelburg?" A shard of fear buries itself in his chest. Something is out there, killing without mercy, and Æthel is right in its path. "Oh God," he says, lapsing unconsciously into Englisc, "I should never have let her go."

Is that *concern* appearing ever so fleetingly on Cadwy's brow? Æthelburg must have spent more time with him than Ine had realized. *Fine. Don't talk to me.* Her words echo in his head and he wants to pummel it for being so dense. He has fretted over the illness and how to hide it—he is so used to hiding—when he should have been speaking to Æthel. Perhaps if they had shared their knowledge, she wouldn't be walking into danger now.

Sun filters through rustling leaves, and it is hard to believe they are discussing murders and magic and stories coming true. With an effort, Ine pulls his attention back to Cadwy. "Even if I allowed you to return home, what could you do to stop this?"

"I am the Heir of Dumnonia." Cadwy swallows. "It is my duty to protect my people, as it was my father's."

"You do not look so certain."

The boy's nostrils flare. "When I stand on the soil of Dumnonia, the Land will recognize me. Father should not have died so far from home."

Unbidden into Ine's mind comes a memory: the sense of Geraint slipping away into the soil, and a power reaching out to enfold him. After that, only agony. He shivers. "I cannot be seen to free you, Cadwy. Your protection was won only narrowly. Most of the Witan want you dead."

"Then let me escape."

"I will not risk it." Ine thinks of the vote, of Ingild sitting smugly in the raised chair listening to petitions. If the boy only knew how tenuous his authority may be becoming... "Besides, if you claim to possess this old blood, you will be safer behind walls."

Cadwy clenches his fists. "I knew you wouldn't understand. You would prefer we all perish anyway, so why not let the killing continue?"

"Do not presume." Guilt has chained his temper throughout, but this is something he cannot let stand. "I have no intention of allowing violence to continue, whatever its nature. Not when its victims live in my lands."

The boy stares at him. Ine cannot read his expression now. "How do you intend to stop it?" Cadwy asks finally. "You may speak our language, but you are not one of us. Your people do not believe in the Otherworld. You consider Herla and her Wild Hunt a story. Your priests condemn magic as *evil*."

It is true. How can he make anyone but Gweir and Æthelburg aware of the threat when even describing it will label him a heretic and likely a madman too? The silver cross around his neck hangs heavier than usual. They need more information, to put a name to the enemy. "If anyone can find proof, it is Æthelburg." Ine does not like it, but he cannot deny the truth of it. *You are always happy to use her,* his own hollow conscience says.

When Cadwy's guards return, Ine has to stop himself from saying the men are there for his own protection as much as to deter escape. The boy's only parting gesture is a baleful glare and Ine sighs. "I am such a fool, Gweir. I should have been honest with Æthelburg. We have so little knowledge of the situation. Even the smallest details matter."

"I am sure Æthelburg queen can bring proof to show the Witan. And she is not alone. I left half my men behind." Gweir pauses. "The horsemaster is with her too."

About to head back to check on Ingild, Ine stops in his tracks. "What?"

"Ælfrún. We found her in Scirburne. Without a good enough explanation, I might add."

The fear in his chest turns to panic. "You think she intends Æthel harm?"

"No," Gweir says, and Ine holds his breath. "She claimed she wanted to help. That does not mean I trust her, however." He grimaces. "I am sorry, lord. Æthelburg queen ordered me to return to Wiltun. Convincing her to take half my men was challenge enough."

"That sounds like her," he mutters, rueful. "She has no concern for her own safety."

"She avoids unnecessary risk, lord. And she is not the target of these killings."

It is small comfort. Ine rubs his forehead again. The heat is seeding a headache behind his eyes. The heat or the worry or the stress of his talk with Cadwy. He considers telling Gweir of Hædde's belief that heathens are at work in Wiltun, but the words stick in his dusty throat. They have problems enough. "Time to make sure Ingild is not making himself at home in that seat," he mutters and leads the way back to the mead hall.

The night is barely cooler than the day. Ine tries to sleep, his head tumbling with thoughts. Æthel is interested in Herla and the Wild Hunt? But who is Herla? He had not known the leader of the Hunt was a woman. Christ, he had not known the Hunt was even *real*. In his sweaty, exhausted state, her faceless figure merges with that of the horsemaster. What are Ælfrún's intentions in joining Æthelburg? Ine knows as little of her as he does of Herla. Unease— and perhaps something darker—creeps through him. His wife had spent the whole of Lammas morning with Ælfrún, their heads close together as they spoke. Now to discover she has followed Æthel to Scirburne, abandoning her duties…Ine swears, unhappily aware of the empty space beside him.

Perhaps it is the heat, the mystery of Ælfrún and Herla, the killings, or the memory of another human fading away into the land, but when Ine falls into a fitful sleep, nightmare reaches out to catch him.

He is lost within the locks of the giant's hair. Without a comb— the comb that sits between the ears of the great boar, Twrch Trwyth—it is a tangled wilderness. He is running from something. The green is thickening. Roots reach for him like the pale, bloated fingers of the dead.

He cries out, and suddenly a light is there, a bobbing wisp; the only gentleness in that great green. It leads him to a glade. He stumbles onto moss, grateful until a sense of scrutiny laces his neck. Behind him, skulls are arranged in a gruesome circle, ringing the glade. He must have come through a gap, but it is closed now. And their eye sockets are filled with wheat.

A voice speaks. He ignores it, frantically pulling out sheaves, spilling them onto the moss. But no matter how much he reaps, there is always more, until he is hip-deep in the bounty—enough wheat to feed a shire, fifty shires, a giant's table. Dimly he is aware of words, but the panic drowns them, as surely as the wheat is drowning him.

Ine gasps himself awake. Silence, save for his own harsh breathing. No glade, or wheat, but he scrambles from his bed regardless and throws himself into the hall and out the doors, neither knowing nor caring if he is seen. The dream urges him on through hushed streets; the impenetrable hush of the hour before dawn. He has the sense that, even if he were to shout, no one would hear. When he reaches the grain barn, he yanks open the door, though it is always kept locked, and races inside, wild-eyed.

In the gloom, the bearded sheaves are drained of colour. Stems sprout from the corners cleared just hours before. And there are more of them, a profusion. With a cry, Ine tries to pull them up, but they are sunk fast in the earth. Seizing an abandoned scythe, he hacks at the shoots until it rains wheat. Tears and sweat streak his cheeks.

Skulls glare at him, or round pots of something repelling pests. He cannot tell what is real any more. The first cock crows outside and, tossing down the scythe, Ine lunges for the door and the dawn. Behind him comes the relentless rustle and sway of new wheat pushing up from the earth.

14

ꝪERLA

Sceaptun, Somersæte
Kingdom of Wessex

They follow the old road, built to aid the remorseless march of the legions. Weeds have defeated the Roman paving, but the sight brings Herla no satisfaction. A gulf separates her from the past, and it is not only time. She cannot remember the woman fighting those battles. She has ridden so far and so fast from herself that the way back is closed. Perhaps it is better off closed.

"Ælfrún."

The queen's blue eyes meet hers, and they look at each other for too long a moment. Herla could spend all day looking; it is Æthelburg who breaks the gaze. "We cannot speak publicly of the Dumnonian heritage," she says. "Word would no doubt get back to the bishops." Six men have accompanied them and Æthelburg raises her voice. "When we reach Sceaptun, find out where the Wealas live. Say the king is making a survey of his settlements."

As the afternoon deepens, clouds build in the north like the walls of a grim fortress. "Ælfrún," the queen says again. Sweat and road dust darken the blonde of her hair; she is a wonderful sight—real and vibrant, the opposite of Herla's bleak thoughts. "You know how to use a sword."

Herla raises an eyebrow at the not-question. She has seen Æthelburg fight, so there is little point in denying it, but blade-wielding hardly fits her disguise. "My mother taught me to defend myself," she says and knows, in her bones, that it is not a lie.

"Your mother taught you a lot of things, it seems," Æthelburg replies drily. A smudge has appeared in the distance, squatting across the wide road ahead: Sceaptun. "Few Saxon women become warriors," Æthelburg continues, "but the Britons do not appear to have so narrow an idea of our capabilities." Her tone turns wistful. "A long time ago, there was a tribe led by a warrior queen. The Iceni."

"Eceni," Herla corrects automatically. She has tensed without realizing.

"Yes." Æthelburg's horse frisks under her and she reaches out to soothe it. "Somehow it doesn't surprise me that you know. Our servant told me about them when I was a child. I decided right there and then to practise the blade, though I knew I could never be a real warrior queen like Boudica." Busy with her reins, she does not see Herla flinch. "My mother did not fight, of course, at least not with swords, but she was the one who gifted me my first set of armour."

"You *are* a warrior queen, my lady," Herla says before adding in a whisper, "as much as she was."

"That is not what they call me in court." The wistfulness has slipped from Æthelburg's face. "And I told you to use my name."

As they ride closer, the queen's horse is not the only one uneasy; the men find their own animals snorting in the gathering gloom. Even Herla's mount pricks up his ears. She squints ahead, but cannot see much yet. Scirburne offered few enough clues, save for the intriguing idea of the old blood: the very same power that fought Gwyn's and caused the dog to leap. At the thought of Dormach, Herla glances round. She does not want the hound near her, but it is worse when he is out of sight. *Who does he obey? Her . . . or his master still?*

Lights crackle to life in the settlement. A dark hill rises beyond, capped by a circle of trees. The road they follow runs right over it, intersecting with another near the top. A crossroads. Herla stares hard in its direction. There is something up there.

"I must find whoever's in charge," Æthelburg says as they reach the farms on the outskirts. A simple palisade wall is all the protection the village has, with a spiked wooden gate set into it. The man busy closing it gapes at them as they ride up, the whites of his eyes plain until Æthelburg reassures him. When he sees the ring on her finger, he falls over himself while ushering them through.

Herla's attention is only half on the scene. Her hunter's sense is tugging her towards the hill. With a lingering glance at Æthelburg, she slips away.

The early dusk carried on the clouds has all but finished shrouding the village. The road she follows runs into trees and crosses the track that leads to Old Sarum in the east. Herla dismounts, skirt snagging unfamiliarly on her saddle. A grassy barrow hides within the copse. Age clings to it like lichen on stone; it was raised centuries before her birth. She passes through pale mist, smelling of the still places under the earth. *Women sleeping in neat, straight rows.* Herla thrusts the image aside.

The peak of the barrow is split. She gazes on that dark fissure and her breath comes cold in her throat. Dirt rims the opening. Leaning down, she drags a finger through the soil. *Fresh.* Slowly, Herla turns to look at the settlement and, in the next instant, she starts to run.

The ancient dead have never concerned her. The forms that lie at rest beneath their blankets of grass and time are beyond her reach. But their echo is another matter. The land has a long memory. It remembers strife. Suffering leaves the ghost of itself behind like a standard fallen and trampled in battle. And there are those who can give it form. Give it purpose.

She knows now how the Britons were killed.

The dark ground flows beneath her as she throws herself towards the flickering, unknowing torchlight of Sceaptun. In her mind is Æthelburg. She imagines the queen, sword in hand, disbelieving as her blows fail to draw blood, but her own red life spills keenly from her. With a snarl, Herla urges her legs faster. Why did she leave the horse? A moment of madness when her thoughts are usually brutal and clear.

She reaches the village as the first screams ring out. The air is taut, on the trembling cusp of rain. She can sense them here, the echoes that broke free of their tomb—and they are not alone. They were woken by something stronger, something that walked the world but recently. Seized with yet another emotion she has not felt in so very long, Herla rounds a corner. She has no name for it, but it makes her heart run wild as a rabbit from a fox.

Æthelburg stands before two people, one prone in the lap of the other. A glance tells Herla the man is dying, slain on the doorstep of his home. The woman holding him has bloody hands, trying fruitlessly to staunch the wound. Æthelburg's lips are pulled back from her teeth. "Ælfrún, beware." Her eyes rake the dirt street and Herla realizes Æthelburg cannot see the shades circling her to reach the woman on the ground. Their forms are barely human, just scraps of spirit held together by will and power.

The drooping thatch of two houses has created a narrow, roofed passage, and a shadow stands in it. Æthelburg must see it at the same instant Herla does, for she gasps a breath and shouts. A moment later, the six men that accompanied them converge on the figure, forcing them deeper into the passage and obscuring Herla's view. She hears the scrape of blades drawn. The night wind carries laughter.

Æthelburg swings. Her sword passes harmlessly through the shades, but it makes them pause. One holds a bone knife, a bloodstained shard, which it slowly turns towards the queen. Æthelburg seems to sense the danger. Throwing herself aside, she does not see Herla raise a hand towards the shades.

They are like scree; it is impossible to gain a purchase on them. She cannot reap an echo. All she can do is dampen it. Herla closes her fist and the shades droop. The bone knife clatters to the ground; Æthelburg jumps as it rolls to a stop. The woman cradling the dying man moans when she sees it. Her eyes travel from the bloodied weapon to the shades, and her lips pull back in a grimace of rage or terror. To be able to see them…she must carry the old blood.

A scream from the passage, where the queen's men closed on

the shadowy figure. Nothing is there now, but another scream comes from somewhere beyond.

"Ælfrún, wait!"

Herla ignores her, heading for the anguished cries. Æthelburg will not be safe until she finds the person controlling the shades. Even without the bloodlust of the Hunt, Herla can feel it: the instant each man's soul slips from its bonds. It is over by the time she reaches the end of the passage. A dark shape marks where each man fell, one in front of the other. The figure she saw stands at the end of the macabre line. A drift of laughter. A glint of gold.

Shadow coils around the man's limbs like smoke, but she sees him clearly: the crown across his heavy brow, the eyeless pits below it. He wears Saxon trappings, fingers encrusted with rings, and multiple weapons at his waist. *"They send women now to challenge me?"* His voice is the hiss of grave-dirt falling onto the shroud below.

Herla frowns; there is no doubt that the man is dead. But not dead in the way of the shades. Inside a body that is not quite solid, she can sense his soul. Gwyn's sword can sense it, and the spirits that burden her sigh as she unsheathes the blade.

A wight.

Into his hand springs a sword as spectral as his form, and he closes in less than a breath, stabbing for her heart. Where common metal would pass through it, Gwyn's blade catches the sword, sends it spinning into the darkness. The wight's eyes burn. He reaches for her, fingers spread, his palm the same pale hue as a fish's belly. To be touched by a wight means death. Herla generously gives him a moment to savour his triumph before her own hand flashes out.

He chokes, thrashing in her grip as she lifts him from the ground. *"Who are you?"*

"I hoped to ask you the same." Herla brings their faces close, turns her will on him. "What is your name? Who summoned you?"

"Cædwalla," the wight says in his grave-voice. *"I was king of these lands."*

"And?"

He shudders, but his bloodless lips remain shut. Anger ignites in Herla: the Hunt-rage is never far away. No soul has ever refused her, has ever resisted. Her grip tightens. "Answer."

"You cannot command me."

It is true, she realizes with no small disquiet. The souls she reaps are free, unchained. This one comes to her bound and her anger falters. Only one person, surely, has the skill to rip souls out of the Otherworld, to return them to a semblance of life. The shepherd, who gave her his blade and cursed her to ride eternally.

"Is he here?" she hisses, paralysed by the thought, excited by it too. *Gwyn. I will find you.* "What does he want?"

Again the spirit of Cædwalla does not answer, and it only strengthens her belief that Annwn is involved. But why? Herla has not forgotten the war camp, the way Gwyn ap Nudd flinched upon seeing her, as if she were a pebble that could bring down a mountain.

"Ælfrún!" Running feet. She has only moments before Æthelburg arrives. Herla regards the wight through narrowed eyes. She cannot command him. She cannot let him go. Destroying him might alert Gwyn. All that is left then is delay.

A snort tells her the horse has found her. "Dormach," Herla snaps, as she throws the wight across the saddle and—to her surprise—the hound appears from the darkness. Time to see if he will obey her. "Find the shades," she orders, mounting her horse. "Carry them back to their grave." The dog's hackles lift. He growls, but turns with a whisk of his tail.

Just as Æthelburg bursts out of the passage between the houses, Herla urges the horse into a gallop and the first roll of thunder buries the sound of his hoofbeats.

The queen is kneeling by the corpses of her men when Herla returns. She is unsure how long the seal she placed on the barrow will hold, but it should buy them a little time. About to step into view, she hesitates, watching as Æthelburg moves between the bodies, closing their eyes, muttering a prayer. Her hands are steady, but her cheeks are wet. One of the men is young, fair hair tangled across his face. Æthelburg smooths it back.

Each small, tender movement, the furious tilt of her head bowed over the fallen… *Watching the light leave eyes open to the sky. Touching torch to pyre. The silence where voices once called and throats laughed and fingers left the imprint of their grip on her arms.* The memories rise from the graves the Hunt put them in, when Herla became it. She presses a palm to her head, her back bumping against the thatch of a house that slopes nearly to the ground. She does not want to see more. It hurts to remember; pain waits in the shadows to bring her to her knees. Just as Æthelburg kneels before the dead.

"Ælfrún."

Without knowing it, she has drifted out into the open, repelled and fascinated. Before, the bodies were little more than obstacles to avoid. But Æthelburg has made relics of them. Herla looks at the fair-haired young man. Peaceful. But it is not the kind of peace he would have wanted.

"What were you *doing*? Your dress…" There is dirt on it from the barrow, Herla realizes, and it is ripped in places.

"I fell chasing him," she says while light blossoms in her chest, lessening the pain of her memories. Æthelburg is safe. Nothing else matters.

"Who?"

"The leader."

Æthelburg's eyes lose their tenderness. "He ran? Why?"

"Because he failed." Herla nods towards where they left the couple. "The other Britons are unharmed."

"Back there…" The queen hugs herself, fingers digging into the cloth of her tunic, and Herla cannot stop herself moving closer, putting a hand over hers. Surprised, Æthelburg glances at it, but does not shake it off. "I know the woman could see whatever wielded that knife."

"You saw the weapon yourself?"

Æthelburg shakes her head. "I heard it fall, but could not see it until it lay on the ground." She glances at Herla's hand again. "Did *you* see whoever…whatever wielded it?"

Herla hesitates, sensing she will not buy a lie. "Yes. They looked like shades. Echoes of the once-alive."

"How?" The other woman regards her narrowly. "Is it because of your gift—as a horsemaster?"

"Perhaps." They are skirting the dangerous edge of truth, and once again Herla considers throwing off Ælfrún. Why does she need the horsemaster any more? Surely Æthelburg has seen enough strangeness not to be frightened. Her heart quickens. She could take her to Glestingaburg. The queen would be safe amongst her battle sisters. She said she hated court life. They could ride every day like she had wanted to—

Herla freezes at the word *ride*. Æthelburg knows the savage story of the Hunt. She knows to fear it. Herla glances at the bodies of the men, respectfully arranged despite being dead. What would she think of Herla, who left nothing in her wake but corpses sprawled where they had fallen? It is *Ælfrún* she trusts. Her hand drops from the queen's. "I heard their leader's name. Cædwalla."

Æthelburg's face turns ashen. "The villagers said he was crowned," she whispers, "like a king. But it isn't possible—Cædwalla is dead." Her eyes are almost pleading. "Can the dead truly return?"

"Why are you asking me?" Herla's agitation is in her voice. Too defensive. A moment later, the seams of the sky finally split. As the first drops strike the earth, the queen lifts the arms of the nearest corpse.

"Help me move them under shelter," she says, nodding at an open-sided shed a short distance away. Herla dutifully picks up the man's legs and together they carry all six out of the rain. "Not a mark on any of them," Æthelburg notes uneasily. "How were they killed?"

"If this Cædwalla has returned, he has returned as a wight. Their touch is supposed to be deadly."

"Wights and shades, the dead walking—these are stories we told to frighten each other at All Hallows." The queen gives a bleak shake of her head. "I never imagined I could be here, standing over dead men without a wound on their bodies."

Herla is sure it is only shock that stops Æthelburg wondering why Ælfrún knows so much. She swiftly turns her back to preserve the illusion of taking flint to the nearest torch, which crackles into life at her willing. "See here." She crouches over one of the bodies, so that the light falls on the man's exposed neck. Five roughly circular marks mar the skin there. "Proof if you wished it. A wight's touch does leave a trace."

"I did not wish it," Æthelburg says faintly. She swallows at the sight and her face hardens. "But proof, as you say, that I am not losing my mind. When I tell them what happened here." She pauses. "Even if you speak for me, as a woman and an outsider, your words will carry little weight. The men of the Witan will opine that Lady Æthelburg, without children to occupy her, has become hysterical."

"Your husband will believe you, and he is king."

"My husband gives away too much of his power." Herla sees anger in the set of her jaw. "Ine has always placed more weight on the opinions of others. Even others who do not have his best interests at heart."

"He loves you." Herla had not meant to say it. The words taste bitter.

Æthelburg stiffens. When she speaks, she stares hard at one of the wooden posts supporting the roof. "I am not so sure of that."

Herla has seen the king and queen together only a handful of times, but despite the tension brewing between them, it is obvious to her that Ine would do anything for Æthelburg. And why would he not? She comes closer, so that a mere step separates them. "Anyone would be proud to call you wife."

Æthelburg stops gazing at the post. When she lifts her eyes, the torchlight picks up a flush in her cheeks. The same heat is flowing through Herla's body, igniting parts of she she had forgotten. And that urge is with her again, the urge to take what she wants. She trembles with it. Her hand starts to reach out—and

Æthelburg steps back. "I...we must check on the Britons." Her voice is husky. "I fear the man has passed already."

They are drenched by the time they reach the house. Drenched and—in Herla's case—disappointed. She watches the queen the whole way. Æthelburg does not run, as many would to escape a deluge, but turns her face up to the sky, as if the water is a baptism to cleanse the truth of what they have seen here. After a while, she begins to shiver. The rain drips off the ends of her short hair, her chin, beads on her lips...

Herla unpins her cloak. "There is no need," the other woman protests when she goes to drape it over her shoulders. "You will be cold."

"I do not feel the cold," Herla says without thinking. "Besides, you are the one shivering."

After a few weak objections, Æthelburg relents. Their hands brush as she tugs the cloak around herself. Before Herla can move away, the queen catches her arm. "Thank you, Ælfrún. For coming with me." A flare of that heat and a quickening of pulse. Herla swallows hard.

The man's body has been taken inside the house. His wife sits hunched on a chest, a sickly cast to her face. At her side is another man, similarly featured. A brother, perhaps. The bone knife is there too, lying rag-wrapped on the floor. When Æthelburg reaches for it, Herla catches her arm. "Do not touch."

Æthelburg blinks. "Why?"

"It is a wight's weapon." The voice comes from the back of the room: an old woman lying in a pile of threadbare blankets. The rain is loud on the ragged thatch; one corner leaks, making mud of the dirt floor. "Not for living hands and not easily destroyed."

"Mother," the man says warningly, but his eyes are tired. "Guard your words."

"Please do not be concerned." Æthelburg bows her head. "I am deeply sorry for your loss. That I could not protect you all."

"Of course you couldn't, child," the old woman snaps and the other Britons look horrified. "Only those with the blood can see the hand of the Otherworld."

"The Otherworld," Æthelburg repeats, frowning. "Is that why the dead walk?"

Laughter fills the room. "Old Gwyn claims his cauldron can heal death," the woman cackles. "But those 'healed' by it become slaves. No power on this earth can restore a life lost."

Herla sucks in a breath, and the old woman's face turns towards her, digging her out of the shadow cast by one crude lamp. She is almost completely blind. "Why come you then beneath this roof, Lord of Winds? We will have none of you."

Into the silence that follows, the man murmurs, "I am sorry. My mother is unwell and speaks out of turn."

"It is of no consequence." How like the King of Annwn has Herla become, for the woman to name her so? Threaded through her rage at the mention of him is dread, and the others—including Æthelburg—are looking at her with furrowed brows. "I will find the person in charge here," she says, newly discomfited by their stares, "and tell them the danger has passed."

"Passed?" the old woman echoes from her nest. She laughs again, a long and rattling sound full of cold humour. "The danger has not passed. It is only beginning."

15

ÆTHELBURG

Wiltun, Wiltunscir
Kingdom of Wessex

The closer she rides to Wiltun, the sweatier Æthel's palms become until she has trouble gripping the reins. That stormy night left no room for doubt, but the searing sun of several days' riding is burning a hole through her conviction. What did she really see in Sceaptun, after all? *Something killed that man,* she reminds herself, firmly rekindling the image of the Briton lying bloody in his wife's lap. *And I saw the weapon that did it.* Ælfrún had taken charge of the bone knife. Æthel notes the shape of it wrapped in rag, sharing space with the blade on her belt. Proof, if the Witan refused to accept her story.

But perhaps I should not show the Witan. Not yet. The thought is more than appealing. She could tell Ine first, leave it up to him to decide how much to share with the others. *He will share everything,* she thinks bitterly. *And it's me they will label as mad.* Maybe Ælfrún will speak for her. She raises her gaze… only to find the woman already watching her. They both look away and Æthel wants to laugh. She does not know why. The horsemaster is altogether strange, no doubt has a hoard of secrets, and is hardly a conversationalist. Why then does Æthel feel so comfortable with her? Is she starved of female company? *Or is it female company that likes the things I like?* A woman unafraid to ride at her side, who does not think her eccentric.

"Will you spar with me, Ælfrún?" she asks abruptly.

Ælfrún raises an eyebrow. "Why do you think I can spar?"

"You said your mother taught you the sword. And the way you move...it is obvious that you can fight." When the other woman does not immediately reply, Æthel adds, "I can see the strength in your arms," and then realizes, to her horror, that she is blushing.

Ælfrún seems genuinely robbed of words, and Æthel seizes the opportunity to hide her face in her ale skin. Just as the silence starts to stretch, the woman says, "I will spar with you, Æthelburg."

"You used my name." Æthel feels absurdly pleased about it. She returns the skin to her saddlebag and, when she glances back up at the road, the golden-tipped roof of the hall at Wiltun has appeared in the distance. Her smile fades. The building holds almost as much dread for her as the events in Sceaptun. She would rather face an invisible foe than the men with their narrow condescension, their words calculated to excoriate without open rudeness. They have become very good at it and the thought sets her fear afire. Æthel clenches her fists. The longer Wessex goes without heir or peace-weavers, the more the men despise her.

"My lady? Æthelburg?" Ælfrún is staring at her angry fists, and Æthel uncurls them slowly. "A favour for your thoughts?"

"I am unsure what to say to my husband's council," she offers as explanation. "They already think me deluded and this will only deepen their poor opinion. I know what I said the other night, but...will you accompany me when I deliver my report?"

Ælfrún shakes her head. "It is not my place."

"What if I ordered you to?"

The other woman half smiles. "Then I must obey."

"I would rather you came willingly," Æthel murmurs, aware that the smile is warming the pit of her stomach. "Of your own free will. I trust you."

Ælfrún looks at her, and the air between them grows taut as the strings of a lyre wound too tight. Inside the other woman, Æthel senses a coiled energy and remembers the way Ælfrún touched her that night in Sceaptun, her fingertips afire. She swallows, aware she has leant over in the saddle, moth to a flame.

"You should not." Ælfrún's voice shatters the moment.

"Why?" Æthel studies the woman's face, but the intermittent sun dapples it, masking whatever is there. "You have proven yourself an ally. I suspect you might have saved my life." She hesitates. "The Briton said the shades that killed her husband just stopped after you arrived. They did not even pursue when she and her brother carried him inside."

"There are those who take trust and slaughter it," Ælfrún says—so harshly that Æthel flinches. "I do not want to see that happen to you."

She is still pondering those words when, an hour later, they ride through the gates of Wiltun. A few people hail her, but not as many as used to. The court's poison has inevitably trickled down to the streets. It would not surprise her to learn of a whispered war waged against her in secret. Æthel straightens her shoulders, lifting the queenship before her like a shield, but no one stands beside her to form the wall. No one save perhaps a stranger come so suddenly into her life.

The first sign of something amiss arrives in the form of a street strewn with pale stems like the floor of a stable. "What..." Æthel urges her horse forward and the sounds of people working grow louder: shouts, bangs, the occasional laugh. When she sees the grain store, her mouth falls open. The double doors are thrown wide and newly harvested wheat lies in bushels all around the building. "What on earth is going on here?"

"It's a miracle, my lady," a man babbles, his tunic freckled with dust. "The wheat—we're running out of places to put it."

"We *thought* it was a miracle," an older man adds darkly. "But it won't stop growing."

Another time, endless wheat might have alarmed Æthel, but now it seems almost trivial. When they dismount at the stables, Ælfrún holds out her hand for the reins. "My queen."

Æthel cannot bring herself to protest about the title. She is a butter churn of nerves at the prospect of explaining Sceaptun, and she hates it—the knowledge that every word she says will be weighed against her gender. It is only while staring at Ælfrún's cool expression that she wonders when it began, the court's ill feeling towards her. She had once been respected. Not understood, perhaps, but respected. She cannot put a finger on when that changed.

"Æthelburg," Ælfrún says, an odd note in her voice. "If you need help, I will offer it. But it will be safer to forget what you saw in the village."

"Forget?" Æthel stares at her, dumbfounded. "How can I forget? People *died*."

"People die every day," the other woman says, apparently unmoved by her own cold words. "This is something that does not concern you." She touches Æthel's elbow. "It is dangerous."

Æthel pulls away. "I rule this kingdom jointly." She is aware of the busy streets behind them, the comings and goings of folk to which it is haven, home. "It is my only concern."

Ælfrún's eyes burn. "There are perils you cannot see. That I may not be able to protect you from."

"When did it become your business to protect me?" Æthel snaps. She is sick of people claiming she needs protecting, cosseting. She had thought Ælfrún was different. "I believed *you*, at least, did not doubt me."

"I do not," the other woman murmurs. "And yet. There are things you do not understand."

Æthel turns away. "I understand more than you think. Give me the bone knife. I will need to show my husband." Although part of her deems it petty to storm off, she wants some distance between them before she says something she might regret. After Ælfrún hands over the weapon—with a warning to keep it wrapped— Æthel takes the steps to the hall two at a time.

News of her return must have reached them, but the only person waiting to greet her is Nothhelm. Æthel glowers and he holds up his hands in mock-fright. "What have I done?"

"Where is my husband?" Unsummoned, worry twists through her. Ine is almost always the first person she sees. *Not* seeing him here, smiling gently, or descending the steps to welcome her home is...disturbing. She searches the length of the hall.

"In his bedchamber, I believe." The King of Sussex grins at her. "You cannot wait even to wash the road dust from your face?"

"Shut up." She pushes past him. Their private quarters adjoin the Witan chamber and she finds Ine alone there, in the dim. He sits on a carved clothes chest, shoulders pulled up to his ears, as if dreading a scolding. He even jumps when she enters. Shadows ring his eyes. "You look awful," she blurts.

A veil seems to lift from his face. "Æthelburg."

"You weren't there to greet me," she hears herself say and winces; the words sound like a pout.

"I...no. I'm sorry."

"Don't be." She tries for airiness. "I thought you'd want to hear my news at once."

Ine straightens from his slump. "I do." A little more clarity enters his gaze, like sun struggling through cloud. "Gweir said you went on to Sceaptun? That was dangerous, Æthel."

She shrugs, as if it's nothing—when she knows she came within a whisker of her end that night. "It has never bothered you. I can cope."

"It has always bothered me," Ine says quietly.

They stare at each other. Pulled up short, Æthel fights to regain her wind. "Fortunate for the Britons there that I did. One lost his life, but the rest of his family was saved."

"What happened?"

It is practice for what she might have to tell the Witan. Æthel gathers her thoughts, attempting to arrange everything she saw into a report that won't see her laughed out of the council chamber. She has barely begun when Ine says flatly, "The horsemaster was with you."

Gweir must have told him. "I did not order her along." Feeling defensive, she wraps her arms around herself and props her hip on the desk Ine likes to read at. "She was useful. Turns out her mother was a Briton and she can wield a blade."

"So, she has been lying."

What is wrong with him? "Wouldn't you?" Æthel says before hearing the heat in her voice. She drops her arms. "I mean, if you did not know how the natives were thought of in the place you sought shelter."

"You seem to know her well," Ine comments, still in that flat voice. If Æthel did not know better, she would call it jealousy. That is ludicrous. He has never been a jealous man.

She grasps for the trailing threads of her narrative. "Gweir was with me in Scirburne. He heard the Britons' stories and can back me up. It was why you sent him, wasn't it?"

"Yes," Ine says, and he still seems a little put out. "I sense he knows a good deal more about the Dumnonian heritage than he admits. Tell me about Sceaptun."

Cædwalla. The dead walking. In the lazy Wiltun afternoon, it sounds like the crazed dream of the ailing. Æthel steels herself—and there is a knock on the door. They look at each other. "Come," Ine calls.

"I must speak with you, lord," Hædde says, breezing in. Æthel scowls, but it is nothing to Ine's reaction. He recoils, as if the bishop is a striking snake. She hopes it is only obvious to her, but judging from Hædde's furrowed brow, there is little doubt he noticed too. "My king?"

Having shot to his feet, Ine links his hands behind him so that only Æthel can see their tremble. *What is going on?* Before he can utter a word, she says, "I was speaking privately to my husband. Why the urgency, bishop?"

"Lady, my apologies." Hædde looks less than apologetic. There is something…excited about him. Focused. As if he is preparing to give a sermon before the Pope himself. "The situation in the grain store is growing serious."

"The miracle?"

"I am afeared it is no miracle." That strange focus in him sharpens. "It is the work of *heathens*."

"Heathens?" she repeats with a chuckle. Ine does not laugh. "You are being rather dramatic, bishop."

"I fail to see the humour, lady." Hædde's tone has cooled. "If they are not rooted out now, the rot will set in. My king, you have worked hard to bring light to your realm and the Church is thankful. You have resources we do not, however, and I beseech you to use them."

"Is the growing of wheat so terrible?" Ine asks, finding his voice at last. "It really does seem an innocent thing."

"It is heresy."

"Ah." Looking sick, Ine stares at the floor. "Just wanted to make sure."

"True, this *magic* is small," Hædde admits, grimacing around the word as if it is an unripe fruit. When he whirls to pace the room, Æthel glares at him. Who does he think he is, treating their bedchamber like his own? Ine has allowed the bishops too much freedom. "Innocent-seeming, as you say. But it never remains so. Have you given any thought to our conversation the other day? To the scop I mentioned?"

Ine picks his gaze weakly off the floor. It makes Æthel want to shake some life into him. "They cannot be found, Hædde. And if they are some sort of…magician, they won't be."

The bishop's eyes blaze at the word. It is unnerving; Æthel has never seen him so animated. "All the good we have achieved, my king. I will not tolerate it being undone."

"I understand. But we may have larger concerns. I will share them with you once Æthelburg has given her report on events in Sceaptun."

From the stiffening of his back, Æthel can tell Hædde is not at all happy. But it is a neat diversion and one he cannot ignore. "Your will, my king."

Once he is gone, Ine rubs his forehead. "I'm sorry. You were saying?"

"What was that about?" she demands, moving closer. "You near leaped out of your skin to see him."

"I'm fine."

"Don't lie to me." Once, they had shared everything. "You have been behaving oddly since Gifle." Memory assails her, making her throat ache. She and Ine holding hands, walking link-armed into the night to watch the stars bloom. Knees touching beneath the table on which the gameboard rested, as she talked him through her most recent victory. How, one Yuletide, he lifted the cup to her lips to drink while trying not to laugh at something she had said. She had not kept her own laughter in; it had leaked out with the wine until both their chins were stained and a younger Hædde glowered.

The distance between them has deepened while her back was turned. Perhaps she has been away from home too much, Æthel thinks. It is the restlessness in her, a savagery born of anger that drives her again and again to the battlefield, to search for an answer among the thrusts and cuts, the desperate struggle for survival. She wished she knew the question.

"Pull yourself together," she says roughly, hearing fear in her voice, unsure to which of them she speaks. Ine drags his gaze back to her face. His own is terribly vulnerable, like a child lost in woodland as deep and dark as the stories warn. "I need you to listen … and not take fright."

He nods and this time looks desperately into her eyes as if she might be the last handhold on a crumbling cliff. Uncomfortably, Æthel unwraps the bone knife, careful not to touch it. Although washed of its gruesome stain, it still radiates violence from its corpse-pale handle to merciless tip. Ine grimaces. "What is *that*?"

"The weapon used to murder Britons who bore traces of Dumnonian magic." It feels strange to speak it aloud, especially in Hædde's wake. "I couldn't see the beings that wielded it, but the Britons described them as shades, drawn out of the barrows of old. You shouldn't touch it."

She waits for Ine to express disbelief at her claim, but his lips are pressed so tightly that they whiten. "However, these creatures were not responsible for the men I lost that night." Her voice drops to a whisper. "All six were killed, Ine. Slain by a wight, a dead soul called back into the world." *Now or never.* "Ælfrún overheard his name—Cædwalla. Of Wessex."

For a handful of heartbeats, Ine only stares at her. Then he staggers up and rushes over to grasp her forearms. Æthel flinches. His grip is vice-like. "*What* did you say?"

"You are hurting me," she informs him, and, after a startled glance at his own hands, he lets go. "You know I would not lie."

"But you didn't hear this yourself. Ælfrún told you."

"And I do not believe she would lie either." Æthel feels a frown beginning to furrow her brow. She had expected him to exclaim over the impossibility. That Cædwalla is gone, that the dead cannot rise from their graves to commit murder. Instead his eyes are feverish and, to her horror, he starts to laugh, a stark, haunting sound. "Ine," she says sharply, frightened. "Stop it."

His laughter halts as abruptly as it began. That unnerves her too. "What is wrong with you?"

"If he killed six men, how did *she* survive?"

Æthel blinks at him. "I...I don't know. She didn't say she confronted him, only that she heard his name."

Pacing, Ine mutters something that sounds like, *It is not just me,* but she cannot be sure. There is a suggestion of the caged animal in his movements. "An old woman lived with the Britons," Æthel adds, remembering the strange meeting in that house. "She said the knife could not be easily destroyed. And she spoke of the Otherworld, of someone called Gwyn."

Ine stops. "Gwyn? Gwyn ap Nudd?"

Æthel feels her frown deepen. "Have you heard the name before?"

"I..." He lets out a shaky breath. "It was just a story that scop told. The one Hædde is searching for."

Marvelling that he answered one of her questions, Æthel catches hold of his arm before he can resume pacing. "What story."

"It doesn't matter." But he does not pull away. "This—*wight*. If he was called back from the dead, who by?"

"I don't know. Someone who wants to destroy all traces of Dumnonian magic?"

"And Hædde believes there is a dangerous heathen amongst us," Ine says faintly. "What is going on, Æthel?" Without giving her time to answer—she does not have one to hand, in any case—he adds, "I wish we had never gone west. This all began with Geraint."

"That was my fault, remember. He only seized the chance I gave him."

"No." Ine reaches out to touch her face, and shock roots her; she stills. "We have Cadwy because of you. We can ask these questions because you risked yourself to uncover them." His fingertips trail across her cheek as he starts to drop his hand, disgust creeping into his voice. "And what do I do but sit here jumping at shadows?"

Her own hand flashes up to hold his. She did not ask it to. Ine watches her through wide dark eyes. They are so close that they are almost sharing breaths, and the hunger in her—Æthel is appalled by its strength and welcomes it too. She does not want to think because all her doubt is still in here with her, coiled and ready to condemn. So instead of thinking, of pausing, she leans in and kisses his cheek. Several days' growth of beard makes it slightly rough. Odd; he never wears one in summer. A small indrawn breath as she moves to trail her lips across his. It is not enough. She wants to be held, to feel warm skin sing against her own, because inside her is an awful cold, a fear that she does not deserve to be warm. Before she can deepen the kiss, however, his shoulders tighten under her hands—an all-too-familiar tightening—and Æthel pulls back.

"What is it?" Her question is a ragged whisper. "You touch me and then you flinch away. What do you want from me?"

He looks helpless. "I...I don't know how to explain it. Not just to you. To myself. To anyone."

Putting new distance between them, she backs into a table, feeling the hard, unyielding wood against her calves. "*Try*, Ine. I am your wife. Why won't you trust me?"

Ine's throat bobs as he swallows, pain in his face. It makes her angry. *Why do I do it? Time after time. Why do I force him to reject me?* He has made his feelings clear—she even told him so. And yet here they are once again, unable to look at each other, unable to be honest. All of it rears up inside her: the shame of being spurned, the doubt that she can be loved at all. She is choking on it. Before he can answer, she says, "I don't have to be."

"Don't have to be what?"

"Your wife. I don't have to be your wife." She dashes tears before they can fall. "All of them want you to put me aside. I hear them. Why don't you? Why are you making us struggle on like this?"

His fists clench and unclench at his sides. "Your life with me is a struggle? I had not realized how… You deserve better, Æthelburg." Ine closes his eyes; it is his response to everything, Æthel thinks. Not to see it. "If you want to separate, I won't stop you."

Heart thundering in her chest, Æthel stares at him aghast, feeling she might be sick. She had not expected him to agree like that, so readily, as if he could not wait to be rid of her. She opens her mouth, but nothing emerges. He has entirely stripped her of words. So it is in silence that she stumbles out, all thought of Britons and wights and heathens gone. Her heart is in pieces, each shard sharper than the bone knife she has left lying in their chamber behind her.

16

INE

Wiltun, Wiltunscir
Kingdom of Wessex

He should have done this long ago. His sister, Cwenburh, had told him herself, before she left to accompany Cuthburh to Northumbria. *She knows, doesn't she? Æthelburg. And she is content?* He had thought her content. Æthel never pushed, at least not in the beginning. Her military duties had always been more important. Or so he assumed. Now, heartsick with the truth of it, Ine realizes it was convenient to assume. He could go on thinking that he had found someone who accepted him. Even though they never talked about it. Even though Æthel never really *understood*. He had not imagined it could lead to this. To the end of their marriage. To the fact that she would be punished, or punish herself for something that had nothing to do with her.

If I tell her… But isn't it too late for that? What would knowing change? Perhaps she would understand. Perhaps she wouldn't. The damage has been done. Ine sinks onto the bed, face in his hands. His cheeks are wet. Is the court's cruelty his own fault? Or does it come from what people expect, what the *world* expects, of a man, of a king? And of a woman too.

Between his fingers, a gleam. Tears fracture it into a dozen gleams and he brushes them away. The weapon Æthel brought lies like a dreadful thorn on the table. Forgetting her warning, Ine leans forward and picks it up.

Noise assaults him. Not just noise: voices. They gasp, they cry, they scream; the sounds people make as they die. He knows they are dead, just as he knows this weapon killed them. The voices are telling him, so brim-full of fear that he wants to run lest he fills with it too. Bodiless, they stretch out their hands: golden roots that tangle with the larger root inside him, and Ine recalls the agony he has tried to forget. Buried in earth, in the giant's uncombed hair. The memory assaults him like the voices, but still he cannot stop himself from reaching back to them, these lost people; the golden light grows so strong it could be the sun blazing into a thousand mornings at once.

When his screams summon guards, they exclaim over the powder, bone-pale, that lies in a ring all around him. Barely able to string two words together, Ine staggers up, unsure if he lost consciousness or not, waving away the men, uncaring that they will talk. Beneath his skin, something is burning, burrowing—the sun or all the small lives that live in the earth. Worrying his own flesh, leaving it sore and red, he makes his stricken way outside. The sky is pink, swift-fading to indigo. He could have sworn it was afternoon.

Ine finds himself on the path to the river. Shouts from the mead hall echo down to him as he goes, grasping onto trees to keep himself upright. Like a herd beast driven to pasture, he does not know what urges him onwards, cannot see the drover behind him. He runs because the *something* inside him tells him to run. And he runs because maybe, just maybe, he can escape it.

The scop stands by the water's edge, as if there at some prior agreement. Ine drops to his knees before them. The bottom of the robe they wear is dew-damp, a hint of bare brown feet beneath. Without realizing it, he has gasped out, "Help me." His fingers curl in the grass, new stems pushing up around him.

"It is your ancestor's fault, son of the Gewisse, for meddling in a land that did not concern you." The voice is chiming, resonant with tones. "Well, it concerns you now."

Elbow-deep in grass, Ine looks up. The scop's eyes are the same terrible blue he remembers, old as creation. No one has used the tribal name *Gewisse* in years. "Who are you?"

"I go by Emrys," that person says. "These days."

"Are you a man or a woman?"

"I am me. Ask a less ridiculous question."

He licks his lips, tastes iron. "Am I mad?"

Finally, Emrys smiles, a faint cool curve. "No. You might wish you were, though, before long, if you truly seek my help."

"She said it was Cædwalla, the one behind the killings." Ine is babbling the thoughts as they come into his head. "And I've felt him watching me. But Æthel is not mad. She wouldn't jest about the dead walking." A part of him looks on in horror as it all spills out. "And the bread I buried will not stop growing and neither will the dreams I keep dreaming even when I'm awake. It is Geraint's fault. *He* did this."

"Are you done?" Emrys says when he finally falls silent. "Firstly, Geraint did nothing except die. Which was hardly his fault when your brother wielded the knife." Ine blinks, but it's not as if Ingild has kept quiet. He is proud to have slain the King of Dumnonia. "Secondly, I am quite sure Geraint was as shocked in his last moments as you were when Constantine's mantle passed to a Saxon instead of his son."

He is still kneeling like a supplicant in the grass. Slowly, Ine rises. "What do you mean?"

Emrys shakes their head. "You are not ignorant of the Dumnonian birthright, except for your part in it." They seem to find it *amusing*. Beyond their name and their talent for storytelling, Ine knows nothing of Emrys, this person who speaks so casually to kings.

"I do not have to listen to you," he says. "In fact, I could have you punished for your conduct."

"Still, you came to me, fell on your knees before me." A breeze stirs their robe; the body beneath it looks slender, easily breakable, and yet Ine senses a will inside it, the merciless and deadly patience of a spider at the heart of a web that encompasses the world. He has taken a step back before he knows it.

Emrys nods. "Quite. You have enemies enough without making

one of me, Ine king. I will answer your questions because ignorance is dangerous, especially for you."

Owls wake with the twilight. Ine jumps at a screech and a rush of wings. It has destroyed his nerves, whatever this is, whatever is happening to him. "If I am not going mad, tell me why I'm dreaming." And in a softer voice that tastes of fear: "Who is the giant?"

"It is the Land," Emrys says simply, "and everything in it. Forest, stone and stream. It is the people who farm it, give and take from it. We come from the Land and to the Land we return. The Dumnonian birthright is the link between the two."

The Land. "We are not in Dumnonia."

"Human borders shift. Nevertheless, Dumnonia is in *you*. Although Cador's blood has taken a long time to show itself."

He frowns. "Cador?"

"Father of Constantine. And father of the woman your forebear, Cynric, brought to Wessex many years ago, as his bride."

"An old name," Ine mutters before it sinks in. "Wait. Cynric's wife was a Briton? I find that hard to believe. It's not written in our histories."

"And why would a woman's deeds be remembered when there are men's deeds to laud?" Emrys says sourly. "She understood what she was doing. I doubt Cynric did."

"You speak as if you knew her." When Emrys does not reply, he adds, "What *was* she doing?"

"Uniting two warring peoples, of course, although she would not see peace in her lifetime. Her own son brought her pain on that account." Their eyes glitter. "But now here you are, the result of the promise she made to her brother. To the Land and all the peoples that call it home."

It is too much to take in. Ine wants to sink back to the riverbank, to lean his forehead against the nearest tree and think. Except that touching the earth terrifies him. "Why?" His voice rasps. "Why me and not those who came before?"

"Cynric's bloodline has forced the heritage to lie dormant." For the first time, Emrys's mouth creases in something like sympathy.

"You are a child of both. It is why the power in you is so volatile."

"Power?" Ine does not know whether to laugh or cry. "Is that what this is? What caused the wheat to grow and that bone knife to shatter?" And then, recalling what happened when he stood in this spot before, "And the river I would likely have drowned in if not for Gweir?"

Emrys nods soberly. "I admit I wasn't sure it was possible until the night I told stories in your hall."

Ine thinks of the demon-eyed boar, the towering citadel. "How did you do that? Make it real?"

"I am a very good storyteller."

It is all they will say and he is not surprised they keep their secrets close. He feels as if his are scattered across the sun-baked earth, that they tumbled from his pockets when he fell at Emrys's feet. The scop could crush them with a step. "You only gave me your name," Ine mutters, clawing for purchase on the here and now. "How can I trust you? Bishop Hædde is searching for you, after all."

Hands behind their back, Emrys takes a slow walk around him. "And will you give me to him?"

"I…" Ine twists to keep the scop in sight. "No. I don't know."

"How that fills me with confidence," Emrys murmurs.

"Hædde is a good man. A good adviser. But once he decides to do something, he's like a dog with a bone full of marrow. He isn't going to leave it."

"Does his goodness stretch to punishing innocent storytellers as heretics?"

Ine shifts uncomfortably. "I wouldn't let that happen."

"Even though it would lift his suspicion? You have felt his eyes on you already."

He cannot deny it. Æthel noticed his flinch when the bishop pushed into their quarters. And yet—"*Are* you an innocent storyteller?"

Emrys stills, as if at some dark memory. "I have never been innocent."

They look at each other. If the voices in the knife had not driven Ine half-wild, he would never have rushed out here. "How did you know to find me tonight?"

"Better to ask how *you* knew to find *me*."

"Can you not answer a simple question?"

"None of your questions are simple, Ine of Wessex," the scop says, "and I am not made of answers. I told you of the heritage because things were getting out of hand." They pause. "It is dangerous and the knowledge that you have it is even more so. Guard it carefully."

Ine senses the looming weight of the hall behind him, full of men always on the cusp of violence. "You said I have enemies enough. What enemies?"

Emrys's eyes stray to the shape of the hall too. "Someone is working to extinguish the Dumnonian birthright, even the traces carried by common folk. They would never expect to find it in a Saxon king. You have an advantage in that."

It is too much. His head is a muddle of dread and an awful dawning realization that all this is unlikely to go away. "What am I supposed to do?"

"Last I looked, you were the king, and quite old enough to make your own decisions." Emrys half turns away. "I am a wandering scop and a heretic. It is hardly my place to advise you."

Ine resists an urge to grind his teeth. "You have quite happily done so up until this point. Why stop now?"

Emrys sighs. "Then I advise you to keep the boy close. They will come for him."

"Cadwy? I thought you said that I—" *no, it is too wild a tale*—"that he is not Geraint's heir."

"They do not know that. You might have protected him from your court, but a political death is not the only one he needs fear."

Ine lifts his hand to his forehead, but catches himself and drops it. "I...have to think about this."

"Do not think too long. You have a capable wife. Why not trust in her?"

He is so rarely angry that he does not at first recognize the feeling rising inside him. But it comes up hot, furious at the words, at something else they uncover that he does not want to dwell on. Emrys hops nimbly aside as the ground beneath them cracks. River water rushes into the gap, swirling like the anger in Ine's chest. He stares at the foam, hears the gurgle of the stream, *feels* the alarmed scurry of something small and fast through the grass, and that feeling—the knowledge of it—withers his fury.

"I don't want this." He sinks down before the new channel, covering his face. "Take it away."

"And make a mockery of her choice?" Emrys's voice is cold. "It's impossible, in any case. If I could do such a thing, I would not need to concern myself with foolish kings set on throwing themselves at my feet."

Ine laughs. It is a dry and slightly desperate sound and it seems Gweir hears it through the night because he calls out, "Ine king?" Tramping of feet on the path above.

"Another person in whom you should trust." Emrys steps back into shadow, so that only the glitter of their eyes remains.

"Wait." He scrambles up. "You cannot leave now. I have questions."

The eyes pause. "One. You may ask one."

Disbelieving, Ine stares into the darkness, breathless with everything he does not know. Just one question. Who is killing Britons? How have the dead come back to life? What is he supposed to do about Cadwy? Herla and Gwyn…are the stories real? Is the Dumnonian heritage evil, as the bishops claim? How can he hide a power he can't control?

Ine wets his lips. "Cynric's wife, who wanted peace. What was her name?"

A small intake of breath. "Her name was Riva," Emrys says, a strange note in their voice. "Perhaps there is hope for you yet."

"Not even a passing mention," he says later to Gweir, as they sit alone in the room where the Witan meets, surrounded by parchment notes and records. It is gone midnight, but the search for something to back up Emrys's claim keeps weariness at bay. "If Cynric's wife was a Dumnonian princess, would that not at least merit a footnote? We have warred with them for centuries." *And why would a woman's deeds be remembered when there are men's deeds to laud?* With the memory of those words comes another: Æthel stiff and proud before the gesiths as they shook their heads over her actions at Tantone. Ine stares hard at the faded ink. He failed her that day.

"Ine king, will you not tell me what prompted all this?" Gweir gestures at the bundles of parchment. "What did the scop say?"

He had told Æthel he trusted Gweir, but with how much? He still has the sense that the gesith is holding something close. Several times, Ine has seen the bird-shadow of it in his face, winging by unspoken. Perhaps it is time they finished the conversation they started several weeks ago on horseback. "Why do you remain here, Gweir?" He uses the Britons' language. Its hushed syllables draw in about them and it is Gweir's turn to look guarded. "Why are you sworn to Wessex?"

"I am not sworn to Wessex," the gesith says after a long moment. "I am sworn to *you*."

"It's the same—"

"Forgive me, it is not."

They stare at each other. A torch sputters, nearly spent. "You have given me a traitor's tongue," Gweir murmurs, a touch rueful. "I meant that I would not serve any West Saxon king but you."

Wonderingly, Ine says, "Why?"

"Why?" Gweir's eyes are defiant. Tension thickens the air between them. "Because you are Constantine's heir. The Heir of Dumnonia."

Where Emrys spoke of heritages and promises, Gweir's statement is stronger for its simplicity. Ine has the edge of the table in a death grip and tries to uncurl his fingers. His mouth is dry when he says, "And do you... know what that means?"

"Yes," Gweir murmurs. "I found you the night Geraint died. When I saw the roots, the way they covered you, I knew."

So it was not entirely a dream. Ine cannot keep down a

shudder. "But you swore yourself to me years before that. You could not always have known."

"I suspected." Gweir smiles weakly. "I could not believe it when my father told me that the royal blood of Dumnonia ran in the line of Wessex kings. It had never shown itself. I was even angry. But then I met you." The gold arm ring Ine had given him in recognition of his loyalty catches what little light remains in the room and holds it close. "I knew you were different from the start and I am not alone. You have many Britons here who trust you for reasons they cannot articulate."

Silence returns and Ine lets it rule unchallenged. Finally he says in a whisper, "The bishops believe the wheat is the work of heathens." He stares at his open palms. "If they realize... I've given them too much power. Hædde has already spoken of bringing more clergy to Wessex. How long can I hide this? And the Britons. I still don't know who is killing them or why." The darkness seems to deepen and a chill like that of Purgatory presses against his back. *I will not turn around.* Before Æthel's report, he had almost convinced himself that Cædwalla was a figment, a symptom of madness. The prospect of him being real is far more frightening. Wights can kill with a touch...

The moment Ine thinks it, he whirls around, unable to stop himself, but there is nothing there. Nothing except a small scrape outside the door, as of feet creeping away into the night. Worn ragged, he faces Gweir again. "Emrys, the scop, believes Cadwy may be in danger. Will you watch him?"

Gweir twitches at the name. "Of course, Ine king. But... did Emrys tell you of Constantine? You seem unsurprised at my words."

Ine nods stiffly. "And you seem equally unsurprised to hear of Emrys. Who are they, Gweir?"

The gesith bites his lip. "They are themselves a story with many names and many faces." His voice is hushed, reverent. "Older than the world, some say, and on no one's side save their own. But they have always been a friend of Dumnonia."

"Can I trust them?"

"I believe so, Ine king. At least if you honour the birthright."

"Honour it?" Only that soft scrape outside stops Ine raising his voice. As it is, he throws up his hands. "I'm terrified of it. I thought I was going mad."

"What is it like?"

Ine stares at him. The other man returns it, his eyes a gleam in the dim. "I..." In his mind, the giant. "It is so huge. A hundred thousand lives." He turns his palms upwards. "I can see the wind. I can hear the grass. A taste in my mouth like loam." He is speaking without thought. "But I do not want to see, or listen or swallow. Because if I do, it overwhelms me. I was lost the night Geraint died. I don't know how I found my way back."

There is a hunger in Gweir's face. "I wish I felt even a whisper of it." His mouth creases. "I suppose that makes me safer than the Britons in Scirburne and Sceaptun."

"You are welcome to it. I think I see why the Church hates heathens." Part of him feels a traitor voicing it. "Laws cannot touch this—this power inside me. It is too big for one person. It can't be controlled."

"Constantine could control it," Gweir says softly.

Ine fixes his gaze over the gesith's shoulder, preferring to stare at a shadowed patch of wall. "I am not Constantine. I am not even of his people. This shouldn't be happening to me." He sounds like a child, but it is hard not to feel helpless in the face of both Gweir's and Emrys's words. They are painting him as something he can never be. "The blood in my veins comes from Cynric and all those who slew their way to power in his wake."

"I don't believe that."

"It's fact." Cædwalla's shield watches him from its place on the wall. "I want Dumnonia, or thought I did, but if this is the price, I have no wish to pay it. The Britons can keep their land and their birthright, and their memories of a king who was clearly a better one than I."

Gweir opens his mouth to speak, but Ine roughly pushes his chair back. The shocks of the day swirl inside him like tempestuous waters, and his head is crowded with voices: Æthel's; the slaughtered souls trapped in the bone knife; Emrys and Gweir telling him the wildest, most improbable tale. And Geraint, spending his last breath on asking, *Who are you?*

For the first time, Ine truly does not know.

17

ᛞERLᚨ

Wiltun, Wiltunscir
Kingdom of Wessex

The queen passes her at a canter, riding her horse too fast through the dirt streets. It is late afternoon and hazy with it, but Herla's eyes are sharp enough to spot one tear-stained cheek as she flashes by. No word from Æthelburg has reached her in the hours since they returned, nor summons to a meeting. The sight of streaked skin, the glimmer of it, disturbs her. She is sure she wept unashamedly too, a very long time ago. The memory is insubstantial. To raise Gwyn's blade meant to walk in a wasteland where nothing grew and no rain fell, not even tears.

But I am not there any more.

Her muscles move before her mind. Or perhaps it is her heart following its fiery instinct. She opens the stall door and swings into the saddle. Heeling her horse, she rides out as carelessly as Æthelburg and almost tramples the woman in the yard beyond. She yelps and Herla reins in with a curse. They both have words balanced on their lips when it hits Herla—the overwhelming sense of *Otherness*. Her eyes widen.

"Where you are going, horsemaster?"

She had not immediately noticed Sinnoch, standing with a coil of rope in his hands. Unlike the others, he has not warmed to her. She is beginning to wonder whether the cause is more than common jealousy. If he is a Briton, he might also be a pagan—and they are far better than Christians at seeing what is in front of them.

Before she can answer, his eyes flicker to the woman. "And you. Alis, wasn't it? You will not find the queen in the stables at this hour."

Herla tumbles from one thought to another. Is the girl an Other-world creature, or merely touched by it? She fair shimmers with the light reflected off the spires of Caer Wydyr, as if it is trapped beneath her skin. Then Sinnoch's words ignite alarm. "Why are you looking for the queen?"

Not taking her eyes off Herla, Alis says, "I drew a bath for her, but she never came."

"Away with you," Sinnoch barks. "And you, horsemaster, back to your duties. You may have Lady Æthelburg's favour, but you work under me."

Although her disguise is enough to fool a mortal, Herla has never tested it against the blood of Annwn. She dismounts and watches the girl return to the hall, her only consolation the knowledge that Æthelburg is not in it. How is she to warn the queen about Alis without revealing herself? She has already said too much. Æthelburg has *seen* too much.

"I do not trust that woman," Sinnoch mutters. A shelf runs the length of one wooden wall; he bends to inspect the tack. "Ean-swith should be back by now."

"And me?" Herla asks, knowing it is foolish to probe. "Do you trust me?"

Sinnoch straightens. "*You* do not speak Englisc with the accent of someone who has dwelt among the Cymry of the old lands."

"Few would recognize that," she remarks.

"Indeed. Few would recognize it." His smile is sharp. "I find it hard to believe a woman from Anglia would."

Neither says anything more. Herla picks up a broom and goes about sweeping as if nothing has occurred, although urgency boils beneath her skin. Sinnoch buffs saddles until the leather gleams. Eventually, however, he tires of their stalemate. With a backward glance, he leaves for the mead hall and food.

Herla drops the broom. *I must find a way to tell Æthelburg of Alis. Before she returns to Wiltun.* But the queen's tears are foremost in her mind as she leads her horse from the stables. Herla tips her face to the wind. She is a hunter, after all, and can pick up any scent. Æthelburg's is like sun-warmed iron and the first fresh sweat of battle. Herla breathes it in, wanting to take another breath and another, as if the scent can fill a vessel locked away inside her that has long been empty.

Numerous barrows mark the landscape beyond the settlement, unhappily like those on the hill outside Sceaptun. There is an army sleeping beneath the king's shire. Herla narrows her eyes. She would not have believed it possible to harness the echoes of those so long deceased. Could her own countrywomen be called back? An unexpected shudder rolls through her at the thought. They have earned their peace.

Tawny hair against tanned and freckled skin.

Herla swallows Boudica's memory like a bitter herb. It lodges in her belly and burns there, and she does not know how to ease it.

Æthelburg's horse has left tracks, areas of trampled grass and a hoofprint in the bank of a small stream. She is close now. The scent is strong. Before too long, Herla hears the *thwack* and grunts of someone punishing a tree. "You will blunt your blade," she calls.

Æthelburg gasps, but to give the queen her due, she swings round in an instant, weapon raised before her. There are no traces of tears now, only beads of perspiration dotting her brow. "How in God's name did you find me?"

Herla dismounts. "I am a good tracker."

"More than good," Æthelburg mutters. She drags a sleeve across her face. "You seem to turn up when least expected."

Herla says nothing, watching as the queen catches her breath. In addition to trousers, she wears only a band of linen tied around her chest. Her tunic lies near the tree stump that was her opponent, discarded in the warm evening. Herla is staring and knows she is, but like the scent tormenting her, she cannot seem to stop.

When Æthelburg raises an eyebrow, she says, "I saw you ride past. You looked upset."

"So you decided to ride after me." She plants her hands on her hips, sword still clutched in her right. "You are without doubt the strangest person I've met, Ælfrún."

Herla eases closer. "Will you tell me what was wrong?"

"Hmm." Æthelburg's blue eyes take her in. "Perhaps, if you spar with me."

"I have no sword."

"Not a problem. I always carry a spare." The queen goes to her horse, busy cropping a patch of long grass, and pulls a sword from a scabbard strapped to the saddle. When Herla catches it one-handed, Æthelburg nods approvingly. "I knew you could fight." She attacks without warning, sending her blade snaking towards Herla's middle, and Herla bats it aside. Undeterred, the queen attacks again, this time feinting left and going right. They shatter the balmy evening with the clash of metal.

"The skirt puts me at a disadvantage," Herla says.

"Take it off then."

"No, or you do not stand a chance."

"Really," Æthelburg says darkly and lunges again.

"You are quick, I admit." Herla dances out of range. "But you cannot rely on speed alone." To illustrate the point, she darts forward and, raising the borrowed blade, brings it down with such force that it sends the queen's sword flying from her hand. For a startled moment, Æthelburg watches it spin through the air, before she throws herself at Herla.

They go down in a tangle. Herla tries to get her feet under her, but the skirt seizes the opportunity to prove its disadvantage and traps her legs in a fold of cloth. The next instant, she feels a sharp point in the hollow of her throat.

"You are strong, I admit," Æthelburg says, breathing hard, "but you cannot rely on the honour of your opponent." They look at each other. After a second, the queen starts to laugh and, oh, that sound—it calls for company. Mirth engulfs the bitter burning memory in Herla's stomach, bubbling up to escape as joyfully as

Æthelburg's. Again, it is not the laughter that shook her when the hound leaped. Or the dark amusement she felt at the curse's weakening. It is the laughter of the soul, even a soul as ruined as hers.

Æthelburg takes her dagger away. "Have we met before?"

Herla falls silent.

"Only…your movements seem familiar." The queen shakes her head and, to Herla's extreme disappointment, climbs off. "Ignore me. I won't pry. You are the one bright spot in my life."

Would she say such a thing if she knew the truth? "Why? What is wrong?"

They sit side by side in the grass and Æthelburg pulls her knees up to her chest. "It hardly matters what I say now, whether I can trust you with it. My husband's council already despises me, thinks me unfit to lead the armies of Wessex." She examines hands grubby from her practice. "I have spent the last decade propping up the borders of our kingdom, hunting exiles looking to usurp Ine and winning battles against them and whatever rabble they raise. But the Witan sees none of that. Because of course I should have been at home having babies." Æthelburg grimaces. Instead of Herla, she stares at the space between the waving stems. "You have spent long enough in Wiltun to hear the rumours, no doubt. They think me barren, or too warlike to conceive."

Herla chooses her words carefully. "Do you want a child?"

"Whether I want a child or not is irrelevant." She plucks a piece of grass and starts to shred it. "We have been married ten years and I could count the number of times my husband has lain with me on one hand." She says it very quickly and shreds the grass even faster.

Herla cannot hide her astonishment. Astonishment and something fiercer that has woken at the words, at the thought of Æthelburg—she pulls her attention back. "Has he said why?"

"When he showed no interest on our wedding night, I thought he was being considerate." The queen gives a hollow chuckle. "He need not have worried."

"And after?"

"After…every time we were intimate, it was because I forced

the issue. Do you know what it's like to be made to feel so undesir-able?" Tears in her voice. "I told myself it was fine. I was busy, anyway. Lying with men leads to children and I did not want a child." Her hand opens, letting the grass fall in pieces to the ground. "I think he has always loved another but is too dutiful to admit it. Our marriage was arranged."

"Have you asked him?"

"Of course," she snaps. "He never answers."

"Do you give him a chance to?"

"Of course," Æthelburg says again, even more unconvincingly. "If he was only honest with me, I could bear it. I would not care if it was another woman—or even a man. I am hardly one to com-plain on that account."

Heart in her throat, Herla studies her closely. "You are… happy with men *and* women?"

"I think I might have mentioned Leofe." Æthelburg leans back on her hands. "You could say she was my first love. We were very young."

She had not forgotten, had in fact already stored that piece of knowledge away. Æthelburg's story is intriguing, but it has not changed Herla's belief that the king loves her. She says nothing. Because gathering inside her is a deepening contentment. She leans back on her hands too, holding the queen's secrets as if they are her own. "Thank you for telling me."

"You must think me a fool," Æthelburg murmurs. "You told me not to trust you."

Their fingers are very close, just half a grasp apart on the grass. The air is becoming dewy. "I did," Herla says softly. "I meant it."

"But I do trust you. I don't know why. Perhaps because we are so alike."

Alike. Herla almost laughs. "No. You are a good person, Æthel-burg. Kind." Again she sees the queen kneeling to close the eyes of her slain men. "You are brave and selfless and you love your people."

"I think you love your people too. I think… you would do anything for them."

At that, Herla turns to look at her. Surprise makes her breathless, steals her words.

"And I think," Æthelburg continues, holding her gaze. "That you have been hurt profoundly. So profoundly that you cannot allow yourself to trust anything or anyone ever again."

A small touch. The tips of the queen's fingers rest against her own. Herla lowers her eyes to look at them, and the flame inside her—the desire—roars up. But with it comes a voice that has been growing in her since Sceaptun; a voice which orders her to take her hand away, to distance herself from the woman she has called selfless and kind. Herla ignores it; the hunter does not waver. So she tilts her face up as Æthelburg's hand covers hers, as the queen leans in. She even closes her eyes.

A horn wails. In the same moment, Herla feels the hooks in her spirit tighten and start to pull. *No.* She jerks back and Æthelburg catches herself on the ground. *It cannot be.* The moon has made a full grim circle to wash up once again on the shores of old age. *And it is impossible.* Surely the curse cannot force her to ride now. Herla scrambles to her feet.

"What is it?" Æthelburg rises too. "Ælfrún, what's wrong?"

She stares at the queen in horror. *Sweet Mother, I will kill her.* "Get out of here."

"I don't—"

"If you value your life, you will mount your horse and *ride.*" The word is a growl. "Ride home. Do not stop for anything." Sudden agony doubles her over, like an arrow shot through her core, and she gasps.

"Ælfrún."

Æthelburg grips her arm, but Herla shoves her roughly away. "Did you not hear me?" She feels them, her hunters. She can hear the familiar cry, *We ride, we ride.* Goddess, not now. In its guise as a knife, Gwyn's sword is singing, growing stronger with every bellow of the horn. The sound fills the night and Æthelburg pales. She takes a shaking step towards her horse.

"*Go.*" Herla throws her bodily into the saddle and slaps the horse's flank. The animal needs no encouragement. Its lips are pulled back and the wailing horn is in the whites of its eyes. Æthelburg turns her pallid face towards Herla as the horse carries her away. Lips seem to shape her name.

Fighting back the red misting the corners of her vision, Herla cannot spare another glance. The illusion concealing her true form wisps away as she drops to her knees. "No." She presses both hands against the earth so that they will not grip Gwyn's blade. But the moon stares down, ancient and unforgiving. It is not alone. In a ring around her are eighteen women on black horses, their faces as merciless as the moon's. *Is that what I looked like?* she thinks wildly. *Is that how I looked when I rode?*

"Rise, Herla." Corraidhín's voice is cold. "Rise and lead us." Only her eyes show Herla the truth: in them is a buried horror. Her words are in the Eceni tongue and hope flutters in Herla's chest. Perhaps the curse cannot reclaim them entirely.

Dormach stands on one of the mounds, a bulky silhouette against the sky. She can feel the hound's stare, rage-filled at her defiance. He throws back his head and howls, and the red mist thickens, spreading to stain the world. Why is she resisting? She is the Hunt and the horn. The wolf driving the deer before her, the falcon on the wing. Gwyn's blade is in her hand, bare to the moon, and she is on her feet. She is swinging into the saddle of a horse as dark as the others. She is lifting her face to sniff the wind, which carries the scent of iron and battle-sweat. She is—

No. With a furious scream, Herla turns her horse away from the settlement and the lone figure racing towards it. Instead, she looks west, to the distant isle of Glestingaburg. It is the only place that can hold her, hold them. As her horse's hooves pound the dark earth, Herla tries to ignore the mass of the souls rubbing against her own. There are more out there, waiting for her blade, Gwyn's blade.

No. Dimly she is aware that she could not have resisted before. It takes all her will to resist now, to keep riding straight and true for the hollow under the hill. *Foolish, I was foolish to believe we were free.* The last month spent among people, beside Æthelburg—what had she been thinking? They are rapidly disintegrating into a dream now, those stolen weeks, absurd and improbable. The Hunt is waking. It is her *real*. She had chosen it for herself, on the shores of another world. She cannot go back.

The door appears in the hill and Herla bursts through it, hunters behind her. But no enchanted sleep seizes her, or dampens the urge to ride. The curse will make her fight for every shred of self. "We will not ride," she screams, falling from her horse to the smooth earthen floor. She lays her palms flat. "We are Eceni. We remember the Mother and the herbs burned in her honour." Somewhere beyond, Dormach is howling. "We remember the blood spilled in the name of freedom." It is little more than babbling, scraps of memory pulled from the person that has begun to take her first steps in a new time. But the others hear it. Corraidhín too finds the strength to abandon her saddle, to throw herself down beside Herla and to place her hands over hers.

Others join them. Hands upon hands, until the call of the Hunt and the baying of Gwyn's hound are overwhelmed by their weight, their warmth, and the musky scent of leather and fur. That is how they stay through the long night, heads close, sharing breaths. Tears streak their faces; none of them are worthy of this; none of them have earned the love of the past that protects them. For the first time since she awakened, the truth engulfs Herla, welling up from that chasm where the people whose souls she reaped reside. *We have lived too long. We have taken too many lives.*

When the sky starts to lighten, Corraidhín whispers, "You did it," and her smile is as brilliant as the sun rising far above.

"*We.*" Herla gathers them all to her. "I could not have done it without you."

"But what does it mean?"

"Yes." Senua uses her spear to push herself upright. "I thought we would not have to ride again."

"I thought so too." Herla's stomach writhes; she wraps an arm around it. Goddess, how close she came. The thought of Æthelburg dead at her hand—of her soul in chains—sickens her. "I was wrong."

"And yet we do not sleep," Corraidhín points out, gesturing at the hall with its polished walls. "We can speak again. We remember ourselves."

"We can fight where we never could before," Gelgéis adds.

"Yes, we can fight." *You should have let the queen be,* the voice of earlier hisses. *Now look at what you have done.* Herla bows her head. "But we cannot walk safely amongst the people of this time. Not when the curse still controls us."

"What did you learn?" Nynniaw asks.

I learned I can never go back. The thought is bleak; she is still full of the sight and scent of Æthelburg. Why did she allow the queen to come so close? She was supposed to be concentrating on the Otherworld trail, locating the— "I did not warn her," Herla says in a whisper, aghast at herself. She meets Nynniaw's eyes. "I found the trespasser. At least I believe the girl is from Annwn. I intended to tell the queen, but..." Æthelburg: perspiring, half-dressed, sword in hand. *Perhaps, if you spar with me.* She winces. "I was distracted."

Corraidhín is studying her. She has always known Herla best, long ago ferreted out her secrets after stumbling across the Queen of the Eceni in Herla's hut one too many times. Herla avoids her friend's gaze and hears the other woman sigh. *You are a fool,* she might have said. *Only a fool makes the same mistake twice.* Can Herla be blamed, though—for seeing Boudica in Æthelburg? Queens of their people, warriors and strategists, married to men who do not deserve them.

She picks up the thought by the scruff and shakes it. *I will not walk this road again.* And yet that hunger is still in her: the hunger of the hunter, the urge to pursue. Herla clenches her fists weakly, trying to master it. She is weary from the night's struggle in a way she has never been before. "During Lughnasadh, did anyone try to cross from Annwn?"

Gelgéis shakes her head, and Herla breathes out. "That is something. But you have been busy nonetheless." Now that the moon has set, she has attention enough to survey the hall. Weapon racks line the walls. A long table runs down one side, and a carved bench sits at the top like the Saxon king's throne. Torches burn in brackets; the fire too silvery to have sprung from common flint.

"Do you like it?" Orlaith asks, on seeing where Herla's gaze has strayed. "We made all the furniture."

The lump in Herla's throat threatens to summon the unnerving pain of remembrance. Eceni emblems spiral across the walls and someone has even woven a battle standard, tied to a fresh-sawn pole. Nynniaw, probably. The earthen floor is softened in places by skins, and horned trophies are scattered about. It is both like and unlike her ancient home. The humble materials cannot disguise the fact that Annwn bleeds into Glestingaburg—the flames, the scent, the pillars built of a glittering rock not to be found in this world. And yet the women have made it theirs, like boundary markers placed in field and fen to say, *This is our land.* And why shouldn't it be? "It is wonderful," Herla tells them, and Orlaith beams. Locked somewhere inside her is the child who went to Annwn before she could fully become a woman.

"So, are you going back?" Corraidhín asks later when they stand alone on the summit of Glestingaburg. The land unfolds beneath them, a green wool blanket of trees and meadows broken by streams catching fire in the sunset. The view is new to Herla. Her curse had bound her to the hollow, not the heights. Now she bathes in the sight of land under sun and thinks, *This is Æthelburg's kingdom.* Her throat tightens.

"Herla?"

"No, Corraidhín." She forces a chill into her voice, just as she forced conviction into that short painful word. "I am not going back."

"What about warning the queen?"

"I cannot." Herla closes her eyes against the beauty. "I cannot face her now, Corra. When I nearly slew her like a beast."

Corraidhín grips her forearm. "You fought it."

"I should never have put her in a position where her survival depended on my fighting. She must know who I am now. That I have lied to her."

The wind, taking advantage of their silence, gusts between them. She told Æthelburg that she did not feel the cold, but Herla can feel it now: a grey whisper on her skin. It is not the only whisper; the souls that burden her murmur like a distant ocean. She grits her teeth, trying to ignore the way they press up against her own soul. They are louder than they were yesterday.

"This woman," Corraidhín says eventually. "She has become important to you."

Hearing it spoken hits like the shock of a squall from cloudless skies. Herla's eyes snap open, but the truth is no better in the light. "I...It is why I cannot go back. Do you understand?"

"Yes," the other woman says. "Sensible. Some would say it is right. And yet—" she gives Herla a sideways look—"you have never been one to do what is right."

She speaks without rancour or blame, but Herla nevertheless feels it settle in her heart like a riven shard of the knife she gave Æthelburg. Was it right to want Boudica when she had a husband and children? Was it right to let her queen use her in the way she did, just so Herla could feel she belonged, ever so briefly, to something other than battle? Was it right to doubt the Eceni? To listen to stories of the Otherworld king? Was it right to seek his help?

Perhaps it was right for me. I wanted to change the ending. But Æthelburg...how can she be right for her? Æthelburg has a husband who loves her, a strong kingdom. And Herla could have torn it all away in an instant. If she had not fought against the curse, the queen would be dead. Worse than dead. Again she feels sick at the thought. The longer she stays near her, the more danger Æthelburg is in. If Herla cares for her, the choice should be easy. But being near Æthelburg is what Herla wants—with a strength that is frightening.

Selfish. She has always been selfish.

"Something I *can* do, Corra," she says, fighting through the conflict in her chest, "is destroy the wight. He was a king of Wessex in life, and he can call on shades. I bound him lightly for fear of alerting whoever summoned him." She hesitates. "You know that only Gwyn ap Nudd has the ability to knit a soul to flesh after it has passed."

Corraidhín hisses. "If it *is* him, what does he want?"

Herla thinks of the murdered Britons, of the old woman with eyes that saw too much. *The danger has not passed. It is only beginning.* She thinks again of Æthelburg kneeling beside the dead, of the queen's ringing voice as she said she ruled her kingdom jointly. Herla will not admit it to Corraidhín, but she will die before she lets Æthelburg come to harm. Even if it means she must keep away from her, she tells her burning heart. Even if it means forgetting how it felt to be touched, how it felt to be human again. She is Lord of the Hunt and her enemy still walks free. "If it brings Gwyn to this world," she says, her words a dark promise, "we will be waiting for him."

18

ÆTHELBURG

Wiltun, Wiltunscir
Kingdom of Wessex

A week passes and Ælfrún does not return. "She was odd and spoke little," Deorstan tells Æthel regretfully. "But the horses miss her."

They are not the only ones. Alone on a hilltop outside Wiltun, with a view of the new-shorn fields, Æthel sits with her knees pulled up to her chest, as she did the night Ælfrún vanished, and revisits everything she saw. *If you value your life, you will mount your horse and ride.* She had not imagined the pain in Ælfrún's face, or the shock. How she pushed Æthel away with a desperate fear. She had not imagined the horns—a call she has heard twice before. The horns of the Wild Hunt. Ælfrún clearly knew what they were and stayed to face them.

Now, biting her lip, Æthel finds she has drawn blood. She runs her tongue over the place and thinks a thought too wild to be true. It is a thought that makes her palms sweat and her heart race. Her face is hot. Æthel rests it against her kneecaps, remembering with dawning horror every candid thing she said. How her fingers inched over Ælfrún's, as if they had a will of their own. The other woman had not pulled away. *Holy God, what am I doing? What have I done?*

When she returns to the hall, the wild thought is safely locked up, even from herself.

Ine has tried talking to her, but the memory of that day has curdled inside Æthel. Neither of them can take back the words they spoke. Besides, her husband has had years to talk to her, and she has grown tired of waiting. Searching for distractions—from Ine and Ælfrún both—Æthel does something she usually avoids, and approaches the women of the court in the corner they have claimed. Conversation ceases immediately and she almost laughs to see their faces, slack with surprise. Then one of them smiles. "Sit with us, Æthelburg." She pats the bench beside her and Æthel tries to remember her name. "How nice of you to join us."

Friendly words cannot hide frost. They think her too proud to join them, and they are right. She has always justified her decision by believing they have nothing in common. Now, as she lowers herself to the bench, where they sit consumed by their words and weaving, she realizes they represent everything she most fears. Domesticity. Irrelevance. A life behind walls.

"You seem troubled," Eadgifu says, who has always been kindest. "Have you argued with the king?"

Æthel's glance is sharp, but it is not such a clever guess, not when the cloud under which she walks covers half the hall. "I suppose," she mutters.

"Men can be stubborn." She squeezes Æthel's arm and seems perturbed when her fingers do not meet around the muscle. "You will make up soon enough. And yet…the king does seem distracted of late."

The way she says it is casual, but Æthel is aware of hands stilling, of gazes fixing innocently elsewhere. They are all keen to hear whatever she has to say. Why not oblige them? "True, he has not been the same since we returned from Gifle. And the incident in the grain barn has shaken him."

"Why?" Thryth asks. She is Nothhelm's wife, and whatever Æthel says, it *will* get back to him. "It's a miracle, is it not? A sign of God's favour."

"Perhaps. But Hædde believes there are heathens in Wiltun, that the wheat is their work."

Thryth's eyes brighten, as if she is thrilled at the prospect. "*Really?*" She lowers her voice and the others lean in. "Is that why they have increased the church services? I heard too that the bishops have requested Winfrid return from Nhutscelle. He is young, but very fierce where pagans are concerned."

Wonderful, Æthel thinks, *another holy man.* Watching the way her news is taken up and dissected, she feels a flash of unease. But what's said is said. "You should join us more often, Æthelburg." Thryth's smile is a small, tightly controlled thing. "Men are rarely circumspect around us. We hear much."

"Like?"

"Like the fact that, about a week ago, my husband's guard found Ine king very distressed one afternoon. To hear him tell it, the king was collapsed on the floor and crying out." Thryth raises an inquisitive brow. "When they tried to help him, he fled."

It is difficult to keep her face blank. A week ago...surely not the day of their argument? Æthel swallows, aware of Thryth watching her, waiting for a response. "He has not spoken of it to me," she says and although some of the women sink back, Nothelm's wife nods thoughtfully. Even an admission of ignorance tells her what she wishes to know. Gossip is a kind of power, Æthel realizes too late—collecting scraps until they make a picture. It is one she never learned to wield.

Another woman is hovering on the edge of the circle. Eadgifu shifts to make space for her. "Have you met Merewyn of Gifle?" she asks, and—Æthel blinks—it is Gefmund's daughter. She remembers those lakewater eyes. "She was at Gifle during the battle."

"You make it sound far more exciting than it was," Merewyn says, seating herself and smiling at Æthel. "I was safe inside. Not like Æthelburg queen."

Someone tuts. Ignoring it, Æthel smiles back. "What are you doing in Wiltun?"

"Is it not obvious?" asks the two-faced woman who invited Æthel to sit in the first place. Æthel remembers her name now: Sælin is Edred's wife. *A perfect match,* she thinks sourly. "Gifle is a backwater. Merewyn hopes to find a husband here at court. She is long past the proper age."

Merewyn is flushed and staring at her knees. Through gritted teeth, Æthel says, "I was asking *her*. I am quite sure she can speak for herself."

"Yes, I am unmarried." The woman looks up, reddening further. "But actually, Lady Æthelburg...I came for you."

Sælin's stitching slows. The other women pause in their work, and Æthel is no less perplexed. "For me?"

"I..." Merewyn avoids all eyes save Æthel's. "I was hoping you could teach me." She draws a breath. "Teach me the sword, that is."

Astonished silence is her only answer. Then Sælin titters behind her hand and, as if it's a signal, the others join in.

"When I saw you in Gifle," Merewyn hurries on, raising her voice over the laughter. "I didn't know women could learn to be warriors."

"Because they can't," Sælin says, amusement dying. Her pale blue eyes narrow. "All they can do is play at it, as a child with his toys."

The venom should not surprise her. Sælin is simply throwing Æthel's rudeness back in her face. They know she looks down on them. Instead of reacting, Æthel sits very still. She is practised at swallowing her rage, packing it into an acid space inside her. But that space is becoming full. She does not know how much more it can take before it ruptures. Before *she* ruptures.

Nerves taut, Æthel looks at Merewyn, as if the two of them are the only ones present. The younger woman's eyes are dark, her expression tinged with a bitterness Æthel recognizes. It must have taken courage to speak that wish aloud, and she feels an unexpected kinship. "Find me later. We'll start with the seax. A woman should know how to defend herself." *But how do I defend myself from* this?

"Lady Æthelburg, the Witan requests your presence."

She blinks at the servant. The interruption could not come at a better time except—"Now?" she asks, frowning. It is early evening, a strange hour to call a moot. When he nods, she rises, the women's eyes heavy upon her. Of all people, they should be her allies, but rather they are wolves circling. She does not like the idea of leaving Merewyn amongst them. Not after the woman's request.

The first person she sees on pushing open the door is Ingild. "I hear you lost another six men in Sceaptun," he says by way of a greeting. "You are becoming quite careless, Æthelburg."

Furious words rise. So too do the bodies of the men who died, laid out white and cold beneath the golden morn. Hastily dug graves were the only reward they received for their service. Her anger falters.

"Nothing to say?" Ingild sighs and exchanges glances with Edred and Nothhelm, the only other two present. "Perhaps you should reflect a while at home," he continues in a soft voice. "We are not made of men."

But you are, Æthel thinks. *This world is. And I am suffocated by all of you.* "I am deeply sorry for their loss. Is Sceaptun the reason we are meeting? If so, Gweir should be here."

"If he considers it important, he will attend," Ingild says with a careless wave of his hand. "However, I am sure you can deliver an equally…comprehensive report."

At any other time, she would be grinding her teeth at his condescension. But a cold sweat has broken out under her clothes. She needs Gweir to corroborate her story. Ælfrún—she smothers her earlier thoughts before they escape—had agreed to support her, but she is gone. No one else was there.

The door opens, revealing Hædde, Ine walking in his shadow. He must have been the one to call the Witan together, but the sight of him trailing behind the bishop makes Æthel uneasy. Once again, she has that feeling of the rules changing in a game she thought she knew how to play.

"We need Gweir," she says and her voice cracks a little. "He spoke to the villagers. He has information—"

"If it is that vital, he can supply it at a later date," Nothhelm says tetchily, taking his seat. "I agree with Ingild that your report will suffice in the meantime."

She does not want to, but Æthel appeals to Ine. "If Gweir cannot join us, it would be better to wait."

"I expected him to be here," he replies—but not before studying each corner of the room, as if to check for assassins. Why has he waited so long to call the Witan together? Does he feel, like her, that the men will not believe her story?

Leofric enters, leading Cenred, and an awful thought strikes her. What if Cenred's illness runs in the family? Ine *has* been behaving oddly. And now there is Thryth's story of finding him in the grip of a frenzy. When Æthel had asked him what was wrong, could this be the reason he refused to answer? That he knows he does not have long? If Ingild has realized too, it might account for his aggressive behaviour—such as killing Geraint of Dumnonia against Ine's wishes. He is waiting to step into the breach.

Still standing, she has to grip the back of her chair to fight dizziness, as her fear about explaining Sceaptun blooms into a greater one. She never…Æthel swallows and forces herself to look at her husband. In no version of this life has she ever believed he could die before her. *She* is the one who stares down death. She has long made peace with the fact that the next battle she fights could be her last.

"Well, Æthelburg?" Ingild's voice reaches her across the chasm newly opened in her chest. "We are waiting."

You are getting ahead of yourself. Straightening, Æthel releases her grip on the chair, the heels of its carvings imprinted in her flesh. "Britons are being killed across two shires," she says—and her voice comes out loud and raw. She lowers it. "The killings look indiscriminate, but they are not. The only people dying are those with links to the old religion of Dumnonia."

She has phrased it prettily, but Hædde knows exactly what she means. After a long moment, he leans back in his seat. "I fail to see the issue."

Æthel glowers at him. "You fail to see the issue with unsanctioned killing in the king's lands?"

"The king is aware," Hædde says, "that continued survival of the old ways will undermine the Church and its status."

"That does not mean these people deserve to die," Æthel exclaims hotly. Edred raises an eyebrow. *Less of the emotion,* she chastises herself, knowing it will be used against her.

Ingild smiles narrowly. "And who is carrying out this killing?"

"I did not see the perpetrators. But I know the name of the one behind them."

"If you did not see them, how do you know they are responsible?" Ingild appeals to the rest of the Witan. "Are we to endure more talk of ghostly women appearing from nowhere?"

"Less of that, brother," Ine snaps, a little fire back in his eyes. "Let her speak."

Æthel looks at them all, caught in their rude assumptions of her character, and it takes more courage to say what she says next than she ever needed on the battlefield. "I have it on good authority that the man behind them is Cædwalla." When none of them react to the name, she adds, "Cædwalla of Wessex."

She is braced for laughter, but it does not come from the corner she expects. Cenred is shaking in his chair. And rather than mockery, Æthel hears something much colder, much darker. Ine is watching his father with a stiff expression that—in the wake of her previous thoughts—she cannot help but see as dread.

"Get the servants to remove him," Ingild mutters to Edred, his smile gone. "He is a nuisance."

Ine would usually come to his father's defence, but he does not speak as Cenred is led, still laughing, from the room. When the door closes, plunging them into uncomfortable silence, Æthel wraps her arms around herself, feeling terribly alone.

"I apologize, Æthel." Ingild's smile is back in place. "My father interrupted the fine tale you were spinning us."

He is utterly at ease. Nothhelm and Edred exchange nods, as if holding their own private conversation, and Leofric studies his clasped hands. As for Hædde...Æthel does not dare look at him. Ingild's smile only lengthens at her silence. "I..." She throws a desperate glance at Ine, whose own silence is condemning her, but he sits frozen in his chair. "I know how it sounds. I struggled to believe it too, but the men lost at Sceaptun did not die natural deaths. And the Britons were killed with a strange weapon, a knife of bone." She almost reaches for it before remembering she left it with Ine. "I gave it to the king."

Doubtful glances are exchanged around the table, but her last words arrest them. Ingild leans forward. "Brother, is it true? Do you have this knife?"

Ine is pale. As pale as the bone knife he is failing to produce as evidence. Æthel looks at him expectantly, but he does not meet her eyes. "I...don't have it any more," he tells his clenched hands. "It broke."

"*What?*" In a lower voice, she adds, "The old woman told me it could not be easily destroyed. It can't have broken."

Ine's face is bleak. "I'm sorry, Æthelburg."

Something hot and bitter bubbles into her throat. "Do you have the pieces?"

Slowly, he shakes his head—and in that small movement is the power to discredit her. Æthel forces the bitterness back down. Why would he do this to her? Surely, *surely*, it could not be a punishment for refusing to speak with him since their argument?

"Ine," she says, her voice grating in her ears. "You at least saw the bone knife. You know I am telling the truth about it. And you must have been concerned enough to share my report with the Witan."

"Actually, Æthelburg, *I* requested this council." Ingild is no longer smiling. "You have delayed your report long enough. This knife should have been shown to the Witan at once."

Suddenly Ine's mood makes sense. *Why didn't you tell me Ingild would do this?* she thinks at him, but she has her answer already. He had tried to, perhaps, and she had insisted on silence. She had even gone so far as to sleep and rise before him, just to avoid the temptation to break it. Only the men's scrutiny stops her growling in frustration.

She must consider the Britons; the families being killed. This is bigger than her and Ine. The wight is still out there. Æthel draws a calming breath. "I apologize, Ingild, for not showing you the knife. But I have been mocked by this council before. You can understand my reluctance."

To her surprise, Ingild gives a sober nod. "And I apologize for my part in that, Æthelburg. But you must see how ludicrous this sounds—invoking Cædwalla's name in such a way. You are telling us that a man has returned from the dead." Before any of the others can speak or scoff, he adds, "You accuse him 'on good authority.'" Ingild's eyes are cold. "Whose?"

She stares at him, trapped by her own words. A week ago, she would not have hesitated to bring Ælfrún into it—any ally against the men—but now... Horns echo in her head. Ælfrún's panicked grip, the expanse of her eyes, the way she stiffened at the wailing call. The instincts Æthel has honed on the battlefield are screaming, *Don't tell him*. But if she does not share it with Ingild and the Witan, she has nothing. Ine has nothing. Hædde will dismiss the matter and more people will die.

Ingild's chill deepens at her silence. "Very well," he says softly. "You cannot or will not back up your claim, which, as I said, is ludicrous in the extreme. What do you expect us to do with a ghost story, Æthelburg?"

"There must be someone who knows more..."

"A witch perhaps? Or a magician like the tales of Myrdhin?" Nothhelm's smile is indulgent, but not warm. "Why do you bring such a story to us? If you fear *we* will mock you, you are doing a good enough job of it yourself."

Æthel slams a fist on the tabletop. "*Someone* is killing Britons—"

"And not just here," Ine says finally. "Cadwy mentioned similar murders in Dumnonia."

"*Cadwy*. He is a child, Ine." Ingild throws up his hands. "Moreover, a child of the enemy. He is not a reliable source of information. He will spin you whatever stories take his fancy."

They are getting nowhere—just as Ingild likely planned. Æthel can feel Ine's gaze; he must be wondering why she has not mentioned Ælfrún. But taking his cue from her, neither has he, and she is thankful for reasons she cannot express.

"First you talk of befriending the Wealas," Ingild says, rising to his feet, "and now some scheme of theirs has succeeded in persuading you to waste Saxon lives. This is not you, brother." All eyes are on him, so all eyes see the way he stares pointedly at Cenred's empty chair before continuing. "Are you quite *well*?"

Lurid hues of anger and humiliation stain Ine's cheeks. He rises too. "I do not give you leave to speak to me so. *You* were the one to insist on this council despite my telling you that we needed more time to investigate. You make a mockery of Æthelburg and me both by forcing us to lay this prematurely before the Witan."

Ingild's expression is ugly. "We should be taking the fight to Dumnonia while it is weakened. Instead, you want to pursue this madness?"

His choice of word is not lost on Æthel. Neither, perhaps, on Ine, who snaps, "I will do what I see fit. As you seem to forget, I am king."

"Then maybe you should act like it."

Ingild's words are delivered with a gravity that well conceals his scorn. The hush that follows them is full of sharp edges. Nothhelm and Leofric examine the walls. Edred sits in Ingild's shadow, and Hædde...Æthel finally brings herself to look at him, but it is odd. He seems to be staring at Ine's hands, gripping the edge of the table.

"This council is dismissed," Ine says. The anger she expects to hear in his voice is only a memory of itself. What's there instead is...fear? "Leave me. All of you."

Ine is looking at *her* too and Æthel, flushed with fury, spins on her heel. The meeting has achieved nothing but to harden opinion against her—exactly what Ingild wants. As to why, she is unsure. What threat does she pose him?

Her thoughts, as she pushes outside, remind her of the day her mother tried teaching her to weave and Æthel became so badly tangled in the threads that she had to be cut free. Her head feels like that now: a knotted mess. She has always been aware of the friction that rubs both Ine and Ingild raw, but the ætheling has never before spoken so boldly. She does not like it. She does not like Hædde's callous dismissal of the violence done to the Britons.

And she cannot puzzle out Ine's decision to withhold the knife. If it broke, as he said, why did he throw the pieces away?

Running beneath it all, the warp thread herself, is Ælfrún. Her absence gnaws at Æthel in a way she is frightened to acknowledge. *You are the one bright spot in my life.* She does not know when she started thinking of Ælfrún as a friend. Can you even call a person a friend when you know so little about them?

She is pulled from her thoughts by the stealthy movements of someone who does not wish to be seen. Although dusk is settling in, there is light enough in the sky to identify the braid on Ingild's cloak as he disappears down the path to the tannery. *What is he doing?* Before she knows it, Æthel has slipped after him.

The building is set apart on account of the stench long soaked into its walls. She grimaces. Of all places, why here? Ingild stops as another, slighter figure emerges from the twilight, and Æthel ducks off the path before they spot her, using the straggling bushes to edge closer.

"Is it done?" Ingild asks tensely.

"What do you think?" The voice is whining, female. Æthel recognizes it instantly: Alis. She frowns at the impudent tone no servant should use. "That half-blood bastard was there. Waiting. As if he *knew*."

Ingild curses. "He could not have known."

"It was your job to clear the way. Can I not trust you with the simplest of tasks?"

Unlike Ine who reddens, Ingild's anger leaves him pale. "Do not forget who I am."

"I could say the same." Wind swells in the trees, cold as a blade on bare skin. Æthel's heart is knocking against her ribs, and she presses one hand against it, frown deepening. What task?

Ingild mutters his next words, seeming chastened. "Then we will try again."

"You know he will go to the king," Alis says, her lip curling. "It will make the task ten times harder—at least to execute with the subtlety you insist upon."

"And what was subtle about sending thugs to do the job? I must be above suspicion, or everything I have worked towards will count for nothing."

Æthel draws a sharp breath. Ingild dallying with a servant wouldn't raise a single eyebrow in court, but this is no dalliance. She does not know what it is, except trouble. And Alis...If she is not a servant, who is she? What is she doing here? Sudden fear for Eanswith courses through her. She has been gone too long.

"Very well." Alis lifts a hand, runs her fingers slowly down his cheek, and Ingild shivers under her touch. "Then first, we will need another—." She stops. Her eyes rake the bushes where Æthel is hiding, though she has not made a sound. Fear for Eanswith turns to fear for herself. There is something wrong in Alis's gaze; it raises the hairs all over her body. She holds her breath, still as a mouse with only bare stems to protect it from the sky. What little light remained is fading fast now; Ingild and Alis are mere shapes in the gloom.

Finally, Alis takes her eyes away. "I will be missed. And *you* have work to do."

Æthel does not emerge until she is sure both of them are gone. Although her mind turns it over, she cannot make deeper sense of the conversation—other than that Alis is more than she seems, and Ingild is planning something. Twice now he has challenged Ine's authority in full hearing of others who would be swayed by his words.

As if that thought summoned him, she almost trips over Ine as he backs out of the hut that has become Cenred's sick room. Built for guests who cannot be housed in the main hall, it is still near enough to benefit from the swift attention of the king's servants. Braziers provide heat instead of a firepit. Through the door, Æthel can see the old lord propped up on pillows stuffed with wool.

"Æthelburg."

Ine's lips are ready to shape her name, but the voice is not his. Cenred is staring at her and, with one crooked finger, beckons her inside. "Father," Ine begins, but something seems to pass between the two men and her husband steps back. Oddly formal, he says, "I think he would like to speak with you alone."

There is an urgency in her to tell Ine what she saw, to wrest the truth of the bone knife from him, but Cenred does not look well. Æthel shivers as her earlier thoughts creep back. *Could* his illness have passed to his son? So she enters the little house, aware of the heartbeat that hasn't entirely slowed. The tips of her fingers are numb and she curls them into her palms. The loss of mind is something she does not know how to fight.

"Are you thirsty, Father?" she asks, recalling how the term once pleased him. Unlike the rest of the court, Cenred has never commented on her suitability as queen. Perhaps his illness has sheltered him from the knives that grind ever sharper during her absences. He does not answer, but lets her drip a few mouthfuls of ale between his lips. Æthel returns the jug to the table and sits beside his bed. His hand, once strong and sure, is uncertain now, lying on the blanket in a half-curl like a question. She forces herself to take it. The skin is dry, warm against her own cold and clammy palm.

Immediately his grip tightens, and Æthel gasps. He is strong; stronger than he should be. With a sudden yank, he pulls her down so that her ear rests against his lips.

"Watch out for my son."

Æthel struggles up in time to see the clarity fade from his eyes. "Of course I will," she assures him, unnerved. "He is my husband." *Even if he does not care to be.*

Cenred's brow creases. He opens his mouth, but the brief light in him is gone. His fingers loosen, and Æthel reclaims her hand, rubbing it distractedly, before leaving Ine's father to his troubled rest.

It is not until the following dawn, when grave-faced servants come knocking at their chamber door, that she learns she was the last person to see the old man alive.

19

INE

Wiltun, Wiltunscir
Kingdom of Wessex

The council table has eight marks burned into it—one for each of his fingers. His thumbprints are less visible, hidden beneath its lip of wood. Ine remembers a hissing in his ears as the anger he felt at Ingild boiled through him, ending at his fingertips. And here is the evidence; not just of his emotion, but of his heresy, as the bishop would call it. The way Hædde stared at his hands as they gripped the table's edge—was that worry for his king, or suspicion? In his panicked state, Ine is inclined to think the latter.

Sending everyone away before they saw had meant sending Æthelburg away too, and he cannot forget her narrow-eyed look of betrayal as she stalked from the room, especially after his losing the bone knife. *Destroying,* a voice in his head amends and he swallows hard, recalling the voices that cried from the heart of the weapon. For an instant, he had felt them in their agony. But how can he tell Æthel that, or the Witan? Silence, however, meant condemning his wife in front of Ingild, and the truth of it is a poisoned shaft in his heart.

The marks show no sign of fading. Taking a deep breath, Ine lays his hands back over them and pauses. *You cannot wish them away,* he tells himself harshly. Who does he think he is—Myrdhin the magician? A scornful laugh escapes as he parts his fingers. The marks are still visible, of course.

That shaft buried in his chest has split it open, and anger froths beneath. Has it always been there, long contained by the excuses he has made to himself? Perhaps by suppressing it, he has given it strength, and now it has him in its grip. Ine raises his fist and brings it down hard on the marks.

With the *clap* of a sudden summer storm, the table cracks.

Aghast, he stumbles back as the halves collapse against each other. The resinous smell of wood is thick in his nostrils, and the anger, so fierce a moment ago, wisps to nothing. Just as it did in tonight's council. Just as it did that evening on the riverbank with Emrys. What if it isn't anger at all?

It is why the power in you is so volatile.

The door crashes open. Gweir and Leofric barrel inside. Gweir takes one look at the table, and Ine is sure he knows what happened. "Lord, are you hurt?"

Ine shakes his head and watches, dread-filled, as Leofric bends to examine the break. "Clean," the gesith muses, "and straight as the Romans' old road." He rises to his feet. "Must have been a fault through the wood. I will arrange to have it carted away."

"Ask the carpenters to come here. It is not above mending." *The fewer who see it, the better.*

Leofric frowns. "Then where are we to assemble in the meantime?"

"I heard a council was called only this evening," Gweir says with an edge to his voice. His hair is mussed, cheeks flushed, as if he has been running. "Surely the Witan will not need to convene again so soon."

Finally, Leofric nods. "I will see to it."

Gweir falls to one knee the moment he is gone. "I am sorry, lord. I heard what happened. The meeting would not have gone so badly if I had been there. But I had no choice."

"Stand up, Gweir." Ine offers him a tired hand. Whatever just happened with the table has drained him. "Tell me everything."

"It's Cadwy," the gesith says immediately on regaining his feet. "I think someone tried to kill him. The men on guard tonight were not the ones I assigned. His door was open and the two were in there with him, armed."

They will come for him. The scop's voice will not leave Ine alone. Years have passed since he last found himself locked in the violent embrace of a shield wall, but he remembers the giving and gaining of ground. The strain of holding up their wooden defiance, the horror of treading on those who had fallen. That is what he feels now: an echo of the sick struggle for dominance. And just as he did then, he has only glimpses of the enemy. Otherwise, it is a faceless force surging against him. Faceless except—"Do you think Ingild was behind it?"

Gweir's anger is clearly a helpless one. "Who else could it be, lord? But I have no *proof.*" He spits the word. "God knows what would have happened if I had not been keeping half an eye on the boy. I stood guard over him myself until my men could be found." His jaw clenches. "They believed *I* gave the order to stand down."

"Until they, until—" Ine forces himself to voice it—"*Ingild* comes out of the shadows, how am I to move against him?"

"By then, it will be too late," Gweir says bleakly. "You must find a way to remove him from court. Disrupt his influence."

He drags a hand through his hair. Is his brother truly prepared to kill for the throne of Wessex? Ingild has always been content in his position as ætheling, or so Ine thought. Something has changed. His gaze falls on the broken table; the rift in the wood is too like the one growing in the Witan. Too like the rift opening between Æthel and himself.

He looks away. "Come. We will check on Cadwy before I see my father."

Gweir lowers his voice as they move outside. "Have you considered sharing what Emrys told you with Cadwy? He understands the Dumnonian birthright, respects the old ways and would do anything to protect them. He could help you."

"But he believes he is heir." The late-summer dusk seems very dark.

"Yes," Gweir concedes. "He will require proof."

"How? Whatever this is, I cannot control it. And Hædde was

staring at me." Ine grimaces. "He already suspects. What if it happens again, right in front of him?"

"You are the king," Gweir says after a long silence. The mournful cry of an owl echoes behind them and shapes swoop overhead. "He cannot easily accuse you of anything, let alone of being a heathen."

Cadwy's prison is comfortable, but comfortable or not, it is still a prison—and he and Ine both know it. "Horseshoe," Gweir says bizarrely to the men standing guard at the door, who nod and step aside without comment. To Ine's raised brow, he murmurs, "Since they believed the order to abandon their posts came from me, from now on, if someone who looks like me cannot give them the correct word, they are not to let them pass."

Ine stares at him. "Someone who looks like you?"

"I heard Nothhelm and Leofric discussing the queen's report," Gweir says darkly. "If the dead walk, we may face other dangers."

Ine detects no amusement in the words and feels a rush of gratitude. He places a hand on Gweir's shoulder. "Thank you. You are a true friend."

"You mean a loyal Saxon hound," a voice says from within. Cadwy is sitting on his straw pallet, elbows on knees, but he rises when they enter. His eyes are red-rimmed. He looks older, Ine thinks with a pang. Grief and anger have worn tracks in his face. He cannot be called a boy any longer.

"There were men here," Ine says without preamble. The hut is sparse, containing only a table, chair and a shelf in addition to the pallet. "They did not harm you?"

Cadwy folds his arms, attempting defiance. "Would you care?"

"I would care very much." Ine sits, hoping to put him more at ease, but Geraint's son remains standing. "Cadwy. What do you know of wights?"

Various emotions flash across his face; he has not yet learned to master it. "Did you come to check on me or interrogate me?"

Ine winces at the truth of that. "I truly am glad to find you unharmed. But—" *a dead man watches me from the shadows*— "Æthelburg says a wight is behind the killings of the Britons."

"Then it is as bad as Father feared." Fresh anger balls his hands into fists. "Do you think it will be content with our blood? The dead come back hungry. The killing will spread."

"Then *help* me," Ine says, leaning forward, remembering Geraint's conviction. "Your father believed that this was larger than us. Larger than our rivalry."

As expected, Cadwy presses his lips together in furious hurt. His voice, when it comes, is cold. "He was a good man. He always put his people first."

"He was a good man. He even warned me about the Wild Hunt that night. The least I can do is resume his search for answers." Ine pauses before adding softly, "The least I can do is protect his son."

Cadwy opens his mouth, closes it. Gweir advised discussing the Dumnonian birthright, but looking at the baleful shimmer in Cadwy's eyes, Ine cannot bring himself to do so. His fists ache with the memory of smashing the table. *Does Cadwy really believe he can defend his home with this power?* All it has done so far is destroy.

"You ask me to help you," Cadwy says eventually, "but you will not help me."

"I already—"

"It is not enough." The prince lifts his chin. He may not have his father's look, but his resemblance to Geraint in that moment is striking. "You will free me."

Ine exchanges a glance with Gweir. The gesith nods slightly, but he is not the one shouldering the consequences of such an action. Allowing the prince of Dumnonia to walk free—return to his people, perhaps raise an army—is tantamount to treason. Ine swallows. "If I agree to this," he begins and Cadwy's mouth falls open. "*If* I agree, you will let me choose the time and means. You will keep to the truce I agreed with your father. You will share any knowledge you have on wights." Ine hesitates. *Do I really want to know this?* "And," he adds tensely, "you will tell me everything you know about the Dumnonian birthright."

From slack and surprised, Cadwy's face hardens. "That does not concern you."

"And yet," Ine says, speaking the same words he did to Geraint in Gifle, "those are my terms."

He is certain he has gone too far when Cadwy turns away. He might be a prince, but a prince of few winters, who watched his father bleed out in front of him. Threatened with death, taken by the enemy. Ine can well imagine the sorts of stories the Britons tell about his people; Cadwy would have grown up hearing them. But someone also ensured he learned Englisc. Why teach him the Saxon tongue if only war with Saxons awaited? So Ine says nothing, giving him time to consider.

Although the anger has not left Cadwy's face when he turns back, something new has joined it: a grim sort of determination. In another echo of that meeting with Geraint, he holds out his hand and Ine does too, and they clasp forearms. Cadwy lets go swiftly. "I do this for my people, who need me."

"As I do for mine."

"I have a name for you, then." Fear stiffens Cadwy's shoulders. He even rakes the small room, although there are no possible witnesses. "You asked about wights. I know of only one person who can bring people back from the dead." His voice drops to a whisper. "He is King of the Otherworld. His name is Gwyn ap Nudd."

Ine's dreams that night are ripples on a lake; there and gone in moments. *Gwyn ap Nudd.* The name is beginning to haunt him, yet he is no closer to understanding. According to Cadwy, Glestingaburg hides a gate to the Otherworld, and the killings drove Geraint to seek it. Despite it being the home of Herla and the Wild Hunt. Despite it lying within Saxon lands. A fool's errand, the lords of Dintagel had told him, and so it turned out to be; he had lost his life in pursuit of it. Why would Ine fare any better?

Herla. The Wild Hunt are Æthel's riders—he is certain of it now. They had been there the night of Geraint's death. Were they a part of this too?

The questions must have chased him eventually into a deeper sleep because the next thing Ine knows is that he is being shaken awake. Æthel's face is stark against a dim dawn. He blinks the mist from his eyes. They share a bed, but she has made a point of not being awake in it whenever he is. If Ine is honest with himself, *he* has made a point of it too. Finding her here now is bewildering. "Æthel. What's wrong?"

"It's Cenred." Her cheeks are pale. "I'm so sorry, Ine."

For a second, he simply stares at her. Then it feels as if a fist clenches in his stomach. "Father...is dead?"

When she nods, he hears himself say, "But he was fine." His tone is oddly inflectionless. "Were you not with him?"

"Ine." Her voice catches. "The last thing he said...he wanted me to watch out for you."

My father is dead. He pushes himself up. Numbness is spreading from his belly to his arms and legs. Every breath he takes is shallow. *You knew he was ill,* Ine tells himself, but the words do not mean anything. All he can think of, oddly, is the time he fell from his horse when the animal spooked at a fox in the grass. Cenred's big hand held his while his leg was poulticed, just as it held Ingild's the day their mother died. "I need to see him."

"They have moved him to the crypt," Æthel says, rising. "It is cooler there."

Nothing about the fact would have disturbed him before, but now Ine feels cold at the thought of his father in that stone space. *Once, our people burned beneath the gaze of Woden.* Pyres hung with burnished rings, weapons kept sharp, the treasure of kings. Not that his father followed pagan ways. He just cannot imagine him laid in the earth, patiently awaiting Heaven. "I must send word to my sisters," he says hollowly.

Seeing he has not moved, Æthel fetches his clothes. "I will do it."

Ine forces himself to dress, pushing his arms into sleeves that feel too tight. He stabs his thumb several times with the cloak pin, a wyvern of twisted gold. The sight of his own blood burns off a little of the mist and, when he finds his feet, they are steadier than he expected. News of his father has spread. "My condolences," someone says when he emerges into the mead hall, but Ine does not spare a glance as he walks through.

The numbness, which he supposes is grief, is even strong enough to handle the sight of Hædde without flinching. For once, the bishop seems as conciliatory as he appears, hands clasped, adorned in black cloth. "Down here, lord."

The air loses its warmth the further he descends. At the bottom of the stone steps is a long, low chamber, not too dissimilar to how he imagines the burial mounds of old, although this crypt is modelled after Wilfred's at Hestaldesige. The walls are inscribed with various names and dates, and lids shelter the bones of long-dead clergy. "I want some time alone with him," Ine says. "Leave me." It is the shortest he has been with Hædde; the bishop's eyes narrow as he goes.

In the corner of the crypt is a stone bier. His father could be sleeping, save that no man sleeps with such an expression. Ine stops breathing. Leaning over, he touches a fingertip to the corner of Cenred's mouth, pulled into a grimace that death has fixed in place. The muscles are stiff. To think his father will wear this grim face for eternity…it is more than Ine can bear.

A sob escapes him. As if the sound has stolen his strength, he finds himself sinking to the side of the bier. Pain as his knees hit stone. He rests his forehead against the unyielding rock, so that he cannot see Cenred's expression. He must have suffered at the end.

It is only kneeling that he spies it: blood beneath his father's nails. Ine frowns. Perhaps Cenred scratched himself in his delirium, but there are no corresponding marks on his arms. No obvious marks at all.

"Brother."

So absorbed is he in the mystery, disturbed by it even, that he jumps at Ingild's voice and stumbles gracelessly to his feet. Ingild wears long sleeves against the chill of the crypt, and his cloak is pinned sloppily, as if in a hurry. "I came as soon as I heard."

Ine studies him, saying nothing until Ingild sighs. "I know what you are thinking." He circles the bier to stand on the other side. "That Father's death means nothing to me. That I am even glad of it." They are bitter words. "It is true we never saw eye to eye.

You were always his favourite. I can't say it wasn't difficult for me." When Ine opens his mouth, Ingild forestalls him. "No point denying it to save my feelings." He lays a hand on Cenred's chest. "He was still my father and I will grieve that his death makes orphans of us."

Ingild seems genuine, but Ine has never been very good at reading his brother. And, as much as it troubles him to admit it, Ingild's words are fair. As the eldest son, destined to be king, Cenred had spent more time with him than any other of his children.

"This place…" Ingild swallows audibly. "It brings memories to mind." He looks away from Ine to gaze instead at the dark stone wall. "This was the last roof she lay under. And I remember thinking, what use is a god who lets a woman with nothing but good in her heart perish—and her child with her?"

According to Æthelburg, Ingild only valued Frigyth for her ability to give him another son. His firstborn, Eoppa, is a frail boy. Ine has always dismissed that cruel assumption, but after yesterday's conversation with Gweir, he is learning to see Ingild in a new and unpleasant light. Perhaps Æthel was right. He looks from Cenred's contorted face to Ingild's carefully arranged one. Even if their father neglected Ingild, surely he deserved more in his final days than his son's scorn. "I don't think God has much to do with it—or us," he says.

"No, you are right." Ingild's eyes glitter. "Better to trust in the powers we know, than in the promise of one we do not."

All at once, the crypt is cramped, suffocating, the peace he expected to find here absent. Instead his mind shows him the wheat, the skulls, the giant. *The Land,* Emrys said. At least the wheat has stopped its mad growth, and has ensured that no one in Wessex will starve this winter, but neither fact brings Ine relief. *Powers we know?* How much has Ingild seen? He is reminded of the tread outside the door the night he raced through their histories searching for proof of his heritage.

"Strange that Father died so suddenly," Ingild remarks as they take the steps to the nave, "when his decline has been slow."

"What do you mean?"

"Wasn't your wife the last person to see him alive?"

Ine stops walking. After the gloom of the crypt, the church is bright, its stained glass a brilliance on the flagstones. There is an edge to his voice when he says, "What are you implying, Ingild? Æthelburg has shown Father nothing but kindness."

"And isn't it a kindness to end suffering?" Ingild spreads his hands. "Do not tell me the expression on his face was of a man who passed at peace."

True, his father had not passed peacefully, but to think *Æthel* had anything to do with it…no, he cannot believe that. He *will not* believe it. For Ingild even to suggest—"You go too far." When Ine resumes walking, his pace is much faster, and a cold sweat has broken out all over his body. "Even if it *was* to end suffering, I do not believe Æthelburg capable of such a thing."

"Oh, brother." There is a thick streak of pity in Ingild's voice. "You have no idea what she is capable of. You have not fought beside her in many years. Writing laws has kept you cosseted, while *she* spills the blood that would otherwise threaten those laws."

How does Ingild know exactly what to say to rob him of response? Again, Ine finds his throat dry. Yes, he has not battled alongside Æthelburg since the days they were first married, when he was newly crowned and eager to prove himself—to her and to Wessex. As the years passed, he came to believe that warfare and killing did not solve the problems they promised to. Now, with the sweat and the church both chilling him, Ine realizes that Æthelburg gave him the luxury to believe it. What has it been like for her—to wield the sword he disdains? *What*, he worries, *has it done to her? To us?* Cenred's grimace lingers behind his eyes. *What might it drive her to do?*

He is disgusted as soon as he thinks it. He is disgusted that Ingild has grasped something so important about his wife. How has he drifted so far from her? Beneath the sorrow for his father, the loneliness of that truth eats away at him.

Ine is still brooding on it when he breaks his fast. Although the bread tastes like ashes, he outright gags on the milk and honey the servants bring him. "What is it?" Leofric asks just as Ine manages to spit his mouthful back into the cup.

"Urgh." He drags the sleeve of his tunic across his lips. "How long has that been sitting?"

"It was fresh this morning." The nearest servant looks into the jug and his face pales. "I am deeply sorry, lord. I will fetch more."

But the other jugs are the same. "And so are the cows," Leofric reports when he returns from the milking shed, the crows' feet at the corners of his eyes creased with worry. "It must be sickness, lord."

"Safest to slaughter them then." Nothhelm prods the jug with a revolted finger. "Glad I only drink ale at breakfast."

"Killing them before we know what's caused this seems unwise." Ine winces. "And expensive. This is a whole herd."

"It is quite obvious what has caused it," comes a voice: Hædde stands behind them. He moves softly for a large man. "I fear Nothhelm king is right. The cows have been touched by the heathen powers that poison this town. It is not the doing of any mortal sickness."

Ine notes uneasily that where the gesiths would once have laughed, they now greet the pronouncement in silence. "I told you, Ine king, that the wheat was only the beginning," Hædde continues, the hard light of vindication in his face. "That it would grow worse."

"At least the wheat was a positive thing." *Too defensive.* "This is ruinous."

"You have hit upon the very danger of paganism. It is often fair of face, just as the Devil lures with promises of wealth and plenty. But turn those promises over and you will see the rot beneath." Hædde pauses. "The scop is not the only heathen in our midst. You are actively sheltering another—Geraint's son."

Slamming both hands to the tabletop, Ine rises and rounds on him. "Firstly—" he holds up a finger—"I am not slaughtering an entire herd of cattle. Secondly, how can a single boy be responsible? He is under constant guard."

"He is not under constant watch, however." The bishop shakes his head, as if at a particularly stupid child. "He does not have to touch the animals to sour their milk. There are spells, charms—"

"The Britons are not responsible for this." Heads turn. "Æthelburg laid her case before the Witan. I saw the knife she found at Sceaptun. I saw…" He chokes back the spectre of Cædwalla. "If there are heathen powers at work, they are not in league with *any* human at all."

Ine knows he has erred when Hædde says, "You entertain things no God-fearing king should suffer, lord. I urge you to guard your mind against the intrusion of such thoughts."

"And I urge you to guard your tongue, bishop." Anger pulses beneath his skin, fighting to escape. "I allow you to speak freely, but that does not extend to issuing demands to my face."

I could destroy him.

The force inside Ine is quick and hot, and the words take root; the spark of an idea igniting into a plan. Staring at Hædde's thin, frowning mouth, he wants nothing more than to raise a hand and—

He stops, doused in a sudden chill. He wants to *what?* Hædde has always been an ally, a worthy adviser. Ine has known him all his life. This anger, new-awoken in his blood, is a pagan power. It would naturally lash out at men of God. But the words are said. And he sees the harm they have done in the lowering of the bishop's head, the stiff retreat as he turns church-ward.

"I will pray for you, my king," Hædde says without looking at him. "I will pray for all of Wessex."

The weather cools, which is for the best as far as Cenred's body is concerned. Hidden beneath a shroud, it waits in the crypt while above Ine waits for his sisters. It is a cloudy afternoon in Haligmonath, holy month, when two horses, surrounded by a dozen armed men, trot through the gates of Wiltun. The leaves are bursting into flame, and the plains beyond the town are sere in the wake of summer. Ine stands on the steps to the hall, forehead banded by the crown of the kings of Wessex. It is not an ornament he wears every day, but now that his sisters are here, the funeral will be held tonight, and he will appear as tradition demands.

Æthelburg stands beside him, clad in a dark dress belted with gold. Fish-shaped earrings glimmer in her ears and a torc wraps her throat. Her hair has grown to her shoulders, longer than she usually wears it. Watching her fiddle distastefully with the strands reminds him of the day he found her, not long after they were married, sitting amidst a pile of blonde, joyfully cutting it off. "You don't mind, do you?" she asked, pausing with shears in hand. "I hated it, but my father said I had to keep it long."

"Of course not," he answered, amused, "it's your hair," and she had gaily resumed the work that would have caused some noble women to faint clean away. It is a happy memory, at odds with the sombre day and the sombre feeling that has grown between them. She has not said anything more of separating, but her distance speaks for her. Perhaps he will have to make the first move. *Foolish*—of course he must. Ine's stomach churns miserably at the thought.

"Brother," Cuthburh says in her brisk manner, as if they have only been apart a season instead of five long years. She offers her cheek perfunctorily for a kiss. "Despite the occasion, it is good to be home."

Cwenburh drifts behind, her large eyes having lost none of their mistiness. In fact she looks more ethereal than ever, clad in a nun's habit with a creamy linen veil over her hair. "Ine," she murmurs. "Æthelburg." Her eyes sharpen as she takes in the too-wide distance between them. There will be questions, Ine knows, but she will not ask them in the way of most people.

"I was sorry to hear of Aldfrith's death," he says to Cuthburh. "He was a good man. A good king."

"Yes." She straightens her own habit matter-of-factly. "We reached an understanding and parted before he passed. I was fortunate to have a pious husband. We continued the Lord's work in our own ways."

"And what of your son while you've been with Hildelith at the abbey? I heard there was some trouble with an upstart."

His sister waves a hand, as if they are not discussing the Northumbrian crown stolen from her own son. "Osred is restored. As king, he needs advisers, not a mother. I have more important work to do. On that note, we need to speak. After the funeral, of course."

Ine swallows a smile. *Poor boy.* Unlike her sister's, Cuthburh's eyes have always been focused on the here and now—and how to make the most of both.

Ine is glad when the funeral is over and his father safely interred. Neither of his sisters had requested to see Cenred, thank God. His father's decaying grimace haunts him.

"How did it happen?" Cwenburh asks. She, Cuthburh, Ine and Ingild are sitting in a pocket of quiet at the top of the hall. Naturally, mead is flowing, as the court toasts their father, the older men regaling the others with stories of Cenred in his prime.

Æthel is absent. "You will want time with your family," she said, sweeping off before Ine could tell her *she* was his family. One flash of her icy eyes and the words would have stuck in his throat anyway. Heavy-hearted, he picks at the funeral feast, sinking his knife into the meat and watching its juices run out. He can feel Cuthburh glowering at him.

"Father had been ailing." Ablaze with golden jewellery, Ingild looks every inch a hero-king. Ine's finery consists of his crown, signet ring and the arm ring Cenred gave him. He feels extremely unadorned in comparison, and knows his sisters are thinking the same. "Brother insisted on his coming to council, however," Ingild continues. "No doubt the stress of it worsened his illness."

"Father deserved a voice in the Witan." Ine's tone is sharp enough to cut through the nearest chatter. "He expressed a desire to be involved in matters of state right up to the end."

"He had the mind of a child," Ingild retorts. "How could he have expressed any such desire?"

"You ignored him." Ine finds his fist curled, remembers the incident with the table and hastily uncurls it. "His mind may have been stricken, but his will never faltered."

"As you can see, sisters," Ingild says with a silky, regretful sigh. "Father is a subject on which Ine and I cannot agree." He pauses. "I admit there may be some ill will on my part because he favoured Ine so."

"Of course he did." Cuthburh redirects some of her disapproval. "Father's time was taken up instructing him. That is the way of things, Ingild. You are quite old enough to understand."

Cwenburh places a restraining hand on her sister's arm. "It cannot have been easy for Ingild, after Frigyth. Have you considered remarrying?"

Ingild shakes his head. "I do not think I could love and maybe lose again. At least I am blessed with a son."

The statement summons an awkward silence. Even Cuthburh, never short of opinions, does not break it. So it's left to Cwenburh to ask, "How is Æthelburg, brother? I expected her to join us."

"She says she wanted to give us time alone," Ine mutters, avoiding her eyes. "To tell you the truth, there have been…worrying developments in the kingdom. Æthel has much on her mind."

"Do not fill our sisters' heads with this nonsense." Ingild skewers a chunk of meat, gestures dismissively with it. "All Ine means is that the Wealas are killing each other and making up stories to slander us, as usual." Ine opens his mouth to protest, but Ingild forestalls him. "We have been over this many times. It bores me and I guarantee it will bore our sisters. We should be toasting Father like the rest of the court."

None of them can argue with that. Ine raises his beaten silver cup only to see the wine in it trembling. His body is seized with a too-familiar cold, every hair on end. Stiffly, as if he is becoming ice himself, he turns his head.

The wight stands in the shadow cast by one of the great pillars that hold up the roof. His garments are dark with grave-dust, and dull gold sits heavy on his brow. Two facts strike Ine at once. The first, that this is not Cædwalla. The second, that he recognizes the features set close together on the man's broad face, although Ine was just a boy at the time he died. He cannot stop the name forming in his mind. *Centwine.*

People avoid the place where the erstwhile king is standing. It seems only Ine can see his eyes, as chill and depthless as Cædwalla's, flicker disdainfully across the hall. He has but to reach out a hand and all those here will join him in death.

"...will you say something?"

Ine blinks, the wight is gone and Cuthburh is speaking his name. "Ine, did you hear me? Will you lead us in a toast?"

He turns to see his sisters wearing twin frowns. Ingild has one brow raised. "Of course," Ine stammers, hoping they mistake the cold sweat on his forehead for the more common type. "Of course."

But the words will not come. In the end, Ingild has to step up, much to the hall's confusion, and give the tribute to his father that Ine should have spoken.

20

꒭ERLA

Glestingaburg, Somersæte
Kingdom of Wessex

"I am going alone."

"No." Arms outstretched, Corraidhín blocks her path to the door. Herla tries to duck around, but a spear appears in her friend's hand and knocks her back.

"Corra." It comes out as a growl. "This is ridiculous. Let me pass."

"What is ridiculous is your desire to do everything yourself. We are your sisters-in-arms, your blood. We want to help."

"I hardly need your help to face one wight."

"It is not about the wight," Senua says softly. "You walked amongst people, spoke to them. We want to do the same."

"And look what nearly happened." Herla shakes her head. "I have already said I cannot go back. None of us can."

"But…"

She holds up a hand and Senua's mouth snaps shut. It never used to. Her battle sisters would once have deafened her with indignation until she laughed and threw an arm around the nearest pair of shoulders. They would have gone together. Now they fall silent at the mere raising of her hand. Herla grimaces. She is Lord of the Hunt, and they are her hunters. Why should she be surprised?

Her time with Æthelburg has distracted her, upended her, made her think *something* could be again when it cannot. Herla stares at their faces. Only Orlaith's still appears faintly outraged. "You came with me once," she reminds them in a hard voice. "Are you so eager to do it again?"

It is Corraidhín who breaks the uncomfortable silence that follows. "A compromise, Herla. Take me. I will be your lookout." But her voice has lost its fire.

They leave after dark, whispers in the larger blackness. Two handfuls of miles to Sceaptun, and the barrow in which she sealed the wight. They pass through the sleeping village, peaceful now, and Corraidhín drinks it in: everything from the squat square houses with their roofs that slope earthwards to the rutted road, beginning to soften under the rains. Her lips are parted, face pale, and Herla wonders whether *she* looked like that on her first morning in Wiltun. Finding the mundane profound, as if a fresh-baked loaf or stinking straw contained the deepest mysteries. Only now is she awakening to the truth that she has not put the hunter behind her. Watching Æthelburg as she bathed, raking her body with her eyes, touching her so boldly...Herla hunted the queen as she had hunted the spy, as if she had the *right*. As if Æthelburg were nothing more than prey to be seized.

Disgust at herself spreads through her like poison. *Gwyn made me an animal, a mindless predator, and that is how I behaved. It is what I am.*

"I sense the wight."

Corraidhín's words arrest her, but they do not chase away the disgust, or the pain of wanting Æthelburg despite everything. It is in Herla's voice when she growls, "Stay here and keep watch."

Her friend catches her arm. "If Gwyn is behind this, how will you avoid alerting him?"

"Gwyn is not here. He must have loaned his power to Alis."

"The servant girl?"

Herla nods. "If we are fortunate, she will not feel it when I free Cædwalla's soul."

Corraidhín looks askance at her. She knows that destroying the binding means adding the soul to the tally that weighs so heavily on Herla's spirit. Every day, it is worse. The voices are louder; she has the sense of a great wave threatening to crash over her. But what choice do they have? *I cannot give you peace, Cædwalla,* Herla thinks, as she urges her horse up the hill. *He did not make me that way.*

"*You appear different,*" Cædwalla says when she lifts her seal on the barrow. He rises adorned with iron and gold, as if from a throne. "*In any case, I know you now, Hunt Lord. Should you not be riding?*"

"Should you not be sleeping?" Herla asks coldly. "You have had your time."

"*And so you have come to put me down?*" Although Cædwalla's words are scornful, she can sense the fear in him. "*I am not done with this world.*"

"You are a puppet, nothing more. Do not tell me you have free will."

The dead king laughs. "*You would know. Lord of the Hunt? You are lord of nothing, Herla. Whose strings do you dance on?*"

Rage surges into her; she bares her teeth. "It is not the chief of Annwn who gives you your orders, is it?" The metal of the wight's sword has an oily, eerie sheen in the darkness. "Alis must be working with someone in Wessex. Who?"

"*Irrelevant. You will not stop what is to come.*"

Herla's eyes widen. Her hand strays to the sword at her waist. "What is to come?"

"*You have played your part in it.*" Cædwalla smiles, an awful rictus, and draws his own blade. "*You cannot change that.*"

Gwyn's sword sings in response, harsh and low. "I already have," Herla says. She raises it over her head.

"How inconvenient."

Herla stops breathing. The voice came from behind her—from the path Corraidhín is guarding. And yet she has had no warning. The only thing holding dread at bay is the fact she can still feel the other woman somewhere below. Their bond is as strong as ever.

Slowly, as if her limbs are caught in dream, she lowers the sword and turns.

He sits on a tree stump, incongruously at ease. The bones in his face are as fine as she remembers, the silver sheen to his skin dimmed only by the fact he is not truly here. Every newly recovered emotion crashes into Herla at once. She is a leaf in a gale. Relief, remorse, revulsion, fear; a storm wind tearing the walls of her self apart. But there is fury too, and she grasps for its familiar hand.

Something *tugs*, and she glances down to see the black blade straining towards the one who gifted it. Gwyn ap Nudd recoils. It is that small movement which gives Herla the courage to say, "Do you not want it back?"

He recovers quickly. "It was a gift. It would be rude to take it back." An instant to look her over. His eyes are like sunlight on the surface of a lake. Before, she had been dazzled by the ripples. Now she glimpses what lies beneath in the dim undertow. "Hello, Herla. You were not so eloquent when last we met."

"Surprised?"

"Somewhat," he admits, rising from the stump. Herla holds her ground while every instinct screams at her to run. Dust and death, the first wild ride where her tongue shaped nothing but savage shrieks. Shuddering, she tries to master herself—but which self? The woman doomed by pride and ambition is hidden beneath the hunter. She does not want either of them.

When Gwyn whistles, Dormach slinks out of the trees, belly dragging. The King of Annwn's face is cold. "You failed me," he says, as if to a person. "Are the mortals of Dumnonia really so potent?"

Herla recalls the golden light sweeping towards her like a fisherman's net cast wide, how Gwyn's sword tried to flee. What exactly had happened in the second before Dormach's paws struck earth? It had been strong enough to weaken the curse, to challenge Annwn itself. If this is the power of the Dumnonian birthright, no wonder Gwyn seeks to smother every trace of it.

She catches her breath. In Scirburne, the Briton had claimed that only the king could commune with the land. But if the king—Geraint—is dead, who holds that power now? Could it have passed to another the night he died…to the son Æthelburg had saved, perhaps? Herla strives to keep her face blank. *If Gwyn finds the boy, it will be over.* Her own power comes from Annwn; she is under no illusions that she can win against Gwyn unaided. Nor does defeating him necessarily mean the end of the curse. A bleak expanse opens before Herla, like the marsh of her homeland in winter. Will she learn to fear the moon? A battle every month for her soul, until one day she lacks the strength to fight and the curse reclaims her?

"I am not ungrateful." Gwyn takes a slow walk around her; she turns to keep him in sight. "You freed me from an irksome duty. You are the single most important part of the dream I have had for so very long." He stops in front of her. "Surely there is something I can offer you, Herla."

"You think I will bargain with you again? You are as wild as the stories say."

Anger flashes across his face and disappears. "Not even the Queen of Wessex?"

Herla cannot help it: she flinches. "You speak nonsense." But Gwyn's eyes have brightened.

"I have always been able to see your heart, Herla, and it has not changed." He pauses, drawing out the moment. "You wish to watch her wither and die, while you remain as you are?"

Does he know how much those words wound her? *Of course,* Herla thinks, while the heart Gwyn can see quite plainly aches. There is a keen, sunlit place inside her that she has forgotten about, and despite her vow to leave Æthelburg alone, a future has been growing there, though the soil is poor. *A doomed future,* Herla realizes now. The queen is mortal; she will grow old just as Gwyn says. She will die. Perhaps on a battlefield, clothed in her own blood. Perhaps as an old woman, in Herla's arms.

She thrusts the image away so violently she almost stumbles. The King of Annwn is watching her, no doubt feeding on the pain he has caused. Just for an instant, Herla yearns for the skins of the hunter, to wrap herself in uncaring brutality. A hunter does not feel pain. "Such is the fate of all humans," she says.

"As you know, it need not be."

"I paid too high a price for my immortality."

"Yes," Gwyn says and there is no trace of mockery in his silken voice. "Which is why I offer you this freely."

Herla laughs, a bitter broken sound. "Nothing you offer is free."

"You shall have your queen. You shall even have your liberty. As long as you stay out of my affairs. As long as you continue to ride at the old moon, to wield the sword and lead the Hunt."

She cannot hide the fierce *wanting* that rises inside her. In the place where a future has grown, Gwyn's offer is water seeping into parched earth. *He is false,* Herla tells herself harshly. *You cannot trust him.* When the urge to ride overtook her, had she not fought against it and won? She can fight this desire too. But it is not the same. Fighting against something she does not want is one thing. Fighting against something she desperately wants is quite another.

She regards Gwyn unspeaking, as if she truly is considering his offer. *Are you not truly considering it?* The King of Annwn even starts to smile before she asks, "What irksome duty?"

His smile is gone. More than gone—eaten up by an emotion so strong that the air around him shivers. For an instant, Herla glimpses the towers of Caer Sidi, their flags stirred by the capricious Otherworld wind. It is disorienting to see him lose control, but it does not last long. In another instant, the air quietens, the vision vanishes, and the brief sense of fear is lost in Gwyn's laugh. "Consider it, Herla. My offer will not remain open forever. If you think I cannot bind you again, strip you of will and language, you are wrong."

Gwyn ap Nudd vanishes before she can utter a word. Herla does not know what that word might have been. She is paralysed by the thought of returning to the mindless cycle of sleep–hunt–sleep. And she is reeling with his offer: a life. *Almost* a life. Trembling, Herla turns to the wight, but the barrow is empty. Cædwalla too is gone.

She wants to curl up. She wants to ride and keep on riding until she finds herself back where it all began. She will fall at

Boudica's feet. She will ask her queen to kill the traitor kneeling before her before she can do more harm.

Instead Herla screams at the sky. It pierces the night, waking the people of Sceaptun. When Corraidhín finds her, she is standing with Gwyn's sword in her hand, the stump where he sat cleaved fully in two. "Hear me, Corraidhín," she says, her voice sore with her scream. "I vow never to stop fighting, *never*, until this sword rests in the King of Annwn's heart."

21

ÆTHELBURG

**Wiltun, Wiltunscir
Kingdom of Wessex**

"I need to speak with you."

Ine glances up from a missive that has given him a grave face. It is the morning after Cenred's funeral, a greyish prelude to colder days, and Æthel can wait no longer. Refusing to break her self-imposed silence to speak with her husband had cost her both support and credibility. She will not make that mistake again.

And yet the last time they talked alone in this room was the day he offered to dissolve their marriage. *Don't think of that now.* Æthel steels herself. "It is not about…us," she says tightly, hearing an entire world in that word. "I need to speak to you as one ruler to another." The mystery of Ingild and Alis is gnawing under her skin.

"Of course." Ine's nod is as sober as his face when he invites her to sit opposite him. Æthel swallows. It is the same table they have always used. Many a dark winter was spent here, the air warmed by braziers, their bodies by the wine inside them, and the presence of another person so close—

She stops. For the first time in a long while, Æthel hesitates in her anger. She had told Ælfrún that she believed Ine must love someone else. But those evenings cannot all have been pretend. *Ælfrún.* A fluttering in her belly.

"What is it, Æthelburg?" Maybe Ine is remembering too because his eyes are sad. The golden flecks in them seem brighter; she has not noticed until now.

"It's Ingild," she says bluntly.

Ine sighs, unsurprised, but his brother's name has deepened the creases in his brow. "What has he done?"

"I fear it's what he is about to do." Æthel outlines the conversation she overheard. By the time she finishes, Ine's hands are white-knuckled, resting on the table between them. "Although Alis may be more than she seems, she is still a servant and can be dealt with." Æthel nods at him. "Ingild is another matter."

"You mean he is my problem."

"That is exactly what I mean."

Ine blinks at his clenched hands, loosens them. "Gweir believes someone tried to have Cadwy killed. I have no proof it was Ingild, but—"

"Who else can it be?" Æthel exclaims, exasperated. "This is treason, Ine. Dissent against the crown."

"It would be if I had evidence," Ine says, and yet his voice holds that familiar hurt whenever he speaks of Ingild. Æthel has heard it before: guilt. The darker side of pity. She wants to shake him. Ingild will take Ine's pity and strangle him with it. Perhaps she does not understand, having no siblings of her own. But neither is she blinded by whatever dazzles Ine when he looks at his brother.

"Ine, listen. He may be your brother, but he is dangerous. He slew Geraint behind your back. You have seen him in the Witan, and now I—and Gweir—are telling you he is plotting something."

"Yes, he is my brother." Ine's tone sharpens, on the verge of anger. "And ætheling of Wessex. How can I move against him without sufficient proof? As you say, he has supporters in the Witan. Edred, Godric, probably Osberht and certainly now Hædde. *Plotting something* is not enough, Æthel. I…" His wind falters. "If I confront him, he will turn it into an opportunity to accuse me of paranoia. Of losing my mind. You know this."

The retort on her tongue fades too when she recalls Ingild asking, *Are you quite well?* She is aware of Ingild's ability to twist a person's words back upon them. She and Ine have both fallen victim to it. But they must do something.

"Perhaps I *am* mad," Ine says bitterly. "The things I have seen, Æthel." He looks up from his hands. "If not for your testimony about Cædwalla, I would think Ingild right."

Æthel slowly sits back. "What do you mean?"

Ine hesitates. Then his breath leaves him in a rush. "I saw Cædwalla. Here in this hall. And not only him."

She listens, aghast, as he describes the chill coming from the shield and the horrific experience of the dead king walking through him. Then—"There are *two*?" She wraps her arms around herself. "*Centwine* was at the funeral feast?"

"I have not seen Cædwalla for some time," Ine says with a shiver of his own. "Not since you brought news of him from Sceaptun."

Æthel recalls the ragged state he had been in that day. Ine's grip on her arms, his fevered laugh. "You didn't tell me," she says, and they have been here so often that instead of anger, all she feels is grief—at watching something she treasured sinking out of sight.

Ine lays half a hand across his eyes, staring out at her from beneath it. "Æthel, I thought I was seeing things. I haven't been… right since Geraint was killed. If it seems I have not taken the threat of Ingild seriously, this is why. Something worse is happening in Wessex."

"I know. But Ingild is taking advantage of it. He's taking advantage of *you*."

Ine slams down the hand that had covered his eyes; she jumps. "We are stumbling around in the dark. The murder of Britons. The old blood. Gwyn ap Nudd. There must be someone who knows more."

"There is," Æthel says softly. The *someone* is still fluttering in her belly like a trapped moth uncertain of freedom.

"Who?"

She takes a moment to master herself before she answers. "Herla." The name trembles on her lips like the first chord of a song. So much for mastering herself.

Ine stares at her, his expression slack with disbelief. "The leader of the Wild Hunt? Æthel, you cannot be serious. The way Cadwy described her…she seems a force of nature to be feared, not consulted. All she wants is blood."

They have said similar of me, she thinks at him. *That I give no quarter, that battle is all I know.* But how can Æthel compare with the glorious figure on the horse, antlered helm and mane of hair cascading down her back, face tipped in triumph to the stars? How can she compare with the woman who clashed blades with her, who said anyone would be proud to call her wife?

The moment she admits it, Æthel stills, letting that unbelievable truth expand to fill the space inside her. That Herla would disguise herself to avoid attention is not surprising, but why had she come to Wiltun? Heat builds in Æthel's face. Whatever the reason, it must have been important. *And I dragged her along to Lammas with me. I told her about…*She is abruptly aware of Ine watching her, but can do nothing to dispel the colour in her cheeks. As if Herla wanted to hear about the troubles of a spoiled noble. Then why had she followed Æthel to Scirburne? Why had she ridden after her that evening the Wild Hunt called? A part of Æthel is frightened of the answer to those questions. Such answers have the power to change everything.

All she can do is take a breath and try to slow her thundering heart. Surely it is loud enough for him to hear. "She was there when Geraint died." Æthel has no intention of telling him about Ælfrún. *If he can keep secrets, so can I.* "The stories say she sleeps beneath Glestingaburg. But something happened that night. I think she sleeps no longer."

Ine shakes his head, as if *she* is the one who has lost her mind. "And you intend to—what? Ride to Glestingaburg, and ask to see her?"

That is exactly what Æthel is thinking of doing. "Why not?"

"My God, Æthelburg." Ine rises to his feet. "Has all sense left you? A few weeks ago, the Wild Hunt was a story. Now you'll risk your life to seek them out?"

"It is *my* life," she says coldly, rising too. "And I do not believe it is in any danger from Herla."

"But…" His shoulders slump. "I need you here. You are one of the only people I can trust. The only person who tells me I am an utter fool for not seeing the truth when it is staring me in the face."

That pulls at her heartstrings; she cannot pretend otherwise. But one thought is repeating over and over in her head: *I must see her.* Æthel takes a step back, and Ine half reaches out to her. Half reaches. It is always half. "I have said what I came here to say." She turns to go. "I will question Alis. Ingild…do as you see fit. I only hope your pity for him does not condemn us both."

I must see her. The urge grows stronger every hour. But Æthel is afraid too: not for herself if she is wrong about Herla not harming her. She is afraid of the words that might pass between them if she is right. With horror and some awe, she remembers her last afternoon with Ælfrún. Saying what she said, doing what she did—pinning the other woman beneath her, a dagger in the proud hollow of her throat. Consumed by the memory, she reaches into her clothes chest without looking, and her hand touches something wet.

Æthel hisses, jerks back. Blood smears her fingers. There is a crow nestled carefully amongst her things, a puncture wound to its heart leaking red. Her breath comes fast. It is still warm, and the blood on her hand is sticky, no different from blood that has coated her before…except it is. Here, seeping into clothes she puts next to her skin, it is grotesque. A sound escapes her, foreign to her ears: a whimper.

"My lady?" Alis peers over her shoulder and gasps. "What is that?"

"*You.*" Æthel grasps a handful of her dress, slams her unmercifully against the wall. "You did this."

Tears fill her wide green eyes. "What do you mean, lady? You are hurting me."

"Drop the act," Æthel snarls. "I saw you with Ingild. I heard you."

Alis blinks at her a moment longer before she smiles and suddenly Æthel finds herself holding nothing at all. The girl stands smoothing the front of her dress where Æthel's fist had bunched it. "Such violence. So much anger. I can see why she wants you."

"Who...?" Æthel starts before realizing it is a distraction. *How did she free herself?* "No." She draws her knife. "Tell me who you are, what you are doing here."

"Why should I?" Alis's voice has lost its girlish whine. It is older now and lilting. "Send me away, if you like, as you would a servant. But you lack the power to keep me out."

"Oh, I will ensure the guards have orders to slay you on sight."

Alis laughs; beads of glass shattering. "How funny that you think you can harm me."

"I know someone who can." Æthel needs help. *Wessex* needs help. Her knife slips in a palm slick with the crow's blood.

Alis does not spare the weapon a glance. "Herla will not aid you in the way you hope. She is a selfish creature, little queen. She has only ever cared for herself, and the things she wants." Her fey eyes narrow on Æthel's face. "Or my lord would never have been able to trick her."

"Your lord?"

"Oh no." Alis shakes her head. "You have had enough of my time, *my lady*. I suggest you forget what you think you heard. I suggest you take the deal when it is offered to you."

"Deal?" Æthel growls. But Alis simply laughs and turns on her heel. Although Æthel is only seconds behind her when she bursts into the hall, there is no sign of the woman. Instead gasps ring out at the blood on Æthel's hand, curled around a bared length of blade. That puncture to the crow's breast is so like the wound made by the bone knife—*curses*. She had intended to ask Ine about it. Did another exist?

By that evening, crows with heart-wounds have spread across Wiltun like a plague. When cooks open the flour bin, and farriers reach into baskets for nails, their fingers come out red. Feathers drift through the streets.

"Must be something in the water," Cuthburh says dismissively, raising her voice over the other more fanciful whispers that fill the court. She fusses with her wimple in a pompous way that is starting to grate on Æthel. "Or in the air."

Æthel can't hold in a scornful laugh. "Something in the water or the air? Have you *seen* the wounds? I suppose if it rained daggers—"

"There's no need to describe it, Æthelburg."

"Nothing natural would target crows alone," Cwenburh says before Æthel can retort. She shakes her veiled head. "Bishop Hædde has ordered them gathered up to be blessed then burned."

"As if that will make the slightest difference." The harshness in Æthel's voice is not all scorn. Although she is far from the only one to have found a dead crow, none of the other noble women have. That horror was saved for her alone. Alis probably, but Æthel cannot help feeling targeted, painted red, like a woman accused of witchwork.

Cuthburh pats her: more obligatory than sympathetic. "I would put it from your mind, Æthel."

Ine's sister seems oblivious to the tides of the court, her eyes fixed solidly on the next task to be done. Even a plague of crows barely distracts her. And the fact that Æthel's unpopularity could earn her enemies would not even cross Cuthburh's mind.

Cwenburh, however, looks thoughtful. She is a softer and stranger sort, most like Ine, and her large brown eyes make her seem absent. Æthel used to have the impression she was watching another lifetime pass before her, a place where Æthel and Ine and all the rest of them were but ghosts. Now what she once considered absence, she recognizes as subtle attention. Cwenburh is good at pretending *not* to listen.

"There is something you should know about my brother," she had said to Æthel on the eve of her wedding to Ine. "You must be patient with him. He may not be what you expect."

Æthel had dismissed those words as a fond sister's worry. Now, faced with the woman, she wonders what Cwenburh had been trying to tell her. That Ine had no intention of touching her in the way of husbands? That maybe he loved another? The thought, coming on top of the dead crow, makes Æthel want to run and keep on running, until she leaves the whole lot of them behind. The court and its callous whispers. The gesiths and their doubts. The husband who cannot bear to be held by her.

I must see her.

Despite Ine's protest, in spite of Alis's insinuation, Æthel spends the evening stuffing clothes into a saddlebag. *This is lunacy.* In a space of weeks, she has gone from sensible queen to a woman made wild by a story. Sensible. She snorts, unsure if the word has ever described her. One thing is certain, however. Neither Ine, his family, nor the court will miss her. She leaves him a note on the table in their quarters, warning him of Alis. Against an unknown power, a warning is all she can leave. He will know where she has gone. He will know why she has gone. *For Wessex,* Æthel tells herself, and tries to ignore the fact that her heart is singing.

She takes the back path to the stables, avoiding the main hall. But she cannot help glancing in one more time. It is late. Meat and drink still clutter the long table: Cenred's funeral feast has lasted several days. Her eyes, curse them, stray to the man sitting alone. The chairs to either side of Ine are empty. The men of the court are clustered instead about Ingild, who seems to be telling a ribald story. Guffaws go up, and Ine looks across, an unreadable expression on his face. Æthel sinks into the gloom before he notices her.

His concerns are not mine, she tells herself as she slips out of the door, saddlebag on shoulder. Ingild is his problem. Wessex is hers. And he is still hiding something from her. Gweir is the only one he lets close. Could it be that—she squashes the thought before it fully forms. *His concerns are not mine.*

When Æthel steps into the deserted stables, she stops. This is where she met Ælfrún; she tries to recall her first impression, wondering if there were clues she missed. The animals poke their heads over their stalls and she smiles. She had certainly missed the largest clue of all: Ælfrún's gift with horses. And then at Sceaptun... the smile falters. Other clues had been there for her to see if she'd only had the wit. Æthel's hands tremble as she straightens her saddle and tightens the girth. Everything from the Britons' sudden reprieve to the wight who had killed six men but vanished at Ælfrún's approach. Why has she not questioned those things before?

There are those who take trust and slaughter it. I do not want to see that happen to you. So, Herla had run from her. It is the first time Æthel has used that name while thinking of Ælfrún, and the thrill of it is like the growing knowledge of a battlefield victory. Does she care for Æthel? That last evening, she had seemed shocked, appalled even, to hear the belling of the Wild Hunt. Æthel had let her horse carry her away only because she heard the rasp of genuine fear in Herla's voice. Fear . . . for her? Æthel swings into the saddle and wraps her tingling fingers around the reins. The leather creaks in her grip.

Brows are raised and foreheads creased when she demands the men open the gates for her. It does not matter; she will be long gone before the news reaches Ine's ears. She points her horse westwards. A few days, no more, to reach Glestingaburg, if she rides hard. "Come on, girl," she murmurs, staring at the dark roll of the land ahead. "Get me a league a two from Wiltun and we will wait for dawn."

The season has truly turned, and Æthel rides through an uprising of colour. The road is fastest, so she takes it, and cries of recognition follow in her wake. It is somewhat surprising to discover that outside the walls of Wiltun, she is not the useless excuse for a wife the court think her. Folk holler, "Lady of Wessex," and others stand with fists to hearts as she passes, as if she were the king himself. These men must have spent time in the fyrd; perhaps farming life has not quite buried their memories of battle-light and blood. *This is my legacy,* Æthel thinks, as one man grips his rake to salute her. Gravely, she nods at him, uncertain how it makes her feel.

The leagues pass too swiftly and too slowly. On the morning she sees Glestingaburg rising out of the mist, her stomach clenches. The tightness stays with her all that day as the hill comes closer, its soft green slopes cut in tiers. How can Herla sleep *beneath* the tor? Are there caverns? Is there a door? How does one enter a hill?

The problem becomes more pressing when Æthel has ridden the entire way around the base of it and found nothing. Lights are being lit over in the abbey, but here the mist is creeping back, a white stirring that seems to follow her. After half an hour, she admits she is lost. The mist does not smell like river, or damp earth. It has the sweetness of rot. Blood starts to pump through her.

The abbey. Æthel can shelter there, try again come morning. In the ghostly twilight, she fumbles in her pack for flint, but the torch only makes matters worse, turning the mist into an impenetrable wall of white. She dismounts, bending to study the grass, thinking that perhaps she can follow her own tracks back the way she came. As soon as the thought crosses her mind, however, a wind blows up, as if something has rushed past her unseen. Æthel whirls round, but there's nothing, and no sound either. Could any sound be loud enough to break that flat silence? She licks dry lips. "Herla!"

The mist eats the name. Her voice is small, barely more than a child's cry. Æthel summons her strength and calls again, "Herla!" This time, the mist twitches, but Glestingaburg is larger than her. It steals the shout, taking it into itself, and dampens all trace. Silence grows, deeper than before.

"Who are you to shout my lord's name so?"

The hollow voice comes with a spearpoint cold on the back of her neck.

22

INE

Wiltun, Wiltunscir
Kingdom of Wessex

"No one saw her leave?"

The men exchange looks. Of course they had, but who would have stopped her? Æthelburg has always done as she wished. Ine stands at the gates, gazing out at fields that appear grey beneath the weak morning sun. There is nothing strange about Æthel riding out, but this time feels different. She never leaves without saying goodbye.

Perhaps because they both know where she has gone. The note hangs limply in his hand. And even though he tries to tell himself she would not leave unless she believed it necessary, his own words return to torment him. *If you want to separate, I won't stop you.* It is all blurring together in his mind. She has left Wiltun. She has left *him*. And she has taken so little with her, discarded her jewellery along with her dresses, and the gameboard he'd made for her, over which they had spent evenings too happy, surely, to have been real. Only her sword, armour and horse are missing— the things she values most. The things that had kept her company in his place.

Ine slams a fist into the gatepost. The guards jump, but say nothing. If the king wishes to break his hand, it is his choice. *Æthel.* He squeezes his eyes shut. Suddenly it all seems unimportant: Ingild, the wights, the heritage—even the part of himself he has hidden away. Without her, it means nothing. Why has it taken him so long to understand what his heart has been trying to tell him? That she is the lynchpin holding his world together.

A man coughs, and Ine realizes belatedly what this must look like. He should not have been so careless. The guards will talk and it will spread: that the queen has ridden off and he does not know where. Yet more fuel for Ingild to heap on the bonfire his court is becoming. An unstable blaze with the power to burn everything Ine has achieved. Rather like the power coiled beneath his skin that no one can—or will, in Emrys's case—explain to him.

"Ah." Hædde wastes no time in accosting him the moment he returns, decidedly sick, to the hall. "Allow me to introduce Winfrid from the abbey at Nhutscelle. I do not believe you have met."

Garbed in a monk's hood and vestments, the young man at Hædde's side leaps up. *Exactly what I need,* Ine thinks, *the paganhunter.* An unfamiliar spear catches his eye.

Winfrid chuckles. "A man cannot be too careful, lord." He pats the weapon like a favourite hound. "I intend to travel widely and I hear the land of the Franks is rife with pagans whose favourite sport is the slaying of holy men."

"Abbot Winbert encouraged this?" Hædde asks with a lick of distaste. "When did weaponry become a suitable study for priests?"

"It is not the only unorthodox study at Nhutscelle." Winfrid's voice is perfectly neutral, but his eyes gleam. "We have men of science amongst us, who practise leechcraft and study the stars. Warriors with blessed weapons sent all the way from Rome. And scholars and scribes, of course. We are quite the community."

Hædde grunts. "This talk of going overseas. Last I heard, Winbert expected you to take over as abbot."

The young man's humour falters. "He honours me. But an abbot's life, while worthy, is not one I would choose. For the most part, our country has embraced God. Now the work must continue abroad." He nods at the spear. "There is still so much to be done, and few men willing to do it."

"Well, Wessex will miss your guidance," Ine says to keep Hædde happy. The bishop has been distant since their argument. "When do you plan to sail?"

"Not until next year." Winfrid glances at his superior. "Bishop Hædde invited me to winter at court. By your leave, of course, Ine king."

They are skirting the real reason Winfrid is here. Hædde has brought him in to spy, to purge the so-called rot from the heart of the kingdom. It is a chance for Winfrid to prove himself before taking his pagan-hunting gifts abroad.

Cuthburh breezes over, her face breaking into a rare smile. "Winfrid. My sister and I heard your praises sung even in Berecingum."

"And you are undoubtedly Lady Cuthburh."

Although Winfrid's answering smile is a force to be reckoned with, his fair locks and warm greenish eyes have no effect on Cuthburh. Rather than blushing, she folds her hands against her bosom and says, "Perhaps you can help convince my brother to let me found a double monastery at Winburnan."

"Wait, Cuthburh." Indignation forces its way through Ine's darker thoughts. "This is the first I've heard of it."

His sister turns with a glower. "I told you just the other day, Ine. I knew you weren't listening."

Perhaps Winfrid foresees an argument because he interrupts with a short bow. "Let me offer my condolences on the passing of your father."

"You are kind," Cuthburh says before Ine can answer. "But he was an old man whose mind was leaving him. His death was a blessing."

Her words could have been Ingild's. *You were not there,* Ine thinks at her. *You did not see his face or the blood beneath his nails.*

Summoned by Ine's very thought of him, Ingild appears in the doorway. "Welcome, Winfrid. Has my brother not offered you refreshment after your journey?" Despite the early hour, he barks for wine and servants hurry in with it, not a few glancing twice at the sight of an armed priest—and a handsome one at that.

"Thank you, Ingild ætheling, but I will have water."

Ingild's face creases with an irritation so fleeting Ine might have imagined it. "Very well."

"And then perhaps we may retire to the chapel." Hædde's eyes meet Ine's. "We must speak privately of the threat to the kingdom."

Where before the rumours of pagans were confined to Hædde's sermons, Winfrid's presence in Wiltun scatters them like seeds on the wind. Suddenly talk of heathens is everywhere. Ine hears it in the mead hall as servants stoke the fire, sees it in the bowed heads of townsfolk hurrying to complete their tasks before nightfall. The milk is still spoiling, no matter the cattle he finally agreed to slaughter, and stories spread that the crow pyre burned with green flame.

He is forced to invent a reason for Æthelburg's absence. News of Ealdbert, bandits on the road to Hamwic. The usual problems. Gweir, however, is not fooled and neither is Cwenburh. "You don't know where she is, do you?" she says in a soft voice when she finds Ine alone a few days after Æthel's departure.

I fear I know exactly where she is. But he cannot tell Cwen that. The streets tumble down from where they stand at the highest point of the settlement. It is a foul noon. Behind them in the hall, there is fire to lift the gloom and voices to banish the grey. It all rings hollow in Ine's ears. Æthelburg is gone, but the dead are not. And although the maid, Alis, has not been seen since Æthel sent her away, he cannot believe her so easily dismissed. Like Herla, like Gwyn, the woman must belong to the Otherworld.

A light touch on his arm. "What happened?"

"It is more about what didn't," he says without thinking.

Cwenburh has their mother's eyes, large and languid. But there is little languorous about them now. "You never told her."

He stiffens.

"Oh, Ine. She would have understood."

"No," he says in hard, choked tones. "She would not. You don't know her, Cwen. You have been away too long. She is passionate, feels everything so keenly..."

"Like someone else I know."

He shakes his head. "We are nothing alike."

Cwenburh laughs. He hasn't heard that merry sound since they were children. "You are only seeing what you expect to see, brother." In a lower voice, "What they have taught you to see."

Ine stares at his open palms, but they have never held the answer. "I cannot give her what she wants."

"Have you asked her what she wants?" Cwenburh sighs at his silence. "I knew you had not."

Ine draws his cloak around him, a shield against the strengthening wind and a chiller one that only he can feel. "Because I already know. She wants..." He stops, feeling his face warm. "I can't say these things to you, Cwen."

"You can say anything you wish to me, brother. I doubt there is another who knows you like I do."

"Why is that?"

It is Cwenburh's turn to be silent. Then, plucking at her nun's habit, she lets out a long breath. "Why do you think? We all find our ways of coping in a world which does not understand. That we do not want as other people want."

Her words are like the sun burning away a mist that has clung to him ever since he can remember. Ine gapes at her, his heart thudding. "Why didn't you tell me before? I thought you always intended to become a nun."

"I was the youngest, so Father never pressed me to marry. Still, the prospect of it hung over my head like a damnable sword." Her voice is carefully dispassionate, but Ine can hear a low note in it, like the hurt he has carried for so very long. "I could not imagine sharing my life with another," his sister continues. "The things that would be expected of me in a marriage. The lies I would have to tell." Cwenburh's fingers stray to the wooden cross resting on her chest. "The Church offered a way out, and it is not a bad life, considering. I have my books and learning. I am a servant of God first, a woman second." She pauses. "It is worse for you. No one questions a nun's lack of desire to find a partner, to sire heirs."

"The court thinks the fault lies with Æthelburg," Ine murmurs around the lump in his throat. "And I—I have done nothing to challenge it. I asked myself what might happen if I did, which men might move against me. But in reality, I am scared." The words are cascading out now and Ine does not fight them. If he stops, he might never speak them to anyone. "I am a coward who would prefer to drive away the woman I love. And now I have finally succeeded." The town blurs until he looks at the world through a haze. "She's gone, Cwen." A salty taste in his throat. "And it's *my* fault. All because I couldn't love her as she deserved."

Twining her fingers through his, Cwenburh squeezes his hand. "Of course she hasn't gone. Æthel is queen and takes her responsibilities seriously. She has simply given herself space to think. For you both to think. But Ine, listen to me. What you have built with Æthelburg is special. Its roots go deep. Don't deny her the chance to accept you for who you are. You owe each other the truth."

Ine drags a hand across his eyes. "Wessex is not safe. She could be in danger."

Cwenburh grimaces. Even she knows that danger and Æthelburg have never been far apart. "What is going on, brother?"

"Didn't you hear Ingild?" Ine says bitterly. "It is only Britons murdering each other, as is their nature."

"You do not believe it."

Outside is an unsuitable place to speak, but he has no wish to re-enter the hall and risk running into the churchmen. "I have seen things. So has Æthelburg. Things that have no place outside of stories. But they are *real*." The word is hushed, desperate. "They have spilled over into Wiltun. People are frightened, and Hædde has been spreading tales of heathens." Fearing what he will see there, Ine meets her gaze. "Tales of magic."

But Cwenburh has no ready laugh this time. Her eyes are serious and dark.

"Worse," Ine rushes on. "I do not believe Father's death was natural." It is the first time he has voiced it aloud and the sound of it only hardens his conviction. "It was a violent end, Cwen. There was blood beneath his nails—as if from a struggle."

"Who was last to see him alive?"

Ine winces at the question. "Æthel. This is why I cannot take the matter to the Witan. Ingild already believes ill of her. That she would murder an old man under the guise of kindness."

"And does Ingild have such influence in the Witan that his word would be taken over yours?"

Ine stares at her. He recalls the words Ingild coerced out of him in Gifle. The vote on Cadwy's fate. The way his brother cleverly belittled Æthel's testimony and mocked Ine's opinion on the Britons. "Yes," he says quietly. "I think it would."

Cwenburh mutters a word he never thought to hear from her. "How long has this been going on?"

"Longer than I realize, perhaps." A slant of unexpected sun ignites the church windows. "But worse since this business with the Britons began. He has found an ally in Hædde, and I fear Nothhelm, Godric and Osberht would side with him too. Edred, of course, is already his." Gaze still on the church whose crypt-stones shelter all that remains of Cenred, he says, "Father helped tip the vote on Cadwy. Ingild never forgave him that."

"The boy," Cwenburh says with a thoughtful glance at the building in which he is being kept. "He is a Briton and a pagan. Has he been able to shed light on the source of the trouble?"

Ine hesitates. How far does Cwenburh's loyalty to the Church stretch? His sisters have spent the last few years under the oppressive wing of clergy like Hildelith and Earconwald. It is painful to admit he might not know them as he once did. "He has...helped. But he is not entirely open with me." That is the truth, at least.

"He could have an explanation for the crows."

"You don't believe the crows the work of heathens?"

"They may be," Cwenburh says evenly. "With the right incentive, the boy could tell you more."

The right incentive is the freedom that Ine has already rashly promised. Wind lifts the hair off his neck, all the better to chill him. "I am going to sit with Father awhile." Grief for Cenred is having to battle for control of his heart. "His advice was always good. Perhaps an answer will come to me."

Cwenburh says nothing, but her parting touch is warm.

Raised voices greet Ine as he nears the church, trailing two men-at-arms. A small crowd has penned in a figure: Sinnoch. The stablemaster's lean form towers over most of those gathered. His face wears its usual dourness, but there is something alarming in his stiff-legged stance, as if he wants to reach for his knife. The crowd grows louder and uglier the nearer Ine comes, until he can pick out individual words.

"And I say he *is*," a man spits, his cheeks ruddy from shouting.

Deorstan elbows his way to the stablemaster's side. "What shit are you spewing, Ceadda? He's one of us."

"One of us?" The man steps forward, raising a finger. "When has he joined us in church?"

"That hardly makes him a pagan." Deorstan's face is reddening too. He holds out an arm before Sinnoch. "He's lived here for years and you've never had cause to attack him before."

"Maybe we should have done," Ceadda says darkly. "Then my wife would not wake screaming that crows are pecking out her eyes. My children would have milk in their bellies."

Cries of agreement from the crowd. "He is not responsible," Deorstan shouts over them. "What proof do you have?"

"Enough, Deorstan." Sinnoch's voice is quiet, but carrying. "You need not put yourself in harm's way for me."

"Yes, Deorstan." Ceadda looks to those on either side for support. "Unless you wish to share what's coming to him."

"He is a good man," Deorstan says desperately. "Wessex is his home."

"But he is no Saxon," someone calls, provoking a chorus of *ayes.* "He is Wealas, born a heathen. He should go back where he came from."

"And how many of you can say you are Saxon?"

Silence smothers the crowd. Heads turn. Ine watches the people part for him, opening a path towards Sinnoch and Deorstan. He takes a slow walk towards them and stops. "How many here can swear they do not have even a drop of native blood in their veins? I can tell you: none. It is in yours and it is in mine." The anger he is beginning to recognize as the two heritages fighting inside him wakes. "And that is because our forebears—our mothers and fathers—came together. They realized nothing divides us except the desire to be divided. Ask yourselves why. What does it bring you?" He lifts a hand to Sinnoch. "This man, for example. What benefit will you derive from hurting him, or driving him out?"

No one answers. No one dares, until Ceadda says, "The wickedness in his blood, the evil that has poisoned our home, will be driven out with him."

There is a collective intake of breath, and an older woman grabs his arm. "When will you learn to guard your tongue? Lord king, I am sorry for my son's—"

Ine holds up a hand. "I will not punish him for answering a question I asked. But—" he lets his gaze rove across the crowd—"I am disappointed. I thought my people were better than this. You turn on a man who has served loyally for years with no evidence to suggest wrongdoing. I know you are frightened." In his mind is the dead face of Centwine. The screams of murdered souls trapped in the bone knife. "I am too. But not of people who live peaceably amongst us. This is a time to unite, not to sow hate and division."

With a deal of muttering, unrest drains from the crowd. Still, some gazes are lowered, or turned sideways to conceal resentment. Ine lets out a long-held breath as people begin to disperse. If he had not arrived when he did, what might have happened to Sinnoch—and to Deorstan for defending him? The stablemaster nods grave thanks to Ine, clothing himself once more in his usual impassivity, but his hands tremble slightly at his sides as he watches the townsfolk drift away.

Someone orchestrated this. The moment he thinks it, the skin between Ine's shoulder blades prickles, and he turns. Hædde stands in the doorway of the church, hands folded calmly into his sleeves. Candles flicker behind him; he is a shadow against their light. How long has he been watching? Long enough, Ine suspects.

Æthelburg is gone because he had been too afraid to speak. Just as he had been afraid of offending the Church, and of confronting Ingild. He and Hædde look at each other, and in the other man's eyes, Ine sees a reckoning. Once he might have felt grief at their lost friendship. Now he welcomes the anger inside him.

Your move, bishop.

23

ÆTHELBURG

Glestingaburg, Somersǣte
Kingdom of Wessex

Not one of her honed instincts had warned her. Covered in gooseflesh, Æthel holds still, mind racing through options and discarding them. Her sword is sheathed, the knife in her boot out of reach. "I mean no harm," she says, barely moving her lips.

"I shall be the judge of that." It is a woman's voice, flint-edged. "Who are you?"

"Æthelburg." The weapon rests against the fragile skin of her neck. Every breath is snatched air.

"A Saxon name. So you are descended from those who invaded our country in Rome's wake." The spear never falters.

"I was born in Wessex, and my mother and grandmother before her." She cannot keep indignation out of her voice. "This is *my* country."

A quiet chuckle. "Is that so? Well, Saxon, you must have a death wish coming here tonight. I will be happy to grant it."

"Wait." Æthel tries to banish an image of that sharp point emerging from her throat along with the echo of Ine's voice saying, *Has all sense left you?* She would hate to die here and prove him right. "I am known to your lord."

"I highly doubt it."

"She came to me as Ælfrún. We fought together."

The unseen woman hisses through her teeth. "You are the queen?"

"Yes," Æthel says swiftly, not yet daring to feel relief. "Then you know of me?"

"Perhaps." The spear tip eases. "Turn around. Slowly."

Æthel does as she says. The pallid mist-light shows her a stocky woman, shorter than her, with coppery hair. A brace of rabbits hangs from her belt and behind her on the ground is the prize of a hunt: a stag so huge that no one person could possibly carry it. The woman's arms are bare to the shoulder, inked like the Britons, but more detailed than Æthel has ever seen. She wears a crude kind of leather armour, a long plait merging with the fur of her cloak.

The stranger seems to have been studying her with equal intensity. "Why have you come here, Queen of Wessex?" she asks finally, planting her spear at her side. "And all alone?"

"I…" She must choose her words carefully. Æthel would not put it past the woman to decide she deserves the same treatment as the stag. *I need Herla's help.* She opens her mouth to say it, but what emerges is, "I needed to see her."

"Goddess." The woman flings the word like a curse to the ground. "My name is Corraidhín. I would strongly suggest you leave."

"No." It is out of her disobedient mouth before Æthel can think better of it, and Corraidhín's brows shoot up. "I mean," she adds, "I have ridden many leagues."

"Then you are used to long journeys." Corraidhín steps aside, opening a path to Æthel's horse. "Another awaits you."

"Not until I see her."

They glower at each other, Æthel's chin tilted stubbornly, until a voice says, "What is this?"

Between heartbeats, another woman stands there, attired like Corraidhín in leather and fur. Her eyes flick to the stag and she makes a sound halfway between growl and huff. "Damn, you got it first."

"Of course," Corraidhín says easily. Her hand tightens on the shaft of her spear. "I was always the better shot, Gelgéis." Before the other woman can retort, she adds, "We have a larger problem."

"Take me to Herla." Æthel straightens her shoulders, sensing that neither woman will respond to pleading. "Let her be the judge of whether to send me away."

"Lord Herla is not to be lightly disturbed." For the first time, Æthel hears a lash of protectiveness in Corraidhín's voice. Her next words are cold. "She left you for a reason."

Æthel's heart beats faster. "What has she said of me?"

"That you are trouble."

"She did not," Gelgéis says, and Corraidhín turns a glare on her. "But the reason stands."

"What reason?"

"For your own protection." Any playfulness has vanished from Gelgéis's tone. "You should not be here. We are not like you."

The mist has parted a little, leaking moonlight into her fair hair, silvering the curve of her cheek. Gelgéis is right, Æthel thinks with a shiver, looking on their faces. Women, yes, but fey, as if the unrelenting chill of winter lives under their skin. If they were human once, they are not now. And yet...Ælfrún's laugh as Æthel pinned her to the ground, the warmth of her fingers linked ever so briefly in hers. Something remains. There is something to be found beneath the warning and the threat and the *otherness* of the power that made her.

"Let me see her," she whispers.

For a moment, neither speak. Then Gelgéis snorts. "Fine. Let her in, Corra. Goddess knows, she needs the distraction."

"Not *this* type of distraction," Corraidhín mutters so quietly Æthel cannot be sure she heard right. The blood is pounding in her head besides, burying the women's voices in a kind of elated dread. She has not felt like this since the eve of her first battle, when every nerve was afire with the possibility of victory...and defeat.

Corraidhín hefts the stag across her shoulders, as if it weighs no more than a sack of grain. "Let me save face and have the rabbits?" Gelgéis asks and grins when the other woman tugs them off her belt with a sigh. Then Corraidhín waves an irritated hand at the mist. It dissipates and Æthel finds herself standing a few paces from the tor. As she watches, hardly breathing, a crack appears in the skin of the hill. Pillars guard a grand archway carved of a stone she has never seen. The doors look heavy, but they swing without sound, spilling light across the grass. "Come then." Gelgéis swiftly ties the game to her own belt, and the humanness of that gesture strikes Æthel anew.

She hesitates on the threshold. There is a difference in the air here, like the nameless boundary near the coast where earth-smell meets sea-smell and mingles. Stories rush through Æthel: of worlds colliding, of bards trapped in elfin courts, and changelings waking by human hearths. But what she sees inside the hill is a long chamber, not so dissimilar from the hall at Wiltun. She bites her lip. The thought of home seems foreign. Walls smooth as river stones, an earthen floor full of tiny gems. Further in, figures sit on benches, or pass to and fro as shadows in front of a great firepit, which burns without smoke. Before either Corraidhín or Gelgéis can call her irresolute, Æthel steps inside.

The doors whisper shut. That closing is a barb in her heart, the clinging fear of being unable to return. Did Herla feel it too when she crossed into the Otherworld? The story never said why she went at all. "Do not worry, little queen." Corraidhín glances back at her. "We have plenty to eat tonight." She laughs and the laugh summons others, who exclaim over the stag and Gelgéis's rabbits, until they spot Æthel. Then all chatter falls still.

Their combined gaze makes Æthel feel small as a mouse flinching from talons. They are the same women she saw mounted, their voices the wailing of horns. More faces like Corraidhín's and Gelgéis's—remote and ageless as the stars. One woman near the front catches her eye. She has the same look as her sisters, but her cheeks are dimpled and rounded, the only signs of long-arrested childhood. She must have been young when she was changed. For some reason, the sight makes Æthel's throat ache.

"What is it?"

The voice that calls from the back of the chamber lodges in her bones like a silk-wrapped blade; Æthel knows she will not be able to remove it as long as she lives. Although the women do not touch her, she finds herself swept along with them, as they traverse the hall. Unfamiliar pennants adorn the walls, and racks of weapons stand ready. Whetstones lie on benches, rags to oil leather—Æthel recognizes the familiar tools of warfare. But here and there are other pursuits: a cup of dice, a small lute, vellum filled with drawings of plants. The items are strangely intimate, as if she spies upon a private scene.

Reddish eyes watch her. The chamber does not seem large enough to contain the horses, but the animals are only there when she looks at them. Otherwise they fade, somehow not quite present. They do not smell like horses, but rather the salt of the sea, the mineral tang of wet rock and…flowers. She is careful *not* to look at them.

The journey seems endless. Her heart races with every step. At the top of the hall is a bench, its back formed of two rearing stags, hooves raised like pugilists. It is a wild seat, and the figure upon it is wild, almost too *real* to look at. But Æthel looks. She has to. Her heart demands it.

Widening amber eyes. A hunter's eyes, fierce and afire, pulled from the wilderness where humans should not go. Stripped of disguise, her face resembles Ælfrún's, but leaner and harsher. Mercilessness would be at home there. And yet the faintest lines around her mouth suggest she laughed once. Her dark hair is a tumble of braids, the odd bead or bone charm woven amongst them. Her arms are inked like Corraidhín's, bare brown skin under blue.

Herla rises slowly and Æthel experiences a powerful urge to fall at her feet. *You are a queen,* she reminds herself, locking her knees, but the urge remains. The sheer presence of the woman before her would be enough to make most men flee. They look at each other for one long and speechless moment before Herla says, "Æthelburg."

"Herla."

The leader of the Wild Hunt closes her eyes briefly at her name. "Why have you come here?"

"I…" Æthel swallows, aware of the gazes crowded on the two of them. Herla does not appear to do anything, but the women, bunched together a moment ago, scatter to their tasks. Almost certainly listening. "How could I not," she says softly, "when I realized?"

"I could have killed you." Herla clenches a fist. "I *would* have killed you. I sent you away for your own protection."

"As I find myself regularly repeating, I do not need it."

Herla says nothing for a moment, but when she next speaks, her voice is cold. "You know that many call me death."

"I am a warrior. I have never been afraid of death." Æthel lifts her head, eyes touching on the other woman's closed fist. "We all take her hand in time."

Herla's face is blank. Then she smiles, a dark curve of her lips, and something in Æthel's chest flutters. Not the moths of earlier, those uncertain wings, but a fearful being whose name, nevertheless, is not fear. "You are an impossible woman, Æthelburg of Wessex."

"I've been called worse."

"So."

Æthel folds her arms. "So."

"You found me," Herla says—and is that a hint of secret pleasure Æthel can hear? The thought makes her heart beat faster. "Why have you really come?"

"Why did *you* come to Wessex?"

The bench is long enough for three to sit comfortably. Herla sinks onto it and gestures for Æthel to join her. The moment they are side by side, Æthel remembers the last time they sat so, their fingers touching, and her cheeks flame. She looks away, down the long chamber, aware that she is being studied. "Seeking something that did not belong," Herla says.

"What do you mean?"

"An Otherworld meddler."

One of the women stirs up the silvery fire. Æthel watches as the stag is split and spitted. "I think I know who it is. Alis, my maid."

Herla's eyes widen. "Did she hurt you?"

"I confronted her." Æthel thinks of that strange conversation. What *had* Alis meant about taking the deal that was offered? "After I caught her plotting something with Ingild."

"By all the Mother holds sacred," Herla breathes. "Do you have no regard for your life?"

"Why is everyone always asking me that? Besides," Æthel adds testily, "if she is so dangerous, why didn't *you* warn me?"

Herla's jaw clenches, and Æthel feels a little regretful over the words. How have they fallen so easily back into the pattern of companions, of simply Æthel and Ælfrún? About to reach out, she falters at the amber glow in the other woman's eyes. Because of course they are not. She is Queen of Wessex and Herla is not even human.

"I intended to warn you when...it happened."

Æthel wishes her face were not afire. She examines the hands that are folded too neatly in her lap. "The stories say that you sleep beneath the tor when you do not ride. Are they wrong?"

"No." Laughter drifts from the group of women, and bickering, as they argue over the best way to roast a stag. "That was how it was," Herla continues, "until the night Geraint of Dumnonia died. When Gwyn's hound leaped down, I thought the curse had lost its power to make us ride." She scowls at something in the corner. "I was wrong. You are fortunate the moon is full tonight."

There is a shape: an indistinct bundle of shadow which growls softly when Herla looks at it. "Gwyn," Æthel mutters. "It seems I am hearing his name everywhere."

"*He* did this to me." Herla's voice drips with venom. "With one hand, he offered power, and with the other, snatched away every reason I sought it." She pauses to gaze into the middle distance, as if the haze of fire and torchlight has made a doorway through which the past spills. "What good is power when you have nothing left to fight for? When you are without a cause?"

Æthel cannot help it. She leans closer, enthralled by the blaze in Herla's face. "What *was* your cause?"

For just an instant, Herla seems to sway towards her. Then,

"You must be hungry." She stands and holds out an arm. "I have tasted your road rations firsthand. Our dwelling and our welcome may be rough, but I can at least refresh you before I send you on your way."

"I'm not going anywhere," Æthel says. Why had Herla sought the Otherworld? Who did she leave behind? *Herla is a selfish creature, little queen.* And what does Alis know that Æthel does not?

Ignoring her remark, Herla strides towards the fire. "Wine for our guest." There are cups warming on the stones around it. Smokeless flames are not the strangest things Æthel has seen lately, but she finds herself staring regardless until a cup is thrust at her and she has to close her fingers or drop it. The wine inside is lightly spiced. Æthel takes a long draught which, upsettingly, goes straight to her head. Unlike Ine, she is usually able to hold her drink. Her insides squirm; she swallows the thought of him in another sip.

Herla raises her eyebrows. "Have some care. You will not have tasted it before."

"What is it?"

"From our homeland." It is the young woman Æthel noticed earlier. Herla gives her a hard stare and she falls silent. Not for long, though. While the meat pops and sizzles, filling the chamber with a rich aroma, the woman says, "My name is Orlaith. Herla tells us you are queen of these lands." When Æthel nods, Orlaith bares her teeth. "It is good to be queen."

"Yes and no." Surprised by her own honesty, she takes another sip. "People expect things of you. Things you might not want to be…or do." Ine's dark and troubled eyes will not leave her alone. *Do not look at me like that,* she tells the shade of him. *I came here for Wessex.* But Æthel cannot deny that she had also come for herself. She had followed the joy she'd felt at having Ælfrún's— Herla's—lean body beneath her own. She had followed the words, *Anyone would be proud to call you wife.* Had Ine ever told her that? Was he proud to call her his wife? Æthel's throat prickles; she wets it with more wine. No, his silences have always spoken for him. That is why she is here in this hall. Because she feels more at home with these cursed women from another world than she does in Wessex among the men, and with him. The prickling has moved to her eyes. She raises the cup again, but a firm hand stops it halfway.

"I said have care." Herla's lips curve in one of her rare warmer smiles. "You have nothing to prove here."

"I wasn't proving anything," Æthel mutters, but she lets Herla take the cup. Their fingers brush, and there it is again: that sweet singing desire. She shakes her head; it's a mess, flitting from one thought to another in the erratic way of one who has had too much to drink. When was the last time she let her guard down like this? The wine is surging through her veins and she feels lighter, as if finally relieved of a burden long carried. "Is that meat done?"

Gelgéis inspects a skewer. "This bit is." Without even flinching, she grasps the hot metal, slides the speared chunks off onto a trencher and then licks her unburned fingers. Æthel blows on the meat, aware that nineteen pairs of eyes are watching her. Thanks to the wine, it does not bother her so much.

"Will you tell me your names?" she asks, knowing she has only half a chance of remembering them all come morning. Grins go round the circle like beacons lit one after another; the women are happy to oblige. Æthel listens to the names they pour out, made ancient by time, and tries to reconcile the scene with the memory of their ride. Horse and spear, savage faces, Herla's cry, the horns of her helm thrown against the sky, as if they grew from her own head. The hairs are standing up on her arms now. She knows Herla has seen, and concentrates on eating. But it's as if the other woman is a turning tide, tugging Æthel away from the land, into the deep. The image frightens her, excites her.

"You are a warrior?" Senua asks; the woman Gelgéis introduced as her blood sister. When Æthel nods, she leans forward, elbows on her knees. "You have come here, claimed your rights as a guest and we have fed you. Will you pay the debt with a story? Tell us of a battle you have fought." She grins. "A great victory."

Æthel blinks. Not once has she been asked such a question.

Only with Ine has she ever sat down and dissected her fights. The gesiths are interested in the outcome alone. *As if the battles won themselves.* Despite the bitter thought, she finds herself grinning too. Using a skewer, Æthel draws three lines in the dirt, marking her archers with a cross, and the start and end positions of her shield wall. Her opponent in the fight had been Uhtric, another upstart exile with designs on the throne. Æthel pushes the twin shames of Tantone and Gifle aside, buries the thought of her losses at Sceaptun. So engrossed is she in recounting the battle, flushed at the memory, bloody and bright, that she momentarily forgets where she is and who she is talking to.

"You slew this Uhtric yourself?" Senua asks, fingers busy stripping the flesh from a bone. "Outnumbered as you were?"

Æthel laughs, but it is strained. "He underestimated me. Most of them do. What I wouldn't give to fight someone who *didn't*." She glances up in time to meet Herla's wolf-eyes across the fire. She cannot read them, but the other woman's face is quite pale.

"You may be valiant in battle, Queen of Wessex." Corraidhín sits on a bench, balancing a sharp skewer between two fingertips. "But your foes are just men. It is dangerous for you to be here. You must leave."

Although Æthel wants to bristle at her tone, Corraidhín is right. Her father-in-law is dead; she should be in Wiltun to offer comfort, counsel. *Ine has his sisters,* she tells herself, aware that Cuthburh is probably the least comforting person she knows. And yet Cenred's words haunt her like a dying wish. *Watch out for my son.* It is time she asked for the aid she came for. "I cannot leave. I need your help."

"Our help," Corraidhín repeats flatly, but the other women's eyes are keen. Senua tosses the bone into the fire and Orlaith cocks her head.

"You said," Æthel appeals to Herla, who sits just outside the circle, "that Alis does not belong here. Nor do the shades and the wights. Yes, my foes are just men, but you have fought these creatures. You must know more."

"Must I?" Herla puts her meat aside. "What I know is that this is beyond you, Æthelburg. It is not a business for humans." She takes a steeling breath, as if the next words are going to hurt her. "You would do better to return to your husband."

Æthel's heart flickers fitfully in her chest. *She does not really mean that.* "People in my kingdom are dying. I should think it very much *is* a business for humans. Don't speak as if you aren't one."

Herla's face tightens. "I am sorry I let you believe otherwise." Before Æthel can reply, she rises and walks towards the blank wall where the doors ought to be visible. From its corner, the shadow uncurls itself into a monstrous hound, white with crimson ears, which pads softly after her. Both of them vanish.

"Let her go," Orlaith says when Æthel makes to stand.

"Why?"

"Because you remind her too much of *her*. You remind all of us."

Æthel turns slowly back to Orlaith. "Of who?"

"Our queen," Orlaith says, ignoring Corraidhín's hiss to be silent. Her eyes are wide and shining. "Boudica of the Eceni."

24

INE

Wiltun, Wiltunscir
Kingdom of Wessex

The crypt is so quiet that Ine's footsteps seem sacrilegious. He brushes his fingers across Cenred's tomb, thinking of his father locked in his stone sleep. One day, more names will letter these walls. Shivering, Ine hopes his own will not be amongst them. Not here. Perhaps, like some of his predecessors, he will abandon the land of his birth to go abroad. To fill his eyes with stranger sights before they have to close forever.

He laughs at himself, softly mocking. "I am a sorry excuse for a king, Father. You would be ashamed. I have not been leading as I should. I've let my brother and the Church decide for me, even when it goes against my better judgement. I've—" his voice breaks—"I have driven my wife away, my best friend and ally. People are dying under my watch, turning on each other, and I do not know how to stop it."

The crypt smells damp, of must and massed earth. He can *feel* it, the weight of the ground above; the depth of the ground below, plunging to the world's heart, or to Hell. Perhaps they are one and the same. If he let the anger out, he might see it: the chasm his blood could create. To strike the earth with a fist and watch it shatter like ice on a winter lake. The church would slide into it, and the town above. Perhaps the hills and flats of Wessex too. And the giant would open its eyes, creased in long repose. "Who am I?" Ine asks the walls, frightened of that violent desire. "Saxon or Briton? Christian or pagan? The world will not allow me to be both."

Time passes and, despite his hope, no answer comes. Inside this ashen prison, an hour could be a day, a week. Eventually his stomach reminds him that he is alive and starving. Joints stiff, Ine goes to leave, but a voice stops him. More than one voice and coming from the nave above.

"I know you agree, Nothhelm king." *Ingild.* Ine freezes.

There is a lengthy silence before Nothhelm speaks. "I agree with your belief that keeping the boy alive is dangerous. But he is protected. Your brother's ruling—"

"—only passed because Ine gave Cenred a vote. He knew how Father would use it."

"Yes," Nothhelm says and, in the crypt below, Ine draws a sharp breath. "But we cannot be seen outright to break it."

"Ah." A pause and the merest shuffle of feet, as of someone moving closer. "We cannot be *seen* to break it. Then we must not be seen."

"Say what you mean, Ingild." Nothhelm sounds tired. "It is past time I was at table."

"Wiltun is in the grip of heathen forces," Ingild murmurs, a careful blend of doubt and scorn. "Why not let them do the work? According to my brother, Wealas are being slain every day."

"You are suggesting we kill the boy and pin it on the pagans? They would not harm their own."

"Who knows their minds?" Ingild retorts. "Cadwy is a heathen. The Church will not object to his death. Neither will the Witan— he is the son of Geraint and natural heir to his lands. Even if it seems suspicious—and there are ways to make it look natural— no one will care enough to discover the truth, or weep for the boy. Except my foolish brother, perhaps."

"Who is also the king." Nothhelm does not sound so tired now. Uneasy, Ine detects a spark of something like interest. "He will not take Cadwy's death well."

"Oh, he will make a fuss about how bad it looks that Cadwy

died without a sword in his hand. And then he will accept it, just as he did Geraint. He'll have no proof we're involved."

Ine's hunger dissolves. *No proof except this conversation.*

"You keep using the word, 'we,'" Nothhelm says. "You have the resources to carry out this plan yourself. Why take the risk and share it?"

"Because my action will benefit us all. It will benefit the kingdom, even if Ine does not see it. While I love Wessex, I am not an altruistic man, Nothhelm. And neither, I think, are you. We will not put ourselves in harm's way for the benefit of others. If I carry the risk, I will also carry the reward." Ingild is breathing heavily. The speech seems to have taxed him, or the daring it has taken to voice.

"And what reward do you seek?" the King of Sussex asks—a question Ine would very much like answered too. Trembling with the effort of leashing his outrage, he creeps to the steps.

"Only to be able to count on your support in the Witan, which is not so great a thing. We already think alike."

"Asking me to vote with you is asking me to vote against the king. When do your opinions ever align?"

"They used to," Ingild mutters and Ine strains to hear. "If I can speak plainly, Nothhelm, I do not recognize him. First his rage over Geraint's death. Then this obsession with a bunch of Wealas peasants and talk of ghosts. Something has hold of him. He is not thinking clearly. If Hædde is right and we are harbouring pagans, they will sense his weakness. Cadwy's presence—"

"—is a spark to tinder, I agree."

"So do I have your support?"

Ine realizes he is holding his breath. He does not let it out until Nothhelm says, "You do," and then it escapes him in a soundless sigh. He leans back against the wall of the crypt, ignoring the chill seeping through his cloak. Kings have exiled their brothers for less. And worse than exile. In harsher courts than his, such sentiments would merit death.

"When will you act?" Nothhelm asks.

"Tonight."

In his shock, Ine pushes himself off the wall and his shoe scrapes stone.

"Did you—?" Nothhelm's next words are louder, as if for the benefit of an approaching clergyman. "I will leave you to pray in peace, Ingild ætheling." Ine listens to his footfalls growing fainter, while his gut twists impatiently inside him. *Tonight.*

Ingild waits until Nothhelm is gone before following. By the time Ine emerges, the sun has set. How long do he and Cadwy have? There is no question of letting Ingild murder the prince. He is crucial to understanding the Otherworld threat. But it is more than that. Despite their differences, and the bloodshed between their peoples, Ine has come to care about him. And he made a promise.

Of course, saving Cadwy means betraying his own people. *Isn't Ingild betraying me?* Ine dismisses the guards left waiting for him outside the church and lengthens his stride, hoping it looks like natural haste. Blood pounds in his temples, alongside the thought that he might arrive too late. He bumps into Gweir outside the hall, and, with a surge of relief, seizes his arm. "Thank God. I need your help."

The gesith is shaking his head before Ine has even finished explaining. "This is enough to condemn your brother and Nothhelm king before the Witan."

"They *are* the Witan," Ine says, raking the gathering dark for witnesses. "Their actions will be seen as right. Ingild knows I only won the vote because of Father, and he is no longer here. The rest want the boy dead."

"I still think—"

"If I do not get him out of Wiltun, he will die. Ingild's is no idle threat. Æthelburg—" Ine forces the words past the pain of her absence—"overheard him planning something, and this must be part of it." He pulls in a breath. "You believe Cadwy was almost slain before. Ingild could make it look like an accident this time, or even self-inflicted. And he is right, nobody will care enough to question."

"My loyalty is to you," Gweir says at once, "not to Ingild. But you

cannot be seen, lord. If the worst happens and we are discovered,
I will take the blame. I am half-Briton. They would believe it of
me—wanting to rescue my own."

"No. This is my decision and I will own it."

"It is the price of my help." The gesith's eyes are fierce. "You must
remain free to act. Free to uncover the truth of the murders. If it
is the doing of the Otherworld, you will need Cadwy's aid...and
the aid of his people."

Ine looks at him helplessly, but time is slipping away. "Very
well. How are we to get horses out of Wiltun without raising suspicion? The gates are closed at this hour."

"They will open them for me. You need not implicate yourself.
I'll meet you between Bryn's smithy and that hole where Leofric
likes to drink." Ine's lips twitch despite himself. "The men guarding
Cadwy are mine," Gweir continues. "I will stand them down and
then you only have to lead the prince there."

"You are a good man, Gweir. God go with you." But the phrase
feels false on Ine's tongue. Instead of following in the gesith's footsteps, he flips up his hood and takes a circuitous route to Cadwy's
hut, giving Gweir time to send the guards away.

The night seems too quiet. Intermittent torches lap at the dark.
How surreal, Ine thinks, to steal fugitive through his own streets.
Unless he actively sends his men away, he is never alone outside
of his chambers. He even feels a flash of exultation, as of a child
escaping a parent's watchful gaze. When he slides the bolt on
Cadwy's newly unguarded door, he finds the prince on his feet,
fists raised. Dark circles ring Cadwy's eyes. For all his youthful
bluster, he must not have slept properly since the failed attack on
his life. Ine pulls off his hood and Cadwy's face slackens. "King
Ine?" he says in his own language.

"You are in danger." He nods at the door. "I had Gweir dismiss
your guards so we could leave unseen."

"Leave? What is happening?" His voice wavers, making him
seem more a boy in that moment. "I thought you persuaded your
council to keep me alive."

"My brother has other plans. If you want to live, come with me."

Cadwy does not move. "How do I know it is not a trick? That you want me to escape so you have an excuse to kill me?"

"No Saxon needs an excuse to kill you," Ine says hotly. How to make him understand? "I gave my promise, remember? I would set you free. But that I would choose the time and means." He kneels before Cadwy and holds out a hand. "Well, it is now... or never."

Cadwy's eyes widen. They gaze at each other, king to prince, until—with a long-exhaled breath—Geraint's son nods. "You are the strangest man I have ever met."

No doubt. Ine gives a short laugh. Then, cracking open the door, he peers out. "Cover your face. Let's go."

A man and boy sneaking through the night might look suspicious, but Cadwy is tall for his age, not much shorter than Ine, and only a close inspection would reveal his youth. So Ine hopes. "Gweir is waiting near the gates and will have them opened," he murmurs as they keep to the quieter streets. "There will be a horse saddled, supplied and ready for you. He is a good man, Cadwy, and can be trusted."

The boy's face is pale beneath the hood. "Why are you doing this?"

Ine stops in the shadow of the smithy. From here, there is a clear view to the gates. "I told you I never desired your father's death. Or yours. Both of us have deadlier enemies." He turns to meet Cadwy's eyes. "Don't you agree?"

"You believe it all then?" the boy asks slowly. "The Otherworld? The murders?"

"I thought I'd made that clear." Ine steels himself. Cadwy had grudgingly promised to tell him of the birthright; now both of them will have to face that truth, or Ine must send the prince away ignorant. His lips are dry, and his mouth too. What will Cadwy say when he learns that Ine has inherited the power he thought was his? *I did not choose this,* Ine reminds himself, but what difference does that make?

Before he can shape the words, however, he hears feet slapping packed dirt and Gweir barrels out of the darkness. "Lord, go back. Quickly!"

Ine takes in his flushed face. "What?"

"There were no guards. Watching Cadwy." He gasps the words between breaths. "I doubled back, tried to find you. I fear a trick—"

"I must say, brother," calls a voice, "you played your part perfectly."

Ine turns. Ingild is standing in the open space before the gates, Nothhelm and Edred at his shoulder. With growing horror, he sees Hædde and the young priest Winfrid making their way down the street too, Leofric in their wake. "What is this thing you wished to show me, Ingild?" the gesith calls before spotting Ine and Gweir. "Lord." He frowns. "What goes here?"

"You may ask my brother that." Ingild's eyes are bright. "He should be able to tell you what he is doing at the gates with a saddled horse and the wealh brat at his side."

Cadwy rips off his hood. "Say that again, pig."

"You intended to break my ruling. The Witan's ruling." Ine is acutely aware that of those present, besides Gweir, only Leofric voted against killing Cadwy. "I heard you in the church."

"You heard what I wanted you to hear." Ingild chuckles. "I knew you harboured unfortunate sympathies for the pagans, but to think you would go so far as to betray us for them." His face sets soberly, all traces of humour gone. "You disappoint me, brother. You disappoint us all."

"Lord." Leofric takes an uncertain step forward. "Please tell me your brother speaks nonsense."

"When does he not?" Ine growls. *How could he do this?* Directing his anger at Ingild is better than feeling the burn of it against himself. A trap, and he had walked right into it. "I am betraying no one. I am preserving the life of a boy who does not deserve to die."

"This grieves me, Ine king," Hædde says, sounding not at all grieved. "To think, after everything you have done for the Church, that you would defend heathen ways." He shakes his head. "It is, as Ingild says, disappointing."

His anger threatens to spill over at any moment. Ine remembers what happened the last time it did and grits his teeth. "This is absurd. It has nothing to do with my sympathies, Christian, pagan or otherwise."

Their raised voices have drawn folk drinking at the tavern on the corner. Whispers travel back and more appear, holding cups and consternation. Torchlight illumines Cadwy's face. Enough people have glimpsed the prince to recognize him, and whispers become exclamations.

"Enough of this." Ingild looks to the warriors gathered behind him and they unshoulder their bows. "Kill Geraint's son."

Ine throws out an arm before Cadwy. "Leave him."

"Brother." The word is cold. "Do not make this difficult."

"Any man who touches him dies," Ine says, and warriors who had begun to nock arrows freeze, uncertain.

"What are you waiting for?" Ingild barks at them. "Do you wish the boy to live to raise an army? To spill your blood on the field? My brother is a traitor and will face justice for siding with pagans."

Why? Ine stares at the ugly mottling on Ingild's cheeks, those words ringing in the chambers of his heart. *What wrong have I done you?*

Metal rasps as Gweir steps between Ine and the men, his blade drawn. "*You* are the traitor, Ingild. I follow the true King of Wessex." He glares at the rest of them. "I thought you did too."

"I am sure it took little to convince *you*, a man with filthy wealh blood in his veins," Ingild retorts, lip curling. Beyond him, however, Leofric's face is strained as he gazes on his friend.

"Leofric." Gweir extends his free hand, palm up. "You know this is wrong."

"Enough," Ingild snarls. "Kill the pagan." His eyes meet Ine's. "And any who stand with him."

The sound of a bow twanging fills the night, fills Ine's ears. The anger inside him flares. Abruptly, he can *feel* the arrow it released, knows where it will strike the unarmed boy. The grain of its wood, the tree it once was part of, the roots that mingle in earth and water, webbing the land. They are veins, he realizes. Veins that lie beneath the skin of a vast being, whose chest rises and falls in perpetual motion like the tide, like the inescapable circle of seasons. All of it flashes across his mind in half an instant before he raises a hand, as if to shield his eyes from the sun.

The arrow bursts into splinters. Ine has a familiar fleeting sense of disintegration, just as with the bone knife, before thunder cracks across the sky. Between his fingers, he glimpses a vast pattern in the heavens, so intricate and beautiful that it steals his breath. Then a force is racing through his blood, unchecked, and lightning roars down to strike the ground a foot from Leofric. Horrified, Ine watches the man thrown aside in a spray of dirt to slam against a building. Smoke rises from his clothes and people start to scream.

"*Leofric!*" His voice is not alone when it shouts the gesith's name.

Hædde's eyes move from Leofric to the splinters of arrow. He draws the sign of the cross, and Ine swallows a wretched urge to laugh. *That will not save you.* He cannot stop staring at the fallen warrior, searching for the smallest signs of life, but Leofric is still. *What have I done?* His hands are shaking, and frightened cries surround him. Neither are enough to curb the disastrous power. Already it is building again. Above him, the clouds burst open.

"You see the wickedness these pagans wield?" Ingild levels a damning finger at Cadwy. "A life for a life. There is always a price."

"I didn't." The rain has washed the snarl from the prince's face. "I couldn't." But the sound of the crowd is growing, a swelter of anger and fear that echoes Ine's. They want blood. Geraint's son backs away as the crowd tightens, Ingild's men leading, and Ine and Gweir are forced to back away with him.

"What is going on—Ine, Ingild?"

"Come no closer, sister," Ingild shouts over the growling sky. "It is not safe."

"I saw light arcing from the heavens." It is the only time Ine has seen Cuthburh shocked. Even on the day their mother died, she had swallowed the news without a grimace.

Cwenburh pushes past, taking in the scene with one sweep of

her dark eyes. Ine watches them flash wide at the same instant the hairs rise on the back of his neck.

The dead flank the gates. Centwine *and* Cædwalla. A chill panic seizes him; he'd naively hoped he had seen the last of his predecessor. But something is different. Fingers are pointing at the wights, and voices clamour in disbelief. Hædde's mouth opens, closes, apparently struck speechless at the sight. How is it possible for others to see the dead when only Ine could before?

A flash of colour catches his eye. Æthelburg's maid is standing atop the roof of the smithy, and she no longer resembles a serving woman. She is clad in fiery silk, its folds whipping round her in the storm wind. Her feet are bare, her skin like crushed pearls, untouched by the rain. Her eyes are the painful green of new spring grass. She blinks them, deliberate; she knows he has seen her.

"Our king will not condemn the pagan," Ingild shouts, pulling Ine's attention away, "or his use of powers that slew a man of Wessex." His brother is flushed. Rings glow in the hissing torchlight as he raises both hands. "So God has called the honoured dead from their sleep to pass judgment instead."

Amidst the gasps of the crowd, the young priest, Winfrid, levels his spear at the wights. "Ine king, do not let them touch you."

They still believe Cadwy did this. One of Leofric's legs is twisted at an unnatural angle. Ine looks from him to the wights, and the power he cannot control threatens to rip down the sky, rupture the very ground on which Wiltun stands. It is too like the vision he had in the crypt.

The freezing eyes of Cædwalla and Centwine are fixed on Geraint's son, as if they have indeed been called to exact justice upon him. Ine searches for Alis, but the roof where she stood is empty. She and the wights appeared at the same time. She must be commanding them.

Cædwalla draws a blade, an exact copy of the bone knife that killed the Britons. There is something ritualistic about the way the dead king raises it in front of his face before he flows forward, inhumanly swift, needle tip aiming for Cadwy's heart.

Ine does not think. He moves faster than he has ever done and catches the wight's arm. The bone blade nicks the chain of the cross about his neck before he wrenches it away. "*I am king here.*" He stares into Cædwalla's cavernous eyes, as icy death shears through him. "*The only order you will obey is mine.*"

"*Can you not feel it?*" Cædwalla whispers. They are face to face and his breath is the reek of an open grave. "*You are dying, Ine. Perhaps our lord will make you one of us, after.*"

He knows the wight speaks truth; the chill inside him threatens to shatter his bones. "I have no intention of being anyone's slave." Agony brings tears to his eyes. "And if I must die, I will take you with me." It has happened so fast. If only he could see Æthel one more time, he would tell her...he would tell her—

The power bucks in his chest and Ine gasps. He has feared it ever since it reached out to seed him with root and bramble. He has run, shied from understanding. He did not want to be changed. *But it has already changed me,* he thinks, as his body shudders. He cannot return to what was. In his mind is the giant...and finally Ine bows his head. He cannot fight it any longer. *I see you.*

Pain is nothing to the shingle and streams of the Land. He *is* the Land. It is everyone here. All lives are small in the heart of sovereignty. He has no other name for it; even god seems lacking. A majesty in the water, in the shape of wind and the beating of wings. In the slope of dark as it bears down on them, and in the stars that burn despite them. It is so vast that everything else recedes.

Everything, that is, except the strange power in the dead. There is a being behind it, holding the strings of soul. Ine opens the Land's myriad eyes to see better and knows he too is being seen. A march of citadels glimpsed across a ghost-grey sea. He recognizes one from Emrys's vision: a cold glass magnificence, sparkling beneath the sun. The nearest flies pennants emblazoned with female figures, nine pairs of arms bearing a cauldron. On its steps is the watcher, and his face is pale with fury. "*Thief.*" A voice as terrible as the towers above him. *"I will find you. And I will rip that pact from your blood myself."*

The vision tumbles away from Ine, slipping out of his grasp strand by strand like the wheat he pulled up in the barn. He has eyes again, a body; bones and blood. Beneath his feet is a golden pool, fed by little rivers welling up from the earth.

Cædwalla's mouth is a grimace of shock. Ine hurls him away with such force that the wight smashes the bar of the gates. Fractures travel through the wood and the hinges buckle. In the silence that follows, Cadwy looks up at Ine, wondering, terrified. "Who *are* you?" The very words Geraint spoke as he died.

"I knew."

Both of them turn at Hædde's voice. The bishop raises his staff of office, as if daring another bolt of lightning to strike it. "I knew it went beyond defending the pagans. How long have you been one of them, Ine king?"

He watches the words borne back, seeded amongst the people of Wiltun. The sky has not ceased rumbling. The rain falls in large merciless drops that promise a punishing winter. Heads turn to him: blurred ovals.

"You have nothing to say? No defence to make?" Hædde gestures at the prone body of Leofric. "This is the price of lowering your eyes from Heaven."

"My eyes see better now, bishop," Ine says. His voice is husky and his hand throbs from touching the wight. "They see how you have poisoned my people, and spread dissent and distrust." The weight of the cross is too much for the damaged chain, which slips from his neck. Hædde watches it fall into the mud. "They see that I am just as guilty for permitting it."

"You are the rot at the heart of this kingdom." The bishop's hand trembles on his staff. "The cattle, crows, who knows what else—"

"He is the only one who can save you from what is coming," Gweir shouts. "No amount of praying will ward off the Otherworld. The dead were not sent by God."

"You speak heresy."

"Call it what you will." Gweir addresses his next words to the people gathered. "If you turn against the king, you doom your-selves and all of Wessex."

It is only Ingild's silence that causes Ine to search him out. His brother's face is drained of all colour, his eyes flicking feverishly between Ine, Cadwy, and the crumpled form of Cædwalla. When he feels Ine's gaze, Ingild's fists clench. "Driving him out is not enough," he calls. "If he is the rot at the heart of the kingdom, we must *cut* him out. He has earned death."

Ine had not listened to Æthel when she questioned his broth-er's influence. Even Gweir had exclaimed over it, and he had pushed it from his mind. When Ingild stepped up to hear the petitions, Ine had let him. Just as he had let him lead the tribute to their father. Is it his own guilt then that opened the door to this? Guilt that Ingild grew up in his shadow, that the moment he found joy, it was snatched away? *These things were not my fault.* But now Ine realizes he never spared the time to understand what they had done to his brother.

"I am sorry, Ingild." He stares into his hate-filled face, knowing the words come too late. "I am sorry for everything."

His brother draws a deep, unsteady breath. For a moment, all Ine senses from him is grief. Then he wraps rage around himself, smothering it. "He cannot stand trial as our laws dictate," Ingild shouts. "He is too dangerous to confine. He should die here. The Witan must agree it now."

Uncertainty parts Nothhelm's lips. "Ingild ætheling. To kill a reigning king is—"

"*Just*, when that king is a traitor." Ingild lifts a finger at the dam-aged gates. "Have you not wondered where the queen is? Why she slipped out so quietly? Like as not, she has gone to incite the Wealas against us. If Ine lives, he will join her and we will have a pagan army on our doorstep."

Ine would laugh at the thought save that, with a sickening lurch, he sees how many brows rise in alarm, how many eyes narrow with anger. Ingild has worked hard to turn opinion against Æthelburg and now it is paying off. Cries of agreement from the crowd, grim nods amongst the men of the Witan.

Perhaps he could have salvaged the situation, but the splintered gates condemn him. Leofric's body condemns him. And Cadwy at his side might as well be the noose around his neck. *Æthel, I am glad you do not have to see us end like this.*

"Ine king, take my horse."

"You are getting out of here, Gweir." Keeping his arm between Cadwy and the crowd, Ine adds, "Go with Cadwy. While you can."

"No." Gweir plants his feet. "If we leave, you come with us, or there is no hope. Seek allies and return. Wessex will need you if she is to survive."

"These people don't need me, Gweir." He can pick out individual faces in the crowd. Gerefa Wulfstan, ealdormen Osberht and Godric, and Thryth with her women, who are begging her to come away. Nothhelm's wife watches avidly. "Look at them."

But the stablemaster, Sinnoch, stands grim-lipped, no trace of scorn or anger in his look. Deorstan is beside him, and he too seems far from violence. Both regard Ine soberly, and do not join the clamour for Ingild's brand of justice.

A hooded figure catches his eye on the edge of the crowd. Even before they raise their head, Ine knows who they are. Emrys nods ever so slightly, a gesture as enigmatic as their person. What does it mean? Can the scop somehow approve of Ine being hounded from his own kingdom like a traitor?

"Then you must show them who you are," Gweir says and it could be Emrys speaking. "You must show them that we are all one people and that the real enemy is the world we cannot see."

Gweir's words in his ears, Ine stares at the crowd, at the faces of those he considered allies just this morning. Then he lunges for one of the saddled horses and pulls an unresisting Cadwy up with him. He can feel the prince trembling.

"Shoot him," Ingild screams, but the warriors hesitate, and it gives Ine the chance he needs. He heels his horse and races for the hole in the gate, Gweir thundering behind. Glancing over his shoulder, it is only then that he sees it. Ingild's sleeves have fallen back, and long jagged scratches mar his forearms. The wounds must have been desperate and deep, or they would have healed by now. Cenred's nails, the congealed blood beneath them. His son's blood.

All the horror of the night seems contained in those marks. *Ingild,* Ine asks the cold wind bruising his face, as the horse carries him away from everything he knows. *What have you done?*

25

ḄERLA

Glestingaburg, Somersæte
Kingdom of Wessex

She stands atop the tor, eyes narrowed fox-like on the night.
Nothing is hidden from her save Gwyn's mind. Whatever his
dream is, she wants no part in it.

Surely there is something I can offer you.

Herla thinks of the woman below, of the desire that has only
grown stronger in the time they have spent apart, and lets herself
imagine another life. What it would be like to have Æthelburg as
her own. Endless summers under the sky, fighting side by side;
winters curled up away from the cold, sharing warmth. Everything
she had wanted from Boudica, and could never have.

But Gwyn is appealing to the hunter in her. The hunter takes
what she wants when she wants it. What would Æthelburg say if
she knew she was a bargaining piece, a prize? The queen would
never abandon her people for a life with Herla. So like the woman
Herla had followed. The woman who had killed herself rather
than live with defeat.

Memory sends her to her knees. *Boudica.* On the day Herla
returned to the world, ignorant of the centuries that had passed,
she had learned that the name belonged to history, not to a person
who had slept in her arms just days before. *She slew herself before
the Romans could do it. Took enough of them with her.*

"I should have died alongside her," she rasps.

"We all should have." A hand reaches down and Herla lets

Corraidhín pull her up. She had not heard her approach; her friend has always moved silently. It made her a great hunter—both of game and of men. And then Corraidhín says, "Another queen, Herla?"

"It is not the same."

"I have seen the way you look at her."

Every day, they are more like the women Herla once led in battle. Spears sharpened to pierce Rome's armour. Tongues that cut as well as jest. Contests of hunting and shooting and songs sung for the fallen—in short, everything that made them human. They are all she has left. Still Herla wishes Corraidhín would not speak so boldly. She cannot bear the flint of her memories, not after hearing Æthelburg speak, watching her teeth flash with her telling, exultant in victory, yet with the same underlying respect for life that Boudica once shared. The respect she lost when the governor's men raped her daughters. Herla trembles, forcing herself to swallow a howl that tastes of black grief and rage. Too animal, like the unthinking shriek of the Hunt.

"It is a bad idea," Corraidhín says.

"Of course it is. I should send her away, but...I can't do it, Corraidhín."

Her friend regards her a little wistfully. "I doubt she would go without a fight. I have also seen the way she looks at you."

Herla turns her face to the wind, letting it cool the heat rising in her. That Æthelburg would want *her*...she has not considered the possibility. What can Herla offer the queen? "She is right, however," she says swiftly. "Gwyn has plans for this land and its people. Do you want revenge, Corra?"

"I did. But revenge will not change the fact that we cannot go back." Corraidhín's voice drops. "And I cannot see how we move forward."

The sentiment echoes her own. "Did you know Gwyn offered me my liberty? *Our* liberty." Herla glances at Dormach; the hound does not obey her order to keep his distance for long. Likewise, the sword at her waist refuses to be parted from her. Herla has tried to be rid of it these past weeks. Left it in the heart of an ancient oak, tossed its dark length into the chasm between two cliffs. Every time it returns, she becomes surer that it is the source of the curse. She will never have true liberty unless she rids herself of both hound and sword.

"At what cost?" Corraidhín asks.

"That I continue to lead the Hunt every moon. That I let him do whatever he wishes to this land." Her heart gives a sick thump of longing. "He will give me Æthelburg if I agree."

"And you are tempted. I do not blame you," Corraidhín adds before Herla can make a doomed attempt to deny it. "But his offers are so drenched in honey that it's impossible to taste the poison beneath."

"Do you think I don't know that?" Herla whirls to pace the summit. The grass coats her boots with dew. "The alternative..." She shivers. "If I oppose him, he will take all of this away." Her gesture encompasses the hilltop, Corraidhín, their conversation. The hall below filled with the work of their sisters' hands. "We will again be animals. Forever."

Corraidhín is silent. Gwyn ripped them from the world that birthed them, and then cast them from the world that changed them. Who are they except the Wild Hunt? The black sword murmurs and once again Herla *almost* wants it back—the predator's oblivion. To hunt without thought or consequence in one unending instant, free of emotion, and the pain of wanting something that she cannot have. "We lived from moment to moment," she whispers. "There is something to be said for it."

"Of course. When is *not thinking* harder? To be unburdened and alive." Corraidhín shakes her head "But I do not believe you want that."

"If—*when* I face Gwyn, will you stand with me?" Herla uses the question to muffle the thought of his offer. Although she blocks her ears, it does not stop singing. "Will you follow me one more time?"

"I will follow you for *all* time, Herla." Corraidhín reaches up to take Herla's face between her palms. "Our sisters too. Remember— we were bound together long before *he* bound us."

Herla swallows roughly. The weight on her spirit does not feel like souls, but tears. Enough to fill the cauldron of Annwn to the brim.

When she masters herself and returns to the hall, Æthelburg is showing Orlaith how to throw an opponent. A light sweat sheens her. Strands of flaxen hair stick to her face. Æthelburg sweeps it carelessly out of her eyes, and the sight makes it even harder for Herla to refuse Gwyn's offer.

"Like this," the queen says. Gripping a strap of Orlaith's armour, she threads an arm beneath the other woman's and—with a seamless turn—rolls her bodily across her shoulder and back. Orlaith hits the earthen floor with a satisfying *thud*. There is pure joy in her voice when she exclaims, "Again!"

Æthelburg laughs. "Why don't you try it on me?"

So recently provoked, Herla's heart is in no state to resist the desire to race. She steps forward. "Or how about *you* try it on *me*?"

"I..." Æthelburg's smile turns nervous and does nothing to help slow Herla's pulse. Could Corraidhín be right? Although they are not touching, she feels the other woman in a way she has only experienced once before, as if invisible fingertips are running lightly over her skin.

Æthelburg gestures at the scuffed circle of earth and Herla moves to join her. "I learned this many years ago." Her voice is a little husky. "When an opponent is heavier or stronger, or if you find yourself weaponless—" her eyes flash to the black sword and then away again—"this can even the odds." The nervousness seems to be in her hands too; her thumb flutters across Herla's collarbone and Herla holds very still. The next thing she knows, she is on the floor, the wind knocked out of her. Æthelburg gazes down, somewhat rueful. How long has it been since anyone stood over her in victory, even in the practice arena? Herla laughs aloud. As if the women were all holding their breaths, there is a great *whoosh* of air before they laugh too.

She lets Æthelburg pull her to her feet. "My turn."

The queen raises pale brows, nods and the laughter dies away. The throw is not a move Herla knows, but she thinks she sees how it is done. The moment she touches Æthelburg, however, she realizes her mistake. She is overly aware of their closeness, of the heart beating just inches away beneath warm skin. She can feel the rise and fall of her chest, the little hitch in Æthelburg's breath as Herla hesitates. Over her shoulder, Corraidhín is giving her a *remember what we just spoke about* sort of look. Herla shakes her head, tightens her grip and—

She is on the floor again, the ends of Æthelburg's hair tickling her cheek. The other woman's knee pins her in place and Herla has no room to wonder what went wrong. Blue eyes look into her own, not icy, but hot enough to set her whole body aflame. She could reach up, could so easily reach up, wind her fingers into blonde hair and pull Æthelburg down to her—

Corraidhín coughs. Æthelburg's cheeks redden and she scrambles off. "Sorry, I couldn't resist." She glances at Orlaith. "There is always a counter to every move, you see."

Chuckling, Senua passes her another cup of wine. "For besting Herla."

"Truly," Herla murmurs. She is trying hard to forget how the other woman felt. A glorious combination of lean muscle and soft skin. A scar marks Æthelburg's upper arm, newly won, Herla thinks, and pink amidst the brown of summer. She knows she is staring, can feel Corraidhín's warning glare on the back of her neck. *It is a bad idea.*

So was Boudica, perhaps. So was Annwn. She seems to be made of bad ideas. Sobering at the thought, Herla sits up and the chatter trails off. "You asked for our help," she says, and Æthelburg's lips part in surprise. "One thing I know for certain is that the Dumnonian birthright is the only power I have encountered that can fight the curse that binds us here—and therefore Gwyn." She remembers the strength of the silver vines. Their touch had, ever so briefly, threshed the Hunt from her mind. And when silver became gold, it was enough to compel the hound to leap, to free her at last from the threat of the earth that had turned Ráeth to dust. "What else might that power do, in the right hands?" she asks aloud. "I think Gwyn of Annwn wonders and fears the same."

"The right hands?" Æthelburg leans forward, her cup of wine forgotten. "Gweir said the Britons believe they have lost their protection. They meant Geraint. The Dumnonian birthright died with him."

"Did it?" Herla shakes her head slowly. "Then what power freed us? Where did the golden light come from? These are questions we should ask."

"We," Æthelburg echoes. Her mouth quirks. "Does that mean you won't send me away?"

"No." But the word is hollow and the queen hears it. "If Geraint's power passed to his successor," Herla hurries on, "we need to find them. I would bet that Gwyn's people are searching for them too. And snuffing all traces of the heritage as they go."

"The Heir of Dumnonia," Æthelburg says thoughtfully. "It is surely his son, Cadwy. The boy even spoke of his duty to his people." She bites her lip. "Alis turned up around the time we brought him to Wiltun. If she is from the Otherworld..."

"He is in danger."

"Eanswith too. At least Cadwy is protected by Ine's ruling so..." Æthelburg stops, her eyes widening. "Oh God. I saw Alis and Ingild together. He wants Cadwy dead because he thinks the boy will incite rebellion amongst the Britons in Wessex. It would not take much to convince him to act, especially if she used... other means to help him."

"And this Cadwy's youth worries me," Herla says. "Gwyn is ancient and cunning. A green boy will be no match for him."

"If he is heir to this power, he's all we have." The queen's face clouds. "Wiltun is no longer safe for Cadwy. It never was." She rises to her feet. "I might make it back in two days, if I ride hard."

Herla rises with her. "It will be faster if I take you."

"You'll come with me?" There is something else besides surprise in Æthelburg's voice. An eager joy that sets Herla's heart aflame once more. *You are a fool,* she tells herself. *The more time you spend with her, the harder it will be to reject Gwyn's offer. And remember what almost happened.* She thrusts the voice aside. Her fear of hurting Æthelburg has not left her, but the moon is weeks to old, and she cannot let the queen return alone.

Naturally the others wish to come. They clamour and gripe, but Herla is unmoved. "We go quietly. If I need you, I will call for you. The gate to Annwn—"

"Can only be opened at certain times," Corraidhín snaps. "And Samhain is more than a month away."

"The walls between worlds will grow thinner and thinner from now until that night." Herla grips her friend's arm. "Who knows what may come through with Gwyn's aid? You must stay here to watch. He will bring a host. I know it. I saw it."

"I will not let you use this excuse again," Corraidhín threatens, gripping Herla's forearm in turn. "The next time, we go with you."

"Agreed," she says because Corraidhín will otherwise cling like the barnacles Herla used to cut her feet on as a child. Scrambling over tide-washed rocks, her mother's admonishments lost in the wind. *Mother.* A face shapes itself out of the nothing that is her past. That used to be her past. Because now it swirls like mist occasionally pierced by the sun.

Corraidhín pulls her away from the others. "I know why you want to go alone," she says with a nod to Æthelburg. "And I have shared my thoughts on that already. But is this really your battle, Herla?"

"What *is* our battle, Corra?" she demands. "Where else should I be? If Gwyn wishes me to sit in this hall and do nothing, then the freedom we have won is meaningless."

"When he sees you aiding the queen, he will know you have refused his offer. How will you face him without us?"

If you think I cannot bind you again, you are wrong. Herla suppresses a shudder. "Gwyn is not here."

"But his spies *are.*" Corraidhín's voice is a hiss. "Once they witness you defending this boy heir, they will know you have defied him."

Herla turns away before Corraidhín can marshal any more arguments. Her friend is right, but she has made up her mind. The only other choice is to let Æthelburg walk into danger alone, and she will not countenance that.

When she rejoins her, the queen raises an enquiring brow. "You should sleep a little first," Herla tells her. "You have been travelling all day and drinking half the night."

"I have not been drinking half the night," the queen replies loftily then ruins it with a hiccup. The women around her chuckle, and Æthelburg shakes her head as if to clear it. "I can't waste time on sleep."

"Then sleep while we ride. I will not let you fall." Corraidhín glares, but Herla pretends not to see. Æthelburg's expression is hidden in her cloak, as she throws it around herself.

Herla whistles. Her horse reforms from the darkness and she remembers, abruptly, that his coat used to shine. Does he miss the herd? Life on the meadow seas of Annwn? Mounted, she extends a hand to Æthelburg and the queen lets Herla pull her up. "I will not sleep," she says in the stubborn tones of someone fighting that very urge. It takes all of five minutes before her head slumps against Herla's chest and her breathing softens.

The distance to Wiltun is negligible. An hour, perhaps, for a steed of Annwn. The woman leaning against her is a warm and wonderful weight and Herla tells herself she dawdles because Æthelburg must rest. But she is not selfless. She has always been too proud. Instead she revels in being able to hold her freely, in the feel of her arm around the queen's waist. Even this makes her new-woken heart beat faster. She should not be thinking these thoughts, or feeling the beautiful disbelief of finding something so rare as love again. Herla recalls the last time she thought of the word, trapped in the dream-hell of Annwn. She could not touch it then, had not language for it, but Æthelburg has given her back the words.

All too soon, the landscape flattens and dawn lightens the dun of the sky. Perhaps the queen senses it, for her eyelids lift and she stares around with a creased brow. Herla's arm still wraps her waist, keeping her in place. Æthelburg turns her head, the flush of dawn echoed in her cheeks. Her lips shape several unknown words before settling on, "It's morning."

"So it would appear." The sight of the waking settlement ahead of them reminds Herla to slip back into Ælfrún, as if the woman were a garment.

Æthelburg draws a startled breath. "I prefer seeing you as you are," she murmurs and lifts what seems a regretful hand to Herla's face. Her fingers brush Herla's cheek before drawing back, suddenly uncertain, and Herla would like nothing more than to catch them, imprison them within her own, bring them to her lips. But the moment passes. "We're here," the other woman says wonderingly. "I cannot believe it." And then, squinting at the still-distant town, "Something's wrong. The gates…"

Herla snaps a word to the horse and they surge forward. "Not too close." Æthelburg gestures at a scrubby stand of trees. "Off the road."

They pause under sheltering branches to watch. Men cluster like flies, and the sound of the saw rasps across the morning. "No catapult or ram caused this." Herla narrows her eyes at the hole blown clean through the wood. "That is the work of power."

"Gwyn?"

"I do not think so. But the scent of Annwn is strong. Alis has been here. The wight too."

"*Wights*," Æthelburg breathes. "Ine said he saw another. Are we too late?"

She makes to dismount, but Herla tightens her hold. "No. We are ignorant of what has happened here and you are too recognizable a figure. Let us go quietly. Invisibly."

"You can make us *invisible*?"

"To mortal eyes. Not to eyes that have looked upon Annwn. It is nothing difficult. A matter of will."

"Oh," Æthelburg says in a smaller voice and glances down at the arm still around her waist. Herla loosens it self-consciously and they both dismount.

Despite the activity, the workers at the gate are subdued, exchanging only the bare minimum of words. Æthelburg flinches as Herla takes her hand and they step into plain sight. When no looks come their way, the other woman straightens her shoulders, but Herla can tell she is shaken. The area around the gates is scuffed, as if from battle. "Don't let go of me," she murmurs, "or I cannot keep you from being seen."

Æthelburg quickens their pace through the streets. "What in God's name has happened here?"

The town has a grim air, and people are cowed. *There is something missing,* Herla thinks, her nostrils full of Annwn's overripe scent. "Otherworld mischief," she says darkly.

Æthelburg's only reaction is to press her lips together until they are as bloodless as her cheeks. When the golden roof of the hall appears before them, it seems dim, as if shadowed by clouds. With a sudden gasp, Æthelburg pulls free of Herla and rushes up the steps.

"Æthelburg!"

Herla only just makes it to the top before the doors swing open. She seizes the queen's hand, hisses, "You will be *seen.*"

"I have to know." Her voice is low and hard. "I have to find him."

The mood in the hall is hardly lighter than in the streets below. But the activity here reminds Herla uneasily of Caer Sidi. Instead of ale, bundles of arrows litter the table. Spears are stacked in racks against the painted walls—at least a dozen more racks than before. The corner is empty of women. Instead, unsmiling servants are oiling armour, re-braiding leather grips and sorting shields into two stacks. Preparations for war.

The doors to the council chamber are closed. For a moment, she is convinced that Æthelburg will kick them open, but the queen just leans her ear against the crack where they join. Herla does not need to; she can hear the voices perfectly well.

"How large a fyrd can you raise, Nothhelm?" The hard tones of the king's brother. "Will the men of Sussex stand with us?"

"Of course, Ingild ætheling. We are sworn to Wessex, but—"

"I knew I could rely on you. And Edred?"

"You have my hundred without question, lord."

"Osberht, Godric, Stithulf?"

There is a longer silence before the men named speak. Ealdormen of Wessex, Herla assumes. "Naturally, we will defend our
kingdom," a dry voice says. "I can gather four score fighting men
at once, but more will take time."

"Time is a luxury we do not have." Hædde, the bishop.

"Surely the Wealas cannot be roused before winter."

"Æthelburg will be in Dumnonia by now," Ingild says. The
queen draws a sharp breath and Herla tightens her grip on her
hand. "She will not wait to strike. We must fortify Wiltun before
taking the fight to her."

"She is only a woman, Ingild ætheling. A woman who—"

"Has won nearly every battle she has fought. She is not to be
underestimated."

A quake goes through the woman leaning against the door,
like a bitter soundless laugh. "We must find my brother," Ingild
continues. "We must kill him before he reaches her. You saw what
he was capable of last night. Together, they will be unstoppable."

It is not a single tremor this time. Æthelburg is shaking. Her
mouth shapes words that do not come; perhaps she cannot bring
herself to believe them. She reaches for the iron ring of the door,
and manages to grasp it before Herla whispers, "Stop."

"I will not stand for it," Æthelburg snarls softly. "Ingild speaks
slander and treason. When the Witan sees me..."

"Who knows what they will do?" Herla holds her tighter as the
queen strains to free herself. She is remarkably strong, the muscles in her arms and shoulders visible through her tunic.
"Something is not right here."

"We have no proof the Wealas will march with Ine," comes
Nothhelm's voice and Æthelburg pauses in her struggle. "We do
not even know where he is."

"He would not have rescued Geraint's son if he didn't have an
agreement with him."

"You knew he was in the church," Nothhelm says, the sharp
edge of accusation in his tone. "You staged that conversation to
force his hand. And you forced me too—to speak treason."

"I am sorry for it, Nothhelm." A pause, as if Ingild is meeting every eye. "It was a risk for us both. But Ine would not have revealed his loyalties otherwise."

"And we would have learned of his heresy too late," Hædde says. "Now, at least, we are in position to fight back. A risk it might have been, Ingild, but for a worthy cause. It was cleverly done."

Silence falls before another voice speaks, a young man's that Herla does not recognize. "It cannot have been easy to condemn your own brother, Ingild ætheling. To me it seems it would take great...strength. Of character."

Æthelburg has stopped straining against Herla's grip. A strange stillness rules her instead, as if her own shock has the power to petrify.

"Thank you, Winfrid," Ingild says, and Herla muffles a snort. The ears of the other men must be stuffed with wax if they cannot hear the falseness in the young man's tone. Whether wittingly or not, he has touched upon the very thing she and Æthelburg had feared—the Otherworld's influence. Ingild has clearly worked hard to build his credibility, but something in that room reeks of Annwn. Herla is beginning to suspect she knows what—*who*— it is.

"Walk with me," Ingild says, and wood scrapes. Before the doors can open, Herla pulls an unresisting Æthelburg behind a pillar. It is well she does: when the king's brother emerges, his body is limned in the same light as Alis's. Fainter, but enough to allow him to see through Herla's glamour.

"Gwyn has him," she breathes, watching the man stride through the hall to inspect the readied weapons, a king in all but name.

Æthelburg says nothing. Her eyes are frighteningly empty.

Herla leads them back through the town, and they piece together the rest of the story as they go. Much of it is confused. Terrified mutterings about the dead returned; a Dumnonian horde; pagans in the streets of Wiltun who have corrupted even the king. As soon as they regain the shelter of the copse, Herla drops her glamour and Æthelburg leans her forehead against a tree. "I shouldn't have left."

"This is not your fault, Æthelburg."

"I was selfish." She spits the word. Her fingers grasp the bark like claws. "I knew Ingild hungered for the throne, but I never thought..."

"Æthelburg. Look at me."

"...he would have the guts to move against Ine like this. I thought... *stupid*." A red mark on her forehead where she is pressing it into the tree. "I should have confronted him."

Herla turns her bodily. "You did not know."

"I all but threw Ine to the hounds." The queen's eyes are no longer empty; they are brimming-fierce. "I'll kill Ingild. This time, I will kill him."

Herla catches the hand that goes for her sword. "Æthelburg, he is up to his neck in the Otherworld. I sensed it on him. He is dangerous."

Her eyes clear slightly. "Alis?"

"I am not saying Ingild is innocent, but she has a hand in this. The Folk are masters of manipulation." A bitter tang floods Herla's mouth. Something she knows all too well. "If the king's brother is ambitious, it would not take much to persuade him to act. To influence him." She looks away. "I cannot escape my mistakes, but perhaps Ingild can still escape his."

"The shit. As if I will give him the chance."

"Did you hear what the townsfolk said?" It is an attempt to distract her. "That the king faced the wights and lived."

"Cadwy must have aided him, stood with him." Her shoulders slump. "As I did not."

"The king is not a child," Herla says and it comes out more harshly than she intended. "You are not responsible for him or his actions. You cannot protect him, Æthelburg."

"What do you know?" She blinks a few times, angrily, as if tears are an enemy she must hold back. "You know nothing about it."

"Perhaps you do not wish to believe he can cope without you."

"He can't," she snarls, taking a few steps away, turning her head so that Herla sees only a flushed cheek. "He is a dreamer. He's never lived in the real world, never understood what it takes to hold onto power. The sacrifices, the toll." Her voice becomes brittle. "He does not know what it feels like to kill in the name of a kingdom. Over and over."

Into the silence that follows, Herla says softly, "But we do, don't we? You and I."

Æthelburg's chest is heaving. When she finally looks up, her eyes are wet. And there is fire in them. She closes the distance, raises her arms—to fight Herla, or to pull her near, it's unclear— but Herla catches her, locking both hands around her bare forearms. Æthelburg struggles for a heartbeat before the fight leaves her. Instead, tears spill down her cheeks. She buries her face in the crook of Herla's neck and sobs.

They sink to the earth. Herla lets Æthelburg slump against her and curves a hand to hold the queen's head. Her fingers want to tangle in fair hair; she keeps them still with an effort. But she has not accounted for the effect of the tears. Her neck is soon wet with them; she feels Æthelburg's every gasped breath as a shudder, as if her grief is calling to the one that pierced Herla long ago, grief the Hunt tried to smother. And the life that went with it. A flame in her heart; a wind through the embers. Light after centuries of darkness.

She can feel her pulse quickening. The hand resting on Æthelburg's hair tightens just a little. But the queen's sobs hitch and stop. In that moment, when all is still, both of them hold their breath. Both know Æthelburg must draw back eventually. When she does, ever so slowly, her face is red and very beautiful. They are so close that Herla can almost taste the salt of tears on her lips.

26

ÆTHELBURG

Wiltun, Wiltunscir
Kingdom of Wessex

"I knew you were no fool, Herla," comes a voice.

Æthel's chin is still tilted, her lips parted. She had been ready to drown in amber eyes, wanted nothing more than to go under and never surface. But Herla jerks. She moves so fast that Æthel finds herself on her knees behind the other woman, a guarding arm thrown across her. "You must be Alis," Herla says, rising to her feet.

Scrambling up too, Æthel peers over her shoulder to see her former maidservant standing implausibly among the trees. They should have heard her approach. *But you had other things on your mind.* Her throat is sore from crying, and her heart too, a muddle. What had she been thinking?

"Don't you recognize me, Herla?" Alis's laugh is like flute song. "I know—it has been centuries to you. Though to me, only scant weeks have passed since we broke bread together in Caer Sidi." Her body frays, shedding her patched dress as if it were a cocoon. Out of it steps a blinding figure. Silk wraps her, a red brighter than madder, like heart's blood. Golden-haired and green-eyed, Æthel would consider her beautiful were it not for the remoteness in her face. Unreal, distant, and with that distance a lack of mercy, of anything resembling compassion. Æthel takes a step back.

"Olwen," Herla murmurs and bows her head, as if in defeat.

The woman laughs, delighted. "I knew you had not forgotten me."

"Where is Eanswith?" The question is out before she realizes she has spoken. Olwen turns those awful eyes her way, and Æthel trembles despite herself.

"Who?" the woman asks sweetly.

She hates the fear crawling through her. "My maid. Where is she? What have you done with her?"

"What makes you think she did not go to her parents like she said?"

"She would be back by now."

The fairy woman shrugs. "I couldn't have her come back too soon. Not while I needed her job."

"You are a terrible maidservant." The words are petty, but bile is rising in Æthel's throat. "*Where is she?*"

"No doubt still in the ditch I put her in." Olwen's eyes narrow. "Are you content now that you have made me say such ugly things?"

With a rage-filled cry, Æthel goes for her sword, but Herla stops her. She struggles; it is like pushing against an oak. "She deserves death. For Eanswith."

Olwen calmly rearranges her silk. "Thank you, Herla. You know how I hate mess."

"I am not doing it for you." Although unyielding, Herla's grip on Æthel is gentle. "I assume you are responsible for what occurred here?"

"Me?" She tips her head on one side. "My part has been small. Cows and crows are child's play, but they are ever so effective at fanning mortal fears."

"Why?" Æthel demands. "What is it you want?"

"Only scraps, my brethren might say, from Lord Gwyn's table." Olwen is not smiling now. "But when Ingild is king, I will rule beside him. Gwyn ap Nudd cannot be here all the time, and men are so easy to influence."

"So you *are* working with Ingild."

Olwen's look is cold, considering. "You would make a fine trap for your husband. A pity I cannot touch you." She directs her next words to Herla. "I assume you have accepted Gwyn's offer? Take your woman and go, Herla. Do not interfere."

Æthel freezes, as if Olwen's look has seeded its chill inside her. "His offer?"

Flinching, Herla releases her, and Æthel steps back. "His *offer*?" she repeats frostily, while the cold grows in her gut.

Olwen gives her fluting laugh. "Do not look so outraged, child. Bargains made between the Folk of Annwn do not concern mortals. Only Herla and my lord Gwyn need know the details."

Herla says quietly, "I am not of Annwn."

"Everything you are, *he* made you. Like it or not, Herla, you are as much a part of Annwn as I am."

"I belong *here*," Herla says, her hunter's eyes blazing. She takes a step forward. "My Eceni mother birthed me, in struggle and blood. My queen shaped me, put weapon and cause in my hands. You say *Gwyn* made me?" She laughs—and it has none of Olwen's music. It is like the victory cry of the owl, the harsh lilting hawk. "It was my own foolish ambition that made me, fairy. Gwyn merely took advantage, as so many of your kind do. But if you think I bear him no ill will because of it, you are wrong. Accept his offer?" She draws the black blade, which swallows the light, until they stand in a world of shadows. "I want his head."

Olwen looks from the blade to Herla and then beyond, into Æthel's eyes. "This is your answer?"

"It is." Herla raises the sword. "And if you do not get out of my sight, we will see whose strength is the greater."

For the first time, Olwen's face pinches in fear. Her eyes do not leave the shadowy blade as she backs away. "You will pay for it, Herla. He will bind you so tightly that you will even forget your own name."

With a whisper of red, she is gone, leaving Herla staring at the sword. The only emotion Æthel can read in her is hate. Then she sheathes it, light floods back into the copse, and with it comes awkwardness. Æthel's palms tingle as she remembers how close they had been, how she could have gazed into the heat of Herla's eyes forever. *Take your woman and go.* She steels herself. "*I* was a part of this offer? But Gwyn is your enemy. Surely you would not have accepted—"

"Why do you think Gwyn offered you if he did not believe there was a chance I would accept?"

Herla's back is towards her, and Æthel is glad; she can feel colour returning to her cheeks. "Was there a chance?"

The other woman stands very still. "What would you say if I told you there was?"

"I…" Æthel's courage finally fails her. In its place is a fearful sort of awe. *She cares for me.* "I don't know." But she cannot deny her heart is racing at the thought.

"Then it is better unsaid." Herla finally turns. Her face is hard, but it is only a shell; Æthel can see the turmoil beneath it. She takes an uncertain step forward and then Herla adds, "Now Olwen knows I have refused his offer, Gwyn will not allow me my freedom any longer. He will come for me."

Æthel lifts her chin. "I won't let him harm you."

"I appreciate the sentiment," Herla says with a wan smile. "But you cannot stop him."

"Then what do we do?" With a nod towards Wiltun, "Gwyn is not the only thing I have to worry about. Ingild is all but calling himself king, and you heard Olwen—they plan to hunt Ine down." She lets out an explosive breath. "Ingild will *not* take Wessex without a fight. I won't allow it."

Herla whistles softly and her horse melts out of the landscape. The sight no longer startles Æthel. "These things are intertwined. It is Gwyn's favourite game—to bargain with mortals. Apart from offering assistance, Olwen must be here to ensure Ingild keeps to his side of whatever deal they have struck."

"Today's praise is the highest Ingild has ever offered me," Æthel says, feeling a ripple of dark humour. "Do I seem like the type to ride headlong into Dumnonia…?" She trails off because she knows exactly who *is* that type. She has been listening to him defending the Britons all year. There had been two other voices missing from the Witan. Leofric and Gweir. Leofric she cannot account for. But Gweir…*If Ine escaped with Cadwy and Gweir, there is only one place they will go. Only one place they can go.*

"This runs deeper than Gwyn's love of chaos. He spoke of a dream he had fostered." Herla grimaces, as if she has bitten into the heart of something rotten. "Our only clue is the heritage. I think our path leads there."

"To Dumnonia?"

"And its Heir." Herla's look is sharp. "Whoever they may be."

She does not like the thought of doing exactly what Ingild believes she has already done. From the small height of the copse, Æthel watches cloud shadows spread like bruises over the land; she frowns. Something is missing; ineffable, but vital as breath.

"Ine may think differently, but I will not flee to a place where I have no allies." She stares at a pale and distant hilltop, untouched by shadows. "I have always put my faith in the people of Wessex. In the strength of their arms, whether wielding the sword or the scythe. And in their hearts. If Ingild believes they will simply accept his overthrow of the rightful king, then I will show him that he is wrong." In her mind is the memory of men saluting her with the tools of their livelihoods. Æthel had not known then how to feel, but she knows now: proud…and humbled. She will not turn her back on them, especially if Ingild is loyal foremost to his own ambition.

"Ingild believes he can raise the fyrds against Ine," she muses aloud. "He has the support of many ealdormen. But there are others who will not be so easily swayed. That is where I will start."

"Start?"

"I have to believe he is safe," Æthel murmurs. "Because there is work to do here. If Ingild plans to march, I plan to stop him."

"You will raise these fyrds first? But how do you know the men will follow you?"

"Many will not. Others might." A grim smile on her lips, she adds, "And I will have to do it quietly."

"Raise an army quietly." Herla laughs and, God, but Æthel could listen to that sound forever.

Was there a chance?

What would you say if I told you there was?

"That is the plan," she whispers. She should be thinking of her task, and of her husband. Of Ingild and Wessex, Gwyn and Annwn. But inside Æthel is the passing of that chance, and what might have happened if Herla had chosen differently. "What will *you* do?" she asks to distract herself.

The other woman shakes her head. "Olwen will waste no time. I must return to Glestingaburg to ensure everything is well. Where shall I meet you?"

"Hamwic," Æthel says at once. "Ealdorman Beorhtric is a friend. He is old and does not travel much to Wiltun, so Ingild has had less chance to turn him."

"That is leagues away and your horse is at the hall." Herla looks at her own consideringly. "I wonder." Her eyes become unfocused, as if the middle distance holds another world instead of the blurred shapes of the nearer one. After a while, the air shimmers again, revealing the glossy flank of a horse the twin of Herla's. "She was Ráeth's, our sister whom the earth took back."

Æthel raises a hesitant hand. The horse is huge, much larger than her own, and when it turns an eye on her, she has the sense of being *observed*. As if the creature is regarding her with as much intelligence as she regards it. "She will carry you swiftly," Herla says.

"I can't ride this." The horse blinks slowly at her and Æthel breaks its gaze with an effort. "I am just a woman. Not like you."

"So I must keep reminding myself," Herla mutters before patting the gleaming flank between them. "But I have asked her and she will bear you."

Æthel's fingers are still raised. Cautiously, she lowers them until they rest on the horse's neck. The coat is silken and not as black as she thought. Colour swirls across it like oil on water; again the smell of flowers and salt.

"Take this too." Herla slides a spear from her saddle. "It will allow you to see those of the Otherworld...and to harm them."

Runic letters march down the shaft of the spear, and its tip is wickedly sharp. Meant for stabbing rather than throwing. Feeling its weight and perfect balance, Æthel does not even think of refusing. "Thank you. These are great gifts."

"May they keep you safe, Æthelburg, until I find you."

Before she can mount, Æthel catches her arm. "Wait." She swallows. "You said Gwyn will come for you."

"He will not find me as weak as before." But Æthel spies the shadow of a terrible fear in Herla's face. "I have the will to fight him."

They look at each other. The events of the morning have driven them from her mind, but now Orlaith's words come thundering back. *Boudica.* It is a name out of legend. How can it be that Herla knew her? Æthel had pressed Orlaith for more, but all the woman had said was, *it is her story to tell.* She lets go of the breath she has been holding. "Why did he do it?" she asks softly. "Gwyn ap Nudd. Why did he curse you?"

A tremor goes through Herla. "Because I asked him to." Her voice is coarse and she breaks Æthel's gaze to stare beyond her. "I asked for power."

"To fight Rome? Orlaith told me," Æthel adds when Herla's eyes widen. "Only a little. Don't be angry with her."

"Yes." Rather than angry, Herla sounds resigned. "We were outmatched and I knew how it would end. The gradual destruction of everything that made us Eceni." Æthel can see the reflection of it in her furrowed brow: the despair at being helpless. "It began with Prasutagus's deal," Herla says. "And it worsened with his death." She laughs harshly. "The governor who ordered Boudica flogged when she refused to give up her inheritance—he had no idea what his actions would spark, the rivers of blood she would spill." She pulls her eyes back to Æthel, away from whatever visions her memory is building. "He underestimated her."

Grief hides in Herla's tone. Not just grief, but rage and regret too. Æthel is stunned by the strength of it, like a poison brewed over centuries until it is potent enough to sicken the world. She cannot find words to respond, except that she knows what it is to be underestimated.

Herla walks a few steps away. "Boudica united the tribes. But what is a tribe to an empire? We needed something to level the field." Her hand drops to the slender, dark blade at her waist. "So I made my own deal. I went to Annwn and accepted every *gift*—" the word is sour with irony—"that Gwyn offered. I thought I was helping my people, but I was dooming them and myself along with them."

The story lies heavy on Æthel's heart. How much must it weigh on Herla's? The other woman's back is turned, pain in the hunch of her shoulders. "I came to him asking to be made a hero." Her voice drops to a stricken whisper. "Instead, he made me a monster."

Æthel's feet close the distance between them. She had not asked them to. Her heart, so heavy a moment ago, is pounding when she winds her arms around Herla's waist. "You are no monster."

Wind fills the silence, catching in Herla's many small braids and making the beads click gently together. Æthel lays her cheek against Herla's back, breathing in leather and something like the scent that clings to the steeds of Annwn. She wants to stay this way. She wants Herla to turn around.

Herla tilts her head to stare at the hands twined at her waist, as if, Æthel thinks, they are the strangest of sights. Still, she does not move, and Æthel's heart is a sun in her chest, scorching her. "Look at me," she says.

"No." A strained whisper.

"Look at me." Æthel releases her hands to trail one up Herla's arm, to turn her, so that she can meet the other woman's eyes. Their amber is dark, like the sun setting behind sky-cliffs. Breathless with daring, she cups Herla's face, thumbs stroking along the strong, prideful jaw. Before those eyes can do more than widen, Æthel kisses her.

Just a brush, a skim across the surface. But even so brief a touch leaves her light-headed. Herla draws a deep, unsteady breath, as if caught in a struggle Æthel cannot see. Then her own hands flash up, one tilting Æthel's chin, another tightening on her waist. Her voice, when it comes, is low. "I said you were an impossible woman, Æthelburg of Wessex."

She has never been kissed like this before. Not just her lips, but her whole body; a sweet, insistent ache in every limb. The palms of her hands burn where they touch the other woman. Her toes curl in her boots. When Herla draws back just enough to graze her bottom lip with her teeth, Æthel snatches a ragged gasp of air and closes the gap again. Herla laughs softly, a wicked sound that fills Æthel's mind with things she has no place in thinking, but she cannot care, she wants what she wants. The fear she has carried for so very long—that she does not deserve to be warm, to have the empty well inside her filled—is gone in an instant. Her hunger is as great as Herla's. This time it is she who breaks away to trail her lips across the other woman's neck, to nip at the skin she earlier wet with her tears. Herla gives a wordless growl, which only fans the fire burning her up. The hand buried in Æthel's hair sends shivers cascading through her.

"Stop," Herla breathes, a moment from her mouth. "Unless you want me to take you here in this field."

Æthel glories in the urgent heat that swells between her thighs at the thought; how long since she last felt it? "What are you waiting for?"

To her dismay, the invitation has the opposite effect. Herla lets go of her, puts distance between them—as if she cannot trust herself without it. "You have a husband."

The word *husband* is like a gust of cold wind in her face. Her cheeks are hot, flushed with desire, and now too with a heat that feels horribly like shame. Defiant, Æthel thrusts it down. "What does that matter?"

"You have already given him your heart."

"My heart cannot be given away like a trinket," Æthel snaps. "It is still mine."

"Many things have come between you." Herla's eyes are afire with regret, and something a little like fear. "I do not wish to be one more."

Stung, Æthel balls her fists. How can a moment be so different from the one before? All the elation of desire has drained away. "If you are trying to make me take back what I said, I won't. I meant every word." Her eyes prickle and she turns them on the horse standing motionless behind her. "I have work to do. I should be doing it."

The animal is huge. She expects a graceless scrabble, but between breaths Æthel is in the saddle without quite knowing how she managed it. She turns the horse south-east, aware that Herla has not moved. *I will not look around.* Perhaps the creature hears her because abruptly they are galloping for the distant coast, and it is too late to look back. Regret is a stone she must swallow, alongside the memory of Herla's scent and the feel of her mouth on hers. God, how she wants—*No.* She will not dwell on it. Better to fill her mind with her task, stoke her anger at Ingild. And yet. *What is this feeling?* Æthel asks of the warmth inside her. Is it only desire?

Leagues pass and the landscape changes. Æthel watches the river widen and wonders at how *she* has changed. A few moons ago, she had barely heard of the Otherworld, or Gwyn ap Nudd. She believed the Wild Hunt a story. Now the muscles of the horse Herla gave her bunch and stretch tirelessly, and she has seen the face of Annwn in Olwen's chill smile. Grief for Eanswith burns her throat. Not just the rules of a game, but the rules of her world are changing. *I will have to learn fast.*

The grey glitter of the estuary pulls her up short. A day's journey, but the horse has managed it in seeming minutes. Hamwic lies beneath a pall, the smoke of its fires drifting up to mingle with the low clouds. Æthel dons her hood. Until she knows what news has reached the ealdorman here…

"Will you stay for me?" she whispers as she dismounts out of sight of the gate. The horse turns its fathomless eyes upon her; she assumes that means yes. There is, however, no way of hiding the spear, and Æthel is not about to leave it behind. It is too short to disguise as a walking aid, so her only option is to secure it unobtrusively to her pack.

Luck is with her. Traders are being waved inside, so she attaches herself to the rear of one group and follows them into the settlement. Hamwic's scents engulf her. Seaweed salts the air, almost covering the doughier aroma of baking bread and the all-pervasive horse dung. Mud makes the streets treacherous for the carts Æthel has to dodge as she weaves her way through the market, ears pricked for gossip. But the faces of folk are grave and there is little to hear. No tongue wants to shape words such as *rebellion*, or *treachery*. No ceorl's tongue, that is. They carry too much risk. So Æthel heads for the mead hall, seat of ealdorman Beorhtric, where such conversations may be had.

The wooden building is almost as large as Wiltun's, although it has but a single floor. Hamwic has profited from the sea trade. Two large braziers burn on either side of the doors, warding off the gloomy afternoon, and guards stand there. Just as Æthel is wondering how to handle them, strident voices reach her. Three men make for the hall, arguing as they go. All are dressed in the fine linen and silver-pinned cloaks of nobles. She ducks around a corner as they pass.

"We wait to see what position Beorhtric takes on the matter," she hears the oldest say. He has suspicious eyes. Never fixed, they sweep the open space around him, as if searching for things that do not belong.

"The old man is not our master," another argues, twisting a burnished ring on his arm. "We ought to look to our own first. If it is advantageous to side with the ætheling…"

"Who has *not* been named heir."

"But is the only possible choice," the third man counters.

"Precisely. Ingild holds Wiltun, which means he commands a sizeable force. Who knows if the king still lives? In fleeing, he is defeated."

The guards turn their backs to open the doors and Æthel seizes her chance. Darting across the space and up the steps, she reaches the doors just as the guards start to swing them closed behind the group. Before the doors meet, before the guards even realize she is there, she kicks them open again. "Not while I breathe."

They gape for a few startled seconds until a voice from within calls, "Æthelburg. I wondered when we might be seeing you."

The swords half-drawn at her action slide back into sheaths.

She pushes past the nobles to grip the speaker's arm in greeting. "Ealdorman Beorhtric. It is good to see you."

"And you, Æthelburg. Although I could wish for happier circumstances."

"Indeed," Æthel says darkly. She cannot keep a furrow from her brow as the nobles cluster in behind her. "I will not waste time on niceties. You know why I am here."

The suspicious man is rubbing the arm she pushed aside in her haste. "There were rumours you had gone to rouse the west Wealas."

"Rumours Ingild started," she points out.

"You deny them?"

"Cutha," the ealdorman barks. "Consider who you are talking to."

"How could I be here if I were in Dumnonia?" Æthel levels a chill look. "Unlike Ingild, I do not believe the people of Wessex are prepared to follow a traitor."

After a tense moment, Beorhtric asks, "The king is alive?"

"Yes." She says it with all the confidence she can muster. *If he wasn't, I would know it. I would.* "He assembles allies, as I must. Ingild's treachery cannot go unchallenged."

"Ingild ætheling has the bishops. With the Church on his side, he can bring in allies from neighbouring kingdoms." Beorhtric's face creases in distaste. "Ealdwulf of Anglia has only to sniff a holy war and he will march to his aid."

"The war is larger than you know." She is overly aware of the clustered nobles, of the women seated on low benches, hands and ears equally engaged. Soft-footed servants add wood to the fire, sweep up bones gnawed to splinters by the dogs dozing nearby. Whenever she meets a gaze, it drops, and yet everyone is listening. She can tell by the false nonchalance, the way tasks are carried out too quietly. Æthel bites her lip. Ine is used to wielding words like weapons, but she has never had the patience. The clever dance of discourse exhausts her.

"Ingild claims the king is a heathen," she says, struggling to keep her anger in check. "This is to disguise the fact that Ine is a man betrayed by a brother he trusted, a brother who has worked in the shadows for years to seize power."

No one is pretending not to listen any more. Æthel raises her voice, so that all can hear. "But I ask you: how has Ingild managed to drive Ine from Wiltun? Assembling a host of loyal men under the king's nose is impossible." She pauses. "He must have had help." Beorhtric is frowning, the hand raised to his cheek paused mid-scratch. "He *did* have help," Æthel continues. "From the very power he claims Ine has embraced."

"The Wealas pagans—"

"No." She cuts Cutha off before the idea spreads too far. "A power that opposes all humankind, whether they be Saxon or Briton. The only difference is the Britons have always accepted it, and feared it." She clenches a fist, remembering the mockery she faced from Ingild and the Witan. "*We* are the fools for calling it superstition. For letting the Church tell us that only a single great power exists. Ingild has turned that belief against us. He has fuelled the bishops' ambition in order to bolster his own...and that of the power he serves."

"For someone who claims *not* to be the wife of a heathen, you surely speak like one." Cutha's words echo in the silent hall. "I have never heard anything so—"

"She speaks truth."

Æthel turns her head to see a man dressed in the simple clothes of a serf. It takes her a moment to recognize him, and when she does, her breath catches. "Æthelburg queen believed me when few others would," the Briton from Scirburne says. She had never even learned his name. "When my town was attacked, and it was not the doing of men. My sister lives because of her, and my mother too."

Cutha glares. "Hold your tongue, wealh. What right do you have to speak in this company?"

"My right," Beorhtric says, extending an arm. "He accompanied his master, who is my guest."

"Master?"

A man rises from the table: Eadgar, gerefa of Scirburne. "If you do not accept his word, will you accept the word of a Saxon?" He bows his head to Beorhtric. "You should listen to her, lord. *Something* brought death to Scirburne that night. And we were not the only settlement attacked. I heard similar tales on my journey here."

Full of gratitude to both, Æthel ensures her voice is harsh when she says, "The dead walk. I lost warriors in Sceaptun whose bodies bore no wound save the touch of a wight's hand. I buried them myself. They were men of Wessex. The power controlling the wights cares nothing for our divisions. It will kill anyone who stands in its way."

Her words render even Cutha speechless—either with shock or genuine horror at the picture she has painted. A prickling silence spreads until the ealdorman breaks it. His brow is full of furrows. "You know the name of this power."

It is not a question, and Æthel is tired of dodging. "The Otherworld." A log splits with a chuckling crack. "And its king," she adds, her eyes on the leaping flames, "Gwyn ap Nudd."

Beorhtric moves their discussion beyond the ears of the many. Evening brings a sense of weight, as the grey noon hardens to iron. Æthel does not need to see the dark to feel it. She has a sense too of the town seething with her words. Some like Cutha undoubtedly think her mad. She should be comforted by the fact that many more do not; she has Eadgar and Neb—the Briton who accompanied him—to thank for that. Convincing the people is as vital as convincing Beorhtric. It is the people, after all, who form the fyrd, who must take up arms.

"This is no ordinary war," Æthel says. They sit at the back of the mead hall on benches set away from the others, to preserve a sense of privacy. "Despite Ingild's desire to pretend it is."

"You wasted few words in making that clear." The ealdorman drags a hand over his beard; Æthel notes a tremble in his fingers and his eyes are sunken. "I never heard such a tale."

"You think I did not have trouble believing it myself?" She stares into her ale, which is a little flat; the still surface tells her that Beorhtric is not the only one who looks weary. "I had to see it with my own eyes. What I did not see was Ingild's hand in it, his alliance with the Otherworld. When the milk soured and the dead crows appeared, he convinced the bishops—and the people of Wiltun—that they were pagan mischief."

"And how do you know they were not pagan mischief?"

"Because pagans have been dying," Æthel says hotly. "Because Ingild accused Ine of being responsible."

The ealdorman considers a moment. "How do you know he was *not* responsible?"

Ready with an angry reply, Æthel falters. Beorhtric might be posing as the Devil's advocate, but the drowned shape she sensed before—of everything she did not know—is rising in a rush, becoming clearer, so clear in fact that her voice fails her.

And its Heir. Whoever they may be.

She remembers Herla's sharp glance as she spoke those words. "No," Æthel whispers—the only thing that makes it out. Too much is tumbling through her head. Ine tangled in roots; that strange sleep; his distance and sudden fear of Hædde; the barn bursting with wheat after the Lammas ritual; his haunted eyes. And the bone knife—a mystery that might now have an answer. *The king faced the wight and lived.*

Like her, Ingild believed Cadwy to be the Heir of Dumnonia. It was why, surely, he wanted him dead. But now…he must have realized the truth. The impossible truth. Æthel knows she is breathing too fast because the torches in the hall swim before her eyes. How can Ine be the Heir of Dumnonia? She is missing a piece, but the rest fits.

"Æthelburg?"

Her reaction has made Ine look entirely guilty of whatever heresies the ealdorman is imagining, and Æthel has no idea what to say to allay suspicion. Instead she draws a deep breath. "Do I have your support, Beorhtric? Whatever else is happening, Ine is the true king of Wessex and has ruled well for over a decade. We are more prosperous than our neighbours. Trade flourishes. Our monasteries produce some of the best writing in the country, and the people thrive. Ingild would ask you to forget this. To throw your loyalty behind a man wholly unproven as king. Someone who—"

"Has he the full backing of the Witan, Æthelburg?"

The ealdorman's expression is sober. While the crown tended to pass from father to son, no man could be sworn in as king without the Witan's support. "Ingild has the bishops," she concedes, "who are ignorant of his…association with the Otherworld. I suspect he has the ability to sway the others, although Gweir and Leofric are absent."

"Both are warrior gesiths with only small hides to their names." Beorhtric's sigh is heavy. "If Osberht and Godric—and worse Nothhelm—side with Ingild, that alone gives the ætheling a frightening advantage."

"One the Hamtunscir fyrd can help balance," Æthel says meaningfully. "Besides, I am not done. I came here first for the sake of our friendship. But there are other settlements that I believe are loyal and will not be persuaded by Ingild's claims. And I have a powerful ally." When Beorhtric raises a brow, she adds, "Someone who could tip the balance in a battle. You know I would not say such a thing lightly."

The old lord does not speak for some time, but sits in his chair with his eyes turned up to the great wooden roof above them, as if seeking the advice of its gods. "Where are you assembling this army of yours?"

"Glestingaburg," Æthel says at once. "Ingild believes I have fled west to gather allies and will march to stop me. I will meet him on the field as he wishes, and I will defeat him. The king does his part. This is mine."

"His part?"

She is not the type to ride headlong into Dumnonia to rouse the Britons. But Ine is. And if anyone can manage such a feat, Æthel knows it is him.

27

INE

The sense is stronger the further west he travels. As the land loses its flatness, woods thicken. Hills swap their gentle slopes for cliffs that rise like the towers of a people lost to time. Granite tors and tarns. Gnarly glades that remind Ine of the one he saw instead of Wiltun's mead hall. Vestiges of the long ago, places of power and passage that the Christian Church has worked hard to erase. But the memory of them lives on in the land. He is beginning to realize it lives on in him. Along with the ruinous power that killed Leofric.

"Tell me again," Cadwy demands, guiding his mount closer to Ine's. They had acquired the third horse by posing as traders. Now, cloaked and hooded against the damp, with Escanceaster on the horizon, Ine does not know whether they have out-ridden the news of his disgraced flight. Part of him does not care. He tugs the hood further over his face.

"You know as much as I do, Prince Cadwy," Gweir says tiredly.

"I was asking *him*."

When Ine says nothing, Gweir throws a worried glance his way. "You were there the night we left. You saw—" He breaks off. "Besides, Emrys confirmed it."

Cadwy's shoulders slump a little. "They *did*? When?"

"They have been in Wessex some time."

The words rob the prince of response. Perhaps he is wondering why Emrys, a so-called friend of Dumnonia, had not freed him. Ine could tell him. He has felt the strands, fine as spider-silk, that Emrys spins around people. Counsel here, a warning there, and then silence to let you believe you reached the decision yourself. How long have they walked this world, an invisible puppeteer? If Cadwy had escaped, Ingild's plan to expose Ine could never have worked. *Is this what you want, scop?* The question batters against the walls of his mind. *You have made me kill, driven me from my home and people. I cannot even hold Ingild accountable for Father.* Those slow-healing scratches are seared into his memory. How Cenred must have fought, lucid enough at the end to know life was being stolen from him. "But why did he do it?" he asks aloud.

"Sorry, Ine king?"

He shakes his head. "Never mind, Gweir. And it's just Ine now."

Cadwy makes a sound in his throat. Expecting derision, even pleasure, Ine is surprised when he says, "That man does not deserve to be king. Do not yield up your title just yet."

"A king needs a kingdom." Ine nods at the deserted hills. "Who rides at my side but a single man, and the prince of a people we call enemy?"

Cadwy's shoulders square, as if preparing for a fight. "I heard enough during the last few weeks to know that *you* do not call us enemy." His mouth quirks. "It has not made you very popular."

Ine straightens in his saddle. It must have cost Cadwy to admit it. "Yes, well. And here we are."

Gweir is not quite fast enough in burying his smile. "What's funny?" Cadwy snaps at him, but the gesith only points ahead.

"Do we stop, lord? We need supplies and food for the horses. Though our funds are running low."

"We would be fine if your king hadn't thrown good coin into the mud," Cadwy grumbles. "Those Christian symbols are all solid silver."

Ine narrows his eyes at the town cradled in the hills. Parts of the Roman wall still stand, although not enough to hold off attack. "We go quietly. Perhaps we may hear news."

"A quarter of Caer Uisc is ours," Cadwy says with a sidelong glance at him. "We could head there."

"Very well." It is the Dumnonian name for Escanceaster, once a capital of their people. Ine well knows that the Britons are relegated to a single quarter—he wrote the laws that make it so. Another Saxon king might have driven them from the town entirely, but that would not aid in bringing their peoples together. Integration must happen. They cannot be at war with the natives forever. Ine grimaces. These are exactly the thoughts that have landed him here. Æthel might laugh.

He pushes the image of her away. Cwenburh is wrong. His wife is not coming back. Not this time. And he should be glad—it would be outright dangerous for her in Wiltun now. But Ine cannot be glad. Her absence is a constant ache. If only he could see her again, he would tell her everything. Even faced with her anger, he would tell her.

Together they will be unstoppable.

With cold clarity, Ine sees what Ingild has done. What he let his brother do. He and Æthel *are* better together. Each has all the things the other lacks. Their marriage was so strong in the beginning, and Wessex stronger because of it. But the secret he has kept from her and the court's hostility towards a woman who wields a sword and does not conceive has opened cracks, allowing Ingild's poison to seep inside. Ine had thought Emrys a puppet master, but the real master has been under his nose the entire time.

He lets out a growl—frustration at himself, rage at Ingild—and the others look round. The horses, however, have carried them into the shadow of Escanceaster's walls, and cries go up. "I will do the talking," Gweir says, manoeuvring his mount to the front.

Ine does not catch all the conversation that follows, but they are waved inside. Although his duties do not often allow him to visit Escanceaster, he keeps his hood pulled close just in case. All of them do—and they are not alone. The face of the year has turned towards winter, and a cutting wind shears between the buildings. Some of the Roman villas have been repaired inexpertly with wood, thatch and salvaged stone. The people they pass are ceorls for the most part, their clothes as patched as the villas. *I should redirect some funds,* Ine thinks before remembering that he is in exile and little better off than the grim-faced inhabitants.

"Lord." Gweir nods at a street churned to mud by the recent rain. More has begun to fall and the afternoon grows dark. "We should seek shelter."

Ine is unsurprised to find the Britons' quarter in worse condition than the rest of the burh and can feel Cadwy's accusing gaze. What do the Dumnonii think of their countrymen who choose to live in Saxon settlements? Shame creeps through him. *I have spent too long at home, listening to men whose ideals I do not share.* If he had accompanied Æthelburg more often, he might have seen the squalor of these places. He could have done something.

With their dwindling coin, they buy food for the horses and the dubious shelter of a stable for themselves. It is only when the rain drops a curtain across the entrance that Ine lowers his hood and lets his head fall back against the greening wood. The hay-smell tickles his nose, doing little to obscure the odour of the place. Unlike the Britons here, wealth and position have shielded him. He smiles sadly to himself, supposing that this is what Æthel meant by the pig. The trappings of wealth are just that—a trap. They have blinded him to what really matters. "I should have been out there with her," he says aloud, slipping back into Englisc. "I would have seen more of the people, and the way they lived. Perhaps I would have seen the power the Church was beginning to exert."

"Have a care," Cadwy snaps in his own language. "We are not among friends yet."

"*Friends.* You are saying the Dumnonii will not want my head?"

"You owe it to us." There is a low flush in Cadwy's cheeks when he adds, somewhat resentfully, "but you took the blow that was meant for me. I owe a blood debt now."

Ine studies his palms. Despite a wight's touch being deadly, he had intervened. Was it instinct? A foolish desire to protect? Or did he know that the Land would shield him? It is there now, beneath the surface of his thoughts: a root system that leads away from him into places he still fears to tread.

The prince must know something of this power, but the question is too raw to ask. How would Ine feel if his bitter enemy received a gift intended for him? *Hardly a gift when it has killed a man.* But that is unworthy of him. Cadwy considers it a gift, one that Ine has stolen. "Cadwy," he says, waiting until the prince looks round. "I will not hold you to any debt."

"I see what you are trying." He picks up a twist of hay, winds it viciously around his finger. "You think that, by being kind, you can undo the wrong you have done me."

"No." Picturing Geraint, Ine feels an unlikely kinship with his son. "But Ingild has robbed us both of a father. And I will see that repaid in kind."

Cadwy blinks at him. "Your brother *killed* his own father?"

Hearing it expressed in his young voice hammers home the cruelty of that truth and Ine can find no words to lessen it. When he says nothing, Cadwy grunts, as if it is exactly the sort of behaviour one would expect of Saxons.

Remembering Cædwalla has brought something else to mind. When Ine had faced the dead king, the Land was not the only life that answered him. He recalls his vision of the silver-eyed man who had raged and called Ine a thief. *Gwyn ap Nudd.* It must be him. Had he been speaking of the birthright? The more Ine ponders it, the heavier his eyelids become, until their punishing ride and the rhythmic patter of rain lulls him into a doze.

At first the voices are part of a featureless dream. But they grow clearer as he listens, until he wakes with a start, disoriented. The roof is not that of his chamber in Wiltun, and the air smells of wet livestock. Then memory falls upon him and he sits up, squinting in the dark of the stable. He is alone. Where are Gweir and Cadwy?

A mocking laugh comes from outside, and quietly, Ine makes his way to the door, cracked ajar. The rain has turned to drizzle, soaking the shoulders of the two groups standing opposed in the street. He cannot tell the hour. Early evening, perhaps.

"It's not enough, wealh," one of the men says in Englisc. A free-man, Ine guesses, from his plain but serviceable clothes. Seven others flank him, dressed similarly with seaxes on their belts.

"We have no more." The Britons are only five and the difference in their appearance is marked. The speaker's tunic is worn thin, and the two women beside him glare at the Saxons through red-rimmed eyes.

"You'll use Englisc in the king's town," the man growls and Ine frowns at his wilful misunderstanding. The Briton's grasp of the language is imperfect, perhaps, but the meaning quite clear. "The gerefa will be happy to drive you from Escanceaster if you cannot pay your share."

"Our share is nearly twice what your people pay," the nearest woman says in her own language. "It is unjust."

The man spits, contempt in the set of his lips. "Are you trying to talk, wealh? All I hear is the bleating of sheep." His hand goes to his weapon. "*Pay.*"

"You cannot harm us." The first Briton pushes the woman behind him. "The king's law protects us."

"Does it?" The Saxons part to let another man through. His arms are folded across a cloak of good heavy wool pinned with silver and his face is faintly familiar. Ine squints, grasping after his name.

"Gerefa, these wretches refuse to yield up the tithe."

"Because we do not have it," the other woman says, using Eng-lisc this time. "Not because we refuse."

The gerefa chuckles and the sound curls Ine's hands into fists. His heart is beginning to thump an angry cadence in his chest. "My men will search every inch of your hovels for coin. And if they find even a penning, I will hang your elders and drive the rest of you out to starve amongst the hills."

"We must eat," the Briton says roughly. "You cannot take every-thing we have. The king's law—"

"Inside these walls, *I* am king."

Ine steps out. "Really, Hewald?" The name has come back to him, along with a wisp of memory. The last time he had travelled

personally to Escanceaster was six years ago, when his laws were
newly written and demanded the appointment of men to posts of
power. Clearly Hewald's had been a mistake. Guilt tastes sour in
his mouth at the sight of the dilapidated homes, the pinched faces
of the Britons. How long has this been the way of things?

"Who are *you*?" the thuggish man demands, pushing forward.
There is no hint of recognition in him and why would there be?
The plain, unembroidered clothes they picked up along the way
do not mark Ine as any more important than the rest of them.
Besides, he grimly reminds himself, who would expect to find the
King of Wessex in a stable, unaccompanied and leagues from
court?

Hewald's eyes widen as they search his face. He stumbles to
one knee. "Lord." The men around him exchange bemused glances
before they bow too.

Ine regards him coldly. "Would you care to repeat what you
said?"

"I—my king, what are you…?"

"Am I such an unusual sight in my own kingdom? Or is Escanceaster yours, as you claim?"

"I did not mean it. But the Wealas—"

"Are people of Wessex," Ine says firmly. "They are here to live
and work, not to line your pockets. Yes, I can easily imagine
where the extra coin goes. You abuse your position, Hewald."

Although the man stammers apologies, suspicion is plain in
the way his eyes rake the darkness for the king's absent guards,
how his tongue wets nervous lips. Abruptly the sense of how *alone*
he is crashes into Ine.

Perhaps the men sense his uncertainty; Hewald rises to his
feet. "Lord, a rumour has reached us. We did not believe it when
we heard. It was that strange."

"You think to distract me with rumours?"

"Where is your party, lord king? Your gesiths and nobles?"
Hewald takes a step closer. "Why enter Escanceaster without
announcing yourself?"

Confusion is thick amongst the Britons, who watch the

confrontation with puckered brows. Ine nods to them. "How long has this extortion been going on?"

Instead of answering, Hewald takes another step. "Why do we find you here of all places, in the quarter given to the Wealas? As you see, it is hardly fitting."

Although they have ridden hard, Ingild's people have ridden harder. Ine refuses to let even the slightest alarm show on his face, but fear for Gweir and Cadwy rolls through him.

"However, if you *had*—forgive me, lord—sworn yourself to the heathens, where else would you be but here, gathering support amongst them?"

"How astute," comes a voice: young, brash. *Cadwy*. Ine turns to see him at the head of a large group: the Britons of Escanceaster. Spotting Ine, Gweir pales and hurries forward. Clearly he was supposed to be safely hidden. A dozen torches spit in the Britons' hands as they come to a halt. They appear a ragged bunch at first glance; lean-faced people whose bellies are never full. But their shoulders are not stooped, their chins are lifted, and the hard glitter of their eyes is reflected in the weapons they bear.

Immediately the Saxons spread out to flank them, leaving Ine trapped between the two groups. "What is this?" Hewald demands. "You are forbidden from owning any weapons larger than belt knives, let alone bringing them into my presence."

"Let it go, Hewald," one of the Britons says. Ten years older than Ine, perhaps, his hair is grey, but thick still, and he has the build of someone who has spent a lifetime swinging a hammer. "We have no wish to spill blood tonight, especially in our own streets." He nods at Ine. "But if you try to seize that man, we *will* spill it."

"Thus he condemns you, lord." Hewald slowly shakes his head. "That you would turn against your own people for the sake of these—" his gesture towards the Britons is contemptuous—"I would be a traitor myself if I stood aside and did nothing."

Ine's palms are sweating; it is exactly the sort of confrontation he had hoped to avoid. *You have only yourself to blame.* What had happened to staying out of sight? But he had witnessed too much injustice lately to let more go unchallenged.

"Cadwy slipped away," Gweir says in a low voice. "I am sorry, lord. I should have been here."

"This is my fault. I did not think." He has no time to ask what Cadwy intended before Hewald draws his sword and the scrape of metal joins the patter of rain on the Saxons' armour. The Britons have no leather to protect them, only threadbare tunics already soaked through. The man who is presumably their leader meets Ine's gaze. What has Cadwy told him? Why are they even here, armed and bearing torches against the dark?

It is imminent. Ine can almost taste the iron, the blood and sweat. Each raindrop thuds to earth with the inevitability of battle. Earth... The sense is with him again: a vast and ancient knowledge given to those who came before. Clearer than it has ever been, untarnished by the anger that accompanied it in Wiltun. Here on soil that felt the feet of the kings of Dumnonia...

Cold. He is crouching, one hand sliding into the mud, and a whole world opens to him. Lines touch, cross, stretch away, like the brief pattern he saw when lightning spat from the sky. This one is different. Younger than the sky but older than any creature living. He can barely grasp the edges of it. The pattern is the snail-slow decay of fruit fallen before its time. It eats seeds, spits out the bones of beast and bird, and the silty crust which marks the place the river broke its banks. The pattern is not only deep; it skims the shallows where grass smothers ruins. Where mosses grow, and shattered things lie half-remembered. It has stones in it, and soft sand, and a hundred sounds for hush.

It feels him, as he wonders at it. And it moves with him as he rises to rooted feet. It uses rain and rock to push itself upwards until there is wall instead of road. Cries in his ears like the tumble of pebbles. He thought his eyes were open until he opens them.

One hand still rests on the earth now towering before him. Without removing it, Ine looks over his shoulder, at Gweir and Cadwy, and the Britons. Their faces are odd things, so expressive against the slow-shifting face of the Land. The wall he has built blocks the street at the stable. He can hear voices behind it. Their owners will go around, find another way to shed blood. He has bought time, but not very much of it, and he laughs because these scrambled moments can hardly be called *time*. Time is the leviathan beneath their feet, each sleeping breath the exhalation of a thousand years.

"We should leave," Ine says—and removes his hand from the wall. He has only an instant to wonder why the world is tilting before it all goes dark.

"You see now, don't you?" Emrys says. The scop is sitting cross-legged on an altar, wearing a cloak of coloured strips, like the wishes tied to trees in pagan days.

"Yes, I see." They are in the glade he dreamed, but no skulls haunt it, and no wild growth either. Just a slant of sun and the motes that drift in its rays. "It is too great for me."

"It is too great for anyone, Ine. Of course it is." Emrys scoops stray dirt from the surface of the altar and lets it trickle through their fingers, blue eyes on the spaces between earth and flesh. "But does that mean we deny it?"

Ine takes three steps towards the ancient altar. Words like *heathen*, *impious*, *heretical*, none have meaning here. "Where does it come from? Sovereignty."

"You have learned a lot since we last spoke," Emrys remarks with a dry sort of pleasure. "The soul of the Land has many names. The names of gods and stars. Poets and priests and men who think themselves wise have named her, but she has no need of them."

"She?"

"She, he, it, they—we are limited by language, but Sovereignty is not. Call her as you wish." Emrys's face is a closed codex, secrets trapped within. "She is why the Dumnonian birthright exists. She forged the pact between the first people and the land they lived on."

"Gwyn spoke of a pact." Ine shivers at the memory of that unearthly rage. "I saw him when I fought the wight."

Emrys nods. "It is because of him that we must speak now."

"Where are we? Is this real?"

"Real enough."

"I had a vision of this place," Ine murmurs, "when skulls ringed it."

"Yes, I suppose you would." A hint of sadness in the words. "It is in your blood, after all."

The edges of the glade shimmer. Beyond them, the wood simply *is not*. What would happen if he crossed that glistening boundary? Ine shakes the thought from his head. "Gwyn then. Who is he? What does he want, apart from my death?"

"He is something very old." Emrys turns a palm up. "Older than everything, perhaps, save Sovereignty. He serves her, loves her, guards her, and is terribly jealous of her power." Their blue eyes are piercing. "It is her power you use to see the world's patterns. When you spoke to the earth and changed its shape."

Little point asking how Emrys knows. "Gwyn would prefer us not to use it?"

"He does not believe you worthy of it. And who can blame him? Much of the time, humans are selfish creatures who do not deserve her blessing. Look how the Church has eroded it." Emrys hops nimbly off the altar. "But it is not Gwyn ap Nudd's place to take it away. And it is the only thing capable of stopping him doing whatever he likes to this world."

Ine's head is already reeling. "You are saying that...*I* have to stop him? Someone like that?"

"And you do not have long. Samhain approaches. The walls between worlds are thin as a dragonfly's wing and the gates will stand wide open to the hosts of Annwn." Their expression clouds. "The Folk of the Otherworld are not kind to mortals."

"But I know nothing of the birthright," he protests, panic rising in his throat. "It is the power using *me*, not the other way around. I have no idea how I changed the earth's shape."

Emrys wears a half-frown. "Do you not?"

"No, I..." Ine stops because it is not entirely true. He *had* recognized the pattern, could differentiate it from the one in the sky. He had seen the weave of it and remembered pulling on several threads until they loosened from the rest. "It's instinct, not knowledge. Like swinging a sword wildly and hitting the target by chance." He swallows his pride and says, as he had once before, "I am not Constantine of Dumnonia."

Expression touches Emrys's face. "In some ways you are alike." The look they turn on Ine is penetrating. "And in others, not. But you share his blood, blood that gives you the right of the Land-rule, which Geraint and his family have held in stewardship for many years."

Ine cannot help wincing at the words. "It is hard on Cadwy. Losing his birthright to a man he sees as his enemy."

"It was never his to lose," Emrys says, unmoved, and again Ine wonders who exactly they are. They speak of Constantine in the same way they spoke of Cynric's wife—as if they knew both personally. Nearly two hundred years have passed since that time.

The glade flickers like eyelids on the cusp of opening. "Wait." Ine lays a hand on the altar, as if touching it can hold it in place. Smooth patches betray repeated offerings, of blood or beast or worse. "*How* do I stop Gwyn, hold back a host? I had the means to raise an army once, but my brother killed our father and drove me into exile." His tone turns accusing. "You were there."

"Are you not on your way to seek allies, Ine of Wessex?" Emrys smiles. "And you are hardly alone. I told you before that you had a capable wife."

He stumbles forward. "Æthelburg? You have news of her? Where is she?"

"Doing what she must," Emrys says soberly. "She and her heart are your hope, Ine."

He wakes to a circle of faces, those words in his ears. Ine thumps the earth, but his frustration at the scop's riddles is a ghostly thing. *Her heart.* His own is beating hard.

"Thank God." Gweir's hand rests on his shoulder. "Are you well?"

Ine nods stiffly. The watchers have drawn back, guarded: Britons from Escanceaster, but they are not in the town any more. Beyond their shadowed faces, pink stains the sky, a gentle colour. Too gentle for the truths he has brought out of his dreams.

"Seems I am not free of you yet." Cadwy offers him a grudging hand to sit up. "This is Maucus of Caer Uisc." One of the men comes forward: the Briton who challenged Hewald last night.

"I have heard and seen some strange things, but this is quite the strangest." Maucus nods to Ine and then to the people behind—about two dozen of them. "Thank you for keeping the blood inside their bodies, Ine king."

He has spoken in Englisc. Ine's throat feels unexpectedly hot. He replies in the Briton's own language, "It was my duty, nothing more."

As if their simple exchange was a sign, others cluster in. Most wear astonishment, some awe and disbelief. With their eyes on him, Ine feels guiltier than ever for letting Hewald impoverish them. He gets to his feet, hoping his knees do not look as weak as they feel. "I am deeply sorry for my gerefa's abuse. I should have looked in." A wind is blowing off the estuary, and he tugs his cloak close. "But why are you all here? And where is here?"

"Because I asked them if they would come," Cadwy says, rising too. His stare is defiant; it must have been terrible to tell the Britons about Ine. A boy raised to believe he would follow his father, wield the knowledge of the Land as power. Ine cannot change that, but he *can* show Cadwy the respect his position demands. He can offer his friendship, even if the prince spurns it. "This is the road to Dintagel."

The Britons' jewel, the unbreachable fortress of Kernow. Ine catches his breath. No person of Wessex has ever set foot there.

"Wipe the dew from your eyes, Saxon." The corners of Cadwy's mouth twitch before he becomes serious again. "Dintagel is not Caer Uisc. My people are proud and a blood debt alone will not buy you welcome."

I need them to do more than welcome me. I need them to follow me. Choosing not to say it aloud, Ine nods, as if he expected nothing else. "How far?"

"Far enough. We must go before your gerefa sends men after us."

"We've only three horses."

"It cannot be helped." Cadwy squints against the rising sun. "With goodwill, I may be able to acquire some along the way."

"I will walk, in that case." Weariness still clings, but Ine straightens his shoulders. "Let another ride. I have slept enough."

Geraint's son gives him the ghost of a smile.

28

ⱧERLⱭ

Glestingaburg, Somersæte
Kingdom of Wessex

It is the most selfless thing she has ever done…and Herla regrets it almost as much as she regrets Annwn. With every league, her horse carries her further from Æthelburg, away from the warmth of her hands and the wonder of her lips. She has not touched another woman in centuries. The Hunt did not even allow for the thought. And her heart…she had believed it ashes. Broken and irrecoverable. But it beats in her chest as fiercely—more fiercely—than ever. Æthelburg had found it in the darkness, had sifted through the charred remnants for something worth saving. The wind dashes away a tear before it can fall.

You are not even mortal, she reminds herself harshly, *despite what you said to Olwen.* She is not worthy of Æthelburg, but the thought of watching the queen grow old and die is more than she can bear. If she accepted Gwyn's offer, she would not have to. They could be together forever.

"Herla!"

The scream is a spear thrown from a great distance to pierce her. She jerks, hands tightening on the reins. *"Corraidhín?"* She has never heard such terror in her friend's voice. Herla urges the horse to greater speed. *"What is happening?"*

"The gate—" It ends in a strangled cry, and Herla gives a cry of her own. Corraidhín is of the Hunt. Nothing in this world can terrify her.

Nothing in this world. A great cold seizes Herla and sickens her new-awoken heart. *"I am coming, Corra. Talk to me."* What other power but Annwn can harm her people? She reaches for her battle sisters, for the bond forged between them, and she *feels* them. They are fighting. They are fury and fear.

"There are too many for us. I am sorry, Herla. My friend, my sister." Corraidhín's voice is a wisp of what it was, the sense of her growing distant.

"No, Corra. I am here. I am here." The green hill of Glestingaburg is before her, and Herla screams as she races for it, her horse's hooves churning the earth.

"Do not come after us. It is what…he wants."

She throws herself from the saddle. The door to the hall under the hill is held fast, but she seizes it with both hands and pulls, the effort tearing another scream from her lungs. The hall beyond is empty, and a mess. The shafts of shattered spears, blood, battle— all of it assaults Herla as she crosses the threshold. She almost steps on a bone figurine, a cat poised mid-leap. Corraidhín's. She snatches it up, holds it in one slick palm, feeling as if she is drowning.

The destruction continues further in. All the gentle work of her sisters undone. Throat burning, Herla reaches inside herself. *"Corraidhín? Senua? Gelgéis?"* Only an echoing space where their presence used to be. The gate to the Otherworld is shut, but the familiar scent of Annwn tells her it opened recently. "I told them to stay," she whispers. Wet on the stone. She crouches and her finger comes up red. "Oh Goddess. I told them to stay."

"Was I not generous?"

The sword is in her hand before she realizes it. But it will do her no good; Gwyn is still only a vision. He stands in the middle of Herla's ruined hall, arrayed for battle. His mail is the scales of the fish that live in the depths of Annwn's sea. His eyes follow her blade with the same wariness as before.

"What have you done to them?" She barely recognizes her own voice. "Where are they?"

"Far away, Herla. Beyond the seven castles and the summer stars." He takes a slow walk towards her. "Beyond the lip of night, in the dawn that is forever. I have them. And you will not find them without my help."

Her first instinct is to scream; she swallows it. Instead, Herla lets ice splinter through her. "Why? Your grievance was with me."

"What else was I to do?" Gwyn stops before her. "I made you an offer. A generous one, I felt. But you are as proud and stubborn as the day we met, Herla. You have damned your sisters a second time."

"I will kill you."

Gwyn's smile is sad. "No, you will not. You will remain here. You will not interfere further in my work and perhaps I will bring them home." The smile turns sharp. "Though I doubt they will be the same."

She cannot help it—she lunges, blade aiming for his hollow heart. But he is gone. The sword plunges into the earth, hilt shuddering to a stop, and Herla falls beside it. The wreckage of the hall wavers before her eyes. All the things they built, that they rescued from their lost lives. Taken again because she had told them to stay. They wanted to go with her and she told them to stay. All so she could be with Æthelburg.

"You are as selfish as you ever were," Gwyn's voice echoes. "It brings me no pleasure, Herla. We are so very alike."

"I am nothing like you," she whispers. Only silence answers her.

She does not know how long she sits, knees drawn up to her chest. Days pass, the sun rising and setting high above. All she can think of is Corraidhín saying, *We were bound together long before he bound us.* Her grip on Herla's arm, the flashing of her eyes. *I will follow you for* all *time.* "I do not deserve your loyalty," Herla tells the memory of her friend. "Or your love." She strokes the bone cat, her thumb as large as its body. Corraidhín wore it twisted into her hair. Only a warrior of Annwn could have cut it loose.

Each dusk, the walls between worlds thin a little more. Light seeps around the edges of the gate. Even if she could open it, she would not find the Eceni. Annwn answers only to its king. And leaving would mean leaving Æthelburg to face whatever Gwyn has planned. Not that he has given her a choice. Herla beats a fist against the floor. If she lifts a finger to aid the queen, she will never see her sisters again. He has her trapped. Æthelburg must be wondering what has happened. Herla had promised to meet her.

She is aware too of the moon ageing, and hugs herself against the thought of the Hunt. Last month, she had fought the curse, mastered the bloodlust in her veins, but only with her sisters' help. She gazes at the space in which they knelt, their foreheads touching, fingers laced as tightly as the reed baskets her father wove. Herla studies her calloused palms. *Born with a spear in your hands.* She cannot remember her father's voice, but she remembers those words. Once they had made her proud. If she had only woven baskets too, how might her life have been lived? Perhaps she'd have died at the end of a Roman sword like him.

"But I did not," she tells the black blade still standing upright where she stabbed it. "You and I crave blood too much."

It is only then that she feels it—the rising of her pulse, the quickening of her breath. Her limbs are lighter, a dark energy coursing through them. Herla backs away from the sword. Horns are calling in her soul and Gwyn's hound reforms from the shadows, belly low and growling. Her senses unfurl like night flowers; her eyes sharper, her nose keener. Saliva pools at the back of her mouth and Herla swallows grimly. "No," she tells Dormach. "I am stronger now. It will not take me again."

But the Hunt feeds off her despair, her desire for oblivion, to forget what she has done. *You owe it to them to remember.* Herla fills her gaze with the bone cat, with the thought of Corraidhín's glare. *She would fight. She would not give in.* Kneeling where they knelt, Herla presses her hands to the earth, fingers crooked, grasping for the memories that once tore at her.

And then her heightened senses pick up a smell, a familiar scent of sweat and iron. She whips around, coming to her feet. *No. Please no.* There, framed between the doors she left open in her thoughtless grief, is Æthelburg, the brittle crescent of the old moon risen behind her.

Herla stares at her. *This is not happening.* Strengthened by her distraction, the curse rears up; her words, when they come, are sharp as arrowheads. "Æthelburg. Get away."

"Herla." No one has ever spoken her name so gently. "I am not going anywhere." And to her horror, Æthelburg steps inside.

Herla backs off, raising a hand. "The others—they are gone. Taken. I cannot fight the curse without them." Pain almost doubles her over. "I will kill you."

Another step. "You will not."

"Please, Æthelburg. Please." She cannot remember the last time she begged. "Don't make me hurt you. Do not make me live with your death on my hands." She rails at her disobedient body, but cannot stop herself from curling her fingers around the black sword. The blade comes free of the earth with a hiss; sinister, victorious. "No," Herla tells the song beginning to swell inside her. It is like telling the sun not to set. Or the mouse not to run from the owl. The Hunt is inevitable. It is older than the world. And she is the Huntress.

Æthelburg draws her own sword. The curse sees it as a challenge and, for a moment, Herla loses her grip. She lunges forward, stops, knees locked. "Æthelburg. You cannot best me. It will not let you. Please. *Go.*" But even as she says it, she knows it is too late. The queen cannot ride fast enough to escape her.

"No." Æthelburg lifts her chin. In that moment, she is more beautiful than Herla has ever seen her. "I will not abandon you to it. I will fight alongside you."

There is no wind this time to dash away her tear. It is the last thing Herla feels before red mists her vision.

29

ÆTHELBURG

She fights for her life.

Æthel knows it. She knew it when she saw the moon withered in the sky. Herla had promised to return, but two weeks passed and she had not come. So Æthel, working her way west in search of allies, had come to her.

Although wind howls outside, it does not blow through the gates of Herla's hall, as if this earthen cave is not quite part of the world Æthel knows. Debris crunches. She kicks aside wood and bone fragments. A battle raged here.

She cannot spare time to dwell on it, as the woman before her launches a series of impossible attacks. Wary of the black sword, Æthel dodges most of them, but dodging is tiring. She must pace herself.

Herla's face is a merciless mask. Her amber eyes flare in the dim hall and she moves like a cat, fluid from stance to stance, never where Æthel expects. "I know you are in there," she shouts at the other woman. Then something rolls beneath her foot, and she has no time to dodge. Æthel catches Herla's next blow on her sword—and it shatters.

Both pause for a splinter of a second. Æthel leaps back, tossing the useless hilt aside, and reaching for the spear Herla gave her. The reprieve does not last long. The other woman advances again, and Æthel blocks the sword with the shaft of her spear. As she hoped, it nicks, but does not break. How many strikes can it take?

"Herla," she gasps. "You must fight it." Her words have no effect, and for the first time, Æthel's heart quails. Overconfidence had led her here, and it would be her end. Why did she think she could face the Lord of the Hunt? Leader of Boudica's armies. A woman who has lived six centuries. *You are a fool,* a voice whispers and she stumbles.

This time, the black sword comes so close that Æthel feels it on her skin, and hears a cacophony of voices crying for release. She shudders. "Herla. Ælfrún." A spasm passes across Herla's face. *Remind her of her past.* "You are Eceni," Æthel gasps, catching another blow on the shuddering spear. "You told Olwen, remember? You said you were born in struggle and blood. You fought alongside Boudica—" a twitch at the name—"to protect your people. That is who you are. Not a slave of the Otherworld."

Herla staggers. When she looks up, her eyes are less red, her grip on the sword less sure. But a growling comes out of the darkness—Gwyn's bloodhound—and Herla's uncertainty fades. Æthel fights the instinct to run, so primal is the fear it raises in her, as if her body remembers a time when greater predators than humans walked the world. The dog is huge, muscled, pale as bleached bone except for its bloody markings. If she runs, it will tear out her throat.

It is fast approaching—the moment she can fight no more. So Æthel does something very stupid. When Herla raises the sword, she ducks beneath the blow and rams her shoulder into her, carrying them both to the ground. The shock of hitting it stuns Herla; her eyes widen. A moment passes when they lock gazes. Then Æthel roughly grasps Herla's face, leans down, and presses her lips to the other woman's.

She is flinching even as she does it—Herla's blade is still in her hand and Æthel fully expects to feel it bite into her unshielded back. Instead Herla throws her off, only to pin her down, their positions reversed. Æthel is breathing heavily, winded from their battle, and for the first time, notices that Herla is too. A reddish haze still haunts her eyes. When their lips meet, there are teeth in her kiss, drawing blood. Æthel runs her tongue over the bitten place, and that iron and salt sets her body aflame. Fist in Herla's hair, she leaves her own mark on her skin, a livid red wheal. Herla claps a hand to her neck, eyes shocked, and then she drops the sword. The thump it makes hitting earth is heavier than it ought to be, but Æthel cannot spare a thought for it. The battle is not over. She throws Herla off her, rolls, regains her position on top. The other woman seizes her hips, gaze drawn to the blood on Æthel's mouth.

She is feverish and Herla's skin is cool; Æthel wants more of it. Both pull at leather and cloth, until all ties have loosened and fallen away. Just as before, there is no room in her to think herself unworthy, undesirable. Not with Herla's nails leaving crescents on the flesh of her thighs, mouth hungry and hot against her. Æthel lets out a ragged gasp, and Herla lifts her head, stilling for the breath of a moment. Beneath their reddish haze, her eyes are wet. She does not speak, but Æthel hears her nonetheless. "No," she whispers in answer, her arms tightening. "I told you I will not let you fight alone."

When she wakes, it is to amber eyes. They are dry and there is no trace of red in them. Dawn filters through the doors still thrown wide, showing her the chaos of the hall. She is lying on furs, another across her. One bare leg is outside. Herla gently nudges it with her own as she asks, "Did I hurt you?"

"Don't you remember?"

"It is...hazy." Her voice is very quiet and she reaches out to brush a thumb across Æthel's lip. "I was not gentle."

Æthel parts her lips, grazes Herla's thumb with her teeth, and the other woman draws a quick breath. Her neck is a battlefield. Æthel touches one of the marks her passion left behind. "Sorry. I am not gentle either."

"No." Herla captures Æthel's hand against her chest. "You are the bravest and most foolish woman I have ever known."

"What about Boudica?"

"Not as foolish as you."

Æthel frees her other hand to punch her lightly, but Herla's playfulness is gone. "She would not have come for me. She would not have risked her life for mine. The cause was always more important than one person. And you risked more than your life last night. You risked your soul."

"For *your* soul. I considered it a fair wager. Besides," Æthel admits, flushing at the memory of what they had done, "it was not entirely selfless."

Moments pass while Herla simply stares at her. Then she moves a hand to Æthel's face. "If I truly believed in the gods, I would say they were watching over me the night I met you."

Æthel tilts her head so that her cheek rests firmly in Herla's palm. Her eyes feel hot. "You were right before, you know," she murmurs, "about my husband. I *have* given him my heart. But I've given it to you too. Does that make me selfish?"

"I do not believe a heart is a single thing." Herla moves her hand to Æthel's chest. "That the whole of it can be given only once. Boudica loved her husband."

Æthel still finds the name incredible. "You loved her very much."

"Yes." Herla turns onto her back. "Not enough to trust in her victory, though. If I had done…"

"We wouldn't have met." Æthel grimaces even as she says it. She is hardly worth centuries of being cursed. "Sorry. That truly is selfish of me."

"Maybe." A brief flicker of a smile. "I am the selfish one, or I would never have put you in danger."

Æthel props herself up on her elbow. "As anyone in Wessex will tell you, I put myself in danger on a regular basis. I need no help from Eceni warriors."

Herla's laugh holds a thread of sadness. "I have not been a member of the Eceni for hundreds of years. In truth, I do not deserve to carry the name of my people."

"No one can take away who we are." Æthel sits up fully and the furs slip down to her waist. "Even the King of the Otherworld." Herla does not answer for so long that Æthel feels compelled to ask, "What?"

"Merely admiring the view."

With a glower, Æthel yanks the furs back up. "Well, you can stop admiring it. I haven't forgiven you for breaking my blade last night."

Herla winces. "I did?"

"You did." She nods at the hilt lying nearby. "It was an heirloom of Wessex. A grey-mark blade."

The other woman sits up too and, despite her own protest, Æthel cannot stop her eyes from roaming the expanse of her skin. The tattoos continue along Herla's collarbones, down between her breasts to circle her navel. "Did those hurt?"

"Yes, but I earned them. The first when I came of age. The rest to mark the battles I fought and the men I killed." She looks away. "We all bore them."

"Will you tell me what happened? Before I arrived."

Herla's face hardens, a brittle shield. "He took my sisters from me. Punishment for refusing his offer and a threat to keep me in line. Annwn is his domain. Only he can find them and bring them back—and he will not if I oppose him further."

Æthel shivers, as if feeling the first flurries of winter snow. "But we need you." She takes a deep breath because this is the first time she has said it aloud. "Ine needs you. Cadwy cannot be the Heir of Dumnonia."

"I know."

Gaping at her, Æthel pushes down hurt. "Then why did you not say?"

"I was still uncertain." Herla meets her eyes, a defiance there. "And I wasn't sure how you would react."

Æthel bites her lip. In all honesty, she does not know what to feel either. "You said before that a green boy would be no match for Gwyn. Is Ine any different?"

Herla's stony face is answer enough. Finding herself on her feet, Æthel reaches for her discarded tunic and trousers, and struggles into them. "If Gwyn comes to this world, Ine is the first person he will kill. You said yourself that the Heir of Dumnonia is the only one with the power to face him."

"Yes," Herla whispers, and it makes Æthel want to grab her, shake some life back into her, rousing the fierceness and passion she saw last night. *Her sisters are the only family she has left,* a measured voice reminds her, but Æthel thrusts it aside. "I have been gathering the men of Wessex," she says tightly. "They come to fight for me. For Ine. But they are just men, Herla. Gwyn and his host will slaughter them. Quite apart from his own army, Ingild has Olwen's aid. He has the wights while I have nothing but my sword. And not even that now," she adds sourly, eyeing the shattered blade. "And you—"

Herla whirls around, half-dressed. "I am his creature," she says savagely. "Any power I have, he gave me. He can take it away."

"Then why hasn't he?" Her hands are shaking and Æthel stops trying to buckle her belt. "If he is so frightened of your interference, why hasn't he taken his power back?"

Herla goes very still. Her amber eyes rove over Æthel's face without seeing her. "He mentioned an irksome duty," she says eventually. "When I asked what it was, he became angry. It is unusual. He is always in control."

"Ine speaks often of duty." Catching sight of a bruise on her arm that was not there yesterday, Æthel feels a guilty pang. "He believes kings are bound by it, freed only when they no longer wear the crown."

"Freed," Herla echoes. Her brow is deeply furrowed now. "He used that word too. And he called me part of his dream."

"He has now made you two offers." Æthel holds up corresponding fingers. "The only time kings make offers is when they are afraid, or believe they cannot crush their opponents by force. Trust me. I do the crushing and I know."

Herla shakes her head. "Not Gwyn ap Nudd."

"He is no different. He fears you, so he makes you an offer and when that is refused, he threatens you and those you love. What he does *not* do is strip you of your power. Why?"

The doubt in Herla's face wavers. Shadows creep across it instead. "They call him the shepherd of souls."

Æthel thinks of the wailing voices of last night. "Is that what I heard—when we fought?"

Herla turns away. It takes Æthel a moment to realize she is staring at the black blade. "He feared it." Her voice is soft. "He recoiled when I offered it back to him. A strange reaction from the one who gifted it."

Put it together. Æthel lays it out like she would her gameboard. One peg for duty. Another for the curse. Three more: Gwyn's fear, his dream, his title: *shepherd of souls.* "What if," she says slowly, trying to hold the pieces steady in her mind, "the curse is really a duty." She is barely breathing, as if too strong an exhale could upend the board. "What if it cannot be broken, only... transferred?"

Herla's eyes widen. "You are saying that he passed it to me? To lead the Hunt?"

"Is not the hound his?" Æthel is overly aware of the chamber's gloom-draped corners, but there is no sign of the beast this morning.

"Dormach is no ordinary creature." Herla is pacing. "He can carry souls. I told him to return the shades to their barrow that night in Sceaptun."

"Why would he be able to do that if it wasn't part of his purpose?"

Abruptly Herla closes the distance between them and seizes Æthel's shoulders. "Could Gwyn be forced to take the sword back? Take the duty back?"

"I don't know."

"Æthelburg." Herla laughs. The blaze in her face is bright, hard hope. "If he wielded it once, there is no reason he cannot again."

Æthel does not wish to snuff the flame, but the tactician in her demands, "How?"

Herla opens her mouth to respond—and the words are swallowed by a horn blast. They look at each other. "I told the men to gather here," Æthel says, making for the doors, pulling her belt tight as she goes. "When Ingild follows through on his plan to march west, we will be in place to stop him."

She rides out to meet the owner of the horn, aware of Herla following invisibly. "Beorhtric. I am glad to see you." Æthel glances over his shoulder. "How many did you bring?"

"Not enough, clearly," the ealdorman says, scanning the deserted skirts of the hill. His eyes are dark. "Five hundred follow me, but Godric and Wintanceaster are loyal to Ingild. I thought you said you could gather allies in Somersæte?"

"Give them time," Æthel insists and hopes he cannot hear the whisper of worry in her voice. "They will come."

"How many?"

"Ealdhelm brings three hundred, Mærwine another two. And Ceolric vowed to rouse Dorsæte. If we can get the men of Dornwaraceaster, we will stand a thousand strong."

"A thousand." Beorhtric lowers his chin, turning up his cloak against the rising wind. "Ingild has Nothhelm's support, which means he has all of Sussex to call upon. Admit we are badly outnumbered, Æthelburg."

She swallows; she has a belly full of stones. "I have spent the last two weeks riding across Wessex, Beorhtric. The people do not follow Ingild and they do not want him for a king, not while Ine lives. I owe it to both him and them to show Ingild that he cannot simply take what he wants."

"Have you had word from the king?"

She could lie. She knows the power of morale, of hope. But her bones tell Æthel that an untruth before a battle is unlucky, and Beorhtric is a friend. "No," she murmurs. "But he *will* come. You have known him all his life. He will not leave Wessex to stand alone."

A long time passes before the ealdorman answers. The wind teases out strands of hair, grey as the sea of his town. "I *have* known him all his life. But I do not know this version of him—the man you believe will lead the Britons of Dumnonia." He blows out a long, shivering breath and turns to signal his men to camp. "I hope you are right, Æthelburg. For all our sakes."

Æthel cannot help looking west where night still leaves its shadow in the mist. *I hope I am right too.*

30

INE

Dintagel, Kernow
Kingdom of Dumnonia

The Britons of Escanceaster are not the Britons of Dumnonia. It should come as no surprise. They have lived under Saxon rule for decades. They speak Englisc. Some are even Christian, although Ine is unsure how deeply their faith runs. Why did they come with him? Because he is King of Wessex or because he is Heir of Dumnonia?

"Because you are both," Maucus says when Ine asks him. They are riding side by side on horses Cadwy borrowed, trading on the joy his return to Dumnonia elicits in the people they pass. They are a fully mounted party now. "In a way no other has ever been, or may ever be. In the same way I am both a Briton and a subject of Wessex."

"Even though Wessex does not love you as she should."

"Wessex is men and men are slow to change. Rather like my kinfolk in Kernow."

"We are not slow to change," Cadwy says, overhearing. "We do not wish to lose our land and identity. Our culture, our language..."

"You will not lose them," Ine protests. "I only seek integration."

"Integration means the death of these things."

Cadwy is not entirely wrong. "Perhaps it is the price of peace," Ine says softly.

"Would you say the same if *we* were the ones calling *you*

foreigners? If we were the ones driving you and your Christian god into the sea?"

"Our own gods were driven into the sea." It is easier to say without the cross hanging about his neck. "We have paid the price of integration already. If we remained pagan, it would invite armies from Rome, and other nations who believe they do God's work stamping out the old religion."

"It makes no sense." Geraint's son nods at the wild land surrounding them. "Divinity is here beneath their feet, and yet they turn their eyes up and away."

A few months ago, Ine would not have had the faintest idea what he meant. Now he thinks of Sovereignty, the soul of the Land that Gwyn ap Nudd protects so fiercely. "They fear it," he hears himself say. "The Christian priests. Because they know it is real when they do not know if their god is real."

"You have been speaking to Emrys," Cadwy remarks and Ine smiles ruefully. "Look there," he adds. "The coast. We have made good time."

The weather is harsher now that the month of Winterfilleth is upon them. The trees are leafier than in Wiltunscir, but all lean inland, bowed by the ceaseless winds off the ocean. Ine has his first glimpse of Dintagel that very afternoon. The great rock stands proud of the headland, and smoke curls up from dozens of structures, the scale of it stealing his breath. Larger than Wiltun, surely. Perhaps larger than any Wessex settlement. He reins in without realizing, struck by the sense beneath him. He can only describe it as *dense*, as if the earth is a codex with boards that cannot contain all the pages inside. They spill out: lives, deaths, summers and winters.

"Are you impressed, Saxon?" Cadwy asks.

Ine looks askance at him, and sees a glitter in his eyes. How must it feel to return without Geraint? *He is a prince of his people and we are at war.* But Ine is painfully aware that he knows nothing of Cadwy's mother, or the rest of his family. And though his hand had not wielded the blade that took Geraint's life, still it seems callous in the extreme for him to be here, riding beside his son.

A great ditch guards the road running into Dintagel. To the left is a cliff of hulking grey slate, supporting an upper courtyard of timbered and thatched buildings; storehouses perhaps. It would take a mind like Æthelburg's to devise a strategy for laying siege to this place. Ine cannot see any weaknesses in its design at all. Between them, the ditch, cliffs and sea make for potent defences, and the road—while wide enough to admit a wagon—is not wide enough to accommodate the men required to launch an assault on the gates. At this hour, they stand open, and their party is spotted at once.

Grim-faced warriors, even a few women amongst them, bar the way ahead. They are better armoured by far than the Britons of Escanceaster, in proper leather, wool trousers and cloaks pulled up to ward off sea spray. Each bears a spear and a bow which they level when Cadwy shows no sign of slowing down. "Halt," the foremost man calls out, a deep Kernish accent almost obscuring the word.

"Eiddon, you fool, don't you recognize me?" Cadwy pushes his hood back. His light brown hair has grown to his shoulders and his cheeks are downy after their time on the road.

The man blinks several times, until Cadwy vaults out of the saddle and rushes at him. "*Prince Cadwy?*"

"No, I'm the Roman Pope," Cadwy laughs. "It is so good to see you, Eiddon. And you, Celemon."

The nearest woman glowers. She cuffs him and, when he yelps, pulls him into an embrace. "Little idiot. We thought you dead. What do you mean by coming here like this—no word beforehand?"

"It is a long story," Cadwy says with a backward glance at Ine.

Celemon follows his gaze, her own eyes narrowing. "Who are your companions?"

"Friends. But I must go to Dinavus."

"No, you must tell us everything." A second man catches the

boy's arm. "We heard only that the king, your father, fell in battle, and that you were taken prisoner."

"Both are true, Brys," Cadwy says, his humour fading. "But things are not as they appear. It is why I must see Dinavus."

"He's at the hall. We will come with you."

The warriors keep up a steady stream of questions, and Ine tries to concentrate on them. But their accents make the language harder to understand, and he cannot stop his attention from drifting to the sights and sounds of the settlement. The buildings are not too different from those in Wiltun, except that each dwelling has its own green plot, and pathways run between houses, linking them together in a way that reminds him of the old Roman villas. The sea is a constant presence—and the wind that scours the exposed rock, softening the musk of livestock and the stench of gutted fish. The Britons have always made their homes in wild places.

Cries of joy mark their progress through Dintagel, as heads turn and people recognize Cadwy. He waves to them, clasping arms with those who rush over, receiving tears and thanks in exchange. How well-loved Geraint must have been. The king's ignoble death is uppermost in Ine's mind, and anger smoulders at the memory. *He came to warn me and look what it brought him. Ingild and a knife in the dark.*

When they reach it, Dintagel's long hall is modest by Saxon standards, with a single floor and only one window cut to espy encroaching ships on the whale-roads. Figures are carved into posts on either side of the doorway, their limbs merging with the branches of a great tree. Ine glances away; it reminds him too strongly of the night the Land laid claim to him.

Here too Cadwy is greeted with delighted astonishment, but a fair few men wear consternation. *They thought they would never see him again.* The thought brings home to Ine the enormity of the risk he is taking; cold sweat covers him beneath his tunic, and the smoky interior of the hall clogs his throat. When Cadwy remembers himself enough to glance back, his expression plainly says he is enjoying Ine's discomfort. How far can he trust the blood debt the prince claims he owes him?

Servants hurry about tasks, while nobles sit on benches around the edge of the hall, much of which is given over to a long firepit smouldering in the centre. There is a table for feasting and several grand chairs, the largest of which is vacant. The king's, Ine assumes. The smaller seat beside it is filled by a hoary man of at least fifty winters. He looks faintly familiar. Despite his age, he is built like a warrior and Ine has a nasty feeling he may have crossed blades with him in one of the skirmishes he fought at the start of his reign. As their party enters, the chatter in the hall dies away.

"What is it now?" The man squints in their direction. "Who comes?"

"I see your sight hasn't improved," Cadwy says, striding towards him. "Hello, Dinavus."

"It cannot be." With a groan, he uses the arms of the chair to push himself up. "*Cadwy?*"

"Did you think I could not find my way home?"

In the ensuing jubilation, Ine and the Escanceaster Britons are all but forgotten. The whole of Dintagel must know of their prince's return by now. "We shall have a feast," Dinavus declares after Cadwy has grasped dozens of forearms. He claps his hands and the servants scurry off.

"We must talk first, Dinavus." Cadwy's smile fades. "And in private. Call the lords together."

The man frowns briefly. "As you say, Cadwy. You seem… changed."

"Yes," Cadwy says in soft, sober tones that only deepen the furrows across Dinavus's brow. Finally, he appears to notice Ine's group.

"Who are your companions?"

"One of the things we need to discuss. They will be joining us."

Dinavus claps his hands again. "Clear the hall."

Nobles drift out reluctantly; no doubt they are all keen to hear Cadwy's tale. When the other lords arrive—a woman amongst them—warriors bar the doors. "You too," Cadwy says to them. "Stand guard *outside*."

"Prince—"

"As he commands," Dinavus orders, and the men leave. Ine looks around the chamber. If this is the Britons' version of the Witan, its members are notably few. Dinavus settles himself back in his chair and the others take seats on the low benches around the room.

"Prince Cadwy," one man says before Cadwy can begin. He is younger than Dinavus, perhaps Ine's age, dressed in one of the short tunics the Britons prefer. "I cannot believe Wessex would release you without even a ransom. How did you escape?"

"I had help," Cadwy says, meeting Ine's eyes.

"Help? From one of our people?"

"Not exactly."

"You are being evasive, Cadwy," another man says. The sword at his side is surely a treasure with its decorated hilt, tooled scabbard and belt. "It gladdens me to see you unharmed, but are we to expect Saxons on our doorstep because of it?"

"I will tell all if you allow me, Ulch of Carnbree," the prince says testily. "First, I have a question. Why have you doubled the number of guards on the streets?"

It is the woman who answers him. "The killings are increasing in frequency, prince. And not only that. Children have begun to go missing. Cigfa believes it the Otherworld's doing. Only three sennights to Samhain remain."

Despite everything he has seen, Ine still marvels at the way the others nod, as if she has spoken of something ordinary—like cattle numbers, or the harvest. If he aired such words before the Witan, they would laugh to his face and mock him behind his back. *Much as they are doing now, no doubt.*

"I take it your father's quest failed?" another man asks. "He spoke of finding the door beneath Ynys Witrin in the hope of placating Annwn."

"Of course it failed." Ulch gives a disgusted snort. "It was always a mad idea to ask anything of Saxons. Look what it earned him."

"Watch how you speak of my father." Cadwy's tone is as cold as Ine has ever heard it. "All that he did, he did out of love for our people."

"I never questioned his loyalty, or integrity." Ulch does not appear much chastened. "I did not share his belief in the honour of Wessex. Saxons have none. If you recall, I spoke stridently against his plan. It brings me no pleasure to be proved right."

"You are not proved right," Ine says, stepping forward. "King Geraint's instincts were not wrong."

Every eye turns to him. Although he speaks the Britons' language, he learned it in the east, from people like Gweir. His intonation marks him out at once as a stranger.

"Who is this?" Dinavus scrutinizes them all. "Who are these people, Cadwy?"

"Britons from Caer Uisc—for the most part. Led by Maucus here."

"Lords." Maucus bows to them. "Lady."

"Are they the ones who aided your escape?" the woman asks. She has something of Geraint's look; his quick hazel eyes and reddish hair. "Caer Uisc is under Saxon control. If their actions have put them in danger, they are welcome to stay here."

"Thank you, Aunt Goeuin," Cadwy says, confirming Ine's suspicions. "But they merely decided to travel with me when I told them what had happened in Wessex."

"Happened?" Dinavus grips the arms of his chair. "Does Ine plan to march on us before the winter?"

Ine's blood had been racing, every nerve taut. But now that the moment is here, calm descends on him. He lowers his hood. "Ine has larger problems than Dumnonia."

There is no immediate reaction from the others. But Dinavus frowns, squinting his weak eyes. After a few moments, they widen. "Cadwy," he says, rising unsteadily from his seat. "What have you done?"

Cadwy does not answer.

"Boy." Dinavus does not take his gaze off Ine. "Tell me why the King of Wessex is standing in this hall."

"A poor joke, Dinavus, even for you."

Dinavus snarls, "I am not mistaken, Ulch." He clenches a fist. "I fought him at Llongborth."

"When I was young and foolish," Ine says quietly. "And did not know the true face of my enemy."

It takes two horrified heartbeats before swords leave their sheaths and he is surrounded by a bristling circle of iron. "Alert the guards," Dinavus says through gritted teeth. "His men are likely storming the gate as we speak."

"No." Cadwy finds his voice at last. "He is alone."

Dinavus laughs coldly. "Thoughtless child. What lies has he told you in order to gain admittance?" He raises his eyes to the Britons, all of whom have been allowed to keep their weapons. "Call the guards *now*."

"I said no, Dinavus. And you, Beruin, stop." The man named has taken a handful of steps towards the doors. Cadwy moves in front of Ine, so that the swords must pierce him first. "I am not a child and he is not here for violence."

"Put down your blades," Goeuin shouts. "For the gods' sakes, put them down. He is my blood and your rightful king."

"He is addled at best and a traitor at worst." Ulch's cheeks are mottled. "Hardly more than two months in Wessex and he's one of them."

"You speak out of loyalty to your country, so I will ignore your words," Cadwy says, his arms still spread wide. "But all of you will listen now."

Ine has stood with empty hands raised before him. Now he pushes Cadwy's guarding arm down. "Thank you, prince. Blood debt or no, if they wish to point blades at me, they have a right to do so."

The hall stills at those two small words. Even the flames seem to skip less nimbly across their peat bed. "Blood debt?" Dinavus asks, looking sick.

"King Ine saved my life." Cadwy does not move away. "When we fled Wiltun, two wights barred our path. They are the ones responsible for the murders in Dumnonia—and Wessex. They would have killed me."

"Even a single wight means death. How is it possible you…" Dinavus breaks off. "The birthright?" he asks wonderingly. "It passed to you?"

Cadwy stiffens, and pity fills Ine's throat, although he knows Geraint's son would hate him for it. The prince lifts his chin. "No, not to me."

"You said *fled* Wiltun," Goeuin says, her eyes on Ine. "Why would the King of Wessex flee his own stronghold with—of all people—the son of his enemy?"

This is his truth. Cadwy should not have to tell it. "The Church decrees that pagans are not welcome in Wessex." Ine touches his chest where the cross used to hang. "Even those baptized as Christian kings."

"Show them," Cadwy says, his voice hard. "They will not believe you otherwise."

The sense of *denseness* is still with him. Coiled beneath the rock from which the hall rises. There is so much he does not understand about the birthright, but it is all around him: in the fire, the people, in the rough salt wind that claws at the planks. Ine closes his eyes to see better, following it through the cliff, and into the wild ravening water. A web linking every life; stone, tree and heart. He catches his breath. Ripping it away, as Gwyn ap Nudd plans to, would rip out the soul of the people.

He opens his eyes at a short choking sound. Dinavus has a hand over his mouth, and gold threads the floor, part of a vaster pattern that they are all too small to see. Standing at its centre, Ine is not alone. Another is with him. He lives in the Land, an echo of its voice. Ine can almost reach him—

"It is true, lords. He spoke to the earth in Escanceaster. In Caer Uisc, I mean."

If it was a spell, Maucus's words break it. The golden web fades from sight, although Ine can still feel it there like a heartbeat. An answering one thrums in his bones.

"*How?*" Dinavus croaks.

Dismay is heavy in the hall, and something darker. Goeuin holds her face in one hand. Ulch's shoulders are slumped and he is staring at Cadwy with a disappointment that borders on outrage. "It is over," he says. "They have taken our land, work to overthrow our gods, and now they have stolen our heritage and dishonour the memory of our kings. Is this why you come here, Saxon? To revel in our defeat?"

"I did not ask for this," Ine says hotly. "One of your own people brought the heritage to Wessex. Constantine's sister."

"She was a traitor," Ulch says, glaring at the fire. "A kinslayer. King Constantine may have forgiven her, but her crimes are writ large in our memory. And now it seems they are worse than ever we knew."

Do not make a mockery of her sacrifice. "She wanted what I want—peace between our peoples," Ine says, recalling Emrys's words. "Whatever else she did, I understand that wish and there is nobility in it."

Silence greets him. He had expected more argument, but Ulch is right. His people *have* taken land that belonged to the Britons. Few in Wessex see them as deserving of equal status. As for the heritage… "Others set today's events in motion long ago," Ine says, his tone losing none of its heat. "I like them as little as you, but because of them, I was hounded from my home by my own brother, who no doubt sits upon the throne of Wessex now."

Heads rise at that. "There is civil war in Wessex?"

"Worse." Ine has almost forgotten Gweir's presence—so silent has he been. But now the gesith comes forward to stand beside Ine. "The civil war is a cover for the more serious conflict beneath. Gwyn ap Nudd has worked in the shadows, but he will not remain there. He will bring the hosts of Annwn at Samhain and it will mean the doom of Britons and Saxons alike."

"I fear he has made an ally of my brother," Ine says and once more pushes down the memory of Ingild's bloody forearms. "Ingild murdered our father, but I do not know why."

"I can tell you why."

Dinavus whirls at the unexpected voice. "Cigfa." The name is stern, resigned. "How long have you been here?"

"I was always here." A waifish girl sits by the firepit, her long blonde hair charcoal-smeared, as if she has stepped straight out of the embers. It is difficult to tell her age. Perhaps she has the same number of winters as Cadwy, although her build makes her seem younger. "Watching."

"Some meetings are private." But from the weary slant of his brows, it is clear this has happened many times before. "What do you have to say then?"

Cigfa looks at Ine. "Hello, King of Wessex. You do not have the eyes of a Saxon."

He cannot think of anything to answer that strange pronouncement, so Ine simply waits for her to continue. "Only Gwyn ap Nudd is able to call a soul back and bind it to a body, but this power can be loaned." The girl skips closer to peer at him. "It takes a life to make a wight. Your brother exchanged one for another."

Ine cannot suppress a shudder. "You are saying he took my father's life to bring Centwine here? What about Cædwalla? Who paid so that he could return?"

"I am a witch, not a seer," she replies matter-of-factly. "I can only tell you how it was done."

Ine feels cold. "If he can sacrifice our father to necessitate killing, he is lost." *Did I ever believe otherwise?* "And it's my fault. I should have seen what he was capable of."

"He is your brother," Gweir says, putting a hand on his arm. "It is hard to believe ill of kin."

"You do not have the armies of Wessex to fight for you, so you come here." Dinavus glares at him. "Are you hoping our people will shed their blood instead?"

Ine shakes his head. "No one should shed blood for a cause they do not believe in. But Gwyn ap Nudd intends to destroy the heritage of Dumnonia."

Dinavus is not the only one to suck in a breath. "How do you know this?"

"Emrys," Ine says bluntly.

The Dumnonii share narrow looks and Ulch's sneer falters. "You have seen them? Emrys has spoken to you?"

"They told me of the heritage, and of Gwyn's plan to strip it from this world. He believes humans are unworthy of it."

Ulch is clearly itching to call *him* unworthy too. "We almost lost the magic of the land once." Ine receives a venomous glance. "If we lose it to Annwn..."

"It will be lost forever," Cadwy says. "Perhaps Father suspected this when he chose to travel to Ynys Witrin."

With a wince, Ine recalls his words to Geraint the night he died. *Perform your heathen rites and then leave my kingdom.* No wonder the Dumnonian king had not been honest with him. "He had the knowledge and the plan—"

"But not the blood," Gweir argues, despite the hostile frowns of everyone around him. "That must count for something, or King Constantine would surely never have allowed his sister to marry Cynric and go to Wessex."

A weight has settled on Ine's shoulders like a cloak whose hem is sewn with stones. Being expected to uphold the legacy of Cynric and his son, the famous Ceawlin, is pressure enough. Now he must shoulder the legacy of Ceawlin's mother too?

"We must speak of this alone," Dinavus says, breaking into Ine's thoughts. "You and those who accompanied you will remain under guard. And you will yield up your weapons."

Gweir swells as if about to object, so Ine swiftly nods. "I understand."

Out on the steps, beneath the forbidding sky, their party attracts whispered questions. Were they not just travelling with the prince? Why are they being treated so roughly now? The light is starting to fade and the sea becomes wilder in the dusk, tossing itself remorselessly against this scrap of land. The ocean's pattern can be heard in the chest rather than the ears, as if Ine's ribs are a sea cave, and his blood the waves that pound against its hollow. "Have you noticed," he says to Gweir, "how people talk about Constantine as if he isn't dead."

"Because he is not dead." Cadwy slips out of the hall to stand beside them. "He is only sleeping. Held close in the Land. You could say he *is* the Land. There is a belief amongst our people that he watches over us, and that he will return when our need is great."

"Is not the need great *now*?"

Cadwy gives him an odd look. "Yes, but you are here. If we survive this, a day may come when we won't even be able to wield the small magics. We have lost so many of our people to the wights. And thanks to the Christians, we may not remember the old ways. How will we face a threat like Gwyn then?"

"You speak as if I am Constantine's equal," Ine says quietly. "As if I can do the same things he did."

Cadwy gives his shoulder a mocking push. "King Constantine has no equal."

It is the warmest he has ever been, and Ine cannot help smiling. "Why are you not inside?"

"They asked me to leave while they talked." The prince's face turns mutinous. "I am rightfully king."

"No one is king in Wessex until the Witan agrees it." His own accession had been a muddy thing. Ine remembers the agonizing wait as the ealdormen conferred. "I am quite sure my family's connection to Cynric was the reason I gained the throne. Lineage is very important to them." He can hear his distaste plainly.

When there is only a slice of sun left in the sky, doors open across Dintagel and women emerge, carrying bowls of milk. They set them down outside with a honeycake and a braid of wheat. Charms are tied to stray twigs that poke from the thatch. "What are they doing?" Ine asks. The movements are like a ritual, each woman's hands placing the bowl just so, securing the knot with a twist and aligning the cake like a sky instrument.

"What we do every year." Cadwy's face is grave as he observes the activity. "I do not think it will please Annwn or the spirits of the dead this Samhain."

Pagan rites, and yet they are similar to those performed at All Hallows, Ine reflects. Not for the first time, he wonders at the Christian festivals and the way they follow the old religion, laying new ideas atop those established millennia before. Clever.

Calculated even. It is another kind of pattern, a very human kind. The pattern of control. One, as king, he is supposed to have mastered.

"Prince Cadwy." It is the guard from earlier—Eiddon. "There is a person at the gate who seeks admittance. Says he is a priest, but he doesn't look like any priest I've seen."

"Describe him."

"Young, fair-haired, middling tall." Eiddon holds a hand level with his own head. "Although he wears one of their crosses, he's armed. Name of Winfrid."

The pagan-hunter. Cold trickles down his spine. "How did he find…?" Ine stops. "How did he know you were here, Cadwy?"

"Let him in," Cadwy says.

Scratching his beard, Eiddon glances in the direction of the gate. "Are you sure, prince?"

"He is a priest." Cadwy shrugs, but his eyes are on Ine, who has begun to pace up and down before the doors of the hall. "Perhaps he has heard of our Father Daire. The man is famous in Éire."

It is a tense wait. Why would Winfrid leave Hædde's side? Unless they have cooked up a plan between them? But Ine also recalls the way Winfrid held the spear, his polite, firm rebuttal when Hædde questioned his decision to travel abroad. Perhaps the young man dances to his own tune.

Winfrid has been divested of the spear by the time he appears, and walks between two guards. He and Ine share a laden glance. "Right." Eiddon glowers. "You are free to deliver your message to the steward, but I am keeping your spear. Holy men with weapons make me nervous."

The young man laughs. "I am sorry for that."

He speaks the Britons' language like a native and Eiddon's brows climb skywards. "Where are you from?"

"Crediantun," Winfrid says happily. "Near Escanceaster."

It is contested land, nominally under West Saxon control, but not a consolidated part of Wessex. *Interesting.* How much does Winfrid know about the Dumnonian heritage? Too much, Ine suspects, but can only wonder what the priest does with the knowledge.

When Cadwy leads them into the hall, a harried Dinavus splutters, "What now? I thought I told…" Then he catches sight of Winfrid. "Who is this?"

"Winfrid of Crediantun," Cadwy says, giving the priest a dark look. "A Christian from Wessex."

"Then speak plainly, priest." Dinavus resettles himself in his chair. "There is no need to protect your king. We know who he is."

Winfrid's curls gleam red gold in the firelight. He looks positively saintly. But Ine is beginning to suspect his angelic head hides a mind like a siege weapon wound tight. "I am impressed, Ine king," he says in Englisc with a short bow. "Your diplomacy is a force to be reckoned with."

Ulch growls. "You stand in this hall at our pleasure, Christian."

"My apologies." Winfrid changes languages. "I am a son of Defenascir and have great respect for the lords of Dumnonia."

"Despite our so-called heathenism?" Cadwy's aunt asks in chill tones.

Untroubled, Winfred links his hands behind his back. "Yes, you are heathens. But that does not mean I dismiss or discredit the Dumnonian birthright."

"You…" Ine is temporarily stripped of words. "That night," he manages, his anger prickling, "you let Hædde condemn me. Why did you not speak up?"

"Because forces—not all of them natural—were arrayed against you. You must pick your battles, king."

"Do the bishops know you're here?" Ine demands "Does my brother?"

"Of course not." Winfrid's tone sharpens. "I covered my tracks. Both those left by my horse and by my words."

Ine cannot get a grip on him at all. He is like an eel always sliding out of the basket. "So why are you here?"

"I bring news of your wife."

His feet propel him to Winfrid's side in an instant. "Æthelburg? Where is she? Is she safe?"

"She is raising the fyrds in your name. Hamwic's ealdorman follows her and she has turned her attention to Somersæte, but large parts of Wiltunscir are loyal to Ingild ætheling who claims the kingship of Wessex."

Warmth grows in Ine's chest amidst a fragile fluttering hope. *Æthel.* She has not turned her back, but summoned men to fight— for *her*, he realizes, as much as for him. For Wessex. Turning to Dinavus, he says, "It seems I *do* have an army, lord."

"An army whose number we can but guess at." Ulch's snort is dismissive. "The priest says your brother controls the heartland of your kingdom. And if he has, as you believe, an agreement with Gwyn ap Nudd, fighting men are the least of his resources."

"Until Samhain, fighting men are *all* he has," Ine counters. "Yes, we must contend with the wights, but our only chance is to face Ingild now, before Gwyn can bolster his army with the hosts of Annwn."

"I would never have imagined to hear such words from a Saxon," Dinavus says, and it is unclear whether the edge in his voice is born of wonder or disdain. "*Contend* with the wights, you say. But they cannot be harmed by conventional weapons. They will scythe through our forces unhindered."

He is right. What do they have to oppose such creatures? *Me,* Ine thinks and his stomach plunges, the same sensation as of missing a step. Here in Dumnonia, he has some understanding of the heritage, but in Wessex it is a sleeping dragon that wakes at a whisper to kill.

"I passed several groups on my way," Winfrid says, breaking into his thoughts. "The men were intending to join the queen at Glestingaburg."

Glestingaburg. "Why…?" He stops. Because he knows why. Æthel told him herself. "Herla." The name is a whisper. "Æthelburg said that Herla no longer slept. She was going to find the Wild Hunt."

"*What?*" It does not seem Dinavus can take many more shocks. "You believe the Lord of the Hunt is free? Then we are lost. We cannot fight both Gwyn and Herla."

"And what makes you think Herla would fight for the King of Annwn?"

Ine had forgotten Cigfa, and could have sworn she had not been there a moment ago. The elfin girl jumps off the barrel on which she was perching and holds her hands to the fire. "What do you mean?" Dinavus rounds on her. "Herla is a creature of Annwn, and an enemy of men."

"Weren't you listening at your mother's knee?" Cigfa says, sounding years older. "Herla was cursed to ride. Who do you think cursed her?"

"Watch your tongue, child. That does not mean she wouldn't fight for him."

"And it does not mean she would."

Dinavus scowls. "Conjecture. We cannot count on Herla remaining neutral."

She and her heart are your hope. Emrys's words are a puzzle at the back of his mind, one Ine keeps returning to in the confidence it might have solved itself while his attention was elsewhere. Now that he sees it, he wishes he did not. A bitter taste floods his mouth. Who stopped the shades in Sceaptun? Who lived where six men had died?

Ælfrún… *Herla.*

The Lord of the Hunt is not neutral. She has been helping them. Ine should feel relieved, but all he can see is Æthel leaning close to Ælfrún, linking their arms and laughing. All he can hear is the bruised tone she used to defend the other woman, and the catch in her voice when she spoke of going to Glestingaburg. He has been so stupid. Worse than stupid. But why did Herla disguise herself? What could she want with Æthel? Ine has never feared the answer to a question more.

"Æthelburg must have made an ally of Herla." Of course she has—Herla has been in this from the start. He grinds his teeth. Wessex is his kingdom and Æthelburg is his wife. If Herla thinks she has a right to do as she pleases with both—"Or she would not be assembling her army at Glestingaburg." If only Ine himself had been honest, Æthel might have told him.

"Ingild held a council of war," Winfrid says into the silence Herla's name has summoned. "He believes Queen Æthelburg went to seek allies in the west." Muttering amongst the Dumnonii. "He ordered that they take the fight to her." He looks around the hall. "To *you*."

"So we have no choice." Goeuin rises. The bleak shadow of it is in her face when she says, "You have brought war to our gates, King of Wessex, whether you wished to or not."

Ine is aware of their eyes on him. He is aware of the thoughts massing in their heads like the sea-born clouds outside. He has only to focus to feel the wings of the wind as they drag their pinions across the exposed hall. "It seems it is the destiny of my people to bring war," he says slowly. "And the destiny of yours to fight back."

Beneath the lives of the folk gathered here are others; those who came before; those who would come after. "Together, perhaps," Ine says, speaking to all of them, "we may do what our ancestors could not." He holds out a hand, palm up. "Put an end to it."

31

Herla

Glestingaburg, Somersæte
Kingdom of Wessex

"Are you certain, Æthelburg?" It is the third time she has asked the question. "I will gladly fight alongside you."

"And I will gladly have you. But not before we have forced Ingild to reveal his allegiance to the Otherworld." They stand in the stark shadow of branches stripped bare of leaves. Æthelburg's army waits on the other side of the rise nearby. "His credibility hinges on his *not* being a pagan, or being seduced by pagan powers." Herla raises an eyebrow and Æthelburg flushes. "Anyway," she says loudly, slamming a knife into a leather sheath on her leg. Two more hang from her belt. "If you are seen at my side, Ingild will use it to strengthen his argument that Ine and I have both defected. He has manipulated us." Her voice is a growl of renewed rage.

"Be still." Herla takes her arm. "Keep a clear head and do not allow him to taunt you."

"I know, I know." The queen's eyes are as icy as the night Herla first saw her, shrouded in smoke and battle. "But I meant what I said. I will kill him this time. If I get the chance."

Instead of letting go, Herla pulls her nearer, cupping her cheek. "I will stay close. I do not share your belief that Ingild will play by the rules."

"He isn't beyond cheating," Æthelburg admits. She lays a hand over Herla's. "But equally he has not been able to refuse my challenge—he wants to be seen as a king putting down a dangerous rebellion. And he believes he has the greater numbers."

"He *does* have the greater numbers."

"Yes. And we have me."

"I admire your commitment to immodesty," Herla remarks, her smile strained. Æthelburg may be a great warrior, but she is still only mortal, and even the strongest sword arm wearies. *I will be there when it does,* she thinks at her. *Whatever you say, I will never be far from your side.* These politics the queen deems so important matter little in the end. She is too young, too fresh in the world, to understand.

Æthelburg returns the smile for a few blazing seconds before clouds cover her face. "Oh God, am I leading these men to their deaths?"

"It is the destiny of men to die," Herla says with a shrug.

"Sometimes you can be extraordinarily unhelpful."

"You wanted reassurance? I cannot give it to you, Æthelburg." Herla lets her hand fall to the queen's shoulder; the other still grips her arm, reluctant to let go. "People die in battle. The question is whether they believe their deaths are worth it."

"No one believes they will die until they do."

Behind Herla's eyes are the fogged centuries of blood and reaping, the weight of the sword as it rose and fell like a butcher's knife. Thousands of faces, names and lives tilted towards ending. "No," she agrees softly. "Which is why we have the courage to fight."

Æthelburg nods, a small tightly controlled movement that plucks at Herla's heart. She pulls the woman in her arms against her, to feel Æthelburg's warmth on her skin. They could still turn their backs on the slaughter that shaped them, start again in some new and distant land where the truth of who they are cannot follow.

She lets the vision go. Æthelburg already has a land to fight for. And Herla is bound here by more than the curse. She has a promise to keep to her sisters…a promise to keep to herself. She thinks of the sword with a blade darker than the space between

stars. *I know your name now. You are duty. But you are not* my
duty.

"I will stay close," she says again, unable to keep the fear from
her voice. She cannot remember ever wanting to protect something so fiercely. The words brush the bare skin beneath
Æthelburg's ear and the queen shivers. "Do not do anything rash.
Please."

Æthelburg winds her arms around Herla's waist. Her kiss,
when it comes, is hard, and sets Herla's blood afire again. She
slides a hand into the queen's hair. After that first desperate night,
there had been shyness between them, but not for long. That
someone could want her—knowing who she is, what she has
done—still shocks Herla. A better person would send Æthelburg
away. *I am too dangerous to love.* But her heart condemns her. It
has no power to send the queen away, just as it had no power to
send Boudica away.

Æthelburg pulls back, says roughly, "You sound like my husband." She dashes a hand across her eyes and all but leaps into the
saddle. Watching her ride off, Herla touches her mouth where the
ungentle echo of the kiss still clings. She has no wish to be com-
pared to the king, not after everything Æthelburg has said of him.
The queen should be loved as Herla loves her: with lips and teeth,
whispers and moans, skin to skin. But does she not know well that
love is more than that?

She clenches her fists and mounts, dark-thoughted. Yes, she
will stay close. Ingild will not use mere men to win this battle.
Why would he risk losing now?

Riding her own mortal horse, Æthelburg bends in the saddle
to listen to a scout's report. Then she straightens, wheeling about
to face the men. "Be ready! Ingild is upon us."

Scanning the lines, Herla notes that not all are outfitted
equally. Most have armour, but only the wealthier men possess
mail, and the ceorls wield weapons of lesser quality. Still, there is
fire in many eyes as the queen draws her sword—one from
Beorhtric's hoard—and holds it high.

"I have long been privileged to fight beside you," she shouts,

riding up and down the foremost line. "Those of you who were
with me when we pushed back the men of Mierce from Readin-
gas, when we fought the exile Ælfgar—you stood bravely and
ensured our *victory*." She yells the last word and the men echo it,
a roar that travels back through the ranks until the field is a shattering chorus. "Today," Æthelburg continues, "we face a more
serious threat. Treason in the heart of Wessex." The men fall silent.
"Seeking the throne for himself, Ingild ætheling has slandered and
betrayed his own brother. Ine cares for this land and would see its
people prosper. Ingild cares for himself. If he wins here today, he
will call it a sign that God favours him. I will *die* before I let that
happen."

And I will die before I let you die. The vow is entrenched in
Herla's being, as deeply as her vow of revenge, as the vow to find
her sisters. She stares at the queen and thinks, wonderingly, *How
did you find me?* How had Æthelburg known that a woman still
fought and dreamed in the shadowlands where Gwyn had
chained her?

A horn stops Æthelburg from saying more, as a long dark line
tops the rise that had hidden it from view. Herla draws a sharp
breath. Ingild's army must outnumber them three to one. Æthelburg's only reaction is to lift her chin, as if the sight does not
perturb her in the least. But Herla watches her hands tighten on
the reins. The queen is worried—and worried that the men will
sense it.

"Beorhtric," she snaps, and the ealdorman nudges his horse to
her side. "Bring Ealdhelm and Mærwine." When the men named
join her, she keeps her head high as she rides out across the valley.
Herla follows, careful to stay behind cover.

Ingild's party consists of his clinging subordinate, Edred;
Nothhelm, the South Saxon king; and two other men who Herla
does not know until they speak. Then she recognizes them as the
lords she overheard in the council chamber. Æthelburg reins in,
forcing Ingild to come to her. The ætheling's lip curls. "You have
been busy, Æthel. Stirring up rebellion, inciting war in your own
kingdom. Because of your actions, *our* people will die today."

"Yield if you care for their lives so much," Æthelburg retorts. "Lay down your challenge, Ingild, or you will not have a people to rule over. Everyone will remember the blood you spill here today."

"Lay down your own challenge, Æthelburg." He nods at the distant men. "Do not lead innocents to pointless slaughter."

"Pointless?" Her eyes blaze. "They fight for the true king of Wessex, who does not dance on another's strings."

Blood suffuses Ingild's face. "Where is the *true king*?" he spits. "He has abandoned his people, just as he has abandoned *you*."

It is a barb that hits home. Herla sees the queen flinch and knows Ingild has too. "Even a fool could see the disdain in which he holds you," the ætheling adds. "We have our disagreements, Æthel, but you deserve better."

Æthelburg has stiffened. "Will you stand down?"

"Come now." Nothhelm's tone is light, but his eyes are troubled as he looks on the queen. "This is unnecessary. Only weeks ago, we broke bread and drank at table together. Why must there be bloodshed between us?"

"When has Ine ever belittled you, Nothhelm?" Æthelburg asks. "He has given you back the power Cædwalla—" Herla cannot stop herself glancing round—"took from you by force. He values your friendship. Your *loyalty*." The word is weighted with the still-sheathed weapons of Nothhelm's men. "Why would you turn against him?"

The King of Sussex shifts in his saddle. Herla would guess it is a question he has already asked himself. "You were not there the night he fled. He is unnatural, Æthelburg. He almost killed Leofric. The man may never walk again."

Another barb, but this one does not strike Æthelburg as deep. "I am sorry to hear it. But you must have cornered him, forced his hand—"

"He was defending a pagan."

"If you are referring to Cadwy, he was defending a boy, Nothhelm, whose only crime was to be born a prince in a kingdom we have long called enemy. But we have deadlier enemies than the Britons."

"You spout the same drivel as my brother." Ingild shakes his head in a way that makes Herla's fists clench. "I am surprised at you, Æthelburg. I did not think you a fantasist."

"But you thought me capable of leaving the people of Wessex to your machinations. You care nothing for these men that follow you," she shouts, hoping, perhaps, that some of them will hear. "You care nothing for the Church in whose name you condemn Ine. You are a puppet, Ingild." She draws her sword, levels it. "Pray we do not come face to face in battle because I will not hesitate." Without giving him a chance to reply, Æthelburg gallops back to her line.

"Kill them all, including the ealdormen, but leave her for me," Herla hears Ingild say. "She has a use. My brother would in fact do anything to keep her safe."

Feeling an uncomfortable kinship with the absent king, Herla circles the army, determined to uncover any surprise pockets of men, but there are none. Which means either Ingild is confident he can win through sheer force of numbers, or he is holding other pieces in check. The hairs on her arms itch to stand up.

It is an ugly thing, as the two shield walls meet. Terrifyingly, she loses sight of Æthelburg in the crush. Men on both sides have friends on the other. Who can fight with their whole heart when the next opponent might have a face they know? The shield wall struggles back and forth, giving ground and then retaking it. Spears stab out between the locked shields and bodies soon darken the field, trampled and tripped over. The sounds of war in her ears, Herla prowls the fringes, her blade keeping Ingild's army from gaining the upper hand despite the press of their numbers. Gurgles, grunts and screams follow her.

At the urging of a horn, the two sides break off. Men gasp, spit blood, drag the bodies of fallen friends away from the carnage where the two walls met. Herla's heart is clenched until she sees Æthelburg, bloodied but grinning. The queen thrusts her sword in the air to yells. Insults are hurled at the men retreating towards Ingild's lines.

"You see," Æthelburg shouts. "They are the ones to call for respite. They are the ones to falter first."

"Send terms," Beorhtric says to her, pushing through the battered men. "Ingild's losses are higher than he expected. No more need die today."

"I'll send them, but he will not back down." Æthelburg leans her shield against her legs to shake out her arm and shoulder. "You heard him. He has no mind for the lives of freemen."

"But we do." Beorhtric's brows lower with his voice. "*You* do. Is there no way to bring this to a swift conclusion, Æthelburg? You claimed you had an ally. At this point, we could use any edge."

"She already aids us," Æthelburg says, her eyes meeting Herla's across the trampled green.

"She?"

"I told her to keep out of sight. Trust me, Beorhtric. She protects us, as she can." Æthelburg smiles at her, and Herla is lost momentarily in the contours of her face, the smudges of battle on her cheek. Her blonde hair is darkened with sweat from the helm.

The respite is short, just enough for Ingild to swap out tired fighters. Most of Æthelburg's men are bloodied. The worst she sends to the back of the wall, while the least exhausted move to brace the front. "No," Mærwine calls to her as she takes her place in the centre. "Æthelburg queen, you must rest."

Grimly, she shakes her head. Herla could have told him that Æthelburg will fight at the fore to give her men hope, no matter how tired she becomes. It is what *she* would do too. For an instant, the advancing wall flickers, becomes instead a bristling guard with burnished arms and breastplates. Spears raised to jam the wheels of the chariots bearing down upon them.

Blinking the vision away, Herla looks to Æthelburg, ready to step in at the smallest stumble. But although the queen's teeth are bared in a permanent grimace, she does not waver, shouting encouragement to her men, and dark words at Ingild's. Ever so slowly, they gain ground, pushing their opponents back across the field, swampy now with blood.

And then, without warning, the line breaks.

"Close the gap!" Æthelburg yells, but half a dozen men are down, others stumbling away from a figure in their midst. The man wears a king's mail, its bright rings stained grey with death. Æthelburg sees the wight at the same instant; her cheeks pale. "Centwine," she hisses.

It is exactly what Herla has been waiting for. "Leave him to me," she says as she passes near the queen. The wight stabs at the face of a fallen warrior, but Gwyn's sword catches the blow and the dead king retreats in a flowing, inhuman step. Gasps tell her the glamour is gone, but Herla cannot stay invisible *and* fight the creature.

Although men rally under Æthelburg's orders, the shield wall has fractured and it is every warrior for himself. Dozens of separate battles break out around her. "I knew Ingild would not play fairly," Herla growls at the wight. "How does it feel to be pulled from death and forced to fight for a coward?"

"You think I do not embrace this?" Centwine vanishes only to reappear behind her. They clash blades. *"I am better now than I ever was in life. Do you not rejoice in the power you were given, Hunt lord?"*

"Rejoice? It was forced upon me." Herla kicks out, her foot connecting with a satisfying crack. "Freedom is more important than power."

The dead king laughs; the drag of wind across a cairn. *"Power is freedom."*

"Power has chained you to another's will."

"Why do you fight, Herla? You are one of us, blessed of Annwn." The wight extends a hand. *"I and the others would welcome you."*

Aghast, she stares at him. "Others?" But almost as soon as the word is out, screams reach her. Not the cries of battle. Stark horror. A glance to her left reveals a figure standing amidst corpses arranged in a perfect circle. She has only a moment to register the rags of a cloak blowing around him and the long blade in his hand before Centwine grabs her wrist. The grip does nothing beyond chill her, but fury erupts, and beneath it, terrible fear for Æthelburg. Inside his defences now, Herla thrusts the sword into his chest.

The wight convulses. Shock stretches his pallid features and his eyes turn glassy as she severs the power that binds his soul in place. The body slumps, dissipates on the wind. But the soul—the weight of it slams into her. She staggers. Herla drags an arm across a forehead beading with sweat, railing at her knees not to buckle. Why? Why does the king's soul weigh so much? She is burning up with cold, the sensation like a dimly remembered fever. Only one more to add to her tally, only one, but it is one too many.

The second wight turns a lightless face towards the queen. "Leave her," Herla gasps, managing a stumbling step. "Your master...wants her alive."

"*I had no master when I drew breath. I have none now.*"

He is not one of the recent dead. The longer they lie in the earth, the more powerful they are when they rise from it. Terror seizes her. "Æthelburg!" Herla screams, just as her legs fold under the weight of the souls.

The wight's mouth stretches into something that might, in life, have been a smile, and continues his irresistible walk towards Æthelburg. Beyond them, Herla catches sight of Ingild, Olwen at his side. In her true form, she is taller than him and her bare feet are stained with blood. She too smiles, a beautiful smile that sparks such panic in Herla that she plants Gwyn's sword in the soil and uses it to push herself upright.

Bright agony as something fractures, a crack spidering through her soul. Memories leak into her, of lives not her own. She sees the plough and the sickle, the laughter of brothers, apples and salt and the tunic a mother sewed. Summers that flew and winters that dragged. Hunger, sickness. The cry of the gull. The first green. They swarm her, and she cannot keep them out. Dustless throats shriek for release, but she has no way of releasing them, and their malice bleeds into her with their memories. *Hunter. Butcher. Murderer.* The pain of it is unending. She took their lives and then she took their peace.

The wight passes her as she stands frozen. It is all Herla can do to stand. Too late she grasps that the hunter in her guarded against this. Dead, her heart offered the souls no purchase. But she has left herself open. *Child of the dust,* they tell her savagely, tearing into it, *we could have lived if you had died.* Their suffering crushes her, or is it guilt that weighs so heavy, greater than all the stone ever quarried from the earth? Greater than the passage of years that took Boudica and the Eceni away.

Help me. But there is no one to help her, and no one to hear her silent screams.

32

ÆTHELBURG

Glestingaburg, Somersæte
Kingdom of Wessex

They had been winning, Æthel is sure of it. Now she watches her victory set with the sun.

She stabs at her attacker and he falls, her knife buried in his eye. She wrenches it free to take another man in the throat. He slumps at her feet with a grunt and Æthel realizes she is tiring. She can feel the lethargy of exhaustion beginning to cool her blood, making her slower, sloppier.

The moment she spots Herla, stock-still amidst the chaos, she knows something is wrong. A dark mist shrouds the other woman, and she does not move when Æthel yells her name. Worse than the agony in her face are her eyes, gone completely black. The sight pierces Æthel. She glances up, but the moon is not yet old.

Before she can take even a step, the men around her fall back. Æthel feels a chill on her skin. A wight. It is the first time she has faced one. Bodies lie all around him. His armour belongs to a different age—over a hundred years old, she would guess—and the blade he carries is longer than the swords she is used to. But it isn't the sword or the armour that transfixes her. It is how much the wight looks like Ine.

Æthel sheaths her sword, raising Herla's spear instead. "What is your name?"

"*Who are you to demand it?*"

Fear is curling through her blood, but her voice does not falter. "Æthelburg. Queen of Wessex."

"*And I was king.*" The wight holds out his free hand. "*But king of a stronger land than this. It pains me to see it thus, made lazy by peace.*"

Æthel takes a step back, keeping a healthy distance. "Peace is the reason we fight now. That you see it in the land means it is one war we have won."

The wight stares at her as if she is a strange and faintly disgusting thing. "*Conquest is the reason we fight, woman. To bathe the gods in the blood they do not have. We fight for spoils and glory. We fight to be remembered in the great stories.*"

"And are you remembered?" Her hands are slick on the spear. *How can I kill a dead man?* "What do we sing of you?"

Instead of answering, the wight lunges.

Æthel leaps aside, but the long sword nicks her mail, slicing effortlessly through several rings. She hisses, opening distance between them again. There is plenty to be had; the fighting continues, but the ground around them is empty, as if they are gladiators in one of the great southern arenas.

"Herla!" she shouts desperately, still to no response. But other eyes find her. Over the wight's shoulder, she can see a red-draped figure, and her breath catches: Olwen. Fear for Herla courses through her, makes her clumsy. She barely avoids losing a hand to the wight's next swing. *Concentrate.* Her heart is a turmoil. The wights have tipped the scales, shattered the strength of their shield wall, and now her men are losing. She can feel the battle beginning to ebb.

No. Æthel feeds her rage into an attack, launching herself at the wight. The spear takes him in the side, not deep, but shock slackens his face as she pulls it free, spinning away before he can catch her.

She is unsurprised to see that his body does not bleed. Nevertheless, he puts a hand to the wound, gazing at the spear she levels. "*What is that weapon?*"

"Herla gave it to me."

"She cannot give anything but death," is all the wight says before attacking again. Æthel dodges. He is not as fast as Herla, a fact for which she ought to be thankful. But she fought that duel while she was fresh, not in the exhausted lee of battle. She fought knowing she risked only herself. Now she is aware of the lives that rest upon her shoulders and on her blade. She brought them here. It is her fault that they are dying here.

"Herla!" she shrieks, pouring everything she has into it. And Herla raises her hanging head. Her face contorts. Her lips shape Æthel's name, but still she does not move. Dusk is blooming red; their bloodshed echoed in the sky. Æthel's breath is a rasp now. Herla, the men and herself—she cannot save them all. The thought pulls a cry from her tired lungs, and she hears her own despair. The wight flows forward.

When another cry rises, she thinks, for a crazed instant, that it is her own death made audible. But it sounds again: a wail from hundreds of throats, and she knows that ululation. As a young warrior, she stood and faced it, and the ones who made it, as they coursed down from the hills. The ground beneath her is trembling. Thunder of hooves, or feet, or drums in her ribcage. The wight's sword hangs over her head like a curse.

Behind her, from the blazing west, they come. The first on horseback, then scores running behind like the wild children of Woden. Spears in their hands, swords at their waists, and a brilliance in their faces that speaks of something greater than either. Mingled with the drums is a war trumpet shaped like a horse's head with lolling tongue. It is borne aloft by a huge man, his chest full of the air needed to sound it. The shriek that emerges from the mouth is a dark parody of a horse's scream. Æthel shudders. Pagans. Britons. The men of Dumnonia. In her weariness, she does not immediately know whose side they are on.

And then a voice behind her, tight with fury, says, "Ceawlin. Get away from my wife."

Although every instinct screams at her not to, Æthel looks round.

At first, she almost doesn't recognize him. Then she realizes it is the context she does not recognize—she is so used to seeing him against the backdrop of Wiltun: a scroll in his hands, a codex, or with fingers steepled in thought beneath his chin. Now there is a scabbard at his hip, a sword in his hand. Fine mail shields his chest, and a cloak with golden clasps hangs from his shoulders. His dark hair has grown in the weeks since she saw him and his eyes are... different. For a start, they are streaked with woad-blue paint. Æthel gapes at him.

The wight reverses his strike, steps back. *"You know me."*

"Of course," Ine says. "You stand on my land, and so I know you." All around them, the Dumnonii launch themselves into Ingild's men, and she is relieved to hear the distant bellow of Beorhtric giving orders to let them pass. Had she truly believed they and Ine would come? The scene before her could be cut from the cloth of a dream.

"You are as bad as my father," the wight says, watching the Dumnonii stream past. *"Cynric was seduced by them too."*

"Neither you nor I would be standing here otherwise."

Æthel has no idea what they are talking about, but Ceawlin's hand twitches on his sword—and that she understands well enough. She catches his lunge, using the spear to turn it aside. Ine yells her name and there is a rumble in the sky and an answer in the earth as it opens, swallowing the wight to the waist.

"So, you are the one he wants dead," Ceawlin remarks when the echoes have died, apparently uninterested in his own predicament. Now that he and Ine are both here, the similarity between them is more striking than ever. *"No wonder he has not succeeded. How many would have looked to Wessex to find Dumnonia's Heir?"*

Æthel had guessed it, but having Ceawlin voice the fact gives it the weight of truth. "Ine?" Her voice is smaller than she would like. Expression furled, he spares her a glance, and Æthel is overly aware of the earth trapping the wight. Her ears recall the sound it made as it cracked without warning, coughing dirt into the air. *He almost killed Leofric.* She swallows hard.

"I destroyed Cædwalla," Ine says coldly. "And though we are of the same family, I will not hesitate to destroy you too."

The wight laughs. *"Cædwalla was weak. You will not find me so."* With his bare hands, he wrenches the ground apart and climbs free, sweeping up his sword once more. When he turns his eyes on her, Æthel tries and fails to master her fear. It struggles in her chest like a bird for freedom. The desire to scream chokes her.

Then Ine takes her arm—and the fear is gone. She lets out a wondering breath. His grip on her is warm, and warmth fills her, until she can feel strength returning to the hand that grasps her spear. "Æthelburg is a peerless warrior," Ine says, his voice ringing. "And the land listens to me. You cannot face us both."

The wight's bottomless eyes flick to Æthel. It is her only warning before he lunges, not with blade this time, but with his bare hand outstretched. Ine pushes her aside and she can only watch in horror as Ceawlin's fingers close around his forearm. In her mind are the men sprawled lifeless on the dirt street of Sceaptun; skin livid with five bone-white marks.

Ine stiffens. Then his free hand grasps the wight's and Ceawlin lets out an inhuman scream before jerking away. It is loud enough to shear through the din of battle. Across the field, heads turn. "I banish you, Ceawlin." Ine raises the same hand, palm turned outwards. Slowly, he makes a fist. "If I cannot destroy you, I can ensure you never set foot in Wessex again."

The sound builds slowly, a thunder from deep beneath the earth. It changes as it climbs, thunder to hum, and then threads of gold—the same gold Æthel saw the night Geraint died—weave their way across the ground. Ceawlin backs off as they grow thicker, but he cannot move fast enough to escape the tightening net. With a last baleful glare, he vanishes. The golden light blazes across the battlefield and weapons fall silent.

The nearest of Ingild's men look to their leader and Æthel spots the exact instant Ingild realizes the battle is lost. His face is curdled fury and his eyes are dark as he turns to stare at his brother across the intervening distance. Still at Ingild's side, Olwen wraps an arm around him.

"Ingild!" Ine shouts, starting forward just as both disappear.

The golden threads whither beneath him, and he stumbles. "I'm fine, Æthel," he gasps when she grabs him. "You can let go."

"You'll fall over."

"Will you let me have this?" he says under his breath. "I am enjoying coming to your rescue for a change."

Æthel laughs and lets go, but only to slap him soundly across the face.

"Æthel! What—?"

There is a knot in her throat. The laughter of moments ago now feels like tears. "How dare you leave without a word to me?" *You left with barely a word to him,* a voice reminds her, but Æthel ignores it. "And take that paint off at once."

His eyes are wide, his face so very dear. She can hardly believe it when his arms go around her and he pulls her against him. "You've earned a dozen pigs," she mutters to cover her shock. "I'm going to put them in that room you call your library."

"Please don't," Ine says with a shudder. "I promise to make it up to you." He draws back, but only to stroke a thumb across her cheekbone. Æthel stares at him. The gold in his eyes is like the gold in the ground. He leans in and—she puts a finger against his lips to stop him. There is pain: the words said and unsaid between them. But underneath those lurks guilt, like a great serpent slowly uncoiling. Æthel pulls away. "I need to tell you something."

Ine looks as if his worst fears have crept from the shadows to stand before him. "No, Æthel. I need to tell *you* something. I have hurt you. I know I don't deserve to ask—"

"Stop," she whispers, taking a step back.

"But I love you." Ine's shoulders slump, as if in despair. "With everything I am."

Shaking her head, she covers her mouth before the knot inside her unravels into a sob. Æthel turns so she does not have to see his face, and sees Ingild's men instead, throwing down their weapons. Many stare dumbstruck at the place their leader last stood, and the battlefield is thick with the moans of the injured and the grieving. *How dare he say it?* a voice inside her is raging. How dare he wait until now—

An agonized scream. *Herla*. Æthel whirls around to see her kneeling on the bloodied grass, fingers dug into her arms like claws, as if she wants to rip herself wide open. The sight sears her heart. Æthel moves so fast that she almost trips over her own feet in the gathering gloom. Ine calls her name, but she does not look back. The dark mist cloaking Herla is thicker. Falling beside her, Æthel sees faces in it with open shrieking mouths. "No," she cries at them, unthinking. "Don't hurt her."

Ine shouts for her again. She pretends not to hear and— ignoring the sword in Herla's hand—pulls the woman against her, lips brushing her ear. "Herla. It's Æthelburg. Tell me what's wrong. Tell me how to help you."

Herla's body is stiff, trembling, she barely breathes. Æthel can hear the same cacophony of voices as when they fought, scream- ing as one. Herla's braided hair falls over her face as she hangs her head, and her eyes are still as black as the blade. "Please wake up. Come back to me." But no matter how she begs, Herla does not stir, not even to scream again.

She hears a tread behind her and turns, still clasping the other woman. Ine stands over them. He looks bleak and Æthel knows that he has puzzled out her secret, just as she had puzzled out his. It almost makes her laugh, miserably. Instead she says, "Ine. Help her."

"Æthel…"

"Geraint's power was enough to weaken her curse. Yours can too. Please, Ine."

"I do not know how."

She shakes her head. "You banished the wight. You must be able to help her."

Still, he hesitates. Why does he hesitate? But it's obvious. Seeing them together like this, the gentle, desperate way Æthel holds Herla against her chest. She wants to scream. Why has he chosen this moment, of all moments, to make his jealousy felt? "We need her, Ine." Her tone is flinty. "Wessex needs her." *I need her.* In a softer voice, "Don't be like this."

"Like what?"

Æthel wishes she had slapped him harder. "This is not about us." Words spoken before. "Think of—"

"Is it not about us, Æthelburg?" Ine says, and Æthel stills. Slowly, she unfolds herself from Herla, rising to her feet to face him. "Because I do not see what else it could be."

Fear for Herla has made her heart race. Now it stumbles over itself. It is a side of him she has never seen. That she has never given him cause to reveal. Æthel does not know how she feels now on seeing it. A part of her is furious—what else can that roiling in her belly be—while another part stands and catches its breath. People are only jealous when they care. Deeply. When they fear that something precious will be taken from them. It was callous to ask him to save Herla, but she cannot unsay it.

Ine's expression is cold. So are his hands when Æthel presses them between hers. "I know what I am asking. If you will not do it for Herla, will you do it for me?"

His brow creases. He lowers his eyes to their joined hands. This is how they had stood at their handfasting, the ceremony before they were wed, when the priest bound them and listened as they spoke their intentions for the first time. Æthel wishes she had not thought of that, is hoping *he* is not thinking of it, but finally he nods and she lets out a long breath. "Thank you."

Ine does not reply. Æthel watches him approach Herla with some trepidation. Seeing them together is strange, discomforting, and the serpent writhes in its dark well. She hugs herself. When Ine touches Herla's wrist, he hisses, as if her skin is scorching. "There are so many."

"What?"

"The souls she has taken," he murmurs to himself. "She cannot be rid of them. They are like those released from the bone knife when I destroyed it."

So that's what happened. At any other time, Æthel would seize on it. "Can you release these too?"

Ine shakes his head. "They are bound to her. They are part of *her* soul," he adds wonderingly. "But they are overwhelming her. She is the only one who can stop them."

"There must be some way." The image of Herla's spirit—that wild bright thing—broken is more than she can bear. Her desperation is plain in her voice. Æthel cannot care that Ine hears it, that it is hurting him. "I *know* you can help her. You're the Heir."

He gives her an unreadable look before closing his eyes. For an agonizing time, nothing happens. Ine frowns, beads of sweat appearing on his brow. Then from the dirt where Herla kneels grow shoots, thick and green, as if nourished by the blood so recently shed there. When they reach Herla's arm, they fuse themselves into a band. The souls' cacophony wanes, and Herla stirs, drawing a shivering breath.

"Herla." Æthel ducks past Ine to seize the other woman, helping her to stand. Sweet heady relief lends her exhausted limbs strength.

Herla tilts her wrist, examining the twisted roots there. Although the black is gone from her eyes, they are still shadowed. "What is this?"

"Temporary," Ine says, sounding strained. He coughs. "Releasing them is beyond me, but this might quiet them. It has something of the Land in it." He coughs again, harder. "To—to remind them of their home." A shudder goes through him and he claps a hand to his mouth. Blood seeps between his fingers.

The sight is a knife to Æthel's gut. *I know what I am asking,* she had said. But she hadn't known and he hadn't told her. His blood is black in the dusk, in the bobbing light of the torches coming towards them. She had not stopped to think that helping Herla could mean harming himself. Before Æthel can reach Ine, Gweir is there, steadying hands on the king's shoulders. "Lord, are you well?"

Ine swallows, wipes his mouth, but his skin is very pale. "Fine, Gweir. Really."

"You are not," Æthel says. "You're hurt." Had she bitterly assumed his hesitation to mean jealousy, when it was in fact fear for his life? Æthel has never hated herself, but she hates the person who would ask one love to die for the other. She cannot draw enough air into her lungs, and pulls roughly at the straps of her mail shirt.

Before Ine can respond, Herla kneels again, laying the sword at Æthel's feet like an offering. "I failed you, Æthelburg. I swore to myself that I would die before I let anything befall you."

It takes Æthel a few moments to master herself, to find her voice. "I did not ask you to swear such a vow. How many times have I said that I don't need protecting?"

"You do," Herla and Ine say at once and then eye each other suspiciously. Æthel swallows a feverish urge to laugh until Herla drops her gaze back to her wrist. "You say this is temporary?"

"Yes." Ine nods at the band. "I've had some experience with trapped souls before. But only you have any control over these."

"I have no control," Herla says harshly. She does not raise her eyes. "I cannot stand beside you in this, Æthelburg. I cannot be trusted. If it were not for the Heir's power, I would still be suffocated by the souls it is my duty to take."

"No." Æthel grasps her shoulders. "It is *his*, Herla. Gwyn's duty. It was not meant for you."

"Gwyn's duty," Ine echoes. "Why does that sound familiar?"

"Because I told it to you, Ine king," a voice says. "Moons ago, in a story fit for your golden hall. 'Higher powers charged him with…'"

"'…a solemn duty,' I remember now." Ine turns and Æthel follows his gaze to where a figure stands. "Emrys."

The scop inclines their head. Æthel has never spoken with them herself, but under Emrys's scrutiny, she feels known. At a glance, the storyteller is unimposing, and yet their presence is even stronger than Herla's, as if their body cannot contain all that they are.

"The Hunt is a perversion of Gwyn's duty, a duty as natural and vital as breathing." Emrys looks to Herla. "For you, it is a curse. Because Æthelburg is right—you were never meant to shoulder it." A pause. "But you know that now, don't you?"

"I know it," Herla murmurs. She is staring hard at Emrys, and Æthel realizes that the men and torches which had been almost atop them do not appear to be moving any closer. "Who are you?"

"A storyteller who has walked these lands too long."

"I do not believe you."

"And I do not care what you believe." Emrys seems unruffled by Herla's tone. "The Land has bought you time, but in three days, the wall between worlds vanishes, and if you have not mastered your curse by then, none of you will be able to stand against Annwn."

"Mastered it?" Anger flushes Herla's cheeks. "If I could master it, I would have done so. I would have been free of it."

"What we perceive as our greatest weakness is often our greatest strength," Emrys remarks, and Æthel scowls. She has never liked glib riddles. "You have his sword, but you are not Gwyn. The sword is a tool, allowing you to separate body and soul." Set deep in their skull, the scop's blue eyes burn. "But you cannot lay those souls to rest, or send them on. When you rip them from life, *you* are the only place they can go. And so with every Hunt, they grow in number, until your own soul buckles under the strain."

Herla's fists are clenched and trembling. "You need not tell me things I already know."

"But you do not know." Emrys comes closer, so that they stand toe to toe, and abruptly Herla does not seem so tall. "You have great power at your fingertips, if only you find the courage to use it. You keep the souls you free, and while they are weak alone, together they are a host. Perhaps large enough to match the hosts of Annwn. Perhaps powerful enough to challenge Gwyn himself. In his ambition, it is something he has overlooked."

Æthel's heart quickens. Colour comes back into Ine's face. But Herla presses her lips together grimly. "No," she says after a long silence. "They hate me. They are right to hate me. They are the burden I bear for what I have done."

Emrys's expression is cold. "Righteous self-pity does not sit well on you."

"They have suffered enough," Herla bursts out, breaking their stalemate. She turns to pace, her ragged fur cloak whipping around her. "It is wrong to ask them to fight after denying them peace."

"Fighting is all they have left. Anger. Resentment. Why not use it?"

"It makes me no better than *him*."

The scop does not answer at once. There is an odd tone in their voice when finally, they say, "It is not your place to judge him."

"But it is my place to kill him," Herla snarls.

"I have said too much." Emrys turns sharply. "I have given more aid than I usually permit myself." Rounding on Ine, they nod at his bloodstained hand. "As for you. It was well done, but do not run before you can walk."

"Saxon!" a young voice bellows. Between Cadwy's shout and his arrival in a skid of turf, Emrys is gone.

"They always do that," Ine says ruefully. "Every time."

"Good riddance." Herla turns her baleful gaze on Cadwy and the prince yelps. His hand goes to his sword.

Æthel catches it. "Peace, she is a friend."

Cadwy mouths uselessly, perhaps stunned at her use of the word *friend*. He has never spoken of Herla without fear, Æthel recalls. "It is good to see you well," she says, hoping to calm him. "What is it?"

He is still eyeing Herla askance. "Ingild's leaders have surrendered. What shall we do with them? Kill them?" he adds hopefully.

"They are my kinsmen, Cadwy."

"Kinsmen who betrayed you for a usurper."

"Who is also my brother. Besides," Ine grimaces, "if I kill them, I'll only have bishops left in the Witan."

Their conversation is almost the banter of friends. What happened in Dumnonia to cause such a change? If Cadwy feels anger over the truth of the birthright, he is hiding it well. Or is it because there is so much at stake? Whatever the case, Æthel is thankful. Too much blood has been spilled already.

"Cadwy," Ine says with a brief touch on his shoulder, "will you bring Dinavus and the others? And Gweir—will you fetch the lords? It is time we spoke with one voice."

In perfectly inflectionless tones, Herla says, "I am in your debt, king. If it is a council of war you want, you are welcome in my hall." She gestures at the distant door, which has stood ajar since the night she and Æthel fought. The night they first…Æthel pulls her cloak close against the wind, hoping nothing shows on her face. The memory is like a burning brand. Is Herla thinking of it too? She risks a glance at the other woman, only to find Herla staring at her expectantly, one eyebrow raised. Her horse waits beside her.

If Æthel thought things could not become more awkward, she is wrong. Ine mounts too and both look down at her. She stands between them, that awful knot back in her chest. She would prefer to stalk across the battlefield on her own two feet, to give herself space, but they cannot spare the time. When she hesitates too long, Ine lifts his eyes to glare at Herla, and it would be funny if it did not hurt so much. *You were the one who did this,* Æthel thinks at him, but that is not entirely fair. And Herla. How must it feel to be an outsider stumbling into their troubles like this, not knowing if—

Æthel is so torn that all it takes is for Ine to offer her a blood-stained hand and he will probably fall off his horse if she doesn't steady him. And what does it mean anyway, choosing to ride such a short distance with one over the other? How ludicrous. Still, she flinches at the narrowing of Herla's eyes—those eyes she could drown in, burn up in—and the whisk of her horse's tail as she leaves them both behind.

Ine is radiant with triumph. "You do not have to look so pleased," she growls, climbing up behind him.

"Don't I?" But his tone is not without some bitterness. Æthel senses words lying in wait for them, and none will be easy to say.

As the horse picks a route across the debris-strewn field, she murmurs, "Thank you for helping her." The grass has all been churned to mud and is treacherous in places. "Why did you not say it would harm you?"

"I did not know it would," he answers, but she knows he is lying. "The Land is harder to reach here."

"Are you a magician now?"

Ine splutters a bit. "No, of course not. At least I wouldn't call it that. I can sense the Land, touch its patterns." In his mouth, *Land* is not just a word. He turns over his bloody palm. "It was easier in Dumnonia, like a well-worn path through a wood. Here… imagine a thicket stands in your way and you must cut a path. No one else walks it except you, and the brambles grow back."

"I am not sure I understand."

"But you do not seem shocked," Ine remarks.

"I worked it out for myself, no thanks to you." Her hands tighten on his cloak. "Why did you not tell me, Ine?"

"Why did you not tell me of Herla, Æthel? She was here in Wessex. With her help, we might have avoided all of this."

"Or we might not have done," she snaps, her anger rising because she knows he is right. She *should* have shared the knowledge that Ælfrún was Herla. *But I wanted something that was wholly mine,* she thinks at him. *I wanted something that you could not give me.* Was that so wrong? "And what of Ingild? I warned you about him so many times."

Gratifyingly, Ine has no riposte to that. "He has been pulling strings behind the scenes in small ways. Undermining me, casting doubt on you…"

"So that was why Edred supported me at Tantone," Æthel says, as it slides into place. "And then challenged me later. He wanted me to instigate a battle that would cost men's lives. Maybe he even thought he could kill me in the confusion." She grinds her teeth. "Herla's intervention unwittingly helped Ingild build a case against me."

"But don't you see, Æthel?" Ine turns to meet her eyes. "It has all been focused on *us*. He knows we are stronger together. He is the one who has driven us apart."

"We have driven ourselves apart, Ine," she says sadly. "Ingild only widened the cracks that were already there."

His back stiffens. He is silent for a long time. "So is that it?" he asks the darkness. "You are content to let him win?"

"Ingild has nothing to do with this, and you know it." Mercifully, they have reached the hall, and Æthel jumps down. It is not a conversation to be had on horseback. Her stomach is beginning to ache—from hunger, or exhaustion, or the pressure of all the words bottled up inside.

"You have been here before," Ine says.

Æthel nods, not trusting her voice. Although it is deeply uncomfortable to see him in Herla's hall, her guilt has flared to defiance during the ride. Why should she regret the touches she and Herla exchanged? The whispers and tenderness, the desire so strong that they could barely keep their hands to themselves. The truths they drew from each other's hearts, and the promises they had voiced in the movement of their bodies. Folded in a corner, the furs they had slept beneath seem to contain them all.

Herla stands in the centre of the hall. A small smile plays on her lips, and in her face is everything Æthel is thinking. She returns the smile, her turmoil easing, before one of the lords of Dumnonia grabs for his sword. "Stop." Æthel throws out her arms. "As I said to Prince Cadwy, Herla is a friend. We are all friends, are we not?"

"Some more than others," Nothhelm mutters. The King of Sussex is not tied up, but his voice is subdued, his usual cockiness missing. The Dumnonii glower at him, hands resting on sword hilts.

"Be quiet, Nothhelm," Ine snaps. "Your actions have deprived you of the right to speak without my leave."

Æthel cannot stop her eyebrows lifting. She is not the only one who has found her defiance. "Why is he here?" she asks.

"He and ealdormen Godric and Osberht are here because they need to know who and what they aided," Ine says. "And because, underserving as they are, I wish to give them another chance." He turns to Herla, adds brittlely, "And I wish to thank Lord Herla for the shelter of her hall. The leader of the Wild Hunt is courteous."

Murmurs break out, and Herla inclines her head. Fear from the Britons, uncertainty from the Saxon lords. Æthel must admit she is an intimidating sight. The ink etched into her skin is dark in the eldritch light; the fur, leather and bone of her armour the savage remnants of a bygone age. Herla is too real, too wild to stand amongst them in this tamer time. Her braids tumble over her shoulders. Æthel had woven her fingers into them, grasped them as she cried out. She bites her lip and looks away.

"I regret that you did not make yourself known to me before," Ine says, choosing to cloak himself in formality. "We could have helped each other, perhaps."

Æthel keeps her expression neutral with an effort. Only the three of them can hear the other conversation taking place beneath this one.

"Likewise," Herla says darkly. "With your help, *Heir*, I could have trapped Olwen, forced her to reveal everything. My sisters need not have suffered."

"Olwen?"

"Alis," Æthel informs him. "Gwyn ap Nudd's hands in this world."

"Hands Gwyn no longer needs." Herla takes a single step forward. Her movement has all the dangerous grace of a wildcat, and more than one man draws back. "In three days, he will lead his host here."

Although the ealdormen look lost, the Britons exchange bleak glances. And—"Who are you?" Æthel demands of the young man she had missed on first entering. He stands quietly, studying the starry walls, chin propped in one hand. Although his garb suggests a man of the Church, the walking aid beside him is unmistakably a spear. When he turns them upon her, his eyes are quick and keen. "Winfrid, Æthelburg queen. From the Nhutscelle monastery."

This is the pagan-hunter Hædde summoned? He is like a vision of an archangel. Even Herla blinks at him.

"It was Winfrid who carried the news to Dintagel," Ine says— far too casually for such a statement. *Dintagel?* Æthel cannot believe he set foot in the place. "That you were raising the fyrds against Ingild, and that he was intending to bring the fight to us."

Which undoubtedly helped persuade the Dumnonii to march here. "Why?" she demands of the priest. "Hædde condemned Ine as a pagan in the name of the Church. I thought you were the bishop's favourite."

"Not all of us are wilfully ignorant of things it behoves us to respect," Winfrid says with a virtuous lift of his brows. "Besides, I may be able to help."

Hardly an answer. Æthel swallows her incredulity. "Help?"

"With a plan," Winfrid says, and the word is like a spell. Heads come up, gazes sharpen. She is sure more than one person is holding their breath.

"What does a priest know of Gwyn ap Nudd?" Herla asks coldly. "Or Annwn?"

"I make it my business to know all things." Winfrid regards her without fear. "Knowledge brings us closer to God."

Ine shakes his head at that. "Even knowledge the Church considers heathen?"

"One can learn a lot from one's enemy."

Into the bristling silence that follows, Herla says, "You are quite the contradiction, priest. Speak."

Winfrid laces his fingers behind his back. "Before I joined the Church, I was raised on stories of Annwn. Even as a child, I realized they were more than stories." He gives a narrow smile. "Truth hides beneath embellishment. I've always had a gift for stripping it away."

Remind me never to make an enemy of him, Æthel thinks.

"The being that calls himself Gwyn ap Nudd considers you his rival, Ine king. Is that right?"

"I doubt I can rival him," Ine says. "*Foe* is a better word. And it is the Heir of Dumnonia he calls such." He looks at Cadwy. "I assume it is why Ingild killed Geraint, and then sought to kill his son. When he grasped the truth—" his fingers open to expose the blood on his palm—"he raised a rebellion against me." Nothhelm and the ealdormen are staring at Ine as if they have never seen him before. "Legitimacy is vital to Ingild," Ine continues. "Despite allying with Gwyn and accepting Otherworld aid, he manipulated our own laws to give his actions the veneer of legality. It is only by confronting him that we have forced him to reveal his true methods. And true allegiance."

"Lord king." Godric clears his throat. "You want us to believe that this Otherworld is real? That Ingild has been in league with...unnatural powers?"

"After everything you have seen today, Godric, you still ask this?" Ine's voice is taut with restrained anger. "You had no trouble believing Hædde when he talked of pagan heresies, but when you stand on the cusp of the Otherworld, here in Herla's hall, it is all too far-fetched?" He trembles. "Ingild sacrificed our father for this. He *murdered* him."

Into the shocked silence that follows, Godric stammers, "How do you know this?"

"I saw the scars on his arms from their struggle. And I learned that to summon a wight, you need a life. Who knows how many others Ingild has killed?"

"Oh God," Æthel says, remembering. All eyes turn to her. "Cenred warned me. Watch out for my son, he said. I thought he was referring to you, but he knew Ingild meant him harm. If I had not assumed..."

"It's done, Æthel," Ine says quietly. "It is not your fault." He turns back to Godric. "This is the so-called king you followed. One who did not mind killing an old man in his bed."

There is another silence, even less comfortable than the last. Osberht glances at the Britons. "You spoke of Dumnonia, lord. What does that land—or any heirs of it—have to do with you?"

"That is a longer story," Ine says. "I am happy to tell you the little I know of it. Now is not the time."

Before the ealdorman can protest, Winfrid picks up where he left off. "If Gwyn ap Nudd considers you his enemy, lord, then it is safe to say you pose a substantial threat." A pause, as he looks thoughtfully towards the back of the hall, to where Æthel knows the Otherworld gate stands. "If you chose a place and issued a challenge, I believe he would answer it."

"You cannot know his mind." Herla's words are a snarl. "He is a trickster. His right hand offers friendship, while his left works mischief behind his back."

"And can we not work a little mischief of our own?" Winfrid unlaces his fingers to point one at her. "The last the Lady Olwen saw, you were helpless. Gwyn ap Nudd will not expect any trouble."

Herla's eyes turn haunted, but she does not speak.

"We cannot know exactly where Gwyn and his host will appear," the priest continues. "The place you choose to face him is as important as the challenge. It must have significance."

"Significance," Ine repeats. Æthel can see each thought forming behind his eyes. Cadwy opens his mouth to speak, but she shakes her head at him. Ine has worn this face many times while shaping an answer, refining it as a smith does a sword from molten metal. To interrupt him now might spoil it. "There must be a reason Emrys reminded me of that tale tonight," he says, almost to himself. "Higher powers summoned Gwyn...to a place called Woden's Barrow."

Æthel blinks. "I have heard of Wodnesbeorg. Records say we suffered a defeat there." She fights down a shiver. "It seems inauspicious, Ine."

"And you would trust the words of this Emrys?" Herla asks, anger in the set of her jaw. "They conceal their identity, speak in riddles—"

"They are also a friend of Dumnonia," Cadwy counters. "Is it not so, Dinavus?"

"Yes," the grey-haired man says in reluctant, accented Englisc. He speaks the language as if it pains him. "Emrys is loyal to the Land and its Heir."

"Loyal? This person stayed long enough to issue demands and then vanished before I could question them."

Dinavus nods. "So is Emrys's way. We treasure their words because there are few."

Herla gives a disgusted growl. Although she wants to support her, Æthel is torn. She cannot help thinking of the souls and that vast anguish she could sense. And if *she* can sense it, what must it be like for Herla? If pain is all they have left, is it not better to

direct it than to suffer it? Uneasily, Æthel recognizes the sentiment as a refrain she has lived by, turning her own pain outwards,
forcing it into her sword arm. She has killed men with her pain.

"The season will turn," Ine tells them all, "and Gwyn's host will
come. These are things we cannot change. But we stand in Britain,
not Annwn, and while he is here, in our land, it must be on our
terms." He nods at Herla. "I will face him, with or without you."

"The people of Wessex stand with you," Gweir says.

Cadwy lifts his head. "As do the people of Dumnonia."

"Mortals are no match for warriors of Annwn. My sisters—"
Herla stops. Her knuckles turn white on the black blade, and
when she speaks again, her voice is husky. "If you face him," she
says, looking at Æthel, "you will die."

"Then I will *die*," Ine shouts. "It is preferable to bowing and
scraping as Ingild plans."

Æthel holds Herla's gaze. What has happened to the woman
who vowed to take Gwyn's head? Why this sudden uncertainty?
The longer she looks at Herla, the more Æthel is convinced she is
afraid. But afraid of what?

"Is it decided?" Ine asks. "We gather at Woden's Barrow three
days from now."

"Who will deliver the challenge?" Æthel asks him.

When Ine replies, there is a note in his voice she has always
sensed, but never heard. Stone mined from the very depths of his
being. "I will."

33

INE

Glestingaburg, Somersæte
Kingdom of Wessex

There are men to burn and men to bury. The Britons have no objection to building a pyre on the summit of Ynys Witrin, as they call it, while the Saxon dead can be interred in the consecrated land surrounding the abbey. "There is not enough wood," Cadwy tells Ine meaningfully. "And we do not have time to fell trees."

The lords of Dumnonia watch him expectantly. But creating the band for Herla took a great deal of strength. *Are you a magician now?* Æthel asks in his head, and Ine presses his lips together before a dark laugh can escape. If only it *was* magic instead of what it really is: reaching into the perilous heart of existence and asking it to change for him.

They want fire without fuel. He is sure Herla could do it, but she and Æthelburg have disappeared, and Ine is failing not to think about them. Even the threat of Annwn cannot quash the memory of their glances. More than glances. He is frightened to wonder how much more, though the answer is plain.

Cadwy nods. The Britons touch torch to pyre. Although Ine steels himself as he reaches out, the struggle he anticipates is absent. *The tor is far older than your god and saviour,* he recalls Geraint saying. Fire is hungry chaos, but it still has a pattern, and here, he need not fear it. When it roars and surges, the Britons step back as one. "This fire will not go out," Ine says, feeling an echo of that hunger. "It will burn as a beacon on Glestingaburg, on Ynys Witrin, to mark that we fought together this day."

Cadwy says nothing, the shadow of Geraint in his face.

The burial of Ine's countrymen is another matter. Their losses are far greater and the survivors are too exhausted to take a spade to the hardening earth. So Ine stands above it, and tries to find the ancient pattern in its heart, just as he did at Escanceaster. This time, the weight of it near-crushes him. The earth moves with a groan and he staggers, falling to one knee, hand braced against the heaving ground. The iron tang of blood threatens to fill his throat.

"You are going to kill yourself." Arms come around him, under him, lifting him back to his feet. Ine draws a shuddering breath. He has at least managed to shift enough earth for graves. "Ine," Æthelburg says more sternly. "You must be careful."

"How will I face Gwyn if I cannot use the heritage in my own land?" He coughs; there is no blood this time. His throat is simply sore, and a part of him realizes he ought to be afraid. He *is* afraid, but it's eclipsed by the much nearer fear that Æthelburg brings with her. "I thought you were with Herla," he says tonelessly.

Æthelburg's look is unreadable. "Come inside and sit down. You have not rested."

Wearily, he lets her lead him. Beneath the abbey's warm lamps, her hair is the shade of honey. She has washed the battle-dust from her face, and though her eyes are shadowed, she is as fierce and beautiful as the day she stood at her father's side and looked a challenge at him across the room. Has he ever spared the time to tell her?

Æthelburg takes him to an empty chamber adjacent to Berwald's. A battle at his quiet gate does not appear to have fazed the abbot, but that might be Winfrid's influence—the priests have been closeted half the night. When they sit side by side on a monk's austere pallet, it feels as it did when they were courting. The awkwardness. The not knowing what to do with his hands. Although they are older now and supposedly wiser, Ine does not feel so. He would not have made so many mistakes otherwise.

"I *was* with Herla," Æthel says in a strained voice. "She left. I called for her."

"You love her." The words are out before he knows it. He had not intended to say them so bluntly, but speaking them aloud is like lancing a terrible pain. It hurts, yet brings relief.

Her eyes widen. "Do not feel you need to deny it," Ine adds quickly. "If I could not read some of your feelings after ten years of marriage, I would be an even poorer husband than I already am."

"I have never thought you poor."

His throat feels hot now as well as sore. "Then you are kinder than I deserve." He shifts on the pallet, clasping hands between his knees. "This is what you wanted to tell me."

"Yes," Æthel murmurs and she looks him straight in the eye. "I do not want it to be a secret between us."

"And...does she love you?" Before Æthel can answer, he blows out a heavy breath. "Foolish question. Who would not?"

"Plenty of people," she says tiredly, as if he has dug up an old argument. "The court hates me. Why do you think I find any opportunity *not* to be there?"

"I see." And he does. He sees the damage his silence has wrought.

She frees one of his cold clasped hands. "You cannot claim responsibility for my heart."

"No." Ine drops his eyes to their joined hands. "But I can claim it for my own. You are my wife. I should have trusted you. I just...didn't want to disappoint you."

Æthel's voice is quiet. "What is it, Ine?"

Silence stretches. Even the difficulty of touching the Land here pales in comparison with that of sharing the deepest part of himself, especially to a person it has hurt. Æthel waits, and her patience—so unlike her usual anger—gives him the courage to begin.

"I cannot be with you as most lovers are." He speaks to the flagstones because it is taking all his nerve to continue. "When it comes to being intimate, I do not feel desire as other men describe it. I feel indifference...a reluctance to share myself in that way.

I don't know what other people feel, or are supposed to feel, because it's always been like this." Ine looks up, his heart beating painfully. "Æthel, I don't want to feel indifferent when I am with you. I cherish everything you are, everything we have. But I've let this…this part of me come between us." The words are tumbling out now; he hopes some of them make sense. "I am sorry that I did not tell you." He pulls in a breath. "I am sorry that I let you marry me, knowing I could not give you everything you wanted."

Æthelburg looks as light-headed as he feels. "So, before. Whenever I wanted to…"

"It has never been you, Æthel. You are perfect as you are." He swallows tears. "There is nothing wrong with you."

"There is nothing wrong with *you*, either," she says, her voice breaking. "And it *is* me. She was right. I have been…angry. Too angry to listen. I thought only of what I wanted. Needed. I didn't think…" Æthel stops. When she speaks again, her voice is a whisper. "I didn't think that we might not want the same things."

He cannot bear to hear her blame herself. "I could have told—"

"You did tell me." The hands resting on her thighs have curled into fists. "Now I see that you told me every time we were together. Not everything must be said in words."

"Æthel." Ine rises only to kneel on the bare stone before her, covering her clenched hands with his own. She makes a protest, tries to pull him up, but he will not be moved. "When I told you I loved you, I meant it. You are everything I wish I was—bold, fearless. You have a wonderful mind." The tears refuse to be swallowed. "To be able to call you my wife makes me the luckiest man in all of Britain." The feeling in his chest is even larger than the overwhelming presence of the Land. Words do not seem enough and his next ones taste bitter. "If this means you cannot stay with me, I understand. I was ashamed, frightened of telling you in case…in case you wanted to leave."

"I thought you wanted me to leave." Æthel frees her hands, comes to her feet, and the chamber is suddenly too small to contain the agitation rolling off her. "You said our life together was a struggle. That day…you broke my heart."

Ine stares at her. *No, no, no.* "I was thinking of you—that it was a struggle for you, Æthel. And it was *your* word. I never said I wanted you to leave."

She stills. "Maybe not. But you never said you wanted me to stay."

"Of course I want you to stay," he bursts out, stumbling to his feet too. When he reaches for her, she backs off, and that small movement sends a shock of grief to his heart. "But it isn't my choice. It is yours, Æthelburg."

"We are *married*, Ine." Her eyes are a dangerous, brittle blue. "Why should I bear that decision alone?"

Ine stares at her, lost. This is not going the way he imagined, and he has imagined it so many times. "I'm sorry."

"I am sorry too." She breathes out. "Thank you for telling me. That took courage and I will not forget it." Ine knows there will be a *but*. Even so, when it comes, he is not ready for it. "But I need time. To think, to…" Æthelburg's shoulders slump. "I need time."

The monk's cell is like a confessional. Æthelburg stands on the threshold and Ine cannot draw enough air into his lungs. *She and her heart are your hope.* Of course they are—they always have been. "Æthel," he says raggedly. "Please. I cannot do this without you. I cannot face Gwyn ap Nudd alone."

She only looks at him. How long it has taken him to realize the truth. When did he put the court's expectations—of who he and Æthel should be—above his own? When had his own feelings of shame crept in and ruined all they had built? "People expect things of you," Ine says, only half-hearing himself, "but none of it matters." He raises a hand to his head. "Why did I think it mattered?"

Æthelburg hesitates, the shadow of something in her face. Then she turns on her heel.

Had he believed the truth could mend years of misunderstanding? That it could erase mistakes made, and hurts exchanged? In his secret core, Ine had thought that maybe it could. Now, listening to Æthel's footsteps echo hollowly on the stone, he understands that she has felt a very different side of that truth. A side as agonizing as his own. Together, they could have made sense of it. Instead, it has driven them apart.

The room wavers, and Ine sinks onto the pallet. Æthelburg needs time, but what time do they have? In three days, he must somehow find the strength to stand against Gwyn and whatever power he brings with him from Annwn. For now, all Ine wants is to curl into the silence that muffles the sound of Æthelburg walking away.

The next morning, he stands alone before the gate to the Otherworld, resting a hand against the gnarled rock. There is a sense on the other side, as of an expanse: a sea or abyss. Every so often, he catches the scent of flowers.

Ine braces himself. He has barely slept. "I speak to the King of Annwn, to he who calls himself Gwyn ap Nudd." He pauses, but nothing happens. "I tell you: these are my lands and I will defend them, and those who live on them, until my last breath."

A whisper. Ine does not remove his hand. "I challenge you, Gwyn ap Nudd," he shouts. "If you wish to strip the pact from my blood, as you have threatened, then come. Soon there will be no walls between us. I will wait for you at the barrow that bears Woden's name."

He is about to take his hand away when light explodes around him, and he finds himself standing on a seashore. Across the glittering waves is an edifice for which he has no name. Vast, with towers sharp enough to pierce the floor of Heaven, its sibling structures echo it, rearing into distance. Pavilions brighten a green sward: a war camp whose preparations are almost complete.

"Why there?" a voice says. Gwyn ap Nudd stands on the steps, silver-mailed, silver-eyed. His face is proud and cruel, humble and gentle. He is very tall. Staring at him, Ine cannot feel his own body.

"It is as good as any other place," he forces out between numb lips. "If you refuse the challenge—"

"I do not refuse."

"Then the next time we meet, it will be there."

"If you seek to trick me," Gwyn says slowly, and all sound in the pavilions falls silent, "you will fail."

"My challenge is no trick." Ine still cannot move, and terror threatens to engulf him. *I am not here,* he repeats to himself, but it is hard to believe when everything looks so real. He fills his thoughts with Æthel, Gweir, all those who depend upon him, and finds the strength to continue. "I will not cower behind walls while my people suffer the blades of your host. Your quarrel is with me."

"It is with all your kind who bear her gift." Gwyn ap Nudd considers him. "But yes. With you most of all."

"Why now?" Ine asks, curiosity forcing its way through fear. "Why not seek to destroy the heritage from the start?" A wind stirs the pennants, ruffles the waves, but his cloak hangs still.

A shadow in his face, Gwyn says, "I was not free to."

His eyes are closed. Ine opens them and finds himself before a blank rock face, limbs stiff from standing. As he lets his hand fall, a last whisper reaches him. *Things are different.*

When he meets her outside, Æthelburg is perfectly civil. Perfectly distant. His insides knot at that cool expression. "You were right," Ine tells her, doing his best to ignore the feeling, to drown it in their larger concerns. "The gate had thinned enough for him to hear me. He accepted our challenge."

Æthel lets out a breath, hands tight on the reins of her horse. Ine blinks at it. "Æthelburg, what is that?"

"Herla gave her to me," she says, patting the silken neck. The animal stands utterly still in a way that is most un-horselike.

Ine glowers at it. "And what other gifts has she given you?" He cannot keep the bite from his voice. He sounds jealous and he knows it.

"I don't see it's any business of yours," Æthel snaps, one hand straying to the spear at her waist. Ine thinks it very much *is* his business, but that same dangerous glint is in Æthelburg's eyes and he chooses not to push. His anger is a fragile thing regardless; thin ice atop a still sorrowful water.

To change the subject, he says, "Gwyn told me he was not free to pursue this war until now."

"You heard Emrys. Herla has taken on Gwyn's duty." Ine cannot help noticing how she speaks the syllables of Herla's name: softly, wonderingly. "If he says he was not free before, perhaps this duty bound him in the same way it now binds Herla."

"And could it bind him again?" Both mount, Ine raises an arm, and the column behind starts moving, snaking north-east towards Wodnesbeorg. It is not a great force; yesterday's battle has cost them dearly. *Ingild,* he vows, *you* will *answer for it.*

"So we hope," Æthelburg says shortly before admitting, "I have not seen Herla since yesterday. She was behaving strangely. The things she said…" Ine tries very hard not to notice the flush in her cheeks. "I thought she wanted revenge. She is always fierce whenever Gwyn is mentioned. But perhaps Emrys's words changed something. They certainly made her angry."

"She will be there." The thought of Herla vanishing for good is not unappealing, but Ine fears they will need her. They will need her when his strength fails.

The thought hits him so suddenly, so brutally, that he half believes it has come from elsewhere, an attack on his mind by the forces arrayed against them. More frightening is that it's his own thought. It is fed by the blush in Æthelburg's cheeks when she speaks of Herla. By the snap in her voice when she told him it was none of his business.

The sky is a pall. Clouds lower like the lids of tombs, and Ine shudders at the image. "If it is vengeance she wants," he says bleakly, "this is her chance."

"Yes." Yet Æthel's frown remains. "Herla is a great warrior, the best I have ever fought. But she is just one. Alone, she may not be enough."

Æthelburg is still frowning when, three days later, they reach Wodnesbeorg, and there is no sign of Herla. The hill has been visible for half the morning. Now that they are closer, Ine can see the grassy shape of a barrow, and he wonders who or what might lie beneath it. The smooth green skin gives nothing away.

From the top, the view is impressive. The country rolls gently northwards until it becomes Mierce. South lies Sarum, its crumbled walls belying the might of the empire that built them. But the most pressing sight does not require eyes. Rather Ine feels it in the soles of his feet. "This is a place of power," he murmurs to Æthelburg. "Something happened here, millennia ago." It is like a tune he half recognizes. It calls him to follow it through silt and sand, past bones so ancient they cannot be more than dust, than memory, until he finds its name.

Æthelburg touches his arm, and Ine lets out a long breath. "Thank you." She does not ask him what he means, but neither does she let go until he nods. "The men are under your command," he says, staring down at them with a growing dread. *How will they stand against Gwyn's host?* "You know best how to position them. Cadwy has charge of the Britons, but you have the experience he lacks. He will look to you."

"She *will* come. She won't leave m— these men to face Annwn alone."

Ine does not miss the slip and narrows his eyes. His jealousy seems petty against the peril they are facing, but like a flea in his shirt, he cannot be rid of it. An apt comparison; the more he scratches, the more it bites and the more his body itches. He grits his teeth. *You cannot afford to be distracted.*

Apart from the whicker of horses, and the rumble, scrape and sigh of the army, it is eerily quiet. The light fails already, clouds bringing an unnatural gloom. Without warning, the weight of it crashes down upon Ine, choking him. What once resembled rebellion has turned into a war for their freedom—their very existence. *Is this how you wanted it, Ingild? Do you truly think he will let you be king?* "Tell everyone to rest while they can," he says to Æthelburg, hearing his brother in the hollow tone of his voice.

The next few hours are some of the longest Ine has ever endured. Torches are lit as the sun sets, until the hilltop blazes like a giant's pyre. *Woden's Barrow.* He paces, full of wild thoughts. *The cross killed our god and we buried him here.* Only the name remains to mark his resting place. Perhaps Woden went into the Land, and his hair became the roots that had tangled Ine; his thick beard the briars that had caught in his flesh. *But I know you now,* Ine thinks, kneeling and brushing his fingers across the cold earth. *You are part of me.* The wall between this world and Annwn is not the only one that vanishes tonight. It is all walls. *Even those inside ourselves. What lies on the other side of everything we think we are?*

A concussion hits him. The hill trembles, and he opens his eyes to gasps. Nearby, Cadwy rakes the night, futilely searching for the source of the sound. Ine could tell him what it is; the Land feels the feet of the bright host, the brilliance of Annwn. When they spill into the world, their throats are full of song.

Ine knows the moment Gwyn ap Nudd steps, rage-filled, onto the soil of Wessex. He catches his breath as the earth itself flinches. *How am I to stop such a person? Who can deny him anything?* He is breathing too fast. Æthel finds his arm and grips it, her knuckles white. She is still searching for Herla, but the Lord of the Hunt is nowhere to be seen. They are on their own.

Light limns the horizon. Not dawn; the colour is wrong. Rather, a stark ungentle glow emanates from the Folk of Annwn as they advance across the field. Some ride while others run, fleet as horses. An unearthly song comes with them. A war cry, made up of their names.

Rhiannon's birds sit on her shoulders. One's song is sleep to lull the living; the other's can wake the dead. Then the brothers: Bwlch, Cyfwlch and Syfwlch, whose shields, spears and swords are brothers too, and cannot be broken by any power in the world. The horse called the Black One with hooves like hammers, its mane a hundred-headed whip. Pwyll and his son Pryderi, whose tales are greater than their lives. And at the fore, Culhwch, greyhounds at his side. In his hand is the axe that draws blood from the wind.

Others come behind them: warriors and retainers; bondspeople; harp-burdened bards here for the stories; druids adorned with golden-green foliage from the forests of Annwn. *So many,* Ine thinks, watching men cower. His throat is tight. *We are the fyrd, warrior-farmers.* The merest cry from Rhiannon's bird will be enough to fell them. The woman has the yellow eyes of a falcon as she surveys the force arrayed against her.

And then a familiar figure. Ingild is like a child pulled along in Olwen's wake. His face is pale, jaw clenched—with terror, or determination? As the Folk of Annwn spread to surround the hill, making an island of them, Ingild, Edred and a small number of men are the only mortals left below.

The truth of Cenred's death is a dark weight in his mind, but still Ine calls, "Ingild! It is not too late. You are a man of Wessex— you belong with us."

For a fleeting instant, Ingild's expression wavers. Then he cries, "I have never belonged with you. Never once have you praised me, or made me feel as family. Neither did Father. Even our sisters treat me with indifference. So I have found others who do acknowledge my worth."

With his back to the Folk of Annwn, he cannot see their scorn or their cruel smiles. But Ine sees it, and so do those who stand beside him. Nothhelm shakes his head. "You are a fool, Ingild. And so am I—for believing your lies."

"You *are* a fool, Nothhelm," Ingild retorts. "If you think you can best Lord Gwyn on the eve when his power is greatest, you deserve the death you have courted."

Ine raises a hand and Nothhelm swallows whatever he intended to say. "Ingild. I swore you would answer for Father. But do not force me to kill you here."

The Folk have stood in eerie silence. Now a laugh ripples out, inspiring another and another, until the night is chiming with mirth. "The mortal has made himself clear," Pryderi calls. It is he who laughed first. "What harm can you do him while he is with us?"

In answer, Ine plants his feet, this time embracing the image of roots about his legs, anchoring him to the earth. *Please. Please do not fight me.* But as he reaches down, something else reaches up, fingers extending to grasp his. His mind opens like a flower, and everything is gold. Lines of light blaze from the spot where he stands, running off the hill like rainwater and down into the land about it.

The Folk of Annwn hiss and leap back, as if the ground has caught fire beneath them. One of Rhiannon's birds launches itself from her shoulder. Soaring above them, it lets out a cry; not the raucous scream of the falcon as Ine expected, but sonorous, far too low a note to come from a bird's throat. Although men sway, they stay on their feet, and Ine realizes: as long as he maintains his connection with the Land, they cannot fall prey to the spell. Rhiannon's expression turns icy and she flicks a hand. The cry comes again; again it has no effect. "A pretty trick," she snarls, colour in her face now. "But it will not save you from the sword."

"Indeed it will not." Pryderi draws a blade of sunlight that is the very opposite of Herla's. When he dismounts, however, it is a graceless motion, and his eyes widen.

"They have lost their advantage," Æthelburg shouts. "With me!" Before she leads the men downhill, she and Ine exchange one searing glance. It is all they have time for, and he wishes, in that terrifying moment, that they were not king and queen of Wessex. That there were no battles to be fought, no duty to fulfil. That there were no swords to take Æthelburg from him in one callous strike. But they are who they are, and Æthel would never turn her back.

Screams pierce Ine as he watches from atop the barrow. Although every nerve urges him to go to the aid of his men, he forces himself to stand resolute, less than certain how long he can hold off the spells of the Folk. Heart in his throat, he spots Cadwy facing one of the three brothers. He cannot pinpoint the exact moment he came to regard Geraint's son as a friend, but the thought of him falling to Bwlch's bright blade is intolerable. Ine grits his teeth. He must not tire before Gwyn takes the field himself, but he will not let Cadwy die. As he did with Ceawlin, he extends a hand, focusing on the ground where Bwlch stands, concentrating his will there. *I banish you, Bwlch. Never set foot in my lands again.* When he clenches it into a fist, the golden light beneath the son of Annwn flares, swallowing him.

Cadwy turns to look up at Ine. They have a moment to exchange nods before twin cries of rage rise above the melee. Ine shrugs off dizziness just as Cyfwlch and Syfwlch launch themselves across the field, their movements almost too fast to follow. Cadwy's hand trembles as he lifts his sword to meet them.

No.

Earth explodes around the brothers. Roots like locks of wild hair surge up, climbing their legs, their arms, twisting across their barrel chests. Their burnished shields are useless. When the roots find their mouths, they stop screaming, and a moment later, blaze to nothing in the wake of their brother. Ine knows they cannot be killed, have only fled to Annwn, but it will take them too long to return. He has bought time.

Looking up at him, Cadwy pales. Ine does not know why until he tastes iron. Blood is seeping from his nose. He coughs; more fills his mouth. Spitting it out, another wave of dizziness hits him and he staggers. Only Gweir's steadying hand keeps him standing. Deep in Ine's chest, the power is starting to buck like a wild beast; he scrabbles for control of it, swallowing the tang of blood. *Who will protect them if you falter?*

Cries go up at the brothers' defeat, a mingling of Brythonic and Saxon battle-oaths screamed in triumph. Under Æthel's orders, the men do not fight alone, but in groups, Britons shoulder to shoulder with Saxons, evening the odds. It is his vision, Ine thinks, and finds himself despairing at the way it has been realized. What lasting peace can he achieve if they are all killed here? He glimpses Æthel, her muscles straining as she expertly wields the spear Herla gave her. What lasting peace can he find in this world if she is killed?

His bones are beginning to groan under the pressure of the Land's power. *It is too great for one person.* Ine does not care. If his life can buy hundreds of others, why would he hesitate? But the golden light is dimming, slipping like sand through his fingers no matter how desperately he holds it. Sick with dread, Ine looks down to see the silver-eyed King of Annwn staring up at him.

Gwyn's form is bright and terrible, wise and wild all at once. He wears the shimmering armour Ine saw in his vision. The host kneels, and men draw back, pressing themselves against the skirts of the hill. "Look at you," Gwyn says into the sudden hush. His voice is musical, elegiac. Ine can hear it easily despite the distance between them. "It is destroying you. It was not made for mortals."

Ine straightens. He has wrapped an arm around his stomach, but now he drops it. "You are wrong. It was gifted freely. It was made for us, given to help us guard and nurture the Land."

"And you think you are deserving of such an honour?"

"No," Ine says honestly. "And one day, I have no doubt that we will lose it. We do not need you to strip it from us."

Gwyn smiles. "If this is what you believe, why not hasten that day? I will even spare the rest of your people, King of Wessex, if you will come down." He tilts his head consideringly. "It should please you—being able to give your life for them. A noble sentiment."

"I would not hesitate." Again Ine grasps vainly for his connection with the Land. Is this Gwyn's doing? "But it is not my place to give back the gift that Sovereignty bestowed."

Between blinks, Gwyn's sword is in his hand. "You dare mention her in front of me? I will have your life and then I will have your kingdom. It will be a plaything for me, no more."

"Lord Gwyn. You swore that *I* would rule Wessex."

Gwyn lashes out. He catches Ingild on the chin and knocks him sprawling. "You think I will let you be king—*reward* you—when you failed to complete the one small task I gave you?" He points at Ine. "There stands the Heir of Dumnonia. All I asked was that you ensured he was dead before this night. That none would challenge me."

"How was I to know it was him?" Ingild wipes the blood from his mouth. "You told me it was a Briton. Geraint of Dumnonia. I succeeded in killing him, as you asked. I would have killed his son too but for my brother's interference."

When was Ingild turned? How long has he worked to manipulate the events that led to Geraint's death? Ine's heart is heavy at the thought of it, at his own failure to see the picture in its entirety. For without Otherworld aid, how else could Ingild have ambushed Geraint?

"This is your excuse? I gave you power, and still you put your own ambition before mine." Gwyn turns away, as if Ingild is no more worthy of notice than a stain on the ground. "That is why you failed. You do not deserve the title of prince, Ingild, let alone king."

Ingild's face is very pale. His bleeding mouth opens and closes without sound. "Enough talk." Gwyn ap Nudd takes a step towards the hill—and the last of the golden light flickers and fails.

"No," Ine hears himself scream as Rhiannon's second bird leaves her shoulder. Feathers drift down amongst the bodies of the fallen, and where they land, limbs jerk. With every flap of wings, the movements grow stronger, until a score of dead men gain their feet. Ready flesh to do Rhiannon's bidding. They launch themselves at their former brothers, who watch them come with wide eyes. They die with wide eyes too, swords buried in their hearts.

Horrified, Ine starts forward, but Gweir catches him. "No. Without you, he has won."

"Without our people, I have lost, Gweir." Ine does not take his eyes off Gwyn. "I must end this."

"Where will your death leave us?" the gesith cries. "As slaves to the Folk of Annwn who will do with us as they wish."

Just as in Wiltun, a flash of red catches Ine's attention. Barefooted Olwen moves up the hill, easily avoiding the swords that come for her. "So Herla does not want you after all?" the fairy woman calls sweetly to Æthelburg. There is blood on his wife's cheek—the sight seeds terrible fear in him. She is favouring her right leg too. "It does not appear you have any further use, then." Slender dagger in hand, Olwen lashes out, and Æthel's dodge is not fast enough to stop it scoring a bloody gash across her arm.

Fury erupts in Ine. He falls to both knees, plants his hands in the soil, searching for the power Gwyn extinguished. It is there, but he cannot grasp it, and a futile scream scorches his throat. All his control is gone, vanished in terror for Æthel, for the men fighting and dying below. And in Olwen's words, which, despite the battle, have woken the sickening grief that he will lose his wife even if they win here.

The moment he thinks it, a horn shrieks across the field. Ine has heard it before—the night he lay trapped in dream by thorn and root. Instead of the bugle favoured by his people, it is a wail, furious and desolate. Shivering, he raises his head.

This time the light that greets him is not a pearly luminescence, but a deep infernal red, as of Hell come riding. Hell is a single horned figure. Her horse is a monstrous black, eldritch eyes afire. The blade in her hand is darker than the space between stars. And the wail she utters is birthed from a thousand fleshless throats.

34

ꝹERLA

Of course, she feels them. The moment the Folk of Annwn surge into the world, trailing their banners and their stories, ready to write another with the blood of mortals. Seated on a mound a few miles from the barrow, the black sword across her knees, Herla lifts her head to listen. The bards are already singing of victory.

When—flayed and raw—she had first awoken in this time, she had thought only of taking the sword to Gwyn's throat and damn all consequences. Æthelburg changed that. Æthelburg and Gwyn's offer. The promise of a new life. Love. So what if she must ride at the old moon? In her secret heart, Herla cannot deny that it is a price she yearned to pay.

But Æthelburg is too like Boudica, wearing duty as a fine cloak rather than the shackle it really is. Even if they yearned for it, neither of them would pay such a price. It is why Herla is sitting here on this hill. It is why she could not tell Æthelburg the truth.

"Herla, wait," the queen had called on the night of the council, and Herla had hesitated. She should not have. But that had always been her weakness.

They leave the men behind, arguing—in the way men do—about nothing at all. Only the king watches them go with jealous eyes. Herla might have smiled were she not so haunted by Emrys's words and the growing fear that she knows what will come of them.

Outside is better. She has always loved the wind on her skin, in her hair. The sky is as dark and slick as a newborn calf. Herla stares into that liquid night and wonders what Gwyn meant about going beyond its lip into the dawn that is forever. No dawn lasts forever. She clenches a fist. Otherworld tricks, riddles to mock her.

Æthelburg picks her fist apart, gently uncurling each finger, and Herla lets herself revel in the sensation, innocent but full of promise. Hand in hand, they walk far enough from the hill to avoid all eyes, for the moment not speaking. Until Æthelburg says, "Will you tell me what troubles you?"

"How do you know I am troubled?"

The queen looses an incredulous breath. "Because the Herla I thought I knew would not refuse a battle with Gwyn. She would stand and scream defiance beside us."

"Æthelburg." She stills at Herla's tone. "I know it is better unsaid. But that was before. Before we…" Naked skin, the deep groan of pleasure that Æthelburg tore from her throat. The sight of the queen atop her, the shape of her breasts, each muscle in her abdomen outlined in the flickering torchlight. Herla swallows. Æthelburg must be thinking of it too; there is dusk in her cheeks, a colour Herla has come to love, as she has come to love everything about her. "By the Mother," she murmurs without meaning to, "you are beautiful."

A glitter in the other woman's eyes. Herla does not stop her as she leans in, pressing their lips together before teasing Herla's apart, sliding a hand around her waist. Herla already wants to drown, to forget what is looming, and it would be so easy to… Regretfully, she draws back, letting her desire escape into the night. It is not something she would have done when they first met. The hunter took what she wanted when she wanted it, but the hunter is not who she is any more.

Æthelburg blinks. "I'm sorry."

"Do not be." Herla brushes a thumb over her cheek where the

dusk has deepened. She pauses, half turns away. "I said I would not ask you. I have no right to ask you…"

"What?"

"Whether there was a chance." She swallows. "That you might come with me."

Silence between them like a breath long held. Herla can see thoughts racing behind the queen's blue eyes, but cannot guess at them. *Forgive me,* she wants to say. *You are already married.* Pride stops her. Always, it is her pride.

"Where would we go?" Æthelburg asks eventually and Herla blinks.

"Do you mean it?" She holds the queen's hands tight. "Despite your kingdom, your people… despite your husband?"

Æthelburg draws a shivering breath. "I… maybe. When this is over. When I know they are safe." She closes her eyes. "I have made the best of the life and privilege I have been given. I am proud of my achievements as queen." She opens them. "When I found Ine the night Geraint died, I thought *he* was dead too, and it hit me. How awful my life would be as a widow. Who would remember the sacrifices I made, those achievements I was so proud of? I would live out my years in a loveless place. But you…" Her voice breaks. "You make me feel loved. At your side, I would never have to fear being alone. It is very hard not to want that."

Atop the dark hill now, Herla tightens her grip on Gwyn's sword. Hearing those words is enough, she tells herself, while her heart screams at her to take Æthelburg and make them so. It is enough to let her do what must be done. Because Emrys, damn them, is right. *If you have not mastered your curse by then, none of you will be able to stand against Annwn.* Ine will not be able to turn Gwyn back without her help.

She had felt peace in the queen's arms. But it is a peace she has not earned. All those she slew, lost in the thrill of the Hunt—yes, they could have lived if she had died as fate intended. The king's binding around her wrist is like sun on a frozen lake. Thanking him for it was galling, but she is glad of it nonetheless. Because beneath is unfathomable cold. Herla can sense the souls in it, fierce and raging. If she breaks the binding, they will paralyse her as they did before.

Unless she listens to Emrys. Unless she finds the courage to let go of her pride.

Herla had forgotten her past and her love for her queen, until Æthelburg woke it with her own love. If repaying the debt means losing these things once more, then Herla should be happy to give her prideful, scarred self for Æthelburg's life. She should be, but still the thought of letting the queen go back to her husband wakes a bitter jealousy in her breast. That and Æthelburg saying, *I have given him my heart.*

Well, let jealousy be lost with the rest of her. "Your true master is Gwyn ap Nudd," Herla tells the sword, a bleak resolve pushing her to her feet. "And it is time he took you back."

Heart full and burning, she thinks of Æthelburg, imagines how the queen will look at this very moment. Weapon drawn, her ice-blue eyes unafraid, mouth set in a grim line. A mouth which kissed Herla's, which told her she was not a monster.

Æthelburg is wrong. Tonight, Herla will give them a monster.

The ground trembles. A glow like the sky-glass of Caer Wydyr. Above her, the old moon is rising. Herla lifts her arms to it, and this time she welcomes the power setting her veins alight. Imprisoned in her own, the souls clamour for release. Until now, she has held them at bay, separate from herself. It is why they paralysed her on the night of the battle. But Emrys called them a host, and a host is strongest together. With her own soul amongst them, to lead them, what might they do?

Once it is done, she does not know what she will be, or whether a way back exists. Before she loses her nerve, Herla steels herself, curls her fingers around the king's woven band…and breaks it.

The moon is old. The Hunt is upon her, and she is the centre of a whirlwind. A swirling mass of rage. The rage of one whose country was taken. The rage of watching a life burn up in hatred. The rage of betrayal. The rage of having her only family torn from her. The rage of vengeance. It is a power, this rage. It is all that's left of a hundred thousand lives. But it is not mindless. Because *she* is not mindless. She burns with the knowledge of six centuries and two loves. Holding them close, she has no fear. *They* have no fear. She is the Herlathing, and her work is death.

She rides for the barrow, and every one of her voices shrieks like a horn wildly blowing. She thunders into the heroes of Annwn, smothering their light with her own, and soaking up their screams. Not only screams. When she stretches out her hand, even the souls of the Folk come to her. *Join us. Ride with us. You will never be alone again.*

A tall man with a golden buckler on his arm is shouting, struggling towards the one still point in the centre of the chaos. She, the Herlathing, recognizes the being standing there. His silver eyes are furious, but it is nothing to her fury, their fury, who have been bound so long. "Fall back," he barks, as the souls of his heroes are torn free, and the Folk's proud eyes fill with fear for the first time.

She swings down from the horse. "You should not have given us your power, Gwyn ap Nudd," she says, her voice the voice of many, and the chief of Annwn's face tightens. "You have left yourself without. Tonight, the moon is old and *we* ride."

"You are not Herla."

"We are." Dark laughter bubbles in her chest. "And we are the souls your blade reaped. Since then, we have found no rest in her soul. She has found none in ours. But this night we are one. And we have come to give you back your gifts."

Gwyn raises his chin. She can taste his doubt and revels in it. "Impossible. No soul can live in another's. Certainly not thousands."

"Your duty is not ours, Gwyn ap Nudd," she hisses. "It was given to you and only you can perform it." She holds out the sword. "Take it back and free us."

The King of Annwn laughs. "Free you? When *I* am the one who is finally free?" He throws out his arms to encompass the hill.

"Why would I give up the chance to rule both worlds, just to free a foolish woman whose pride doomed her from birth?"

"You think you have a choice?" The Herlathing consider him. "You cannot kill us here, for who would do your duty then?"

Drawing a sword from a scabbard of air, Gwyn lunges, but she is ready. The black blade bats the blow aside. His own sword strains towards him, and he leaps back further than he needs to. "Are you afraid, Gwyn ap Nudd?" she asks in a thousand cruel voices. "Is your duty such a terrible thing? Was it not gifted by the power you claim to love, the same power who gave the gift of the Land to mortals?"

"Mine was no *gift*." The word is a snarl. "Why should humans wield such wondrous magic and *I* be cursed as a slave to their souls?"

"Have you asked her?"

He growls, strikes again, and this time draws blood. The Herlathing do not spare it a glance. Gwyn bares his teeth. "She said it was her greatest gift. But how is it a gift? Bound to a land I can never shape, to the souls of undeserving creatures?"

"And yet these creatures fascinate you." They circle each other, keeping a precise number of steps between them. "Or you would not make deals. You would not cajole and trick and flirt with lives that to you are as fleeting as a fire without fuel."

"Do not speak as if you know me." He throws out a hand and a shining silver chain wraps her, lashing her arms to her sides. She looks at it with contempt.

"You seek to bind us? When we have been bound for centuries? We have worn the sword's chain so long that it has become part of us." Her bloody radiance flares and the enchantment shatters without sound.

"If you strike me, you doom yourself," Gwyn says soberly. "You will dissipate, Herla, like chaff on the wind." He shakes his head. "You are too proud to deal yourself such an ending."

The Herlathing laugh and raise the sword, unflinching. "She is but one. We are many, and wish an end to it."

Pryderi throws himself in front of his king, but the black sword passes through him to pierce Gwyn's chest. Pryderi vanishes; his flailing soul becoming part of the Herlathing. And then there is silence, a shocked silence, broken only by Gwyn's harsh breathing. The sword is buried so deep that several slick inches of it emerge from his back. Although he falls to one knee, still he throws his arms out wide, keeping his hands away from the blade that shudders with every beat of his heart.

"If you do not draw it out," the Herlathing say, "we will have your soul. You can feel it. Already it strains towards us." Fingers still wrapped around the sword's hilt, she plucks at that glorious soul, vaster than any other, and Gwyn lets out a gasp. "We will have it, Gwyn ap Nudd. We are very good at taking it."

"Never," he snarls. "I will not be bested here, not by you."

She lowers her head to whisper in his ear. "You might be the shepherd of souls, but you unwittingly made us the guardian. And we *will* guard your soul, Gwyn. For eternity."

"A trick." She draws back to see horror in his silver eyes. "You cannot do this, Herla."

"I can," the Herlathing say. "Because I am not only her. I am them. I have almost been you. And, as you are so fond of saying, *We are so very alike.*" Smiling, she lets go of the sword.

For an endless moment, nothing moves, not even the cold Samhain breeze. Gwyn ap Nudd turns his head. A few steps away stands the one called Emrys. They look on Gwyn with sorrow in their eyes, and an answering sorrow fills Gwyn's. He bows his head. Then his right hand flashes up to grasp the black sword's hilt. With a scream that is more despair than rage or pain, he pulls it free of his chest.

The blast flattens all those standing. Blinding white billows from him; mist wreathes his limbs. His blade becomes snowy, as beautiful as the day she first saw it in his hand, in the long-ago halls of Caer Sidi. Antlers crown his head, his long hair tearing free of its ties. Under the old moon, his scream becomes a howl. Arrow-straight to his side runs the hound, Dormach, bloody muzzle lifted in joy.

Gwyn ap Nudd extends a hand, and the souls of the Herlathing flow towards him. "We want only oblivion. Give us peace. We are nothing and no one any more."

"Herla!"

It is a woman's voice. The Herlathing have heard it raised in anger and fear, in desperation and passion. Arms come around her. "Herla. Remember who you are, and all that you love. The sisters you swore to save."

As the souls tear free, they pull another ever closer to the sword, and in Gwyn's howl, that soul hears words. *Come with me, daughter of the dust.*

No. Never again. But whether she goes willingly or not, Gwyn is right: she can feel herself coming apart. Her knees give way and Æthelburg catches her as she slumps to earth. The queen is warm. There is another warmth somewhere; a treasure room with contents more precious than the loot of the battlefield, than gold or gems. They are all that remains of a life. A person. Memories. Emotions. Names. And she wants them back. Before the end, she wants them back.

The last of the souls answer Gwyn's call, and she is merely Herla again, and she feels *light*. She will drift away with the next gust. Or crumble under the weight of a raindrop. Called by the spirits of those his host have slain, the shepherd turns his back on her. She lets out a long breath and her eyelids flutter shut.

"No, Herla…"

She opens her eyes again, cradled in Æthelburg's arms. The queen glares down at her. Tears scatter across Herla's face and she lifts a hand. "You are so beautiful."

"You think that excuses you?" Æthelburg's anger is no thicker than a skin scraped for writing. Herla can see other words beneath it, a whole sea of words. Her heart aches, and she finds the strength to sit up. "Nothing for days, and then *this*."

"I should have died many years ago."

"Not good enough." She holds Herla against her chest. "I will not let you go so easily."

Herla twines her fingers through Æthelburg's. "Then come with me," she whispers.

The queen draws a sharp breath. Her eyes move from their joined hands to Herla's face. "Where would we go?"

"Away. It does not matter, if we are together." The sounds of battle are fading. Panic cramps her heart, as the world grows insubstantial. The ghost of another lies tenderly on the familiar grass and trees, and yes, Herla knows that world. If she comes to it washed clean of pride, perhaps it will be kinder. She is weeping now, holding fast to Æthelburg's hand. "Come with me. If I must go, I would not go alone."

35

ÆTHELBURG

**Woden's Barrow, Wiltunscir
Kingdom of Wessex**

Come with me.

Herla's amber eyes are dim, her grip ferociously tight. Æthel loves her and is furious with her, and she is dying, and none of this is real. Behind her, battle. Before her, death. God, but she is sick of death.

Come with me.

Where would they go? Away is not Wessex. Away is a place Æthel has never seen, will never return from. Perhaps it is also a place for a woman sick of death.

Come with me.

If she went, she would be a queen without a realm. She would not even be a queen. She would be Æthelburg, who loved and was loved. No more would be asked of her, and no less.

Come with me.

"I can't," she says. They stare at each other, united in that instant by shock. Æthel has spilled the words and they are everywhere. Only two words, but she cannot retrieve them. She cannot force them back into the heartbroken place where they belong. She is a thing of shards now.

"Selfish," Herla whispers, the colour fast fading from her skin. She is ashen and somewhat unclear, a ghost among the living. "He always said I was selfish."

"Yes." Æthel clasps her closer. Tears fight their way through the tightness in her throat. "To make me choose like this. I want to come with you, but it is not time. Do you hear, Herla? It is not time for either of us."

The woman in her arms laughs softly, sadly. "It is time for me, Æthelburg. Although I have no right to ask...is it him you stay for?"

Inside her are memories; those she cherishes and those she yearns to forget. But that, Æthel realizes, is what sharing a life *is*. "We choose to love anew every single morning," she says, catching one of Herla's tears on her fingertip. It glints like the rarest pearl, and somehow it comforts her, as if their tears have the power to bind them together. "Some mornings are more difficult than others. Yes, I stay for him. But more than that—I stay for me. This is where I am supposed to be. This is who I am." She turns her head to look up at the hilltop. "I have no special power in me, no command over the land or its people other than being their queen, but that is what I will continue to be, as long as I live. As for what comes after—" she smiles through her tears—"only the fates know."

Herla's own smile has faded. "You humble me, Æthelburg. Washed clean of pride indeed." She bows her head. "This is a fitting end for the story I started."

"It is not the end," a voice says.

The storyteller, Emrys, stands over them. Looking upon Herla, their face is unexpectedly gentle. "Beyond the seven castles and the summer stars. Beyond the lip of night, in the dawn that is forever, they wait for you."

Herla draws a pained breath, as if the air has become too heavy for her to breathe. "My sisters?"

"Samhain." Emrys's eyes are a sky, and in that sky is another and another, leading back to some distant beginning. "I am certain that you can find your way to the shore."

"I know you now," Herla murmurs, her own eyes fixed upon Emrys...or on a place just beyond. For a moment, Æthel can hear the sway of the sea. "I will find it. I will find them."

The weight in her arms lessens. The dark ground is visible

through Herla's chest and Æthel's tears are choking her. "I was looking for you," she forces out brokenly. "Even if I did not realize it at first. I was looking for you."

"And I for you." Shockingly Herla laughs and surges up, reaching to take Æthel's face between her palms. "If you think I will not find you again, you are mistaken, Queen of Wessex." Waves roar in Æthel's ears as Herla kisses her, a burning kiss that lingers even after she opens her eyes and knows that she is alone.

"No." She staggers to her feet. "No!" But the waves are fading along with the scent of the sea. Maddened, Æthel throws back her head. "Run fast," she screams into the night. "Run fast, Herla. And do not look back."

A whisper comes. A whisper and no more, and she is empty, just as her arms are empty. She can still feel the shape of the woman in them. She can hear the faltering beat of her heart. Perhaps it is her own heart, wild and sick with grief. She presses her hand against it, trying to keep a wail inside.

The night abruptly is full of lowing and keening, as if every beast of the land and air has come together. An owl's cry, a wolf's howl. The cattle and sheep of the steads gouge furrows from the earth in their disquiet. It is a welcome and a farewell. Dread-stiff, Æthel turns her head.

The Lord of the Wild Hunt towers over them all. His aspect is different now. Gone is the vision of the silver king surrounded by the heroes of centuries. Now he seems *realer*—in the same way Æthel thought Herla real—and vastly present. The heart of wild things. Animals, seasons, storms and change. Lord of Winds, the old Briton had called Herla, mistaking her, Æthel realizes, for Gwyn ap Nudd. And indeed the wind blows fiercely, calling up the dark half of the year that awaits them.

The host of Annwn looks different too. Their faces seem remote, veiled, and their forms less bright. Their eyes glitter. Gwyn's wildness is in them, as they turn their heads to regard the hill, and the king who stands atop it. The golden light is gone, and all is dark.

Please. I cannot do this without you. I cannot face Gwyn ap Nudd alone.

Taking a deep breath, Æthel breaks into a run.

"It is in me to ride." Gwyn's call is the eagle's, as it echoes between high crags. "Why should I not take you with me, Ine of Wessex?" He raises a hand. "Join us and live forever."

"While it would be an honour to ride with the Lord of the Hunt, we all have our duty." Æthel should not be able to hear Ine through the wind, but his voice reaches her clearly. Although his words bely it, she can sense his weariness. And beneath weariness, fear. She pushes herself faster. The fighting has stilled, leaving her to navigate a slope dark with dead. She thrusts the butt of Herla's spear into the earth to keep herself upright.

"Duty." Gwyn's whisper is equally distinct. "Mine is to sweep away the ashes of the dead year. The ashes of lives lived. In the wake of chaos is peace."

She is close now. She sees Ine bow his head. "Then we will surely meet again. I may even go with you. But not yet."

It is such a perfect echo of the last words she exchanged with Herla that Æthel's stomach turns over. *Not yet,* she thinks. *Not yet.*

"You may have the blood of the kings of Dumnonia, but its opposite also runs in your veins, and I am in my prime. If I want you, I will take you."

"You will *not*." Æthel reaches the summit of the hill, and—as if he knows exactly where she is in the darkness, as if they are one being—Ine swings round to take her hand and pulls her to his side. "If you want him—" she lifts her spear—"you will have to go through me."

"Æthel?" he murmurs wonderingly, and his eyes are very bright. "What are you doing?"

"Did you believe I would let you stand alone?" But of course he believed it; Æthel watches expression crowd his face. He had seen her with Herla. He had seen her wild grief. They are still holding hands. "This is my land too," she tells Ine and then, acting on the instincts that have always served her well, she pulls him down so that their joined hands touch the earth.

Threads of light creep through the ground like roots searching for sun. They twine about Ine's arms and legs, and then around Æthel's, until both their figures are ablaze. She can hear a heartbeat as vast and deep as the world. She can smell green after rain and turned earth. In her mouth is the sweet tang of blackberries fresh from the briar. Behind her eyes are plains, wide open to the sky, and evenings where twilight vies with the warm yellow light of lamps lit too early. It is everything she loves: the ties that bind her to this place, this world. And to this person gripping her hand as if she is more precious than all of them.

"Ride you may, Gwyn ap Nudd, but you trespass in our Land." Ine's words thrum with the same low rumble as thunder. He meets Æthel's eyes and they rise to their feet together. "We will not allow you to harm those who live in it. You came for glory, yet there is none in killing. None in conquest or cruelty. Tell your stories, Folk of Annwn," he addresses the gathered host, "but do not make them here, from the blood and bones of our people."

"Refuse me you may, Heir, but your power is almost spent." Gwyn's gaze shifts and for the first time Æthel sees Emrys sharing the hilltop with them. "One day, when it is gone, and you mortals have turned on the land that nourishes you, pray to your distant god that my heart has come to know mercy."

The horse beneath him rears, and he swings around calling, "We ride!" The host echoes it. Harpists pluck the first chords of a hunting song. Archers unshoulder their bows. The great white hound howls, and those bastard birds shriek, but Ine's power renders them harmless. In Gwyn's hand is the sword, and in his face is the hunter, and the wind sharpens as he lifts his eyes to the sky. The Wild Hunt wheels upwards, their hooves trampling clouds still saturated with night.

Movement snags her eye. Two figures—Ingild and Edred—struggle at the foot of the hill before the ætheling breaks into a desperate stumbling sprint. Edred follows, shouting for him, until a whistle and *thunk* end his cries. Cadwy lowers the bow; it was an excellent shot. A glimpse of his face shows it hard and bitter; revenge does that to a person, Æthel could have told him.

Ingild glances over his shoulder, spots the body of his friend, but does not pause. There is terror in his pale cheeks, and no wonder: tonight he is the prey of the Wild Hunt. Now Æthel understands why Cadwy aimed for Edred. One of the riders drops lower, right behind Ingild, until she can stretch out a delicate hand to seize his cloak. Olwen sweeps him up effortlessly, dumping him across her saddle. Ingild's scream is swallowed in her laughter and the laughter of the host, as they gallop after Gwyn, higher and higher, until Æthel can no longer see them. Horns and hoofbeats dwindle into dawn.

In the wake of the Wild Hunt, a few flakes of snow drift down. One lands on her lips, and Æthel tastes winter. "She asked me to come with her," she hears herself say, staring at the place where she cradled Herla in her arms. "She asked me to come, so that she didn't have to go alone." Her knees hit the cold ground as agony saps the last of her strength. "Oh God, what have I done?" And she cannot care, in that moment, what Ine thinks as she curls in upon herself. All she can feel is the chasm where her heart used to be, and all she can hear is the lonely song of the wind.

Three days later—days that pass in a haze for Æthel—they bring the remnants of their footsore army home. Every man who survived the night returns with a pouch full of the king's silver, and a head full of a tale no one will believe.

Wiltun looks strange beneath the milky sun, as if the buildings are bare walls waiting for paint. The real world is behind her eyes, in her memory. The real world was wild and beautiful and had a heart too deep to know. Furiously, Æthel blinks away the tears that want to flow. She will not cry in front of men who lost friends to Gwyn's host. She will not cry in front of Ine.

Something is different between them. She is aware of him in a way she was not before, and when she looks around, it is always to see him watching her with uncertain eyes, as if she might disappear were he to drop his gaze for an instant. Ministering to the dead has given them little time or inclination to talk about themselves. They are like a half-healed wound, Æthel thinks; one they are frightened to touch and yet cannot leave alone. Grief has scraped her raw; it is hard to feel anything outside of it.

Come with me.

The worst thing was watching the light die alongside the life in Herla's eyes. Familiar smells in her nose: hay, manure, yeast. A washed-out sky. Coarse laughter from a tavern. The rattle of a cartwheel on a broken shaft. She could have gone, but this is what she chose. A joyless world. An uncertain husband.

A cloak wraps Æthel before despair can. The wool is warm from Ine's body, and she numbly pulls it around herself. *You are the one shivering.* Her mind is full of Herla, just as the world outside is empty of her. *I never told her I loved her. I never said the words.*

"Æthel," Ine says softly, as they stand together at the gate. "When I rode to Dumnonia, you raised the fyrds, trusting me to come back. I should have trusted you to come back. But I thought...I thought we had hurt each other too much."

She says nothing.

"And yet you came back." He pauses. "Do you know what Emrys said to me? They said you and your heart were my hope."

A pale finger of light filters through the grief. She raises her head. "I know what they meant now," Ine continues, tentatively taking her hand. "Herla would not have had the courage to confront the souls without you. I would not have had the strength to refuse Gwyn at the end. Without you." He squeezes her hand. "You led the men to victory when the odds were stacked against us. You are the hope of so many, Æthel." She lets him bring her hand to his heart. "To have the privilege of loving you, I must be blessed... and Herla too."

Æthel gazes at him, that rawness inside her aching. To hear him say such words, after seeing her and Herla together at the end. And she remembers how he had helped Herla, despite the pain of realizing Æthel loved her. More than likely he had done it for her. Still, he had done it.

So she says, "You were our hope too," recalling how he had held off the Folk, giving her men the courage to stand firm. He had found his own courage. A will to fight which the years had snuffed out. She does not know whether it is because of Herla, or the Dumnonian birthright. Perhaps it is both. "You've changed."

Ine is about to reply, but it is all the conversation they are allowed before the world intrudes and the challenges begin.

Mere hours after their return to Wiltun, a story spreads among the people. It tells of how the pious king and his steadfast queen—though maligned by traitorous kin—held back the forces of the Devil himself when he came a-calling on All Souls' Night.

"This is Winfrid's work," Ine says to Æthel that same day as one of the minor clergymen bustles out of the hall to distribute the tale further. "Who else would turn Gwyn's invasion into an opportunity to blow the Christian trumpet?"

"*And* counter the stories of you being a pagan." Æthel still holds the priest in some suspicion. "Do you think he planned it?"

"It would not surprise me. Neither would his achieving sainthood one day. In the meantime—" Ine raises his eyes heavenwards—"we should spare a thought for the Franks."

She almost smiles. "Bishop Hædde does not believe his story."

"Of course not. He denounced me as a heathen and is far too stubborn to go back on his word." Ine's expression sours. "As much as I dislike him, I don't want him out of my sight. How can I trust him not to bring the whole Christian world down upon my head?"

"The whole Christian world has other things to consider than you, Ine king." Winfrid's timing is preternatural, Æthel thinks, as the young man comes over to join them. "And you might be wanting this back." He drops a small silver cross on a chain into Ine's palm.

"Yes, I suppose I will." Ine puts it on. "Best to keep up appearances."

The priest raises a brow at that. "How will you explain Ingild?"

Ine turns to gaze at his brother's empty seat and Æthel remembers her last sight of him, dumped like a sack across Olwen's saddle. She suspects his death will not come quickly. "I wish we could have talked," Ine says. "Just once, with no lies between us."

He pauses before adding quietly, "The ætheling fell in the battle he brought. A fitting fate for a rebel."

"My king." Gweir bows his head. "Cadwy and the lords of the Dumnonii are here."

"Everything is ready then. Let's get it over with." The weariness that would usually accompany such words is absent, Æthel notes. Instead, there is a glint in her husband's eyes as he leaves the gloomy Witan chamber for the brighter hall. Not before turning and offering her his hand, however. She clasps it and they walk into the hall together.

It is full to groaning. All the ealdormen are here, save for those lost on the field: Mærwine, Godric and, to Æthel's sorrow, Beorhtric. Without the old lord's support, the others would not have followed her so readily. Nothhelm's humour is much reduced, probably because Ine is threatening to strip the sub-kingship of Sussex from him. He sits with his son instead of the other ealdormen, the sleeves of a long woollen shirt pulled down to cover his missing rings.

The Britons are unmistakable in their short tunics, tattooed arms folded aggressively across their chests. The fact that Ine has allowed them to keep their weapons has not gone unnoticed. The warrior gesiths sit with hands on hilts, as if expecting a fight to break out at any moment, and many a noble face wears consternation.

Ine leads Æthel to their seats, but does not sit, and the hall falls silent. "No doubt you are wondering at my guests," he says, and holds up a hand to stem the murmurs. "They are under my protection. I hope I do not need to say it again." No murmurs this time; everyone hears the iron in his tone. Ine has never cultivated the warlike reputation of his predecessors. Æthel has taken that part for him. But the events of the last few months have woken something in him. Not warlike. *Unyielding.* Looking out at the sea of faces, sensing a thousand hidden thoughts, Æthel acknowledges: not every battle is fought with swords. When it comes to words, Ine is as much a veteran of the field as she is.

"My brother's rebellion has failed. And not only that—so too have the alliances he made with folk who have no right to set foot in Wessex, let alone rule it." He pauses while that sinks in. "My wife, Æthelburg, raised the fyrds in my name, but she is the one the people fought for. Although she has led them to countless victories, bringing them home again is the true victory, or we would not have a kingdom to call home. More than you or I, *they* are Wessex."

Ine turns to her. "Æthel." His next words are soft, only for her. "Thank you." And he kneels before her.

Æthel only just stops her mouth from falling open. A rustle of clothing, a scrape of benches, and the rest of the hall follow suit. The Dumnonii do not kneel, but nod at her. Cadwy smiles. Confronted by an expanse of lowered heads, her face feels hot, and her heart a little lighter. She draws a breath. "Please stand." As they do so, one figure catches her eye: Merewyn, the gerefa's daughter. She beams at Æthel. They'd had time for only a few lessons with the blade, but the woman is a quick learner. When Æthel smiles back, a blush climbs up Merewyn's neck and she drops her eyes.

Once the hall is settled, she says, "I thank the king for his praise." *There is another who deserves it more. Whose role in this will never be known.*

Ine bows his head, as if he heard, before turning to the assembled crowd. "Many here have earned praise, not least those who gave their trust and fought beside me despite the bloodshed between our peoples, and many wrongs done. There is no amends to be made for the death of a father." A flicker of sadness creases his mouth. "All I can offer Cadwy king, if he accepts, is friendship and a promise that Dumnonian lands will be ruled by the Dumnonii, as long as I live."

No one misses the title. Cadwy's eyes are huge. The Britons are not the only people looking at Ine as if he has lost his mind. Every one of her countrymen wears a similar expression. But Æthel is pleased to see, on a growing number of faces, *relief.* The kind of relief people feel when they are told that there is one less enemy outside their doors. One less enemy they will be called upon to fight. *This will take time*, she thinks at Ine, *but if anyone can build a lasting peace, you can.*

"I accept Ine king's offer of friendship." Cadwy seems to have mastered his shock. "I think perhaps we have much to learn from each other, after all."

"I think so too," Ine says before his smile fades. "There is one more matter I wish to speak of. On the night my brother called me traitor and drove me from this place, a loyal man lost his life. Leofric served me well for many years. I fear his blood is on my hands." He clenches one. "Believe of me what you will, but do not believe I am a faithless friend and lord. To atone for this wrong, I will pay wergeld to his family, and I will accept a penance of their choosing."

"That will not be necessary, Ine king."

When Gweir reaches him, his embrace nearly knocks Leofric off his unsteady feet. The gesith leans heavily on a staff, but appears otherwise well. Ine blinks at him for a few stunned instants. "You thought he was *dead*?" Æthel murmurs.

"You didn't see what I saw." He raises his voice. "Leofric, I cannot express how happy I am that you are still with us. And how sorry I am that you came to harm."

"I will mend, Ine king," the gesith says, sober voiced. "I had my part to play in the evils that occurred here."

Gweir's joy catches like kindling and the hall is soon full of talk when it becomes clear the king does not plan to say more. Instead, the doors are thrown open to allow platters of roasted meat inside, and mead is soon flowing. Æthel sometimes suspects it is what their people do best: drink. "A nice idea," she says to Ine, as he steps down to greet Leofric. "Everyone likes a feast."

"If they have a cup in their hands, they can't hold a sword," he replies with a smile that is almost mischievous.

The whole of Wiltun seems to be making merry. Æthel knows that the generous bounty for the townsfolk is a calculated move on Ine's part. A lot of confused stories will be circulating about him, not helped by whatever Hædde has said in his absence. A lot of stories are likely circulating about *her* too. Æthel does not want to think of that. She is struggling not to think at all.

When she ventures outside later, her skin is flushed with food and ale, and the fires burning in the hall. Shivering lute notes follow her. It is clear and cold, and the stars are very bright. *Too sharp to be the summer stars.* Tears brim at the thought and, finally, Æthel lets them spill over. A keening comes from her, too low to be heard over the sounds of revelry. But her own ragged noise makes her cry harder. *How can you have done this to me?* she wants to scream at the sky. *To make me love you and then leave me?* As they dry, her tears are sharper than the stars. Æthel cries more, one hand covering her face. They drip through her fingers. *Would you be ashamed if you saw me now, Herla?*

She does not know how much time passes before a careful touch eases her hand away from her face. He says nothing, simply stands behind her, holding her cold cramped fingers in his until they soften. "You know that this is the only thing I have of her now?" With her free hand, Æthel pats the spear that hangs in a special sheath at her hip. "A weapon." She gives a rasping laugh. "How very Herla."

"I was thinking, how very *you*."

"Yes. You can hardly see me with a lock of hair, or a flower."

"That is a shame," Ine murmurs, "because I cannot grow spears." At her feet, the ground splits and a small shoot worries its way upwards. Watching its uncertain progress, Æthel holds her breath. Thorns sprout from the stem and a large rose blooms just beneath her hand. "This is the best I can do."

The tips of her fingers brush its petals. Silk concealing spines. "How very me, I would say." Her voice breaks. "Save that it is much prettier."

"I am so sorry, Æthel."

She turns and he opens his arms, and she lays her face against his shoulder, so that she does not have to see the stars.

By dawn, the sea inside her has dried up, and the newly revealed expanse is scattered with a host of undiscovered things. Ine has held her unspeaking through the night. She does not remember when they returned to their quarters at the back of the hall. Now, feeling her awake, he stirs too, and moves away, so that they lie facing each other with several handsbreadths between them.

"Is it too late?" Æthel says eventually.

"Too late for what?"

"To learn to be with each other again."

Ine catches his breath. "Æthel, I love you. But I cannot be all that you want. All that you need."

"I know." She thinks of those firelit evenings they shared, the walks they took, the conversations they had; the comfort she had always felt with him beside her. "Haven't we found other ways to be with each other?"

"Yes," he says softly. "And yet. It is not fair to ask you to give up a part of yourself for me. I saw you with her. If there is ever another like her, with whom you feel…" He stops. He does not have to say it because she understands, and she cannot quite believe it. A complicated emotion throbs in her chest. There will never be another like Herla, but there could be another. Unbidden, she thinks of Merewyn's lakewater eyes and the smile she seemed to reserve just for Æthel.

"You would be…content with such a thing?" she asks Ine. "Not jealous?"

"I am happy if you are happy. I was jealous because…" He tentatively inches a hand across the empty space between them. It lies there like an offering; the same offer is in his eyes. "I thought she would take you from me."

Æthel looks at his hand, and that complicated emotion in her chest is really her heart, beginning to mend. It is not the heart she had a few months ago. It is a wounded thing, a bone broken in battle. But bones, given a chance, heal stronger than before. She inches her own hand out, and their fingers touch.

"There is one thing we have never spoken of," Ine says, "which has caused you pain." He swallows, gathers himself. "Yes, I cannot be all that you need, but a child, Æthel, a family…if you want it, this is something I will do. For you. For us."

In the eyes of the court, her childlessness eclipses all she has achieved. *I don't know,* she had told herself in answer to that question. But now Æthel does know. At least she knows that the need to bear a child is not in her, but in their world. How easy to confuse what the world wants for what she wants. She squeezes Ine's hand, knowing that it is a sacrifice he is willing to make for her. "Thank you. Perhaps one day. Regardless of how I feel about it, I know we must name an heir."

"It is my responsibility too. And I have a few ideas." He squeezes her hand back. "We will find an answer, Æthel. Together."

For the first time since Samhain night, warmth—true warmth—spreads through her. She shifts closer on the bed, so that Ine can put his arms around her. He kisses her hair and they lie like that, not speaking, for many minutes. It is early still. Few things move beyond the walls of their room. "I've missed you, Æthel," he murmurs against her. "So much. You don't need to be a lone wolf, although I understand it is easier than constantly working to prove yourself to those who do not value you." His arms tighten. "I am sorry I did not speak up when I should have. You had to fight alone."

"*You* have had to fight alone too. I am sorry I believed you could not cope without me." Æthel is reminded unwillingly of her conversation with Herla. She had been right about many things. "I told myself that every battle must be fought with swords, and that you were weak for choosing other ways. That belief has made me very angry."

"Sometimes swords are necessary." He lets out an amused breath. "But not every door needs to be kicked in."

"Then again," Æthel mutters, thinking of Hamwic, "some doors *do.*"

"Your judgement has always been impeccable on that account."

A tremor, maybe laughter, goes through her, and she turns in his arms so that she can see his face. There is something new in his eyes besides the gold. "Æthel," Ine whispers. "You cannot help but cast a long shadow." He touches her cheek. "And even if I stand in it, I would be nowhere else." His finger traces a line from her temple to her jaw, thumb brushing a scar there, a faint white line. She remembers the day she got it. How he had been horrified at the thought of her bearing it forever. She remembers what she told him. *My first mistake. It will remind me to make it my last.*

Æthel has made many mistakes in the years since. If her scars must remind her of anything, it should be that mistakes are part of living. Her husband smiles gently at her, and she moves her hand to his chest. Beneath her fingers, his heart is quick and strong, the same determined beat as her own.

EPILOGUE:
THE SUMMER STARS

When I come to the shores of the Otherworld, I come not as the Herlathing, or Lord of the Hunt, for I have given up all three gifts: fleetness of the wind; mastery over soul; immortality. Neither am I wholly Herla of the Eceni. I wore Gwyn's mantle too long and made his purpose mine. Perhaps I was doomed at birth to wear the mantles of others. The weight of Boudica's drove me to the Otherworld, after all.

Now, filled with the scént of sea pollen, and the hazy rose of the sunrise, I am light. Naked of purpose save the one I hold in my heart. From the place where worlds touch comes a voice. *Run fast*, that voice cries. *Run fast, Herla. And do not look back.* All that is mortal in me feels a terrible loss. A grief like the one that seized me when I heard she was dead. My lover, my queen. But Æthelburg is not. She will live and she will blaze even more brightly than Boudica. And maybe, if the fates are kind, we will meet again. "Farewell," I tell the wind that blows across the gap between worlds. My stuff is too fragile now to stand the rudeness of the land that bore me. Only the fine bones of Annwn offer shelter.

I turn to face it and I do not look back. Not this time.

The sky beckons. Petals wash up at my feet. If I stepped into the swell, I could drift on its white current forever. Is this what death means? Is this the peace I took away from so many others?

Drifting is not for me. Neither is the empty always of the sky. For the first time, my purpose is my own. I whistle, a long rich note, and hold breath I no longer have until he comes. His coat is as snowy as the day I first saw him running with his herd siblings. "You did not have to," I whisper to the animal cursed to sleep when I slept and to ride when I rode. "You are home now."

He blinks as if to say, *Then why did you call me?* I lift a hand to his neck. "Because there is a journey before me, friend. Annwn is vast and eternity is long, and I have need of company along the way." He bows his head. I climb upon his back, and we turn westwards over the waves.

I have heard tell that out past the castles of the Folk, across centuries of water, there is a place where foaming crests become mountains. Soft stars bathe those peaks, but behind them the sky is utterly dark. I have lived in the eye of the dark, and will not fear it. Beyond its curled lip, they say, is another dawn. One that never turns to day.

Half blanketed by shadow, half blessed by light, none know the name of that land save Gwyn, perhaps, and the power he serves. Its grasses are whipped by the shins of girls with muddy feet. Rivers ramble instead of roads. Dew-drenched fields lie paling beneath the sky. And Corraidhín's smile is like the flare of the sun forever on the cusp of rising.

acknowledgements

Perhaps starting the most ambitious creative project of my career in the second year of a global pandemic was not the best idea. It has been a long and challenging road, and there are many people to thank for helping me walk it.

Firstly, my agent, Veronique Baxter: you continue to be here for me and I can't express how grateful I am that we are able to work together.

To my editors in the UK & U.S.: Bella Pagan, Priyanka Krishnan, Holly Domney, Sophie Robinson and Tiana Coven. Bella, Priyanka—thank you for both your insight and patience while I wrestled with this story, and for believing that I could write it. Holly—thank you for guiding my characters to be their best (and most emotionally tense) selves! You understood them clearly from the start and helped me to understand them better too. Sophie and Tiana—thank you for supporting this book as it took its first steps into the wider and scarier world outside of my head.

A lot of people are involved in publishing a book, from desk editors to production to rights and publicity, many of whom I have not met and cannot thank personally. To the teams at Pan Macmillan in the UK and Orbit/Redhook in the U.S.: you have helped turn this story into something readers can hold in their hands, and I am hugely grateful for the care you have taken. Thank you to Crush Creative and Lisa Marie Pompilio for the most astounding cover designs. And to Kevin Sheehan for producing a phenomenal map of Wessex.

Between May–June 2023, I was beyond fortunate to spend three weeks at beautiful Vil·la Joana in Barcelona, focusing on the structural edit of *Song of the Huntress*. Thank you to Anna Cohn Orchard and the teams at Exeter and Barcelona UNESCO Cities of Literature for providing this unforgettable opportunity.

To Susan Stokes-Chapman and her friend: thank you for helping me with the Welsh part of the pronunciation guide. Thank you to my patrons: your support and encouragement means the world to me. And to everyone who bought, read and shouted about *Sistersong*: I was able to write and publish *this* book because of you.

I couldn't do any of this without my family and friends. Thank you to my parents for their unwavering love and support. My sister, Laura, always picks up the phone even though I'm usually calling to moan about something. Spending time with the university crew—Reda, Josi and James—is a highlight of my year, even though it's never enough. A special shout-out to my D&D group who keep me sane every Wednesday; to podcasters-in-arms Megan Leigh and Charlotte Bond; and to Dr. Victoria James for not only indulging my Welsh castle obsession, but for gifting me a Balrog skull, which only the truest friend would do.

Finally, to all the Ines, Æthelburgs and Herlas of this world: you are enough. Run fast and don't look back.

MEET THE AUTHOR

Laura Madeleine

LUCY HOLLAND is the acclaimed author of *Sistersong* and *Song of the Huntress*. She has a BA in English and creative writing and an MA in creative writing, both from Royal Holloway, and twelve years of bookselling experience at Waterstones. Lucy is also a cohost of the award-winning feminist podcast *Breaking the Glass Slipper*. She lives in southwest England on the red shores of the Jurassic Coast with a black cat and a bedroom full of books.

if you enjoyed
SONG OF THE HUNTRESS
look out for

SISTERSONG

by

Lucy Holland

In an ancient land steeped in wild magic, three royal siblings fight to keep their kingdom safe from the warriors who threaten its borders—and their bond—in this lyrical debut of spells and song, sisterhood and betrayal.

In the ancient kingdom of Dumnonia, there is old magic to be found in the whisper of the wind, the roots of the trees, and the curl of the grass.

King Cador knew this once, but now the land has turned from him, calling instead to his three children. Riva can cure others but can't seem to heal her own deep scars. Keyne battles to be accepted for who he truly is—the king's son. And Sinne dreams of seeing the world, of finding adventure.

*All three fear a life of confinement within the walls of the hold,
their people's last bastion of strength against the invading
Saxons. However, change comes on the day ash falls from the sky.
It brings with it Myrdhin, meddler and magician, and Tristan,
a warrior whose secrets will tear them apart.*

*Riva, Keyne, and Sinne—three siblings entangled in a web of
treachery and heartbreak, who must fight to forge their own
paths. Their story will shape the destiny of Britain.*

1

KEYNE

*Imbolc—a festival celebrating
the end of winter*

I will tell you a story.

Seven years ago, when I was a child of ten, I became lost in the woods. My sisters and I had been travelling the road that skims the coast like a stone from Dintagel. I loved our summer home—a spume-silvered rock of houses and workshops, its docks piled high with amphorae. But there is a place, many leagues to the east, where the road slows, turning inland. It loses itself amongst the trees, straying into giant country. Branches interlace here; it is easy to slip away into the green space between a giant's fingers. Easy for a careless child to disappear.

Looking back, I wonder whether it truly was carelessness. Perhaps it was *her* doing. Given everything which came after, that would make sense.

Between one scout's holler and the next, I am lost, a prisoner of the wood. I feel no fear, more an irritation that I've let the trees trick me. I can hear my father, the king, calling me and the irreverent footfalls of men rending foliage.

I wander so long, it feels as though I've crossed some hidden boundary. I've left our world for *theirs*—the nameless land where goddesses sing to the stars, where lost spirits linger in the twilight. Dark quills scratch me; I am surrounded by yews, the terrible grave-trees which grow from death. I shiver, as irritation turns to fear. Deep voices seem to call my name, anthems to lost children. And now I *am* lost, hopelessly so.

The sky darkens and with the light goes hope. Hunger claws at my stomach; I am old enough to know I cannot survive long without food and water. Tears well. What if I die here and the yew grows stronger, roots curling through my bones?

Despair is a sharp scent and I suppose *she* smells it upon the air, for suddenly a woman stands before me. She is old, but not so old as Locinna, our nurse. Eyes peer beneath a heavy brow, blue, and piercing as a gull's. She wears rags, tattered and rent, but after a blink, these become a cloak of moths, their wings a-flit in the evening. Another blink and it's just an ordinary cloak, albeit a strange one made of patches and ribbons fluttering free.

She extends a hand and I realize I've collapsed to the leaf mulch, the seat of my skirt now damp through. My legs wobble as I stand. Her fingers are rough, calloused like a smith's. I wonder what strange trade might have marked them.

"Are you a witch?" The dangerous question is out in the open before I can stop it.

She smiles. "Perhaps." Looks me up and down. "Would you like me to be?"

"No."

"And why not?"

"Because witches are to be feared."

She pauses. "A good answer, if not entirely true."

"I want to go home."

The witch tilts her head, her gull's eyes narrowing on my face as if it were a fine fat fish. "I wonder if you do."

"Of course I do." But I glimpse her meaning. I have never felt at ease in my home.

"You are wet through. Come and get warm."

They are such inviting words. And I'm freezing, it's true. But she's a witch. "My father must be worried."

She steps back and something jingles—her stick-wrists gleam with silver bracelets. My eyes widen; only Mother has silver like this. Where hers is solid and silent, however, the witch's bracelets sing. I feel a desperate urge to touch them, to capture those chimes between my palms, as if I could draw the melody inside me.

She notices my gaze, smiles again. "Would you like one?"

Throat dry with want, I shake my head.

"Here." She slides off a single band, passing it over gnarled brown knuckles. Before I know it, my fingers have closed about its shining curve.

"I can't..."

"But you already have."

My cheeks flush. Shaped like a horseshoe, the band is too big, hanging on my wrist like the crescent moon above us. But it shrinks to a perfect size even as I watch, and I catch my breath at the tingle of magic. When I look up, she's half turned her back. "Wear it when you are ready to find me again." And she is gone, returned to the forest that birthed her.

The forest I am no longer within, for I now stand upon a wide road, and voices—human voices—are shouting my name. One laughing, one crying, my sisters rush towards me.

I remember burying that silver bracelet, sweating and fearful. I hadn't planned to hide it, but inside Dunbriga, our capital, I began to question my gift. It felt nothing like the spells spoken over hearth and home. Not even akin to Father's ability to spark a flame or ask the skies for rain. It was otherworldly. It had come from the dangerous heart of the forest, warmed by a witch's skin.

And yet for all that, the bracelet was mine now. My parents would surely take it away if they found it. So in the shadows cast by Dunbriga's oldest yew, I gouged a hole in the raw earth and dropped the silver in, weeping to see my shining crescent amidst the dirt.

I've ventured into the forest many times since then and have never once glimpsed the witch. As the years pass and the magic fades, she seems more and more a figment of a fevered mind. "Just a fancy," I tell the wheat doll taking shape between my hands. She is nearly finished—a shoulder shy of complete.

"Keyne!"

I twitch. I should have seen Mother coming, sitting as I am at our hill fort's highest point. A waft of rosewater precedes her and then she's towering over me—her shadow blotting out what little sun struggles through the clouds. "What are you doing?" she demands.

My blasphemous fingers are busy weaving a brideog. We make the goddess's dolls every year for the festival of Imbolc. Gildas, the Christian priest, doesn't like it, but I find the work soothing; it takes my mind off other things. And from my perch on the steps of the great hall, I can watch the hold tumbling out below me down the hill. Cattle on the lowest level are tiny as a child's toys.

"I told you to put this practice aside," Mother says sternly, and I hear the priest in her words. Beneath the queen's skin runs the blood of old Rome, the jewel of the empire that abandoned us to our fate. Father took her for her blood; he thought it might give him strong sons to guard his lands and legacy. Instead he has two daughters…and me. Rome's last laugh, I suppose, before the legions left our shores for good.

"We are not prepared for Candlemas on the morrow," she adds, and the word forces my head up. Bright fox fur frames my mother's shoulders, her curls tamed into an elegant braid. Her skin is a shade browner than my own, though we share the same dark hair. "And do try to sit graciously. This"—she waves a hand at my trouser-clad legs—"open sprawling is improper."

My hands clench around the wheat woman. "We've always made brideogs, Mother. I don't see the harm in it."

"Brigid is no longer our concern. We need candles for the ceremony, enough for every woman who—"

"Why is it only the women who must be 'purified' at Candlemas?" I snap, imagining what my sisters might say. Wild Sinne would scoff at the thought, eyes sparkling with some planned mischief. Riva would probably grit her teeth and bear it while murmuring prayers to the old gods under her breath. I almost smile, but it dies when I think about Rome's god and the way his priests seem to delight in punishing women. Gildas believes all

Britons sinners, despite being a Briton himself. He condemns our festivals, our traditions, even our little wheat dolls. But every tale he spins, of revelation and ruin, pushes his Christ further away from me. Gildas's Saviour is a stranger who died long ago in a hot land I have never seen.

Mother's gaze briefly strays from my own: part of her agrees with me. But when she says, "Make candles, Keyne," it is Queen Enica who speaks.

"Let Riva do the candles. You know she cannot weave the—"

"Riva is making them already. And when I find Sinne, she will join you."

She won't find Sinne. My younger sister has a talent for making herself scarce whenever there is work to be done. And to Sinne, everything looks like work.

Our home, Dunbriga, is a smudge of smoke on the edge of the world. I know it's not really—Armorica is just across the water, and ships come from further still, bringing us oil and olives, the taste of sun-drenched lands to the south. I like to imagine cargoes of silks and spices cocooned in ships' holds, waiting to be abused by our rough hands and palates. But when storms keep the ships away, the walls of Dunbriga close in and the fort seems to shrink. We need travellers to remind us that there's a world beyond our borders.

I make my way to the workshop, feeling the holdsfolk's customary stares as I pass. The brideog is coming apart in my hands. I don't know why I care, except that she's an antidote to Christ and his earnest suffering. I am tired of being called sinful. Half my father's hold already thinks me so. I need no help from Gildas and his followers.

At the creak of the door, Riva looks up, her good hand coated in tallow. She's wearing a bandage around the other, hiding the scarred flesh she cried over every night for years after the fire. No one knows how it started, except Riva herself perhaps, and she claims she doesn't remember.

"So," Riva says, as I take the stool beside her in the dim room. "Mother found you." She's as tidy as Sinne is tangled, her chestnut hair braided neatly, sober dress crease-free. Riva has a stillness in her that soothes me. She listens where my younger sister would speak.

I nod. "Now she's after Sinne."

"She won't catch her." We share a fond smile before my sister's eyes stray to the tattered figure in my arms. "...Brigid."

I let her fall. "Mother forbade me. I'm to help you with the candles instead."

Riva scoops the brideog from the rush-strewn floor. The doll is a sorry sight, broken wheat sticking out of her like pins. "Finish her, Keyne," my sister says. "It's important the goddess feels welcome here. I'll see to the candles."

I force myself to protest. "There are dozens. And you don't like fire."

"I am coping." A tremor in her face. "You can help when you're done."

"Thank you." The words hiss from my lips and I sound ungrateful. I can't seem to sound any other way these days. Riva, however, just nods and returns to her shaping and dipping.

I know she's watching as my fingers flash in and out of the brideog, perhaps mocking the dexterity she no longer has. But I don't move, because it's warm beside the stinking tallow and the fire that keeps it soft. And that stillness I love in my older sister is here in the room between us. I can feel my earlier anger slowly seeping away.

An hour passes in companionable silence. I stare at Brigid's blank face. She could be anyone. She doesn't even resemble a woman, just a figure with arms and legs, trunk and head: human. That's something we all share. That's what really matters.

Isn't it?

Raised voices pull me from my thoughts. Riva and I exchange a glance before we creep to the workshop door. We don't want to be seen. People clam up around us, the king's children, as if we're his spies. I grimace to myself. It might look that way, but Father doesn't listen to us as he used to do. These days only Mother, his lords—and Gildas—are welcome to speak.

"Hush, Siaun. If someone hears and tells the priest—"

"Then we'll know who's a traitor."

I put my eye to a crack. Three men lurk outside, one checking the yard is empty. I guess they'd never dream of finding the royal children with their hands in a tallow vat.

"Do you *want* to be caught? The king will lock you up...or worse."

Siaun snorts. He's a slight but rangy man in a farmer's overall and his cheeks are lean with hunger. Last summer's harvest was the poorest in years and the winter has been hard. "Lock me up for speaking truth?" he demands.

The other man shakes his head. "For speaking against the priest."

"Whose side are you on?"

"It's not about sides, Siaun," the third man hisses from where he's keeping watch. "Plenty of folk are beginning to listen to the priest. The king listens, so they do too."

"The king is *wrong*," Siaun says, and I hear Riva draw a startled breath beside me. Her eyes are wide in the dim space.

Siaun's friend clamps a hand over his mouth. "Holy Brigid, Siaun. Say that any louder and you'd be lucky to escape with a whipping."

I swallow tightly. Siaun's expression doesn't change, but his fists are clenched and trembling.

"Will you die for this, Siaun?"

The farmer turns so I can't see his face. "Our women don't need purifying for the festival of Imbolc, so why is this Candlemas different? Would you let the priest shame them?"

"Of course not, but what can we do when 'tis the queen's will for us to follow new ways? Besides, Gildas is not all bad. I hear he's building proper houses for Brys and his family. Times have hit them hard. And not just them."

Riva mutters something under her breath and I think, *Candlemas is only the beginning.*

Once Siaun's friends have bundled him away, I meet my sister's eyes. "Is it true what they said? That there are already people who follow the priest?"

Bandaged hand held close to her chest, Riva says, "Gildas doesn't care a wit for them, so why build them houses? It must be part of his plan to convert us all." Her face firms. "We should talk to Father. Not to tell tales," she adds hastily when I open my mouth to protest. "About Gildas. Father allows Mother to honour the priest's festivals, but perhaps he doesn't know how far it's gone. That people are prepared to give up the old ways altogether, that Gildas is essentially bribing them to do so..."

"What if Father does know?" The stink of candles clogs my nose. *And what if he doesn't care?*